NIGHT TIDE

A DESIGN YOUR DESTINY NOVEL

KORY M. SHRUM

TIMBERLANE
PRESS

NIGHT TIDE

AN EXCLUSIVE OFFER FOR YOU

Connecting with my readers is the best part of my job as a writer. One way that I like to connect is by sending 2-3 newsletters a month with a subscribers-only giveaway, free stories from your favorite series, and personal updates (read: pictures of my dog).

When you first sign up for the mailing list, I send you at least three free stories right away.

If giveaways and free stories sound like something you'd be interested in, please look for the special offer in the back of this book.

Happy reading,
Kory

For Charlemagne "Charley"
Here's to a long life, my little friend.

INSTRUCTIONS

This is a different kind of novel. It requires an adventurous mind and inquisitive soul to fully enjoy.

Unlike most stories, you can read this one in many different ways, depending upon the choices you make.

You can make selections based on what you would do in a situation and see where that gets you. Or you can track every choice you make and make sure you've left no stone unturned. This is a great way to uncover as many secrets as you can about this strange town and its stranger residents.

Or you can choose *not* to choose. In the back of this book, on page 349, is a chapter called "Author's Choice," which is written in the traditional novel style (from beginning to end, no choices). If you select Author's Choice, you will not get *all* of the story but it will be a complete story. This is a good option for those who want to visit Castle Cove but don't want to explore it.

If while reading you see the letters **(ES)** beside a choice, it means that choice leads to explicit sex. If you're not interested in that experience, that's your warning to make a different selection.

When you reach the end of a story path, you can create a new story or redo your last choice.

No matter how you choose to approach this story, I hope you enjoy your stay in Castle Cove.

SELECT YOUR AVATAR: WHO WILL YOU PLAY?

Reese

A 26-year-old woman and longtime resident of Castle Cove. She works as a bartender at Alpha's, a werewolf bar not far from the Castle Cove University campus. She is a shifter.

For Reese go to page 1

Grayson

A young man who lives in Castle Cove with his parents. Today is his eighteenth birthday. He recently graduated from Castle Cove High School with plans to attend university in the fall. He is human. For now.

For Grayson go to page 9

REESE

Reese's feet hurt and the muscles between her shoulder blades were beginning to knot into a single, dull throb. The bar room around her was in full roar as patrons laughed with their friends. Balls clanked along the surface of the pool tables before bouncing into soft pockets. The bitter tang of alcohol was softened by the smell of fresh popcorn, oil slicked and salty, blooming behind her. The latest batch was almost ready. And a good thing because they were running low.

Despite her sore feet and aching back, Reese had to keep an eye on the room. Her best friend, and the owner of Alpha's bar, Kristine, was counting on her.

Tonight was the full moon. That meant Kristine and all members of her pack were in the Wayward Woods. On nights like this when the moon held her sway, they would run the forests until dawn.

That meant that tonight the bar was full of humans. Vulnerable as they were, it was up to Reese and Nick to keep them safe. Nick—the bouncer guarding the door—was a shifter, like she was. They were physically stronger than humans and impervious to magic of all kinds. That meant that demons and witches weren't much competition. The oldest creatures in town obeyed the treaty set forth by Ethan Benedict. Ethan, whatever corner of hell he crawled out of, was the peacekeeper, mayor and founder of Castle Cove. It was rumored that he served Vendetta herself as her direct attendant.

Reese wasn't sure how true all of that was. But she'd felt the magic rolling off Ethan herself, and it had been enough to let her know that she had no desire to see how deep his power trenches were.

Once in a while, something truly ancient and terrible would roll through town and Ethan would handle it. Everything else was usually some low-level menace too stupid to play by the rules. So while there were a handful of demons in the bar and even a couple of living vamps and a table of shifters, Reese wasn't worried. There wasn't anything here she couldn't handle.

Except maybe her ex.

A woman with bright purple eyeshadow and dark red lips stumbled up to the bar and placed her empty martini glass on the bar top. The clatter broke Reese's concentration, pulling her out of the overheard conversation.

"Can I have another dirty martini, please?" the woman hiccupped.

"You sure?" Reese asked, taking the empty glass and putting it in the plastic bin out of sight. It was about time for Bethany to come up and do a round of bussing.

Reese watched the drunk girl's gaze shift to a couple in the corner, on the wall behind the nearest pool table. A man and woman were kissing like there wouldn't be another sunrise for either of them. The girl's face pulled into a sneer.

"Actually," she began. "Can I add two shots of Cuervo to my order?"

She slapped a twenty on the bar top.

With a sympathetic smile, Reese poured three shots,

including one for herself. The woman kissing the face off the guy was her ex, Violet. *That* merited a drink.

Reese clinked glasses with the girl and threw back the shot. "Cheers."

Reese made the martini and slid it toward the customer. Then, with a sigh, she stepped out from behind the bar and moved toward the couple on the wall.

There was no protecting humans from humans, but she had to do something about the demon.

"Oh God, no." The girl with the martini grabbed Reese's arm in a panic. "Don't say anything."

"I have to," Reese said, gently removing the red lacquered nails from her flesh. They left a ring of tiny crescent moons in their wake, but Reese didn't mind. "Nothing will happen to you. Don't worry."

She wasn't sure if the message was getting through those glassy eyes and slack jaw, but the girl let Reese go without further protest.

The pool players, all of whom knew Reese, parted for her like water. Several gave friendly smiles. No doubt, they thought it couldn't hurt being friends with the bartender. They weren't wrong.

Reese stopped in front of the couple on the wall. "Violet."

The girl pulled back. For a moment, hellfire danced in her eyes before they softened to a sweet, caramel brown. "Reese. What is it? Want some kisses too?"

The demon named Violet sounded almost hopeful.

"You know the rules," Reese said, slapping away the flirtation. She had a lot of practice as bartender—and with Violet in particular. "No feeding on pack grounds."

"I don't know what you're talking about." Violet batted her eyes as the guy moved from Violet's mouth to her neck without pause. He hadn't even registered Reese's arrival.

Violet raised her chin to accommodate him.

"You *absolutely* know," Reese said and grabbed her arm. "Stop it or I'll stop *you.*"

The hellfire returned to Violet's eyes. She pinned Reese with that menacing gaze. But her magic had no effect. Shifters were immune to demonic guile.

"Last time I'm saying this. Let him go, or I'll walk you outside," Reese said calmly. And she would have to. She couldn't let a demon enthrall humans without consequence. If rumor got around that Alpha's was lax on the full moon while the pack was out running the woods, then it would only invite more trouble. And to be clear, Violet was just being greedy. Not only had she enthralled the guy and fed on his lust, but she was milking the girl's jealousy as well. Reese could feel it.

"You're no fun anymore, Reese," Violet said with a deep eyeroll.

Reese felt the magic shift around them and the man stumbled back as if shoved. He stared at them, frowning.

"Go see your friends," Violet commanded.

The man stumbled away, on unsteady legs.

"Now what am I supposed to do with the rest of my night?" Violet crossed her leather boots and then her arms, leaning against the wall. She pouted up at Reese. "Were you even jealous? I was trying to make *you* jealous."

Reese wasn't and Violet knew it. Violet couldn't drink a shifter's jealousy as well as she could a human's anyway.

"Because if you were jealous," Violet said, leaning forward with a devil's smile. "You know I can kiss that and make it better."

She flicked her eyes down Reese's body suggestively.

Reese turned back toward the bar.

"Ouch." Violet laughed behind her back. "Rejected."

"You better cut it out," one of the demon boys said, giving Reese a wink as she passed him. "Or she'll stop making your Jager bombs."

"Hey," Violet said. Her smile was sweet again. "You going to tell your precious Kristine about this?"

Here Reese heard the tone of bitterness loud and clear.

"Behave and I won't have to," Reese said with an equally sweet smile before stepping back behind the bar.

The demons had a reason to be scared of Kristine. It wasn't just that she had more power and magic than Reese had seen in an alpha in a long time, nor that she was fiercely loved by her pack members in a way that made her seem untouchable. It was also Cole.

Cole was the oldest demon that Reese had ever met and he considered Kristine a dear friend. If he found out that the demons were giving her a hard time, they would be very, *very* sorry.

The rest of the night passed without further incidents. Reese threw a few furtive looks in Violet's direction, but from what she could tell, the demon had turned her attention to her friends and their pool game. Then they left thirty minutes before close.

"Good night, Reese." Violet had winked on her way out. Minutes later, Reese heard the chorus of motorcycle engines rev to life outside.

Only then did the rope of muscle in her back relax.

They closed quickly. All the tabs were settled. The drawer was counted out and bagged. Bethany—a single-mother and witch with the local coven—bussed the room and Nick locked up.

Reese bid her coworkers good night and stepped out onto the cobblestone sidewalk.

She considered going home, putting on the television and taking a long, hot bath before falling into bed.

But despite her aching feet and back, her mind was too restless.

"A swim," she said to no one in particular. "That would be perfect right now."

It would do wonders for unfurling the tight coil of her mind too, which kept circling back to her demon ex-girlfriend and the drunken hellfire in her eyes when she'd been kissing that guy.

If she swam for a couple hours now, by the time she fell into her bed at four or five in the morning, she would sleep like the dead.

Reese walked three blocks to her red pickup parked in front of the closed froyo station. The truck still had some of the evening heat inside it as she climbed in and turned the key.

It rattled to life, grumbling like an old man who'd been awakened from a deep slumber.

She drove east until it connected with the main strip outlining Castle Cove University campus. Then she turned right, heading south. She'd drive out of town and take Canyon Road. There she could pull off and walk down to the water.

Following the ridge, Reese enjoyed the view of the white, frothy waves and luminous moon. It hung in the sky, bright with milk-white light. The waves crashing against the shore seemed violent. Then she remembered the scrap of conversation she'd heard from the booth in Alpha's.

"A guy died, Trace. Fuck." She'd tracked the voice to a booth against the far wall. Two guys and two girls had sat in it, nursing the long-necked bottles between them.

"I'm just saying it's weird. Why wouldn't they announce it? Why do they have to act like it's a secret?"

"Maybe they don't want to freak people out," the woman had said. She'd turned her beer in her hands, her thumbnail picking at the label.

"If sirens were killing people, I'd want to know," the other guy had agreed.

A guy died.

She hadn't heard about anyone drowning or getting hurt in the water. Could they have been mistaken? Or had something happened that Ethan or the others were keeping quiet for the time being? Usually if true danger cropped up in Castle Cove, the police would issue a city-wide alert. There were too many humans living in Castle Cove not to put them on their guard. It was easy for drifters or new arrivals to miss these important updates, simply because they didn't know where to look. However, long-time residents were savvy. They knew what dwelled within the city limits—let alone the ocean and woods bordering on all sides.

Reese pulled off Canyon Road and parked her car on the gravel shoulder.

Looking both ways, and seeing only moonlit pavement as far as the eye could see, she crossed the street to the beach. Carefully, she slid down the sandy dune to the wet-packed sand below.

The sharp smell of salt overtook her. Her skin prickled in anticipation. Each crashing wave against the shore seemed to call her magic to the surface of her skin. It danced as if alive.

Ocean spray misted against her skin.

"Just a minute," she told herself as she shed her clothes. She folded them up neatly and put them on a jagged boulder at the base of the dune. They should stay dry there until she returned.

She waded naked into the surf. Cool water slapped against her calves and then her thighs. She shivered.

A trill of laughter caught her ears and she turned toward the sound of it. Her eyes adjusted to the dark and the distance. Even so, she could just make out three kids sitting on Heart's Rock. They were playing chicken with the sirens no doubt.

Reese thought the rite of passage—the tradition of swimming from Hunter's Beach to Heart's Rock—was too dangerous. But who was she to say?

The water rose to her chest and she almost couldn't contain

it anymore. She gave herself over to the magic thrashing beneath her skin. Slipping beneath the wave, she transformed.

Her body softened and elongated. Her limbs merged with her torso, becoming a single lithe form of muscle. Two blinks and her eyes adjusted to the watery depths. Sensations radiated along her skin, taken in by her flesh in a way that her human skin could never manage.

Reese was a black-tipped reef shark.

She was a fixed shifter, meaning she took only one form, unlike the doorman Nick who was a chimera.

And in moments like this, when she was in her shark form and one with the water, she wondered if she'd ever really been human at all. Her life on the land slipped away, becoming little more than a dream in her mind.

She felt powerful here. Strong not only in body and speed but in spirit. She often wondered if there may come a day when she simply wouldn't want to change back. What if she stayed in the ocean and lived here forever? She knew she could.

But that decision was for another day.

Reef sharks like herself preferred to trace the drop off, patrolling the place where the life-rich shallows met the deep expanse of sea. That had been her original aim when she'd driven to this stretch of beach after the exhausting night tending bar.

But now that she was here, she also had the option of swimming through the cove toward the kids. That was deeper water, and held some danger. But maybe the kids needed someone looking after them. After what the patrons had said about the sirens, maybe the kids were in danger.

Reese Choice 1
Swim south toward the drop off - go to page 22
Swim east toward kids - go to page 25

GRAYSON

He stood on the beach and stared out at the moonlit horizon. White light shone on the iridescent waves. The salt stung his nose and the wind rolling off glowing crests pulled tears from his eyes.

Someone laughed farther up the beach. He turned and saw Landon and Abigail trying to get the bonfire going. They were bent over the kindling. Abby's lighter sparked, once, twice in the dark. Both times it revealed their faces hard with concentration.

"Birthday boy!" Landon yelled. "Get your ass over here and help us."

Grayson's bare feet sank deeper in the cool sand with each step. It squished up between his toes as the sea sprayed water onto his bare calves.

"I thought the point of having a birthday was so people would do things for me," he said. But he extended his open palm toward Abby.

She handed the lighter over too willingly. "You're better at this shit than the rest of us. Weren't you a wood scout for six years or something?"

"Or something," he said. Eight years was more like it. He

struck the lighter and caught the soft brush on the first try. They'd been trying to burn the sticks themselves, not the soft nest he'd made for them out of dry grass and kindling. That was where they'd gone wrong.

"I can't believe your parents let you go into the Western Woods as a kid," Landon said, dragging his hand under this nose. He sniffed. "My parents *still* forbid me from going in there."

"There's a big difference between the Western Woods and the Wayward Woods." Grayson fanned the sparks. "Even scouts don't go in the Western Woods."

In truth, the entire forest spanning Castle Cove County was called the Wayward Woods. But there was a clear distinction to all who knew better.

"Here we go," Abby said with a teasing smile. He elbowed Landon in the ribs. "We're about to get a lesson from Professor Richt."

Landon snorted, settling down onto the sand beside her. The fire grew, illuminating both their faces with the warm orange glow.

Grayson affected a prim English accent and smoked an invisible pipe for comedic effect. "Yes, children, well, it is all about the territory line. If you go *west* of the territory line you will find yourself in the *Western Woods*. If you stay east of the territory line, and I highly suggest that you *always* stay east of the territory line, then you remain in the Wayward Woods. During the right times, and with the right company, the Wayward Woods are safe enough. You can't be foolish out there, but you'll likely be all right. However!" He pointed his finger into the air. "Under no circumstances should *anyone* cross the territory line into the Western Woods. Do you understand, children?"

"Yes, Professor Richt," they both chimed. They always loved his impressions of their junior year history teacher. All Grayson was missing was a shock of wild gray hair and a mustache Mark Twain would be proud of.

"There are creatures in those woods. Old, ancient and *hungry* creatures. They will devour you alive. Or drag you screaming to their lairs, where they will eat you. Slowly."

Landon shivered.

Then all three laughed.

Grayson dropped the act and sank down onto the sand beside them.

It was true he'd spent his summers scouting the Wayward Woods. He learned more about the flora and fauna of those woods than he thought possible. More about the seasons and cycles of the earth and what it meant to work in harmony with the land. But this education wasn't the result of generous parents. Rather, they fully understood the dangers of living in a place like Castle Cove and they wanted their children well-equipped against any danger that might arise.

We can't always be there to protect you, they'd said as they kissed his cheeks and sent him off into the woods. *The people who get hurt are the people who aren't prepared or who don't understand what is going on around them. We want to raise you strong, Grayson.*

Grayson knew that most parents kept their kids out of the darkest corners of Castle Cove. Abigail's mom hadn't even let her outside after sunset until she was sixteen. Landon's parents still never let him go anywhere alone without at least two or three friends in tow.

By comparison, Grayson's parents must seem like free-range hippies.

Maybe it was because both of his parents were from Los Angeles. To them, anywhere in the world could be dangerous. It didn't matter if it was drugs or violence in LA or monsters in Castle Cove. Living required intelligent precautions.

Grayson watched the flames dance on the pyre, the wood

crackling. His mind wandered. Eighteen. Tonight he was eighteen and he had to decide what he would do next.

He'd told UCLA that he would attend in the fall. He spoke of his love of nature in his admissions essay and was granted a scholarship to their conservation program. However, he also had an open invitation at Castle Cove University where his mother taught folklore.

Two paths were laid out before him. Two worlds offered him a place.

He had to decide which road he wanted to take.

His family had moved to Castle Cove when he was eight. He'd been in this town for ten years. He could stay here, and keep living this extraordinary life full of mystery and surprise, a life where unimaginable creatures and magic were very real. Or, he could leave and see what it was like to live in the outside world, a world he barely remembered.

Abigail pressed the bottom of her foot against his. The sand rubbed between their toes. "You trying to think of a way out of this? Because you're going in the water, birthday boy."

Grayson smiled. "I was thinking about school."

"You excited about UCLA?" Landon asked.

"Maybe."

"We'll miss you," Abby added. She'd pulled her bottom lip into her mouth when she said it. The look in her firelit eyes made Grayson's heart hitch. She wasn't supposed to look at him like that. Not with her boyfriend sitting beside her. But it was also the way she worked her lower lip. It was her *I have something to tell you* face, and yet she wasn't speaking.

Grayson managed a smile. "I'll be back before you know I'm gone."

"Doubt it," she said, looking out over the dark water.

"You'll be busy at CCU," he said. "Engineering is a rigorous program."

She shrugged, trying for nonchalance. But Grayson saw the tightness in her shoulders.

Landon put an arm around her. "You'll rock it, babe. Your brain is bigger than my stomach which we all know is *enormous*."

It was true. He might be rail thin, but Landon ate enough for four grown men.

"And I've got that internship with your dad this summer," Abigail said. She was looking at Grayson, searching his face as if hoping to see something there. "He's going to teach me to calibrate the machines in the lab."

"I think he's more excited than you are." Grayson was careful to keep his smile neutral. Perhaps if Landon wasn't sitting so close to him, he would've dared a real smile. "When do you start?"

"In three weeks," she said, tucking her hair behind her ear. "Will you be working there too?"

"Maybe."

Grayson hadn't missed the subtle advances she'd made in the last few months. The three of them had been friends since middle school. They had classes together, ate lunch together, and hung out together after school and on the weekends when Grayson didn't have scouts. When Abigail and Landon started dating in tenth grade, he hadn't been jealous.

But now...

In the fall, she'd joined the yearbook and school mag, *The Circuit*, which Grayson had worked on since his freshman year. His love of photography was second only to his love of nature. He knew Abigail didn't care about either. At first he didn't understand why she'd want to spend an extra two hours after school every day, until he started to notice *the look*.

Then she tried out for and made the crew team during winter. She took—surprisingly, position seven, which had been vacated by a graduating senior the year before. By doing so, she'd become his able lieutenant to his position, stroke.

He'd known she was a good swimmer, and she'd always come to watch his team compete in the May races. But it was still clear why she was really there.

The only problem was Landon.

He loved Abigail even more than he loved food and had since second grade. If she dumped him for his best friend—for Grayson—*no*.

Just no.

Grayson knew it wasn't worth it. Even if Abigail was beautiful and smart and brave and—

Abigail stood up from the fire and pulled her shirt over her head. Firelight danced across her bare breasts.

"Come on, birthday boy" she said, meeting his eyes.

Grayson did his best to keep his gaze fixed on hers.

Don't look down, he thought. *Don't...*

But her lips had already quirked into a smile. She knew she'd won. "You're not getting any younger."

"This is going to be cold," Landon whined. He stood and shrugged off his shirt. He slid out of his shorts and stood in boxers.

Abigail offered a hand to Grayson, helping him to his feet. Grayson was reluctant to leave the warm fire, but Abigail was right.

Castle Cove teens had a rite of passage.

On their eighteenth birthday, they came down to Hunter's Beach and swam the 800 feet from the shore to Heart's Rock. If they chickened out, there was Coward's Clutch, a small rock off to the left, a mere 350 feet from shore.

But the goal was to swim to Heart's Rock under the mournful gaze of the full moon. Doing so would ensure that Castle Cove would always be your home. You could leave town and never worry that it would disappear on you, as it was wont to do for outsiders.

It just so happened that Grayson's eighteen birthday was a full moon.

It wasn't the swim itself.

It wasn't the sharks, or jellyfish, or even drowning that he worried him. It wasn't the idea of floating out there in the dark waves alone—because Abigail and Landon had both wanted to come with him. That was *their* tradition.

Landon was the first one to turn eighteen last October. After standing on the shore for fifteen minutes, it was clear he'd been afraid to get in the water. So they'd each taken one of his hands and pulled him in. Then the three of them swam to Heart's Rock together.

He had wanted to take the detour to Coward's Clutch, but they'd urged him on, staying beside him until he'd reached Heart's Rock.

When Abigail turned eighteen in April, they'd done the swim again. Abby hadn't been afraid, but they'd entered the water with her anyway.

Now it was June and Grayson's turn. The waters would be warm and the swim pleasant.

So why was his throat thick with fear?

In a word: sirens.

Abigail seemed to read his face as she stood naked in the surf. "They don't come into the cove. They might come onto the rock, but that's when we jump off. No problem."

That's what they had done on Abigail's birthday. A male siren had come onto the rock and sang to her until Landon got his fingers into her ears and pulled her back into the water.

Grayson kept his eyes on hers, but was hyperaware of her bare breasts glowing in the moonlight.

Landon wasn't even trying to hide his gaze.

"Babe, real talk." Landon cracked his neck to one side. "Are you going to be pissed if I fuck a mermaid?"

"Are *you* going to be pissed if I fuck a mer*man*?" she retorted. Landon frowned.

"Sirens just want love too." Grayson tried to break up the tension forming between them.

Abigail snorted and walked out into the water. She beckoned Grayson forward. "You first birthday boy. This is your party."

It was true that they were likely safe. This inlet was supposed to be off-limits. It was supposed to be safe. But sirens did come to the beach and there was a real danger of being raped or drowned by them.

Abigail was staring at him. He looked down, and saw the blade.

"Why do you always bring that?" she asked him. "This is the third time we've done this swim. Nothing happens."

He looked at the six-inch blade strapped to his left forearm. He could see how it seemed paranoid. They'd completed the first two birthday swims with no need of a weapon. However, just because they hadn't run into trouble before didn't mean they wouldn't find some tonight.

"Better safe than sorry," he said, and stepped through the first wave. Cool water slapped his torso and he bent over protectively as if that would spare him.

"It's June," Landon whimpered, wading into the surf after him. "I thought it'd be warmer."

Once it rose above Grayson's thighs, he dove in.

He found a rhythm quickly. His freestyle crawl helped him stay on top of the waves as they buoyed and dropped him.

Salt stung his eyes, but it was bearable. The deeper the water got, the cooler it felt beneath him. He tried not to think about that. He tried not to think about sharks hunting the inlet for their nighttime meals. He tried not to think about what might be circling below.

He kept swimming.

A splash on his right made his heart lurch. But it was only Abby. She had caught up to him and was gaining.

He swam after her and tried to remember why they were doing this. It was a silly superstition. Or it would be, if this was any other town in the world. And the story was given credibility because it had been his mother—the head folklorist at CCU, who'd told him the story of Heart's Rock.

Castle Cove is a unique town with its own history, she's said. *And all myths stem from fact.*

Two myths centered on the large bolder jutting from the dark sea ahead.

First, there was a belief that Castle Cove only invited certain citizens. One had to be chosen in order to even find the town on the map, to even see the exit from the highway. Both his mother and father had been offered jobs here, though they hadn't applied for them. The head-hunting scout had worked hard to sell the town to them. And once they'd arrived, they quickly realized why this town was…*unique.*

The second myth that made swimming 1600 feet beneath a full moon remotely tempting, was the idea that in order for children to remain in the town, in order to *remain* chosen, they needed the cove's blessing—and that was only achieved by touching Heart's Rock, the metaphorical and perhaps literal, heart of Castle Cove.

And while Grayson wasn't sure he wanted to stay in this town, he also wasn't sure he wanted to chance being cast out of it either.

His knee scraped something rough the same time he slapped the granite surface of the rock. He pulled, hefting himself out of the water.

His arms burned. His chest ached. The swim felt harder than it should have been. The waves were doubling in size now. Or perhaps the tide had turned against them. He looked up at the sky and saw thick gray clouds rolling in. It masked the moon like a shroud.

Abigail hauled herself out of the water a minute later, coughing. He offered an arm and she took it. Her skin was cold to the touch.

"Whew," she said, laughing. "Refreshing."

"Where the hell did that storm come from?" he asked, wiping water from his face. He looked out toward the horizon and saw the spiderweb of lightning spread across the sky.

"Right? Those waves are crazy."

He checked his arm and found the blade snug in its sheath. Maybe he would look stupid for bringing it after all.

"Gray—" Abby said. "I need to talk to you, okay?"

His heart crept up his throat. "About what?"

"Something important. Not tonight, but we need to talk."

"Okay."

"Without Landon," she said. She searched his face. "So don't say anything."

"Okay," he said, feeling like a parrot.

He looked out over the water, searching for Landon almost guiltily. He was struggling with the last ten feet.

"Come on," Grayson said, clapping as if to cheer him on. "You can do it, buddy."

When he got close enough, they heaved him out of the water.

"Man," he said, coughing. "Was it me or did it feel like swimming upstream there at the end?"

Grayson pointed at the sky. "A storm is coming in."

"We'll rest before swimming back," Abby said, dragging a hand down her face to clear the water. "But not for too long. My nipples are going to freeze off."

"I can help with that," Landon said. But his teeth were chattering.

Abby snorted. "Worry about yourself, Jack Frost."

Grayson looked north over his shoulder at the cliff face. There sat the castle ruins for which the town was named. It was a dilapidated structure cutting the sky. Something flew above the highest remaining spire.

Bats, he thought, but whatever it was looked too large to be a bat, even if it was flying like one. Perhaps a nightjar then.

A deep ache formed in his chest.

He would miss Castle Cove. As strange as this place might be and perhaps as unsafe for a human like him, it still felt like home.

A cold hand brushed his arm and he looked down, half expecting to see a siren pulling itself out of the water onto the rock that marked neutral territory.

But it was Abigail. She squeezed harder and gave him a smile. "Happy birthday, Gracie."

Instinctively, his eyes darted toward Landon, but the other boy was trying to blow something out of his nose.

"God, I hate salt water," Landon grumbled, hacking into the sea.

"We have a lake," Abigail said. Her voice was perfectly calm as if she wasn't holding Grayson's hand at all.

Landon laughed. "With water demons in it. No, thanks. I'll stick to the city pool."

"The pool's haunted," Grayson said. He marveled at how calm his voice was—as if his heart wasn't knocking wildly in his throat.

"I'll take my chances."

His hand was warming in hers. He was about to withdraw when she let go and stood.

"Okay boys, let's go get some slices at CC Pizza after this. Last one back pays."

She dove into the water. Her pale skin flashed iridescent before disappearing beneath a black wave.

Landon stood, looking into the water. "Man, I'm in love with her."

"I know." Grayson felt like he'd been kicked in the gut.

The grin on Landon's face was sweet and so goofy that Grayson could only laugh. "Go get her then, man."

Landon's grin widened as he jumped off the rock. "Cannonball!"

Before Landon surfaced, a shimmer caught Grayson's eye.

A shark fin stuck three or four inches out of the water. It cut beneath the wave. It had a distinguished black tip, so it was only a reef shark. Luckily, the underwater rock barrier kept all big predators out of the cove. But it was still a shark and a bite was a bite.

The fin had been moving north across the cove and if it kept to its course, it would directly cut across Abby and Landon's paths.

But that didn't mean they were in danger. Shark attacks happened so rarely. In Castle Cove, they'd never had someone even bitten by sharks, let alone killed by one. It was vampires, werewolves and other land creatures one had to look out for.

And he had the blade.

He stood, stretched his arms overhead and readied to take the plunge.

That's when he saw the real danger.

Three shimmering forms darted around Heart's Rock. They glimmered and twirled beneath the water. The three bioluminescent forms swam in tight formation toward Abby and Landon. Then they split. Two followed Landon, one rushed toward Abby who was more than halfway to shore.

She might make it before it reached her. Or not.

Landon definitely wouldn't make it.

Sirens. Inside the territory line. Inside *the cove*. That wasn't supposed to happen.

And what was Grayson supposed to do? Stay on the rock

and wait for a better moment to swim to shore? Or jump into the water and try to reach Landon before the sirens did?

Grayson Choice 1
Stay on rock - go to page 80
Jump in and swim for Landon (ES) - go to page 34

REESE: SWIM SOUTH TOWARD THE DROP OFF

Reese decided to stick with her original plan. She longed to patrol the moonlit waters along the drop.

So she swam south through the reef. She swam in a hypnotic rhythm as she slid along the ocean floor. Her body enjoyed the slow steady drag of the water over her skin. She felt weightless, becoming one with the currents.

The tips of her fins registered the moment the reef dropped away and only an expanse of ocean stretched out before her. She hooked right around the reef, tracing the outline of its slumbering form. Ethereal moonlight cut through the surface, ghostly beams illuminating the coral. Nighttime feeders darted into available nooks and crannies as she passed. No one wanted to be the evening meal for a reef shark.

She might be a predator in these waters, but reef sharks were small, comparatively. She was a little large for a reef shark, reaching six feet. But that was nothing for a tiger or bull shark that might come toward shore.

Castle Cove waters had the usual flora and fauna of a shallow reef ecosystem—and then also creatures that did not exist in other parts of the world. Apart from the shapeshifting sirens they also had a resident *Bake-kujira*, a skeletal ghost whale. Reese felt it in her electromagnetic field and could hear its long, mournful song. But she had not seen it with her own eyes. It was far out in the deep blue sea. Reese wasn't interested in becoming someone's meal just to satisfy her curiosity.

Apart from sirens and *Bake-kujira*, there were also undines who swam these waters. Undines were tricky little water demons. Playfully luring a human into a riptide, causing them to drown, was their idea of a good time.

But the ocean was quiet tonight. Reese saw nothing out of the ordinary as she swam the reef.

Until magic rippled across the water, and her sensors shifted into high alert.

A massive burst of magic ejected from somewhere overhead. She darted west, tracing the reef until it opened up, giving her a path to the shore.

Thunder rolled across the sky, intensifying the strange electric feelings cascading over Reese's skin. The pressure in the ocean changed.

As inconspicuously as possible, she transformed from shark to human in the warm shallows.

Slowly, she stood up in the water, dripping. There, crouched beside a large boulder, was a dark-haired woman. Reese kept low, using another boulder to hide her position as she inspected the scene. Despite the heat, she wore black gloves, boots, and equestrian pants. She looked ready to ride a horse, not go for a swim.

Open on the sand in front of her was an enormous book. Something glinted, sparking with reflected moonlight.

A knife, Reese thought.

The storm raged stronger. A bolt of lightning tore across the sky, illuminating the woman's pale face and black eyes. She was whispering something to the dark, waiting.

Except nothing happened.

The woman cursed and threw the blade into the sand.

She stood and kicked the earth, sending a spray of sand arcing into the water. She gathered up her book, shook the sand from it and started to march away.

After a few feet, she returned and grudgingly picked up the knife again. Obviously displeased with its performance. She looked ready to throw it into the ocean.

Performance, she repeated in her mind. Maybe it wasn't a knife then, but an athame, a ceremonial tool for magic. Reese could certainly feel the magic still dancing along her skin, though now it seemed to be dissipating. The storm overhead was quieting, too. The wind eased its assault on her hair and ears. The woman was halfway up the dune, sand shifting under her boots. Had she caused the storm? The surge in magic? What the hell had just happened?

What was Reese going to do about it?

Reese Choice 2
Follow strange woman - go to page 120
Go home - go to page 174

REESE: SWIM EAST TOWARD KIDS

Swimming in deep water, especially the waters surrounding Castle Cove, wasn't the safest bet. But Reese's mind kept replaying the conversation she'd overheard in the bar. *A guy died...if sirens are killing people, I'd want to know.*

On one hand, she had it all wrong. The kids would prove to be safe, and then she'd retreat to warmer waters. If not, if there was something to the story she'd overheard, she'd regret not being there when they needed her.

So she swam east. Her body enjoyed the slow steady drag of the water over her skin. She felt weightless. No, *powerful*—as she patrolled the deep slowly, her senses wide open to any disturbances in the water.

She felt it through her entire core the moment the reef dropped away and only cold, deep water spread out around her.

Still, she kept her course, gliding toward Heart's Rock, at the outermost edge of the cove.

The humans thought Heart's Rock was a single, solitary boulder in the middle of the sea. But in truth, which Reese could see fine with her shark eyes, a wall of rock rose from the ocean floor. This impenetrable stone wall obstructed most of the cove, cutting it off from the open sea. Only a small gap, on each side of Heart's Rock, would allow something from the open sea into the cove.

In the distance, far off from her right side, she sensed something in the water. Out at sea, something very large moved through the deep. But it was quite far away. A larger shark maybe, but she didn't think so. There was no gentle rhythm to its movement, which Reese knew well.

And knowing Castle Cove as she did, there could be anything out there, moving through the depths.

Something was wrong with the ocean. Reese couldn't be sure, but it felt like a storm was brewing overhead, changing the pressure and ferocity of the waters churning around her. Electricity sparked along her skin, making her fins itch.

Was that magic? If so, it was an enormous flare of power.

But where was it coming from? If she had to guess she would have said west, further along the shore. Something out there pulled on her spirit the way a tide might pull at one's legs.

Before she could puzzle out the mystery, a second starburst of magic seized her mind. It made the end of her nose and the tips of her fins tingle. Then she saw the momentary flash of bioluminescence as three sirens squeezed through the gap surrounding Heart's Rock.

With the flash, three forms were illuminated in the black waters. The fishlike sirens transformed themselves into something more human. Reese thought *more* human because their telepathic glamours wouldn't fool her in her shark form. She saw the webbing between their paddle-like hands. She saw the strange fins protruding from each side of the face and the hexagonal scales shimmering where skin should be.

Then her nose detected three more bodies in the water. The electromagnetic fields around their forms pulsed, giving her a clear sense of their location in the cove. All three were human.

All three were swimming for shore. She could tell by their scent and as well as the clumsy way they splashed in the surf.

The sirens were moving in on them.

Despite the fact that sirens had never—to Reese's knowledge—crossed the Heart's Rock barrier—now they surged forward as if swimming from the gates of Hell. They would reach the kids in moments.

Two of the sirens were female, and unsurprisingly, they seemed bent on reaching the male swimmers. The third siren, and the one farthest from Reese, was male. It must be targeting a female. The male siren would rape her, if he reached her before she found the surf. Not just rape her, but likely drown her in the process. Male sirens were very aggressive and had little concern for a human's need to breathe.

Without a second to lose, Reese used all her power and strength to torpedo her body forward. Her head and tail worked together to cut the water at incredible speed. It took her only seconds to cross the cove and slip herself between the siren and the girl.

The siren collided with the side of Reese's body. The impact stopped them both in their tracks, rippling the water around them. Her body absorbed the impact painfully. Reese felt her fin rise above the surface. The night air licked her dorsal, cooling it.

The siren steadied itself.

Reese almost wished the glamour did work on her kind. Sirens were far from pretty. Their fish faces were hideous. It was their oversized, liquid black eyes, flat and unblinking.

The scales were luminescent with collected moonlight as it circled her once.

Bioluminescence flashed and its legs congealed with one another again, into a single powerful fin that made it look much more like the mermaids Reese knew from legend.

He wants the tail for speed, she thought. *So he can catch up to the girl.*

The thought was barely out of her mind when he shot forward, trying to pass Reese.

Reese darted out, blocking his path again.

The siren moved back, hissing its fury. The screech skittered along Reese's body, prickling her sensors.

He came in again, his hands bent in claws as if he wanted to tear Reese apart. Maybe he did. But Reese had the advantage of being the more dynamic of the two. She outmaneuvered the siren easily, leaving him to grasp only dark ocean water.

Something was coming up fast behind her, its bioelectric field striking Reese before the actual creature did. She dove toward the ocean floor, and the female siren cut overhead a second later, blue bubbles rippling in her wake.

Great, she thought. Two on one.

But the siren didn't seem to notice her. She was swimming for Heart's Rock as if her life depended on it.

Then she smelled it. Blood. It bloomed like overripe fruit in the water. The scent was sweet, intoxicating.

It took considerable will and the clarity of her human mind to bring Reese back to herself.

Blood in the water meant trouble. One of the kids must be hurt.

As exciting as the blood was to her, it was equally terrifying to the sirens. They fled the cove. She spotted the third siren squeezing around Heart's Rock before disappearing into the open waters beyond.

Maybe it's not the blood, she thought. Maybe something else was in the water.

She made her way toward shore. When her belly scraped the sand, her fin cutting the night air, she transformed. She stood, water beading on her skin.

With a soaked hand, she pushed her hair back from her face, coughing.

A girl was screaming. Naked on her hands and knees in the sand, she howled at the rolling surf.

Then Reese saw it. The dead kid.

His shredded body was rolling in the white frothy waves.

"Christ." She bent and grabbed the dead boy and hauled him onto the sand. It wasn't easy. His slick limbs were difficult to grab a hold of and his body was heavier than wet sand. Yet Reese managed it.

"Who the—" the other boy began. But another wail from the girl swallowed his words. He bent and wrapped his arms around her.

"Do either of you have a phone?" Reese asked. The water was beginning to chill on her skin. "We need to call someone."

"It's in my clothes." The boy pointed toward the smoldering bonfire.

Reese found a cell phone in the pocket of a grey dust jacket. She called the police. As she listened to the first ring, a glint caught her eye.

On the upper ridge, not far from where she'd parked her car, something shiny caught the light. A piece of jewelry maybe? If Reese squinted, she thought she saw a woman, marching up the dune toward the road.

"Castle Cove 911. What is your emergency?"

REESE RETRIEVED HER CLOTHES AND STAYED WITH THE KIDS UNTIL the police arrived. It seemed like a long time before Reese saw the red-blue flash of police lights from above. She stayed and answered every question that the police had. She went over her story no less than four times before she was finally allowed to leave.

Her legs were wet, aching noodles as she climbed the dune for her red pickup. By the time she reached the door, she all but collapsed into her truck.

For a long time she just sat there with her head on the steering wheel. She hadn't even made it back into town before she'd begun crying.

"At least it wasn't all three of them," she said, but it didn't abate the guilt. One kid had died. She'd been there, and hadn't been able to save him. It was her fault.

Don't take on responsibility that isn't yours, she heard her aunt say. *We have enough to be getting on with.*

But no matter how many times she said this to herself, she felt no better by the time she rolled up outside her house.

Reese parked her red pickup outside the Georgian three-story home in Cliffside. Across the street, she could see the light on at Cole's place and knew the demon and his vampire husband were no doubt awake despite the late hour. Normally she would go say hi, if the light was on like that. But after the night she had, she just wanted a hot shower and her bed.

She could smell the blood in her hair.

Reese unlocked the front door and stepped into the gorgeous foyer. A high ceiling and bright crystalline chandelier greeted her. The space was sparsely furnished in impeccable whites and ocean blues.

This gorgeous home belonged to her aunt Constance. Constance was an oceanographer, currently on a research expedition. The scientist was studying the degradation of coral in the Indian Ocean. The fact that Constance was a shark shifter no doubt helped that search and the fact that her crew were all supernaturals meant she didn't have to hide what she was or her purpose in trying to salvage what was left of the ocean.

It's our home, Aunt Constance often said. *Where our souls live. If it's lost, that will be the end of us.*

Reese went straight to the first floor bath, afraid to drip blood and heaven knew what on any other surface in the house.

Fortunately, the first-floor bath was just past the living room on the right. All the towels, soap and necessities were present and accounted for. Reese had only to strip out of her sea-soaked clothes and into the hot water.

She washed her hair twice before adding conditioner. Her tired mind wandered. Would Aunt Constance have any information on the sirens? It seemed like a topic the woman would be well-versed in. She could call her, but it would be early evening on the Indian Ocean. Her aunt would be out to sea. Perhaps she could call her tomorrow and get her insights on what went so horribly wrong that a kid died.

Clean, Reese stepped out of the shower and collected her clothes from the floor. She was tidy by nature, a habit instilled in her by her orderly aunt as well as a sense that this wasn't her house. Not really. The clothes went in the hamper. The water she'd tracked in was cleaned up with a mop.

Once every trace of her entrance had been removed, Reese changed for bed.

Out of habit, she knocked on her aunt's study door before pushing it open. The woman wasn't home and there were no ghosts in their Cliffside address—as far as she knew—but it seemed respectful somehow.

"It's just me," she announced, creeping into the room.

She shut the study door behind her. Crossing to the bookshelf, she gazed lovingly at the smattering of spines. Some books were ancient, nearly falling apart. Others looked as if they'd been made yesterday, their bindings never broken. Knowing it would take too long to go shelf to shelf, Reese crossed to the wooden card catalogue adjacent the large picture window.

She pulled out the drawer labeled S. A few flicks of her fingers found the word Siren. "Left case, Fourth shelf, box eight," she read aloud. She crossed the enormous bookcase, repeating the location over and over in her head until she found it. There were four books related to sirens tucked there. Reese plucked them all from their spots on the shelves and carried them to the desk.

She read until the sun rose in orange, pink, and red over the ocean horizon behind her. All eastern facing houses in Cliffside were afforded this beautiful horizon view. Reese loved it, had loved it since she came to live with her aunt as a child over twenty years ago.

A phone was ringing somewhere in the house. Reese, her neck and shoulders stiff, rose, groaning. She placed a hand on the back of her neck and hissed. She knew better than to fall asleep on the desk with only books for a pillow. It hadn't felt great when she did it as a child. It was even worse now that she was in her twenties. Her neck would kill her all day.

The ringing phone was her cell phone. Reese found it on the desk and turned it on.

"Hello?" she groaned. Her voice broke with the effort.

"Reese?"

It was Kristine. She didn't sound so great either. Of course, running the woods all night would do that to a woman.

"Yeah, it's me. What's up?"

"I'm calling an emergency pack meeting. A kid died in the cove last night. He was torn apart by a siren."

"I know. I was there" Reese dragged a hand down her face. She turned the desk chair to peer out at the open sea. By the look of the sun it was past three in the afternoon. According to her cell phone, it was 3:43.

"Were you? What happened?"

Reese recounted the night to her boss and friend.

"Well," Kristine said finally. Her sigh made the woman sound much older. "We need to know what's going on."

"I went through Aunt Constance's books but I haven't found anything that would explain their behavior."

"I called to see if you could watch the bar until I get there. I realize it's not your shift and I'll pay you double for that. But now that I know you're a witness, I wonder if you should be part of the discussion. I'll leave it to you to decide."

Reese Choice 3
Go to pack meeting - go to page 51
Hold down the bar - go to page 67

GRAYSON: JUMP IN AND SWIM FOR LANDON

Grayson spotted Landon swimming toward shore. His strokes were wild and uneven. No wonder he wasn't even halfway there. It wasn't until this moment, when Grayson was terrified for his life, that he realized how terrible of a swimmer Landon was. It didn't matter. He had to reach him as quickly as possible.

Grayson fixed the path in his mind and dove. The objective was to reach Landon on the heels of the sirens. Perhaps they were only curious. Hopefully they would swim around or tug playfully on their legs.

Of course, Grayson knew better.

Sirens had one objective when it came to humans. They wanted to mate.

As Grayson swam furiously toward his friend, he tried to remember everything his mother had taught him about sirens.

"The males are more aggressive than the females. They are more likely to accidentally drown their human mates than the females, though they are also incredibly strong. You have to understand that the males are only looking for sexual gratification. The females, however, are hoping to procreate so they must be more careful with their prey."

"Why in the world would they want to mate with humans?" Grayson had asked.

"Male sirens are sterile. Therefore, a healthy population of the sirens is entirely dependent upon females successfully mating with humans."

"But how do you fuck a fish?" his little brother Tanner had asked.

His father had slapped him gently on the back of the head. "Don't be crude."

"I'm just asking. I thought they had fish tails!"

"They are like shapeshifters," their mother explained. Her face had soured. She hated it when Tanner cursed. "They can take humanoid form long enough to mate."

"Humanoid," Grayson had repeated. Because they didn't really look human. Not without their glamour.

Cold seawater hit the back of Grayson's throat and he choked, coughing. But he'd almost reached Landon.

"Landon," he cried. "Landon!"

Landon stopped swimming, turning toward the sound of his voice. "What—oh shit."

Two streaks of bioluminescence cut beneath them leaving shimmering blue bubbles in their wave.

"Landon, listen to me." Grayson wanted to make his instructions clear before the sirens started singing. "They're probably females looking to mate."

"Oh man." Landon couldn't suppress his goofy grin. "I hear they turn into—"

"Listen!" Grayson spat. "You need to get to shallow water. Don't stay here or she will drown you. Do you understand?"

Landon was watching one of the sirens rise from the depths to the surface.

"Landon!"

"Shallow water. Got it!" He began to paddle to shore half-heartedly.

That's when Grayson saw he had his own problem. A young woman surfaced six feet between him and the shore. He began to paddle toward her. It wouldn't be smart to try to flee into deeper water, nor could he tread the waves all night.

But she didn't look ready to move aside either.

He closed the distance—four feet, three, just two—

He cut to the right, giving himself room. She moved into his path. It looked like Abigail. It *wasn't* Abigail. He *knew* that.

"I'll do it," he said, hoping she understood. "But not here. Okay? Not here."

If the sirens could get into his head well enough to find his perfect image of a mate, surely, it could understand these thoughts too.

But she didn't look like she was going to let him pass.

She began to cut a circle around him, not unlike a shark.

A shark. He'd forgotten all about it and it hardly mattered now. They wouldn't come near the sirens or anything else that smelled of magic.

He dared to look away long enough to check on Landon. He was closer to shore. That was good, though his siren was already practically on top of him.

Grayson felt a hand on his penis and froze in the water.

When he glanced away, the siren had seized the opportunity. She stroked him. Slow and gentle, trying to conjure an erection. So these sirens really did know how it worked.

It was Abigail. It was Abigail touching him.

"No," he said. "No, *not* her."

The anger in his voice startled her. Her grip faltered. She moved back a little as if afraid of him. Of course, her advantages far outweighed his. But she was obviously confused about her failing glamour.

He was in waist deep water now. The silty bottom met his

toes and relief rushed through his body. Abigail's red hair and deep blue eyes fell away. It was replaced with luscious blond locks, pouty lips and green eyes.

He almost laughed, but he kept backing toward shore.

"All right, Mrs. Miller," he said. "You'll do."

It was ridiculous. Mrs. Miller had been his ninth grade geometry teacher and he'd dreamt about her nearly every night that year.

The siren, smiling again, wrapped her body around his. Her grip was so strong, it pulled him under the waves. But the hand was on his penis again, furiously working.

When that didn't seem to have the desired effect, her head dipped below the surface. Lips fastened onto his penis with a suction so intense a moan was pulled from his throat.

He tried to elbow crawl toward the shore. He needed to be in the shallows or he was going to die getting blown by a fish girl with baby fever.

By the time he got his head above water, his erection was fully formed. Her mouth released him the same moment that hands grabbed onto his hips, pulling him toward her.

He realized she was trying to mount him.

Not here. God, not here.

Three or four feet of water was plenty to drown in, especially if his back was ground into the sandy ocean floor.

This was his chance. He could scramble for shore and hope he made it onto the sand before she caught him, or he could pull his knife and cut her. Cutting her would buy him more time to clear the shallows, but it might escalate the situation. His mother had said sirens could be violent when afraid.

Grayson Choice 2
Cut her with the knife - go to page 77
Get to shore (ES) - go to page 38

GRAYSON: GET TO SHORE

Instead of pulling his knife, Grayson committed to getting to shore. There was no escaping really, and if he struggled, it would only cost him.

So he wrapped his arms around Mrs. Miller, knowing Mrs. Miller smelled like Clinique and not ocean water.

He stood up. Her legs wrapped around his torso, welcoming his embrace. She sighed into the hollow of his throat.

He kept one hand on her back, as he waded through the shallows toward the shore. This was difficult to do with her relentless enthusiastic hand, but at least she wasn't heavy.

When she finally managed to slide his erection inside of her, his step faltered.

He fell forward into the surf. A wave crashed over them, pummeling his back.

But when he rolled, body aching, it was dry sand under his head. The pounding waves were only covering his legs and groin. At least he wouldn't drown.

For a moment, it was only the strange storm clouds above, sparking with heat lightning. Then she mounted him.

Her body glistened with ocean water. Sand clinging to her breast and arms looked like crystals in the diffused moonlight.

She stayed astride him, grinding her hips into his. The sand scraped his back and buttocks. There was a rock or shell of some kind pushing into his tailbone. But he knew the best option was to lie still and indulge in his ninth grade fantasy come to life.

He turned his head, looking up the beach. He hoped he would spot Abby and Landon both safe on the shore. But the bonfire had died down and with only momentary bursts of lightning, shadows prevailed.

It looked like there was something happening at the other end of the beach—bodies moving. But it was too far to see.

Mrs. Miller picked up her pace. As she bent forward, and her cool breasts brushed his face, all thoughts were shoved out of his mind. Everything disappeared but the stormy night sky and Mrs. Miller's dripping, hard nipples.

He came and for a moment he was the one holding onto her hips, rocking against her.

But before he even caught his breath, the weight lifted and she was gone.

Two splashes and a bright flash of blue bioluminescence beneath a wave—and she was gone.

It wasn't his best sexual experience. It had been too quick, and the shells under his back had no doubt scraped his skin to hell. He also preferred his partners warm rather than as cold as a sea slug.

He tried not to think of what she must've looked like in her true form. He'd heard sirens resembled the fish monster from the Black Lagoon. If that was true, then the telepathic glamour was a blessing—even if he would find it hard to look Mrs. Miller in the eye again. *Ever.*

Grayson wanted to rinse himself in the ocean, but decided against it. The ocean water would burn like hell with the cuts stinging his back. Plus, now that he knew the sirens had breached the Cove's rock barrier, it was entirely possible that a second female could approach him and he—*no*. He couldn't do it again.

He'd have to put his clothes on as he was and worry about cleaning himself later.

Screaming tore the night in two.

Grayson's heart rocketed into his chest and before he knew what he was doing, he was running down the beach as fast as his unsteady legs would carry him.

It was Abigail. Abigail was screaming.

He pulled the knife from his forearm sheath, afraid he would have to fight a siren after all.

Abigail was still naked on the sand, her hands and knees sinking into the wet shoreline. Her face was contorted. Her mouth hung open, before another wave of sound tore through her.

"Abby—Abby!" He bent to pull her away from the water. But he saw no siren. A flash of bioluminescence sparked a hundred feet away, swimming in the direction of the ruined castle and the cliff it rested on. If it was the male siren, he was swimming away from them.

That wasn't what she was looking at.

Her eyes were fixed on a strange tangle of limbs tumbling in the ocean surf.

"Landon." Grayson's voice cracked.

It was Landon's body tossing in the white waves. Wave after wave pummeled him into the sand.

Grayson forgotten about his plan to stay out of the ocean and went into the water. He grabbed a slick limb and dragged Landon onto beach.

He wanted to turn him over, do CPR, or pound on his chest until water spurted from his mouth the way it did in the movies.

But Grayson knew his friend was dead the moment he

touched his skin. There was something unnatural in its weight. The living had a lightness to their being. Landon's lightness was gone.

Yet Grayson turned him over on the shore anyway, aware that Abigail was still screaming though the sound had become a distant annoyance. It was a fly buzzing in the other room.

Grayson was shoving the heel of his hand into Landon's sternum. He was tilting back the chin so he could pinch the nose closed and blow into the mouth. But the lips were cold. The chest wasn't moving. The heart wasn't beating.

Landon was dead.

THEY DRESSED BEFORE THE POLICE ARRIVED. THEY'D HAD ABOUT fifteen minutes between the moment he'd pulled his cell phone from his pocket until he saw the flashlights first sweep the sandy dunes.

Then the police were calling out their names and Grayson found a way to call back, though his throat was raw and burning.

Abigail's mother was first on the scene. As an officer at Castle Cove PD, she would've heard the call come into the station and would've taken it upon herself to drive straight to Hunter's Beach.

What he hadn't expected was that his own parents would be a close second.

It was his father who threw a gray wool blanket over his shoulders. It was his mother who squeezed him so hard he couldn't breathe.

"Are you all right?" she asked. "Are you—Christ, you're trembling."

"I'm fine," he managed, yet his teeth were chattering. "But Landon—Landon."

His voice broke and his father pulled him into his embrace.

He wasn't sure how long they held him, cocooned by his parents on either side. Someone was stroking his wet hair.

When they finally released him, dozens more had arrived. There were officers in jackets, but also paramedics. They wanted to give both Abigail and Grayson full physicals.

One shone a penlight into Grayson's eyes.

"I'm fine," Grayson insisted. But they still sat him and Abigail down against a rock. She hadn't stopped crying. "Forget about me. Check on Abby."

"We need to know what happened," Officer Una O'Reilly said. Una was Abigail's mom.

"Grayson," his father said. It was the one-word command he'd heard often in his life, but never delivered with such tenderness.

Grayson told the story. He began with their plan to swim to Heart's Rock and then go get pizza.

"It's his eighteenth birthday," his mother interjected as if defending him.

"Then they came around the rock," he said. "Three sirens."

"Onto the rock?" Officer O'Reilly corrected.

"No," Grayson shook his head and cold water fell from his hair on to his cheek. "Around the rock. They passed me and swam straight into the cove. They were chasing Abigail and Landon. The females split off for Landon and the male went after Abby."

Officer O'Reilly stiffened. Her face pinched.

"I thought the inlet was safe," his father said, searching the detective's face. "I thought this tradition was harmless."

"If you call the threat of rape harmless," his mother Lillian countered.

Officer O'Reilly seemed to struggle, but finally found her words. "There was also a siren attack last Saturday." She pointed south, down the beach. "While they do visit the southern beaches from time to time, they've never crossed into the inlet before. We will have to investigate what would drive them this far into the cove."

"If there was another attack, why haven't we heard about it? Why didn't you issue a warning?" his mother demanded.

"There hasn't been time," the detective replied.

"It happened last weekend. Why didn't you let us know they were agitated? The community deserves to know if our children—"

"Lillian," his father said. He squeezed her arm, and to her credit, she seemed to regain control of herself.

"We thought last weekend's attack was an isolated incident. We did report it to…the proper authorities. But we haven't heard any new information on the situation. Frankly, we didn't know what was going on and therefore weren't sure what to report."

"Tell that to *them!*" Grayson's mother pointed at the couple further down the beach. Landon's parents were surrounded by police. It looked like they wanted to come over and talk, but the authorities weren't allowing them to come any closer.

"You could have reported that there was an attack," Lillian said stiffly. "At least tell people to stay off the beach."

"You're right. We will have to now," Officer O'Reilly conceded.

"Landon is dead." It was Abigail speaking. "Landon is dead."

"I know, sweetie." Una stooped and wrapped her arms around her daughter. "I'm so sorry."

Grayson heard the unspoken relief in her voice. *At least it wasn't you.* That must be what she was thinking. Someone's child had died tonight. But it hadn't been her child. And though both of their parents knew who Landon was to Abby and Grayson, they couldn't hide their own gratitude. They might have seen Landon grow into a young man, they might've had him over for dinners and playdates, but none of that meant they would sacrifice their own children in his place.

A man in a dark blue jacket stood awkwardly to one side, waiting to get Officer O'Reilly's attention.

She spotted him. "What is it?"

"We just wanted to let you know that the markings on the body and the water in the respiratory system are consistent with a siren attack. There was no ejaculate present—"

"Christ," Grayson's mother swore.

"—it was likely washed away in the surf."

Una held up one hand. The other remained on Abby's shoulder. "That's enough for now, Darryl. Thank you."

"Lillian, Wade, I hate to ask but could you take Abigail home, please. I will need to stay here until the scene is processed. The kids are both cold and—"

"I don't want to be alone," Abigail said. She lifted her head and dragged her nose across the blanket draping her arm.

"You can come to our house," Lillian said, tugging the blanket tighter around her. Then turning her face up to Una she said, "We'll be with them."

"Thank you." Una helped Abby to her feet. "I'll come get you as soon as I leave here. If it's too late, I'll wait until the morning. I'm sure you're all exhausted. Don't wait up for me."

"Text me either way," his mother told Officer O'Reilly. "I'll be awake."

In silence the four of them climbed the steep ledge to the parking lot above. Grayson and Abby followed his parents, shoulder to shoulder, to the parking lot beside the castle ruins. No one spoke as his father unlocked the car and they climbed in. In the dark back seat, Abigail snuggled close to Grayson's side, crying quietly.

"Are you hungry?" his father asked.

Grayson met his eyes in the rearview. "I don't know if I can eat now."

"We will pick up something anyway," his mother said,

regarding him with one of her stern faces. "You don't have to eat it. But it will be there if you want it."

"Not pizza," Abby said softly from her corner of the car. Her voice was thick with tears. "Anything but pizza."

They picked up Chinese from the Moodle Noodle shop on the west side of campus. His father went in and paid while his mother stayed in the car.

No one spoke. The radio remained off. But distant music from a closing bar reached them.

It was Abigail who broke the silence first. "When I get to your house, can I please take a shower?"

"Of course," his mother said, turning in her seat to gaze at her. "Of course you can."

"Where's Tanner?" Grayson asked. His parents wouldn't have brought him to a murder scene, but it couldn't have been easy finding a sitter at two in the morning.

"He had a sleepover with Will." It was like her face was drinking him in. "We will tell him what happened later."

Don't say it, he thought. He could practically see the *I'm just so glad you're okay* written on her face. But if she said it, Abby would begin to cry again and she'd finally started to quiet down.

"All right," his father said, climbing into the car and handing a brown sack to his mother. "We have enough chicken and lo mien to feed an army. Anything else?"

"A shower," Abby begged.

His father favored her with a weak smile. "Coming right up."

His father waited for a trio of drunk coeds to cross the street before he pulled away from the curb into the post-bar traffic.

Grayson's parents had bought a house in historic Midtown. This was a vintage neighborhood with beautiful restored Victorian homes and small shops. There was a coffeeshop and bookstore and it had the feel of a small antiquated town, complete with a local grocer and old-fashioned video store, where people could still rent DVDs and video games.

This neighborhood's insular seclusion was one of the reasons Grayson had been allowed to roam so freely as a child. Everything he could have wanted—candy or ice cream, a park or playground, his friends—were within a few blocks of his house.

The porchlight was on when they pulled into the drive, illuminating freshly stained steps and the railing. The house itself was a deep cherry red. He and his father had just repainted it the previous summer. It had taken them all three months, and it wasn't like his family didn't have the money to hire a team to do it faster. It was simply one of his father's "bonding" projects—of which there had been many over the years.

But seeing the house had the effect Grayson suspected his father wanted.

Every time Grayson saw it, he felt proud. Proud of what a good job the four of them had done together, and proud of his family.

This was home. He was safe here.

When he threw open the car door, he had tears in his eyes. His father saw them as he was closing his own door.

"I know," his father murmured quietly. "I know."

He squeezed Grayson's shoulder hard, and pulled him toward the house.

His mother got the door open, ushering Abigail over the threshold.

"Honey, get some towels," she said, tossing her keys and purse on the bench beside the stairs. "When you get out of the shower, Abigail, I'll have something clean for you to wear. It'll be a little big on you."

The shirt would be fine, but Abigail wasn't as tall as his mother. The pants would have to be rolled up and perhaps belted at the waist.

"It's fine," Abigail managed, looking small and worn under the gray wool blanket. "Thank you."

His mother carried the food into the kitchen and disappeared through the swinging door.

"Grayson, show her how the taps work," his father instructed, putting two fresh towels in his hand. He took the blanket off Grayson's shoulder. "And make sure there's enough soap and all that."

"Come on." Grayson took the lead on the stairs even though Abby had been visiting his house since the fourth grade. Of course, she'd never stayed the night before.

The wooden staircase creaked under their weight. When they reached the top of the stairs, he turned left and then left again to his own bathroom at the end of the hall.

He placed the towels on the sink, aware of Abigail standing beside him.

"It's backwards. You turn the handle this way for hot, and this way for cold. If it sputters, it's just air in the pipes. It'll kick back up in a second. Don't let the rattle scare you."

He left the tap on hot and pulled up the stop. The water was diverted from the spout to the showerhead, spraying the basin in a gentle rain.

Abigail handed him the blanket and began to undress.

He shouldn't care. He'd seen her naked about half a dozen times in their life. But he still backed toward the door.

"I'll put the clothes outside the door," he said.

He thought it best to look her in the eyes, rather than chance staring at anything else.

But when he looked into her eyes, she was crying.

"It was you," she said, standing there naked in his bathroom, with the hot water running into a cream-colored tub.

His heart hammered in his chest.

"When the siren—I wanted it because—" She bit her quivering lip. Her hand fisted on the burgundy shower curtain. "When he was—he looked like you."

Then Grayson understood what she was trying to say. The male siren *had* caught up to her and she hadn't resisted him.

It was Grayson she'd been making love to as her boyfriend was killed.

"I'm sorry," he said. He wasn't sure what he was apologizing for. Probably all of it. The whole shitty situation. But she'd already climbed inside the shower and had pulled the curtain closed between them.

Grayson showered in his parents' bathroom.

Then after he put the fresh clothes on the sink for Abigail—she hadn't finished yet—he went downstairs to find his parents sitting around the dining room table.

Grayson had always loved this table. It was strange and ornate and looked more like a table built for 1920s seances than for family dinners. But it was one of the many charming features of their restored home.

"Come sit with us," his mother said. She was trying not to sound desperate, which Grayson appreciated. A swell of affection filled his chest.

After his shower, he found he could eat after all. The headache building behind his eyes and the shaking in his exhausted limbs begged him to eat something. "Let me grab some food first."

He went into the kitchen and pulled a white ceramic plate from the shelf. He loaded it with pineapple fried rice, lo mien, General Tso's chicken, and three pieces of crab rangoon.

He grabbed a sparkling water from the fridge and carried it into the dining room.

He sat down between his parents, knowing that was where they wanted him.

"Your father and I talked and we decided to waive the no-girls-sleeping-in-your-room policy," his mother said.

"Good call. I don't think she'll sleep alone."

"But we want you to leave the door open," his father added.

Grayson didn't even fight them. He didn't care.

His mind kept replaying the image of Landon tossing in the surf, his pale body thrashing in the waves.

"We don't have to talk about what happened," his mother began. Her words had the practiced air about them. She was a professor, but Grayson was certain that it was also because she liked to rehearse what she would say in her mind long before saying it. He was like his mother in this way.

And when had she composed this speech? In the car on the way home? When he was in the shower? Or maybe even in the car on their way to retrieve their *almost* dead son.

"Especially if you're tired," his father added. "The swim alone must've been exhausting, not to mention—" There was a jerk under the table and Grayson was fairly sure his mother had just kicked him. His father grimaced. "We just want you to know we're proud of you."

"Landon is dead." Grayson pushed the rice around on his plate with the back of his fork.

His father reached out and squeezed his shoulder. "You couldn't do anything about that."

"I should've done more. I should've—"

"If anyone is to blame for Landon's death, it's the authorities," his mother interjected. "They should have told the town about the siren attack. There should've been a notice to stay out of the water. This town—"

"Lill," his father said and her mouth snapped shut.

"I'm just saying. How are people supposed to stay safe if they aren't properly informed?"

His father fixed him with his gaze again. "You're not to blame for what happened and we're proud of you for handling the situation the best you could."

"Please stop saying that," Grayson said. He couldn't sit at this table with his Chinese food and be congratulated by his parents as if he'd won some prize. Landon was *dead*.

Landon was dead and—

"Keeping your cool in a dangerous situation is everything." It was his mother speaking. "It's going to take a long time to get over this. Maybe you'll never completely get over this loss. But we wanted you to know that we are here and we'll do anything we can to help you. If you need something, tell us."

This loss.

They weren't even saying his name.

He understood all of the words coming out of their mouths. He even understood that the reason he was here at the table while his best friend was dead on a beach was because he'd been blessed with smart, patient parents who'd prepared him to survive.

And it was more than that. He'd gotten lucky. He'd been *damn* lucky.

Then why was he so angry? Why did he feel like he shouldn't be the one in the chair? Why did it feel like it was unfair that Landon should be dead and that he should be alive? Why did he want to trade places with him?

I wanted it to be you, Abby had said.

"If you need anything—" his mother was saying again.

He exhaled and pushed away from the table. "I need some air."

"We'd rather you stay in the house," his father said.

His mother shot him another look and his father grimaced as if expecting another kick.

"But we won't tell you what to do," his mother said. "But why don't you go to bed? You've had one hell of a night."

"A hell of a birthday," he murmured. "I think I'll…"

Grayson Choice 3
Go for a walk - go to page 100
Go to bed - go to page 152

REESE: GO TO PACK MEETING

"I'll come to the meeting," Reese said. She dragged a hand down her face. "When does it start?"

A short rustle of fabric made Reese suspect that Kristine was moving the phone to her other ear. "In an hour. We'll be at the amphitheater in Sunset Park."

Reese glanced at the clock. It was shaped like a great white shark, the white belly shining in the afternoon sun. She'd slept most of the day away. "See you there."

Kristine murmured her goodbyes. Reese considered her needs in order of importance.

Food and a shower were at the top of the list. She decided on the shower first.

She dressed in freshly laundered clothes that reeked of fabric softener.

Brunch, she decided, was a can of tuna on dry toast. After finishing her toast and throwing the rinsed can in the recycle bin, she brushed her teeth for a second time. She unwrapped two sticks of mint gum and washed her hands just to be sure.

The drive to Sunset Park was quiet. It was that calm hour between afternoon and evening. Most of the daytimers hadn't left work yet, and the evening crowd hadn't yet woken. The streets were nearly empty. In Cliffside, a few people were walking their dogs, their headphones on as they strolled down the white-washed sidewalk.

When Cliffside gave way to downtown, she saw more students. Kids that were enjoying their summer breaks hung out in clusters in front of their favorite haunts. The Magic Bean coffeeshop seemed particularly busy, but there was also a cluster outside the burrito shop on the corner. When she turned left just before Red Light, a burst of nature sprung into view.

North of campus and Red Light, the town was completely undeveloped.

Sunset Park was the most manicured part of it. Beyond that, the Wayward Woods sat wild and welcoming. It had its trails and many of the park rangers had even laid wood chips down to manicure the paths.

But no shifter or werefolk worth their salt would be fooled by something as simple as a clean cut path. The nature magic rolling through the Wayward Woods was palpable. But it was a friendly magic, unlike the magic one could feel if they got too close to the West Territory line, or Goddess forbid, the Western Woods themselves. That magic was hungry and wanting.

Reese parked her rattling red pickup in the parking lot at the edge of Sunset Park beneath a large maple tree. She fished the shimmering visor out from behind her seat and unfolded it across the dash, blocking the windshield completely and filling the car with shadows. She hoped it would control much of the heat from building in the truck. She wasn't sure how long this meeting would last, but they had hours left in the day before sunset fell. And the old leather seats in Reese's truck seemed to hold onto heat the way a dying man holds onto his last breath.

She counted the cars in the lot. Thirty at least. A few more and all the spaces would be gone. Were they all werewolves and shifters? Or were other park visitors milling about?

Reese followed the path from the parking lot. She could have gone left, heading toward the trails and woods beyond. Instead, she took the right fork, watching the path snake around a bend before opening up on a large stone amphitheater. More than a hundred people filled the amphitheater. Most of the people were sitting on the stone seats, talking to one another. A ripple of power erupted on the right, drawing some attention.

Ninety percent of the people here were werewolves, unified under Kristine's leadership as their alpha. Once upon a time, there had been multiple packs in town, but once Kristine became alpha, the packs consolidated. Reese suspected that was due to Kristine more than anything. The alpha had worked hard to create a more integrated community.

Not only had she folded all the werewolves into a single pack, but she also worked to bring in other shifters, whom Reese spotted in the crowd. There was an emphasis on sitting not with your own kind, but with those least like you. For this reason, Reese took a seat between a werewolf and a bird shifter in the middle of the amphitheater, off to Kristine's left side.

The alpha had also worked to dispel the separation between bitten and born shifters, which Reese was glad to see was working. The mix was well done, with bitten and born, pack and non-pack spread evenly through the amphitheater. Reese suspected that there were some traditionalists among them who preferred the old ways, but they kept their dissent to themselves. If they were giving Kristine grief, they were doing so behind the scenes.

In the past, the bitten were frowned upon as lesser. Werewolves who had been born of other werewolves were considered stronger and purer. The same was true of shifters like Reese, who had been born with their animal dispositions.

Ironically, those who could change their form at will—to any animal or human they desired—were ostracized. Chimeras like

Nick—Alpha's bouncer—were criticized for their lack of connection to a particular animal spirit.

Right on the hour, Kristine raised her hand. The crowd quieted immediately, turning toward the alpha with deference and expectation.

"I want to link up, before we begin." Her dark hair shone in the light. Her golden eyes were wolf eyes. To the other shifters she added, "Please join us if you like."

Reese felt the alpha's magic ripple over her skin. She let it pass over her without connecting to it. While some reef sharks did group up, generally they were not pack animals.

The magic was simply too different. Reese's magic felt like a formidable ocean wave. There was a rhythm and deep, cool current. Kristine's magic—pack magic—smelled like the earth, not the sea. It flowed like a breeze, not waves. It was sunlight on the skin, not water. The smell of fresh air, falling leaves and warmth intensified. It invoked images of deep, unknowable woods. A forest, a packed-earth floor, and a running river.

Kristine regarded her pack with golden eyes. Those eyes were always wolf eyes now, as they held that space between human and animal, filled with the magical fire of transformation. It was a show of power and a reminder to all who the alpha was.

Seems exhausting, Reese thought and was glad again that her mind and spirit were not linked completely to the creatures around her. She didn't want to have to guard her thoughts all the time, especially since they seemed to move on their own ocean currents.

The moment their alpha's eyes opened and the magic settled, the pack opened their eyes. They gazed lovingly at their leader, their bodies rapt with attention.

Reese shifted against the stone seat beneath her, trying to alleviate the pressure against her tailbone.

"Last night another boy was killed. By another female siren,"

Kristine said plainly, and not for the first time, Reese appreciated how little she wasted words. "He was drowned by two female sirens in the cove."

A murmur of disbelief circled the amphitheater. A few werewolves shifted uncomfortably.

"We don't know why this happened or what is causing the unrest, but we need to address the problem nonetheless."

"Why?" asked a young man in the front.

If Kristine was bothered by this interruption, or a question to her authority, she kept the emotion perfectly hidden.

"Our relationship with the humans depends on it. To the human mind, it's simply us and them. Right now, we—the monsters—are responsible for a boy's death, whether we like it or not. For that reason alone, we will need to pool our resources and help with the investigation. Ethan Benedict is looking into the problem and we will offer him any assistance that we can. If he approaches you, or one of his—envoys—approaches you, do what they ask, within reason."

She said it as if anyone in this town would refuse Ethan Benedict anything at all. The demon was terrifying by most standards. Giving him whatever petty requests he desired seemed preferable to the alternative.

"Let's start by opening the floor for comments. Has anyone heard, seen or smelled anything strange in the last week? I know most of you were with me last night," she said, alluding to the pack-wide run that happened every full moon. "But it seems the sirens' restlessness began a week ago."

A young woman, eighteen or nineteen years old, raised her hand. Kristine nodded in her direction.

"Last week Trick and I," she gestured to the young man on her right. His hand was on the woman's thigh, giving Reese the impression they might be a couple. "Were down at the beach until sunset. As we were leaving, we saw a car roll by several times."

"What did the car look like?"

"It was a black BMW," she replied, scratching her nose. "It wouldn't have been weird except that it passed by several times."

"And it would slow down as it was passing us," the guy named Trick added. He had rings through his nose and eyebrows. "At one point I called out, 'What's your problem, man?'"

"But it just drove off," the woman added.

"Are you sure it was the same car?" Kristine asked, folding her arms over her chest. "A lot of demons drive BMWs."

Kristine was right about that. They drove Mercedes or BMW and black or red was the color of choice.

"It was the same car," the two kids said at the same time. "It was leaking transmission fluid. I could smell it."

Kristine folded her arms across her chest. "And a man was driving?"

"No," the girl said.

"Yeah," the boy said.

They exchanged a look.

"We didn't actually see the driver," the girl clarified. "The windows were tinted."

"Maybe a vampire?" someone added. "They like dark tint."

"Demons also hate sunlight," someone else argued from a row higher behind Reese. She turned to see who was speaking, but they'd already fallen silent.

"It's the asshole's car of choice."

This caused a ripple of laughter to echo through the theater.

"We'll let BMW know for their next ad campaign." Kristine flashed a reluctant smile. "Did you see plate numbers or anything?"

The kids shrugged, apologetic. It was clear they didn't want to disappoint their alpha.

But Kristine was smiling. "Thanks for telling us. We never know what might help. Anyone else?"

No one spoke for a long time.

Kristine looked ready to speak when a woman in the front interrupted her.

"The storm," she said.

The woman had bleached blonde hair in a pixie cut. When she leaned forward, putting her elbows on her knees, the hair fell into her dark green eyes. Reese admired her form from where she sat. She was built like a military commando. Reese half expected her to be in cargo pants and combat boots. But the woman wore dark jeans and sneakers, her massive arms poking out of a sleeveless T-shirt.

"That storm," she said again, looking into Kristine's eyes. "Don't you remember it? It rolled in last night too. And the week before."

"I remember it," Kristine said, frowning. "Both times it came in really quick."

"What connection does that have to the sirens?" the inquisitive boy asked.

"It means there's magic involved," Kristine said.

The blond snorted. "That really narrows it down."

She had a point. Most of the supernaturals in town could directly or indirectly control magic.

Reese thought of the storm that had rolled over her head the night before. Though she'd been in the ocean, she'd felt its power.

Reese spoke up. "I was in the water last night and felt the magic. Someone was definitely using it."

A few murmurs bubbled up along the rows. Kristine considered her for a long moment before adding, "Then we are looking at someone who can call magic. A witch or a demon."

"Or something older," the blond commander said.

"Would you agree it came from the sea?" Kristine asked.

Reese nodded. "Yeah. It rolled in from the south."

Voices rippled through the amphitheater. Several shifters

turned in their seats, looking toward the back of the theater. Reese followed their gaze.

A vampire had arrived. Uninvited.

Liam stood under an oversized black umbrella, his dark eyes fixed on Reese. He motioned for her. Reese faced front again, only to find Kristine observing the exchange.

"We're almost done here, Liam. One minute." Kristine seemed neither surprised nor offended by the vampire's arrival. "Does anyone else have anything to add?"

When no one spoke up she said, "That's it for today then. Remember what I said about keeping your eyes and noses open. If you learn something, I want to be the first to know."

The magic covering the amphitheater faltered and broke. The warmth receded and Reese stood from the stone bench, grateful to be done. Sitting any longer would've made her ass fall asleep.

Even so, her legs tingled as she politely pushed through the crowd, smiling and excusing herself when necessary.

She stopped short of the vampire with his shock of thick dark hair and piercing blue eyes. She wasn't exactly friends with the living vampire. They knew of each other and had spoken on several occasions. But they weren't inviting each other to game night or anything. Liam owned a bar, The House of the Setting Sun, in Red Light. Like Kristine, he was one of the primary fixtures of Castle Cove.

Therefore, it was more than a little strange that the vampire should come to a pack meeting and single her out. Why would he want to talk to her and not Kristine?

"What's up?" Reese asked, glad to hear that her voice was calm and curious rather than anxious.

"Ethan heard you were in the cove last night," he said. His ocean blue eyes fixed on hers. "He wants to talk to you."

"Where?" she asked. The idea of refusing Ethan Benedict was incomprehensible. Not only because he had built this town with his own two hands and a hell of a lot of magic, but because of every creature in this town, he was by far the strongest. If he wanted something, he would have it. And Reese could see no reason to make enemies with a man like that.

"He's at home. Do you know where that is?" Liam asked. His pale white hand adjusted itself on the umbrella handle.

Reese admitted she did not. Ethan protected his privacy fiercely though Reese thought this sentiment was ridiculous. It wasn't like anyone in Castle Cove would dare approach the demon at his own home, even if they knew where it was.

Kristine had a different theory, which she'd shared one night after Alpha's had closed. They'd both just thrown back a shot of tequila when the alpha said, "It isn't about the townspeople."

She'd poured a second shot.

"It's about outsiders. Ethan doesn't want the first blood-sucking rogue to roll through town to be able to pull anyone off the street and get directions."

Liam tilted the umbrella to better block the sun, dragging Reese's attention back to the present. "I'll ride with you then. Where are you parked?"

"In the lot. Just let me say goodbye to Kristine."

Reese found the alpha surrounded by her packmates. Rather than interrupt her, she offered a distant wave. Kristine returned it and shook her phone. Reese took this to mean, *I'll call you.*

As they walked down the path to her car she asked, "Are you okay out here?"

She gestured to the fading sun. They still had a couple of hours before dark.

"I'm tired," he admitted. "And nauseous and I have a headache."

Reese smiled before she meant to. It was sweet hearing such an open, honest response. "Sounds rough."

He shrugged. "This is important. We need to get on top of these killings."

She unlocked the truck and reached across the seat to do the same for the passenger door.

Liam collapsed his umbrella and slid inside as Reese took down the visor and slid it behind the seat. He tucked the umbrella between his legs and pulled the heavy door shut with a clank.

"Take Canyon Road as if you're heading for the interstate," he instructed.

Reese turned over the engine and reversed the truck. She waved at several pack members shuffling to their cars and waited for the young couple—the girl and boy who'd been on the beach the night of the first attack—to cross to their car.

The traffic had picked up in the ninety minutes between leaving her house and the pack meeting. The night creatures hadn't awakened yet, but the humans were now off work and searching for their dinners.

Liam said nothing on their drive through town. She didn't press him for conversation. Instead she rolled down her window to let in the warm ocean breeze. She hoped the fresh air would quell his stomach.

When he visibly relaxed, she took that as a good sign.

At the stop sign across from The Crossroads, he lifted his right hand and pointed straight ahead. "Keep following this to Midnight Pass."

She did, casting longing looks out over the water. The waves had collected the orange-pink of sunset. As the road bent toward the setting sun, Liam grimaced.

"Open your umbrella," she suggested. And he did. It was too big to fully expand even in the spacious cabin of her old red truck, but it threw blessed shadows across his face. He sighed.

"There should be a road up here on your left. Do you see it?"

It was another twenty or thirty feet before the road sprang into view. It seemed to not be there one minute, then appeared the next. Reese wasn't sure if that was magic, or simply a tricky shape of road that had hidden the drive well.

Either way, she turned left onto the road per Liam's instruction.

She drove slowly, careful not to hit any potholes at full speed. But the road was remarkably smooth. And something stranger happened. The branches overtaking the road, at first scratching at the sides of her red pickup, suddenly pulled back.

They bent away from the car as if held by an invisible force.

"What the—"

"Ethan," Liam said, matter-of-factly. "He knows it's us."

Reese didn't want to ask how Ethan knew it was *us*, or how the demon had the power to bend back tree limbs thicker than her body.

She had suspicions though. She'd heard the rumors that circulated through town.

If they were a mated pair, they would share a telepathic bond. She knew that demons did that from time to time—took mates. Violet had made casual offhand remarks as if testing Reese's thoughts about the idea. And her neighbor and friend Cole had soul-mated with his now-husband Dominic.

She'd seen Ethan and Liam together often and knew they were *together* in some capacity.

But Ethan was also a known playboy. In fact, many thought it was a badge of honor to have slept with Ethan Benedict and many people claimed to have done so. He owned a bar in Red Light too, the Labyrinth, and it wasn't uncommon for humans or supernaturals to disappear for a few hours in his care.

Like most demons, he probably fed on lust or sexual desire in some way. Violet seemed to think he actually ate their souls. The general population seemed to think this was a small price to pay for such an encounter with the hottest creature they'd ever beheld.

How Liam felt about these dalliances, Reese could only guess.

Either their relationship was open or Liam was the forgiving kind.

The trees broke open and a two-story Spanish villa sprang into view. The dirt road turned to beautiful paving stones that circled in front of the house. In the center of the roundabout was a fountain bubbling softly with turquoise water.

Reese parked her truck in front of the marble steps. Ethan was standing on the porch as if ready to receive them.

"Welcome to my home," he said as she stepped from the truck. "It's a pleasure to meet you, Reese."

He took her hand and brushed a kiss across the knuckles.

Liam stood beneath his umbrella, frowning.

"Get inside and rest, my love" Ethan said. "And eat something."

Liam entered the house, closing the umbrella as he went. That left Ethan and Reese on the steps of the great villa.

She looked up into the demon's face. He had dark features and a strong jaw. She'd thought his eyes were blue, but today they were nearly black.

"Are you hungry?" she asked. The words were out of her mouth before she meant to speak.

He grinned. "Are you offering?"

"No," she said, perhaps too quickly. "You just…look hungry."

He pouted his lower lip. "Too bad. And yes, I am, but I will rectify that soon. Would you come inside and keep me company? I want to discuss a proposal with you."

She followed him into the mansion, her boots clicking on the marble behind him.

"Can I offer you something to eat? Drink?" He threw a mischievous grin over his shoulder. "I can accommodate any taste, I assure you."

Heat rose in Reese's face against her will. "No, thank you."

Ethan looked mildly disappointed as he passed through the enormous foyer toward a door near the back. It proved to be a kitchen.

Ethan pulled a bottle of red wine from the counter, uncorked it and poured himself a glass. He flicked his eyes up to meet hers. "You're sure?"

"Positive."

Reese wanted to keep 100% of her wits in the presence of Ethan Benedict. She didn't think he would hurt her—intentionally. But he seemed the opportunistic sort. Dubious consent didn't seem out of the question...

He headed for an adjacent door with his glass of wine. "It is my understanding that your true form is a shark," he said. "Is that correct?"

Reese followed him into the other room. "I can change into a shark, yes."

He flashed a wry smile. "It is said that Vendetta herself created shifters. She so loved nature and its beauty, that she bestowed many animals the ability to take human form and move about the humans as if they were one of them. If we are to believe that, then it would mean that truly you are a shark who takes a human form."

Reese wasn't going to argue with him.

"What kind of shark?" he inquired.

"A black-tip reef shark."

He looked over his shoulder and smiled. "Yes, your hair. I can see it. One might think it was dyed that way."

"Most people do." She'd heard her hair described as blond pigtails dipped in ink. But it wasn't ink or even dye, only her natural coloring. She wasn't sure why this trait was exhibited in this way, but it was the same for her Aunt Constance as well. Her aunt's hair wasn't blond, rather a deep auburn red, yet it still had the black tips.

The room around them could've been a library or a study. It

had a desk with a laptop and folders on it. The walls were replaced with floor-to-ceiling bookcases and given how high these ceilings were, Reese was certain she was looking at tens of thousands of titles. At least.

In front of the large window, she saw the sea, reminding her of the window in her aunt's own library at home. If Constance saw this room she would be in love. Likely with Ethan as much as the room itself.

But Ethan was standing by the French doors leading out the back of the room. "Would you like to come out into the garden with me?"

"I thought demons didn't like sunlight?"

He smiled. "Do you think I'm a demon?"

That stopped her in her tracks.

"That's a good guess," he said, grinning wickedly, sipping the wine from his crystal glass.

He offered no further explanation before pulling open the French doors and motioning for her to follow.

They stepped out into an assault of freesia. The high, heady fragrance of a thousand flowers assaulted her. She felt paralyzed by them, her mind unraveling like a pulled string.

Ethan found a wooden bench nestled into a grove of roses. He settled down into it, pointing to the padded chair opposite. Reese took her seat, enjoying the last of the day's heat on her skin as well as the peach garden rose hanging inches from her face.

She'd bent forward to sniff it before considering if that was all right.

But Ethan was smiling at her. "Could you tell me what happened last night?"

"I did my closing shift at Alpha's and then drove to the beach for a swim."

"Yes," he said, in agreement, turning the glass in the light. It sparkled in his hand. "And then?"

She recounted the night for Ethan with as much detail as she could recall.

When she finished, he was regarding a blush rose by his face and nodding as if it had spoken to him.

"Yes," he said finally. "It's clear that the sirens are unhappy. Unfortunately, this could be for any number of reasons."

He turned those dark eyes on hers. A shiver crawled its way up and down her spine. Had his eyes been that color earlier? She couldn't be sure. Ethan had the sort of face—it was beautiful the way lightning snaking across the sky was beautiful. She could feel the electricity there, churning, inviting her in.

His smile widened as it watched the emotions dance across her face. It occurred to her he must be able to read her mind.

"I wonder if you would do something for me?" He wet his lips. "It is a task well-suited to you."

She sat up straighter, trying to gather the reins of her mind. If he was telepathic, she couldn't let it roam so freely in his company.

"The sirens live in a cavern beneath the eastern cliffs. If you swim across the cove and then around the cliff face, you will find it. You need only follow the rocks until it opens. The sirens will not bother you as long as they believe you are a shark. They revere and respect all sea creatures. Therefore they shouldn't react to your presence."

Her mind began to clear. "You want me to swim to the caverns and check on the sirens."

"Yes," he said, taking another long draught from his glass. "See if anything looks amiss and report back to me. Maybe by visiting their territory, we can get a sense of what ails them."

"I wouldn't know what to look for," she said, shifting on the bench.

Ethan smiled. His eyes were filled with soft flames now. She was certain his eyes had not been full of hellfire earlier.

"It doesn't matter. Just use your eyes," he said. "I have ways of extracting what I need."

"And they won't hurt me for swimming into their territory?"

"No," Ethan said, perhaps too quickly. "Of course, if for some reason they do realize you are a woman..." He took another sip of wine, his eyes never leaving hers. "My advice is to swim away as fast as you can."

Reese Choice 4
Agree to go to the caves - go to page 93
Refuse to go to the caves - go to page 109

REESE: HOLD DOWN THE BAR

"I'll hold down the bar for you," Reese said. She didn't believe she could be much help at the pack meeting, but she did know that she could keep Kristine's business running smoothly while the alpha helped the community. It seemed like a better use of her time.

"Great," Kristine said. The relief in her voice was clear. "I'll be there as soon as I can."

"Will you fill me in later?" Reese asked.

"Of course." A short rustle of fabric made Reese suspect that Kristine was moving the phone to her other ear. "When can you get to the bar?"

Reese glanced at the clock. It was shaped like a great white shark, the white belly shining in the afternoon sun. And it really was afternoon. She'd slept most of the day away. "Within the hour."

"Perfect. We'll talk later."

They exchanged their goodbyes and terminated the call. Reese considered her needs in order of importance.

Food and shower were at the top of the list. She decided on

the shower first. Under the hot jets, she gently slapped her face, trying to spark some alertness in her.

She dressed in freshly laundered clothes that still reeked of fabric softener.

Breakfast, she decided, was a can of tuna on dry toast. After finishing her toast and throwing the rinsed can in the recycle bin, she brushed her teeth for a second time. She unwrapped two sticks of mint gum and washed her hands just to be sure. She hoped the fish smell wouldn't linger.

The drive to Alpha's was quiet. It was that calm hour between afternoon and evening. Most of the daytimers hadn't left work yet, and the evening crowd hadn't yet woken. The streets were nearly empty. In Cliffside, a few people were walking their dogs, their earphones in as they strolled down the white-washed sidewalk.

When Cliffside gave way to downtown, she saw more students. Kids that were enjoying their summer break by hanging out in clusters in front of their favorite haunts. The Magic Bean coffeeshop seemed particularly busy, but there was also a cluster outside the burrito shop on the corner.

Reese parked her rattling red pickup in the parking lot across from Alpha's and crossed the street to the bar. She was the first one to the bar, using her key to open the door and begin prep work for the night.

She'd just restocked the pint glasses when Nick showed up to bounce the door. Early bird patrons requesting beer and popcorn arrived a few minutes later. After that, it seemed her shift passed quickly.

Reese looked up the moment the vampire crossed the threshold and entered the bar entrance. Not just any vampire, but Liam, one of the oldest residents in town and a good buddy of Kristine's.

Reese motioned the vampire forward. He obliged, stopping at the bar. He placed a black umbrella on the wooden top.

"Want a drink?" Reese asked. Alpha's carried blood packs that could be heated or mixed into certain cocktails.

Liam's piercing blue eyes considered her for a moment.

"No," he said finally. "I can't stay long."

"Oh. Well Kristine is down at the park. I'm not sure when she's coming in."

It was strange to see the living vampire before sunset. Unlike their undead brethren, living vampires could move around in the day. They would not explode into dust if sunlight touched them. However, they were nocturnal. Being up during the day taxed their bodies and strength. Whatever Liam wanted, it must've been important enough to disregard the nausea for. "Is it important?"

"I went to the park first," he said. "She said you were here."

She paused in the middle of the tequila sunrise she was making. "What do you want me for?"

Reese liked Liam, but they weren't exactly friends.

His ocean blue eyes fixed on hers. "Ethan heard you were in the cove last night. He wants to talk to you."

"When?" The idea of refusing Ethan Benedict was incomprehensible. Not only because he had built this town with his own two hands and a hell of a lot of magic, but because of every creature in this town, he was by far the strongest. If he wanted something, he would have it. And Reese could see no reason to make enemies with a man like that.

"He wants you to come by the house." His pale hand adjusted itself on the umbrella handle. "When can you leave?"

"I can't leave before Kristine gets back," she said, topping off the glass and sliding it across the bar to a werewolf who looked like she needed it.

Liam pushed back from the bar and brushed his hands over the front of his jacket. "I'll be outside when you're ready."

Once the vampire stepped out into the late afternoon, Reese's mind went into overdrive. In fact, her brain was so busy building up scenarios for how the Ethan Benedict conversation might go that by the time Kristine walked into the bar an hour later, she was in a proper state.

"Calm down," Kristine told her, taking the broom from her hand and the rag from her shoulder. "He just wants to ask about last night. We need eyewitnesses."

This changed nothing.

"Go on," Kristine said, nodding toward the bar door. "Liam's waiting out there for you."

And he was. Reese found him on the sidewalk, leaning against the brick face of Alpha's.

"I wanted to give you directions. It isn't easy to find his house," Liam said by means of explanation. Full twilight was upon them. The umbrella was closed, hanging from his wrist. "Where did you park?"

Reese pointed across the street. "The red pickup is mine."

They looked both ways and crossed when the light turned red.

"Have you been out in the sun this whole time?" She frowned at him. "You okay?"

"I've felt better. But we need to get on top of these killings."

She unlocked the truck and reached across the seat to do the same for the passenger door.

Liam slid onto the bench seat and tucked the umbrella between his legs. Then he pulled the heavy door shut with a clank.

"Take Canyon Road towards the interstate," he instructed, pulling the seatbelt across his chest.

Reese turned over the engine and reversed the truck. The street population had tripled since she'd started her shift hours before. Humans were wrapping up dinner and the night creatures were taking to the street for their nightly hunts. She waved to the supernaturals she knew as she passed them.

Liam said nothing on their drive through town. She didn't

press him for conversation. Instead she rolled down her window to let in the warm ocean breeze. She hoped the fresh air would calm her.

At the stop sign across from The Crossroads bar, Liam lifted his right hand and pointed straight ahead. "Follow this up to Midnight Pass."

She did, casting longing looks out over the water. The waves were purple with early evening light. A faint waning moon sat above the horizon.

"There should be a road up here on your left. Do you see it?"

It was another twenty or thirty feet before the road materialized in her view. It seemed to not be there one minute, then appeared the next. Reese wasn't sure if that was magic, or simply a tricky shape of road that had hidden the drive well.

Either way, she turned onto the road per Liam's instruction.

She maneuvered the truck slowly through the dense brush. Then something remarkable happened. The branches that were overtaking the road, at first scratching at the sides of her red pickup, suddenly pulled back, offering her a clear path.

They bent away from the truck as if held by an invisible force.

"What the—"

"Ethan," Liam said, matter-of-factly. "He knows it's us."

Reese didn't want to ask how Ethan knew who was a quarter of a mile away from the house, or how the demon had the power to bend back tree limbs thicker than her body.

She suspected that if they were a mated pair, Liam and Ethan would share a telepathic bond. She knew that demons did that from time to time—took mates. Hadn't Violet been the one to hint that such a thing was possible—if Reese was interested.

She'd seen Ethan and Liam together often and knew they were *together* in some capacity.

But Ethan was also a known playboy. In fact, many thought it was a badge of honor to have slept with Ethan Benedict and a few people claimed to have done so. He owned a bar in Red Light too, called the Labyrinth, and it wasn't uncommon for humans or supernaturals to disappear for a few hours in his care.

Like most demons, he probably fed on lust or sexual desire in some way. Or worse, their souls. Most humans seemed to think this was a small price to pay for such an encounter.

How Liam felt about these dalliances, Reese could only guess.

Either their relationship was open or Liam was the confident and forgiving kind.

While she shouldn't care—none of this was her business after all—Reese would've been lying to herself if she said she wasn't curious.

The trees broke open and a two-story Spanish villa sprang into view. The dirt road turned to beautiful paving stones that circled in front of the house. In the center of the roundabout was a fountain bubbling softly with turquoise water. The fountain was lit with submerged lights, changing the water from purple to a rose pink to turquoise again.

Reese parked her truck in front of the marble steps. Ethan was standing on the porch as if ready to receive them.

"Welcome to my home," he said as she stepped down from the truck.

He regarded Liam and his face pulled into a distasteful frown.

"Get inside and rest, my love," Ethan said. "And eat something."

Liam gave a dismissive wave and went inside

Reese stood on the steps looking up into the demon's face. Kristine had once called Ethan's looks *smoldering*. And this close to him, Reese had to agree. It was the sensual pout of his lips to be sure. The strong, square jaw and cat-like eyes. His dark hair had fallen forward, drawing attention to those eyes.

"Come in," he said with a mischievous grin. "Let's see if I can't make your visit...pleasurable."

With heat building in her guts, she followed him across the threshold into the house. Liam was nowhere in sight as Reese was led through the foyer to the door nestled between the twin staircases.

"Can I offer you something to eat? Drink?" He threw a mischievous grin over his shoulder. "I can accommodate any taste, I assure you."

He pushed open the door to reveal a massive kitchen.

"No, thank you." No one needed to tell her that getting drunk with this guy was a bad idea. And though she could *drink like a fish,* as she often joked, she didn't want to take any chances. Not with Ethan Benedict so close at hand.

Ethan pulled a bottle of red wine from the counter, uncorked it and poured himself a glass. He flicked his eyes up to meet hers.

"You're sure?"

"Positive."

Wine glass full, he motioned toward the adjacent door. "It's my understanding that your true form is a shark." He held the door open for her, forcing her to brush her body past his as they moved into the next room. "Is that correct?"

"I can change into a shark, yes."

He flashed a wry smile. "It is said that Vendetta herself created shifters. She so loved nature and its beauty, that she bestowed many animals the ability to take human form, so they could walk amongst them as she pleased. If we believe this tale, it would mean truly you are a shark who takes a human form, not a human who takes shark form."

The room around them could've been a library or a study. It had a desk with a laptop and folders on it. The walls were replaced with floor-to-ceiling bookcases and given how high these ceilings were, Reese was certain she was looking at tens of thousands of titles. At least.

In front of the large window, she saw the sea, reminding her of the window in her aunt's own library at home. If Constance saw this room she would be in love. Likely with Ethan as much as the room itself. Her aunt had no sexual qualms about bedding whomever she wanted.

"What kind of shark?" Ethan inquired. His gaze was intense.

"A black-tip reef shark."

He grinned. "Yes, I can see it. One might think your hair was dyed."

"Most people do." She'd heard her hair described as blond pigtails dipped in ink. But it wasn't ink or even dye, only her natural coloring betraying her true form. It hadn't mattered when she'd bleached her hair. The black tips remained. It was the same for her Aunt Constance, though her hair wasn't blond, rather a deep auburn.

Ethan placed a hand on the handle of the French doors behind him. "Would you like to come out into the garden with me?"

He didn't wait for her to answer. He pushed opened the French doors and motioned for her to follow.

They stepped out into an assault of freesia. The high, heady fragrance of a thousand flowers assaulted her. She felt paralyzed by them, her mind unraveling like a pulled string. The cloying sweetness had a narcotic affect, dulling her mind.

They followed a small lit path to twin benches.

"I love sitting in the garden in the evenings," Ethan confessed. "Beneath the moon, it's lovely.

Ethan sat on a wooden bench nestled into a grove of roses. He settled down into it, pointing to the padded chair opposite. Reese took her seat, enjoying the last of the day's heat on her skin as well as the peach garden rose hanging inches from her face.

She'd bent forward to sniff it before considering if that was all right.

But Ethan was smiling at her. "Can you tell me what happened last night?"

"I did my closing shift at Alpha's and then drove to the beach for a swim."

"Yes," he said, in agreement, turning the glass in the fading light. It sparkled in his hand. "And then?"

She recounted all that occurred as she swam the waters the night before.

When she finished, he was regarding a blush rose and nodding as if it had spoken to him.

"Yes," he said finally. "It's clear that the sirens are unwell. Unfortunately, this could be for any number of reasons."

He turned those dark eyes on hers. A shiver crawled its way up and down her spine. Had his eyes been that color earlier? She couldn't be sure.

His smile widened as he watched the emotions dance across her face.

"I wonder if you would do something for me?" he asked sweetly. He wet his lips. "It is a task well-suited to your abilities."

She sat up straighter, trying to gather the reins of her mind and the strange electricity rippling along her skin.

"The sirens live in a cavern beneath the eastern cliffs. If you swim across the cove and then around the cliff itself, you will find their nest. You need only follow the rocks until you come upon the opening. The sirens will not bother you as long as they believe you are a shark. They revere and respect all sea creatures, it seems. Therefore they shouldn't react to your presence."

Her mind began to clear. "You want me to swim to the caverns and check on the sirens?"

"Yes," he said, taking another long draught from his glass. His lips were dyed red with the wine. "See if anything looks amiss and report back to me. Maybe by visiting their territory, we can get a sense of what ails them."

"I wouldn't know what to look for," she said, shifting on the bench.

Ethan smiled. His eyes were filled with soft flames now. She was certain his eyes had not been full of hellfire earlier.

"It doesn't matter. I only need you to look around." His grin turned wicked. "I have ways of extracting what I need from the mind."

"And they won't hurt me for swimming into their territory?"

"No," Ethan said, perhaps too quickly. "Of course, if for some reason they do realize you are a woman..." He took another sip of wine, his eyes never leaving hers. "My advice is to swim away. As fast as you can."

Reese Choice 5
Agree to go to the caves - go to page 93
Refuse to go to the caves - go to page 109

GRAYSON: CUT HER WITH KNIFE

The siren pulled on his legs, bringing him farther out to sea. His head sank under the next wave and he was swallowed by dark water. Sand scraped his back and bare legs. She was latching onto his body, settling her weight against him. If she mounted him here, she was going to pin him against the ocean floor until she was done with him—however long that took—and he would die.

And she seemed unaware or uncaring of this fact as her free hand groped frantically at his groin.

With his lungs already burning, and his pulse radiating down each limb, Grayson knew that if he didn't do something—anything—to buy himself time, he would die.

He didn't want to open his eyes in the ocean. The salt would sting his eyes, and blind him. It was also possible that the consuming dark water would be too absolute to help him see anything anyway.

By touch alone, he reached across his chest, brushing the siren's cold flesh as he went. He found the edge of the blade tucked against his forearm and traced the handle until he felt the place where the sheath unsnapped. Careful to hold the blade with his fingers so he didn't drop it, he used his thumb to unsnap the blade.

It came free in his hand just as the creature slid his penis inside her. The siren worked herself into a fever pitch at the promise of success.

Red sparks pressed in from the corners of his vision. It was now or never.

He thrust the blade forward into the abdomen of the siren. A wretched screech, which he heard both in the water and inside his head, tore through him. It was felt like a physical blow, like razor sharp nails scraping down the front of his body.

But the ruthless grip released. He slipped out of her.

Without thinking, he shot toward to surface.

As soon as he broke a cresting wave, he sucked in a deep breath. There was the beach. There was the moonlit shore. He just had to make it there.

He managed only four or five propelling steps when a rough tug yanked him under the water again.

No, no, no. He pivoted underwater, and swung the knife outward. It arched slowly through the water but it connected with nothing.

A deep, fierce burning consumed his left leg. He reached for it, knowing the siren must be fighting back. Of course she would. Why did he think stabbing her wouldn't provoke her? Perhaps she'd bitten him with teeth that crunched through crustacean shells. Or maybe she cut him with her claws. He would inspect the damage once he got to shore.

Right now he just had to get out of the water.

Only, he wasn't moving. His body took on a strange weakness. He grew heavy.

Confused, he reached for his wounded leg. But his hand swiped through water. He felt nothing. Where his knee or calf should be was nothing.

Oh God. Ohhhh God.

He had to see. He had to. He drew his torso and leg as close as possible before opening his eyes. They burned, but there was enough moonlight cutting the water to highlight the blurry outline of his severed thigh.

Most of his left leg was gone.

His leg was *gone*.

The weakness in his limbs, the deepening cold—he understood now that it was rapid blood loss. Had it been the shark after all? Had it been drawn to the siren's spilled blood and bitten him because he was the slower, weaker prey?

Or had the siren torn his leg off?

He supposed he would never be sure.

But he thought he had his answer when twin sets of razor-sharp claws shot forward through the dark.

The End

Create a new story - go back to the beginning

GRAYSON: STAY ON ROCK

Grayson came up onto his hands and knees visually following the trail of bioluminescence. The three shimmering forms had to be sirens. His mind rebelled against the idea, certain it was impossible. Sirens didn't come into the cove. Heart's Rock was part of an elaborate underwater rock formation.

They shouldn't be here.

But they were.

The twin trails of bioluminescence rocketing through the dark water reached Landon in a matter of moments. They circled him like a cyclone beneath the water.

No, no, no, Grayson thought. *Get to the shallows. Get to the shallows or they will drown you.*

But even from this distance Grayson saw the impossibility of the task. Landon wasn't a strong swimmer. Even if he had been, that look on his face, the naked desire. He was already drowning in desire.

The appearance of the creatures was entirely dependent upon the telepathic connection between predator and prey.

He wanted to shout at Landon and snap him out of it, tell him to get to shore before it was too late. But shouting would only draw attention to himself and the whole point of staying on this rock and out of the water, was to give himself a chance to escape.

If he got into the water now, the chance was high that he would only be drowned, too. He wouldn't save Landon, nor himself.

But what about Abigail?

A flash of lightning revealed her in knee deep water. The male siren was only five or six feet away from her and advancing. It was mostly his broad back that Grayson could see from this distance. He couldn't discern any details of its appearance because of the darkness or because Grayson wasn't the siren's intended target.

But Abigail was lying down on the beach. Abigail was—

A crack of thunder made him jump. His hand slipped on the rock, cutting it. Blood bloomed across his palm.

He swore, pulling away from the water's edge. That was all he needed. If sirens in the water weren't enough, a gaping bloody wound would sure draw the sharks. A large shark couldn't get into the cove but a small shark from the reef would be trouble enough.

Bioluminescence illuminated the dark water around him.

This is it, he thought. If the two females were coming for him, they would pull themselves out of the water and onto the rock now. He would do his best to stay on the hard, unforgiving surface because the water on all sides was too deep.

But light split from one to two streams and went around the rock, out to sea. They were headed toward the cliffs holding up the distant castle.

Either they didn't want him, they were scared off by something else, or had achieved their objective.

Grayson regarded the dark water for a long while. His eyes

searched the undulating waves. He didn't see Landon, nor did he see any shark fins protruding from the waves.

He couldn't stay on the rock all night or he would freeze to death. The water droplets on his naked skin chilled him. He was already shaking violently from the cold filling his bones. He should've been fine on any other June night. But this strange and sudden storm had dropped the temperature unexpectedly.

He needed to get to shore and get his clothes on. He needed to get that bonfire going again.

Landon, his mind begged. *Please, please be okay.*

He took a deep breath and dove into the water. With every stroke, with every burning breath, his heart pounded in his ear. He kept expecting to see a shark rise up from the depths and swallow him whole. Or perhaps a forest of hands—siren hands, webbed and desperate—snaring him in their ruthless grips and pulling him down into the black depths.

He was nearly hysterical halfway through the swim. When his foot grazed the sandy bottom of the ocean, he did cry out. He was certain the lick of sand scraping his skin was actually the tongue of some enormous beast.

But he was out of the water and he was alive.

When Abigail saw him, she screamed.

"It's me!" he said, hands out in surrender. "Abby, it's just me."

But she kept screaming. He realized her gaze was fixed on something behind him. He whirled, pulling the blade from his forearm sheath.

It was Landon. Or rather, it was Landon's body. Wave after wave pummeled him into the sand.

"Landon." Grayson's voice cracked. He dropped the blade and it stuck into the sand.

Grayson grabbed a slick limb and dragged Landon further onto the beach.

He wanted to turn him over, do CPR, pound on his chest until water spurted from his mouth the way it did in the movies.

But Grayson knew he was dead the moment he grabbed onto the boy. There was something unnatural in his weight. The living had a lightness to their being. Landon's lightness was gone.

Yet he turned him over on the shore, aware that Abigail was still screaming though the sound had become a distant annoyance. It was a fly buzzing in the other room.

Grayson was shoving the heel of his hand into Landon's sternum. He was tilting back the neck so he could pinch the nose closed and blow into the mouth. The lips were so cold. The chest wasn't moving. The heart wasn't beating.

Landon was dead.

They dressed before the police arrived. They'd had about fifteen minutes between the moment he'd pulled his cell phone from his pocket until he saw the flashlights first sweep the sandy dunes.

Then the police were calling out their names and Grayson found a way to call back, though his throat was raw and burning.

Abigail's mother was first on the scene. As an officer at Castle Cove PD, she would've heard the call come into the station and would've taken it upon herself to drive straight to Hunter's Beach.

What he hadn't expected was that his own parents would be a close second.

It was his father that threw a gray wool blanket over his shoulders. It was his mother who squeezed him so hard he couldn't breathe.

"Are you all right?" she asked. "Are you—Christ, you're shaking."

"I'm fine," he managed, yet his teeth were chattering. "But Landon—Landon."

His voice broke and his father pulled him into his embrace. He wasn't sure how long they held him. Someone was stroking his wet hair.

When they finally released him, dozens more had arrived. There were officers in jackets, but also paramedics. They wanted to give both Abigail and Grayson full physicals.

One shone a penlight into his eyes.

"I'm fine," Grayson insisted. But they still sat him and Abigail down against a rock. She hadn't stopped crying. "Check on Abby."

"We need to know what happened," Officer Una O'Reilly said. Una was Abigail's mom.

"Grayson," his father said. It was the one-word command he'd heard often in his life, but never delivered with such tenderness.

Grayson told the story. He began with their plan to swim to Heart's Rock and then go get pizza.

"It's his eighteenth birthday," his mother interjected as if defending him.

"Then they came around the rock," he said. "Three sirens."

"Onto the rock?" Officer O'Reilly corrected.

"No," Grayson shook his head and cold water fell from his hair on to his cheek. "Around the rock. They passed me and swam straight into the cove. They were chasing Abigail and Landon. The females split off for Landon and the male went after Abby."

Officer O'Reilly stiffened. Her face pinched.

"I thought the inlet was safe," his father said. "I thought this tradition was harmless."

"If you call the threat of rape harmless," his mother Lillian countered.

Officer O'Reilly seemed to struggle, but finally found her words. "The sirens have been acting strangely the last few days. There was also an attack further south last Saturday. While they do visit the southern beaches from time to time, they've never crossed into the inlet before. We will have to investigate what would drive them this far into the cove."

"If there was another attack, why haven't we heard about it? Why didn't you issue a warning?" his mother demanded.

"There hasn't been time."

"It happened last weekend. Why didn't you let us know they were agitated? The community deserves to know if our children—"

"Lillian," his father said. He squeezed her arm, and to her credit, she seemed to regain control of herself.

"We thought last weekend's attack was an isolated incident. We did report it to...the proper authorities. But we haven't heard any new information on the situation. Frankly, we didn't know what was going on and therefore weren't sure what to report."

"Tell that to *them!*" Grayson's mother pointed at the couple further down the beach. Landon's parents were surrounded by police. It looked like they wanted to come over and talk, but the authorities weren't allowing them to come any closer.

"You could have reported that there was an attack," Lillian said stiffly. "At least tell people to stay off the beach."

"You're right. Obviously, this isn't an isolated event," Officer O'Reilly conceded. "We need to tell people to stay out of the water after dark until this is solved."

"Landon is dead." It was Abigail speaking. "Landon is dead."

"I know, sweetie." Una stooped and wrapped her arms around Abby. "I'm so sorry."

Grayson heard the unspoken relief in her voice. *At least it wasn't you.* That must be what she was thinking. Someone's child had died tonight. But it hadn't been her child. And though both of their parents knew who Landon was to Abby and Grayson, they couldn't hide their own gratitude. They might have seen Landon grow into a young man, they might've had him over for dinners and playdates, but none of that meant they would sacrifice their own children in his place.

A man in a dark blue jacket stood awkwardly to one side, waiting to get Officer O'Reilly attention.

She spotted him. "What is it?"

"We just wanted to let you know that the markings on the body and the water in the respiratory system are consistent with a siren attack. There was no ejaculate present—"

"Christ," Grayson's mother swore.

"—because it was likely washed away in the surf."

Una held up one hand. The other remained on Abby's shoulder. "That's enough for now, Darryl. Thank you."

"Lillian, Wade, I hate to ask but could you take Abigail home, please. I will need to stay here until the scene is completely processed. They're both cold and—"

"I don't want to be alone," Abigail said. She lifted her head and dragged her nose across the blanket draping her arm.

"You can come to our house," Lillian said. "We'll be with them."

"Thank you," Una said and helped Abby to her feet. "I'll come get you as soon as I leave here. If it's too late, I'll wait until the morning. I'm sure you are all exhausted."

"Text me either way," his mother told Officer O'Reilly. "I'll be awake."

In silence the four of them climbed the steep ledge to the parking lot above. Grayson and Abby followed his parents, shoulder to shoulder, to the parking lot beside the castle ruins. No one spoke as his father unlocked the car and they climbed in. In the dark back seat, Abigail snuggled close to Grayson's side, crying quietly.

"Are you hungry?" his father asked.

Grayson met his eyes in the rearview. "I don't know if I can eat now."

"We will pick up something anyway," his mother said,

regarding him with one of her stern faces. "You don't have to eat it. But it will be there if you want it."

"Not pizza," Abby said softly from her corner of the car. Her voice was thick with tears. "Anything but pizza."

They picked up Chinese from the Moodle Noodle shop on the west side of campus. His father went in and paid while his mother stayed in the car.

No one spoke. The radio remained off. But distant music from a closing bar reached them.

It was Abigail who broke the silence first. "When I get to your house, can I please take a shower?"

"Of course," his mother said, turning in her seat to gaze at her. "Of course you can."

"Where's Tanner?" Grayson asked. His parents wouldn't have brought him to a murder scene, but it couldn't have been easy finding a sitter at two in the morning.

"He stayed the night with Will." It was like her face was drinking him in. "We will tell him what happened later."

Don't say it, he thought. He could practically see the *I'm just so glad you're okay* written on her face. But if she said it, Abby would begin to cry again and she'd finally started to quiet down.

"All right," his father said, climbing into the car and handing a brown sack to his mother. "We have enough chicken and lo mien to feed an army. Anything else?"

"A shower," Abby begged.

"Sleep," Grayson said.

His father favored him with a weak smile. "Coming right up."

His father waited for a trio of drunk coeds to cross the street before he pulled away from the curb into the post-bar traffic.

Grayson's parents had bought a house in historic Midtown. This was a vintage neighborhood with beautiful restored Victorian homes and small shops. There was a coffeeshop and bookstore and it had the feel of a small antiquated town, complete with a local grocer and old-fashioned video store, where people could rent DVDs or video games.

This neighborhood's insular seclusion was one of the reasons Grayson had been allowed to roam so freely as a child. Everything he could have wanted—candy or ice cream, a park or playground, his friends—were within ten blocks of his home.

The porchlight was on when they pulled into the drive, illuminating freshly stained steps and the railing. The house itself was also a deep cherry red. He and his father had just repainted it the previous summer. It had taken them all three months, and it wasn't like his family didn't have the money to hire someone. It was simply one of his father's "bonding" projects—of which there had been many over the years.

But seeing the house had the effect Grayson suspected his father wanted.

Every time Grayson saw it, he felt proud. Proud of what a good job they'd done and proud of his family.

This was home. He was safe here.

When he threw open the car door, he had tears in his eyes. His father saw them as he was closing his own door.

"I know," his father murmured quietly. "I know."

He squeezed Grayson's shoulder hard, and pulled him toward the house.

His mother got the door open, ushering Abigail over the threshold.

"Honey, get some towels," she said. "When you get out of the shower, Abigail, I'll have something clean for you to wear. It'll be a little big on you."

The shirt would be fine, but Abigail wasn't as tall as his mother. The pants would have to be rolled up and perhaps belted at the waist.

"It's fine," Abigail managed, looking small and worn under the gray wool blanket. "Thank you."

His mother carried the food into the kitchen and disappeared through the swinging door.

"Grayson, show her how the taps work," his father instructed, putting two fresh towels in his hand. He took the blanket off of Grayson's shoulder. "And make sure there's enough soap and all that."

"Come on." Grayson took the lead on the stairs. The wooden staircase creaked under their weight. When they reached the top of the stairs, he turned left and then left again to his own bathroom at the end of the hall.

He placed the towels on the sink, aware of Abigail standing beside him.

"It's backwards. You turn the handle this way for hot, and this way for cold. If it sputters, it's just air in the pipes. It'll kick back up in a second. Don't let the rattle scare you."

He left the tap on hot and pulled up the stop. The water was diverted from the spout to the showerhead, spraying the basin in a gentle rain.

Abigail handed him the blanket and began to undress.

He shouldn't care. He'd seen her naked before. But he still backed toward the door.

"I'll put the clothes outside the door," he said.

He thought it best to look her in the eyes, rather than chance staring at anything else.

But when he looked into her eyes, she was crying.

"It was you," she said, standing there naked in his bathroom, with the hot water running into a cream-colored tub.

His heart hammered in his chest.

"When the siren—I wanted it because—" She bit her quivering lip. Her hand fisted on the burgundy shower curtain. "When he was—he looked like you."

Then Grayson understood what she was trying to say. The male siren *had* caught up to her and she hadn't resisted him.

It was Grayson she'd been making love to as her boyfriend was killed.

"I'm sorry," he said. He wasn't sure what he was apologizing for. All of it, he guessed.

But she'd already climbed inside the shower and had pulled the curtain closed between them.

Grayson showered in his parents' bathroom.

Then after he put the fresh clothes on the sink for Abigail, he went downstairs to find his parents sitting around the dining room table.

Grayson had always loved this table. It was strange and ornate and looked more like a table built for 1920s seances than for family dinners. But it was one of the many charming features of their restored home.

"Come sit with us," his mother said. She was trying not to sound desperate, which Grayson appreciated. A swell of affection filled his chest.

After his shower, he found he could eat after all. The headache building behind his eyes and the shaking in his exhausted limbs begged him to eat something. "Let me grab some food first."

He went into the kitchen and pulled a white ceramic plate from the shelf. He loaded it with pineapple fried rice, lo mien, General Tso's chicken, and three pieces of crab rangoon.

He grabbed a sparkling water from the fridge and carried it into the dining room.

He sat down between his parents, knowing that was where they wanted him.

"Your father and I talked and we decided to waive the no-girls-sleeping-in-your-room policy," his mother said.

"Good call. I don't think she'll sleep alone."

"But we want you to leave the door open," his father added.

Grayson didn't even fight them. He didn't care.

His mind kept replaying the image of Landon tossing in the surf, his pale body thrashing in the waves.

"We don't have to talk about what happened," his mother began. Her words had the practiced air about them. She was a professor, but Grayson was certain that it was also because she liked to rehearse what she would say in her mind long before saying it. He was like his mother in this way.

And when had she composed this speech? In the car on the way home? When he was in the shower? Or maybe even in the car on their way to retrieve their *almost* dead son.

"Especially if you're tired," his father added. "The swim alone must've been exhausting, not to mention—" There was a jerk under the table and Grayson was fairly sure his mother had just kicked him. His father grimaced. "We just want you to know we're proud of you."

"Don't be," Grayson said. "Landon is dead."

He pushed the rice around on his plate with the back of his fork.

His father reached out and squeezed his shoulder. "You couldn't do anything about that."

"I should've done more. I should've—"

"If anyone is to blame for Landon's death, it's the authorities," his mother interjected. "They should have announced the attack. There should've been a notice to stay out of the water. This town—"

"Lill," his father said and her mouth snapped shut.

"I'm just saying. How are people supposed to stay safe if they aren't properly informed?"

His father fixed him with his gaze again. "You're not to blame for what happened and we're proud of you for handling the situation the best you could."

"Please stop saying that," Grayson said. He couldn't sit at this table with his Chinese food and be congratulated by his parents as if he'd won some prize. Landon was *dead*.

Landon was dead and—

"Keeping your cool in a dangerous situation is no small feat."
It was his mother speaking. "It's going to take a long time to get
over this. Maybe you'll never completely get over this loss. But
we wanted you to know that we are here and we'll do anything
we can to help you. If you need something, tell us."

This loss.

They weren't even saying his name.

He understood all of the words coming out of their mouths.
He even understood that the reason he was here at the table
while his best friend was dead on a beach was because he'd been
blessed with smart, patient parents who'd prepared him to
survive.

And it was more than that. He'd gotten lucky. He'd been
damn lucky.

Then why was he so angry? Why did he feel like he shouldn't
be the one in the chair? Why did it feel like it was unfair that
Landon should be dead and that he should be alive? Why did he
want to trade places with him?

I wanted it to be you, Abby had said.

"If you need anything—" his mother was saying again.

He exhaled and pushed away from the table. "I need some
air."

"We'd rather you stay in the house," his father said.

His mother shot him another look and his father grimaced
as if expecting another kick.

"But we won't tell you what to do," his mother said. "But why
don't you go to bed? You've had one hell of a night."

"A hell of a birthday," he murmured. "I think I'll…"

Grayson Choice 4
Go for a walk - go to page 100
Go to bed - go to page 152

REESE: AGREE TO GO TO THE CAVES

"I'll go tomorrow," Reese said, shifting against the creaking bench. "Once the sun is up."

It wasn't only the dangers of night swimming across open waters that concerned her. It was also that she was dead tired all of a sudden—she wondered if Ethan could be blamed for this immense loss of energy.

His mischievous grin betrayed him. "That is very wise. It will be best to go during the day when the sirens are tired and sluggish. They are as nocturnal as we are. Actually I suppose you are crepuscular, aren't you? My apologies." He took another sip of wine, his lips even redder than before.

Quite kissable, Reese thought. She wondered if it was the fragrant garden—or Ethan that was going to her head. Danger a little voice warned. *Danger, Reese. The voice sounded like Violet's.*

"Observe as much as you can and report back to me tomorrow evening. I will compensate you however you wish."

This stopped her in her tracks.

His grin turned wicked as if sensing her excitement. "Do you have a preference as to how you are compensated?"

Reese didn't want for money. Her aunt was generous and

doting, and Reese made good money as a bartender. All of this was made easier by the fact Reese had few needs.

But this was Ethan Benedict she was speaking to.

"I would like a favor," she said.

He leaned back, his smile amused. "And *I* long to please you. What is your wish?"

"I don't know." Now she was the one grinning. "But if I ever find myself in trouble someday, it would be nice to know that I can call on you for…assistance."

Ethan considered his glass of wine for a moment before taking another slow, luxurious sip. When Reese saw the fire spring into his eyes, another chill seized her spine. Had she overstepped? Had she asked too much?

He extended his hand. "In exchange for your help with this situation, I offer my protection. No harm will come to you on my watch."

"Deal." She slid her palm into his.

Quick as lightning, his hand seized hers and pulled. She was yanked from her seat forward across the lit walkway and into Ethan's lap. Her body collided with his. He was warm, the way living vampires were warm after they'd fed. His chest didn't give as she pushed against it.

But it wasn't just his arms around her, or the press of his chest against hers.

It was his lips.

His soft, pillowy lips overtook hers. Her surprise came out as a sigh, or moan before she could stop it.

"This is how I seal my pacts," he said, his breath warm on her face.

Reese stood, stumbling back from the demon. He let her go with a lazy, triumphant grin on his face.

"You have my word, Reese. Should you ever need me, I will be happy to help you."

"T-thank you." She tugged at the bottom of her shirt which had ridden up to reveal her stomach.

He pointed at the French doors with the empty wine glass. "And now I'll lead you out."

His tone brooked no argument.

She'd made it all the way to the front door when she turned and saw Liam descending the right side staircase. His hair was wet and curling. He was buttoning the cuff on a clean white dress shirt that he'd tucked into tight, dark pants.

Reese realized she was staring.

"He's very beautiful, isn't he?" Ethan whispered into her ear. The warm breath made the hairs on her neck rise. "You should see him on his knees."

Heat shot through her body, tightening muscles low in her core.

"Don't let him get to you, Reese," Liam said. His eyes were on Ethan. "He likes to play with his food."

Ethan tsked. "I haven't fed on her, my love. Much."

Reese had become aware of how close Ethan was standing behind her left shoulder. And with Liam standing in front of her, she was practically sandwiched between the two men.

"He likes shifter magic more than any meal in the world," Liam explained. He was giving Ethan a wary look. "It reminds him of Vendetta."

"Telling all my secrets, my love?" Ethan asked. It felt like his lips were micrometers above her skin.

"She deserves to know she's the prey. It's unfair when they think otherwise." He turned to Reese. "He'll get drunk on you if you let him. Better get out of here before he drains you dry."

"I wouldn't do that," Ethan said, in mock outrage. But he was practically purring in her ears.

Reese fumbled for the door handle, her face so warm she thought she would begin to sweat.

Liam took pity on her and threw the door wide, offering her

the night. She burst out onto the porch, the fresh air hitting her with all the force of an ocean wave.

"Good night," she managed before the door closed behind her.

She breathed deep, letting the cool air beat back the magic. For a moment she turned and stared at the front door as if she expected Ethan to come after her. But the front door remained closed. In her mind, she imagined Liam leaning against it, barring the demon's path.

Why had he helped her?

Whatever the reason, she owed Liam and she knew it. Whether or not he was the sort of person to draw on such debts, she didn't know. But the tally mark had already been made in her mind. With a slight tremor in her arms, which she recognized as falling adrenaline, she climbed into her truck.

The tree limbs blocking the road pulled back reluctantly this time—or was she only imagining that? Just be glad they pulled back at all, she thought as she pressed the gas pedal a little harder.

THE NEXT DAY SHE ATE AND DROVE TO THE BEACH. RATHER THAN park on the side of the road, she decided to park in the South Beach parking lot. This gave her a view of the dilapidated castle on the cliff. It looked like a tired, weathered beast on the edge of suicide. With its cold stone crumbling, it looked ready to throw itself into the sea.

She'd heard the story of the castle, like any other long-time resident of Castle Cove. Once it had belonged to an evil queen who had starved her people with her incessant greed and endless campaigns of war.

Vendetta alone had been granted the power to destroy the queen and bring down her queendom. Reese wasn't sure how much of that was true or embellished. But here were the ruins.

She descended to the beach carefully, doing her best to keep her footing in the sliding sands.

Once she reached the water's edge, she looked around to ensure she was alone.

She walked the eastern edge of the beach, hoping this little nook close to the cliffs would render her invisible to anyone on the ledge above. Here she stripped, placing her clothes on a large rock that seemed safe from any oncoming waves or rising tides.

She waded out into the water. It was cool, no doubt because of its depth, but not unbearable.

Once the water reached her thighs, she dove under the next wave. Her body transformed. Her muscles thickened. Organs moved. Her face elongated and her limbs condensed themselves into a single, streamlined form.

That instant calm enveloped her, a feeling she only experienced when in this form.

With gentle side-to-side motions, she propelled herself forward. She established an easy rhythm, cutting through the aquamarine waters. She would have to swim south until the rockface ended. Then the plan was to hook around it and swim north-northeast, following the cliffs as Ethan had suggested until she came upon the mouth of the underwater cave.

Her senses stretched out before her, scanning the waters for any other forms of life. She detected a school of fish feeding on even smaller fish off to her right. And also something with a slow, steady rhythm ahead. A turtle, she suspected. Nothing large, nothing dangerous loomed.

She slid through the rock wall using the gap beside Heart's Rock. Most of her dorsal fin had to break the surface to manage it, but if someone on the beach saw her shark fin, what of it? She was far enough away not to frighten any swimmers.

On this side of the rock wall, the ocean felt vast. Far more vast than she was used to. Reef sharks preferred the tight confines of the reef buffered by an ocean floor. It offered protection on most sides. They were, after all, the big fish in a little pond, so to speak.

Here, with nothing but miles and miles of deep waters on all sides, Reese knew she was exposed. She would have to keep her wits about her, or she could very well end up as lunch for a larger, more opportunistic creature.

She stayed close to the cliff face, scanning the waters around her with unease. After twenty minutes of swimming at a steady pace, the cliff face opened beside her, revealing a deep cavern.

Here, the waters were not so dark. In fact, they shone with crystalline light.

She swam into the cave, marveling at how bright the waters were and how warm as well. There was some light source coming from below.

Then she spotted the sirens. They were sleeping, half in, half out the water. Their tails stretched out behind them on the rock ledges like seals sunning in the late afternoon. Reese swam as close as she dared, trying to get a better look at them.

This close, she saw strange black markings on their skin. Rashes or growths, these patches of abnormality were embedded in the skin.

They're sick, she realized. Would a sickness make them desperate enough to aggressively seek mates on shore? Or maybe the sickness had made them confused about where they were and what they were doing?

She wasn't sure.

But they were restless even in repose, most fidgeting on their rocks as if they couldn't get comfortable. One sleepy siren picked at the open sore of another, the black pus oozing into the water like oil.

Reese circled the cave several times and took inventory of the numbers and condition of the sirens. Very few looked untouched by whatever disease this was.

On her last pass in the cavern, she spotted something at the back of the cave. A partially submerged staircase led out of the water. Where it led, she couldn't be sure from her vantage point beneath the surface. Should she go up and investigate? Maybe she would learn something about the sirens' environment that would help. Of course, there was the danger they would see her shapeshift and know that she was no mere shark.

Reese Choice 6
Go up the stairs - go to page 142
Swim back - go to page 160

GRAYSON: GO FOR A WALK

"I think I'll go for a walk. I need some air," Grayson said. Fearing that his parents might try to physically restrain him, eighteen years old or not, he walked out into the night before they could object.

The cool night air cooled his wet hair as he walked, his hands stuffed down in his pockets. He didn't look back until he'd reached the stop sign at the corner.

His dad was on the porch, watching him go. He lifted his hand to wave. Grayson met his wave with one of his own, hoping it would reassure him.

He didn't want to scare his parents, or put them through undue stress. Grayson understood he had it made in the parent department. They respected him and treated him like an adult, which was more than a lot of his friends could say.

But he also understood that the phone call they'd received tonight must've scared the hell out of them.

It was a good indicator of their self-restraint that they let him walk away without dragging him back as Abby's mother might have done. That woman had no chill. Of course, as an officer of Castle Cove, she probably saw more of the dark underbelly of this town than his parents did. And after Landon...maybe they should all be afraid.

Grayson wasn't really sure where he was going, but the night air felt great on his face. Unlike by the water, it felt warm now that he was insulated by the city buildings. It had become a proper summer night.

He passed the corner store and considered going inside for a slushie and a candy bar. But his stomach turned at the idea of that much sugar this late into the night. So he kept marching north-northeast until the narrow streets of Midtown opened up on the North Quarter, or what the kids at Castle Cove High liked to call Red Light.

This strip of town was known for its dark bars and raucous nightlife. The chances were high that Grayson would encounter more vampires than humans if he went down this road. Every single one of the bars were full of blood drinkers. He knew a few other supernaturals must be mixed in. Werewolves, shifters, and demons were here too, but this was definitely vamp territory.

Usually his sense of self-preservation kept him from wandering around these parts of town late at night. But he was eighteen now and he was more than curious.

If I'm going to stay in this town, he thought. *It's about time I see the place for what it really is.*

Because a dead best friend didn't have a clue, another voice chided. *And look where it got him.*

He turned left and walked toward the thickening crowds.

There seemed to be a bar for every type of party-goer. He passed several upscale establishments with men and women queued at the door, dressed to kill. He passed a couple pubs that seemed more casual with patrons wearing jeans or floral skirts.

Then Grayson stopped dead in his tracks.

A Victorian mansion loomed in front of him. It was massive, taking up half of the block on the north side of the street. It looked like a frat house going through a moody, gothic phase. Spires stretched skyward from its roof and the sharp slopes. Rock music blared through the open windows into the night. There were people lying on the grass in the yard talking and laughing. Grayson could smell the pot from the sidewalk.

The sign read *House of the Setting Sun*. By the front door, a guy stood, bare chested except for the fringed leather vest hanging open. The vest matched his leather pants and he was barefoot, which struck Grayson as a strange outfit for a bouncer.

Grayson mounted the wooden porch steps anyway.

"ID?" the guy asked. He held out a long, slender hand toward Grayson, expectantly.

Grayson hesitated. Maybe he had to be 21. "How old do you have to be?" he asked.

"Eighteen."

Grayson slipped his hand into his pocket and pulled out his wallet. It took him a moment to get the plastic card out of its holder and hand it over.

"Happy birthday," the doorman said with a mischievous grin. Grayson caught the glint of fangs in the moonlight and his heart stuttered in his chest.

The vampire took Grayson's hand in his and put two large black X marks, one on the back of each hand.

The light brush of his fingers made Grayson's heart beat faster. The vampire's smile only widened.

Because he can probably hear your heart in your chest, he thought and wondered if it was true. It was impossible to tell if this guy was a living vampire or a dead one.

They were different, living vampires and undead vampires. The living vampires were those who had not died as a result of their attack and transformation. Their hearts never stopped. Therefore, the virus living inside them had more of a symbiotic relationship with its host. It gave the host strength, and eternal youth. They were not allergic to sunlight. They simply preferred the night. Their bodies emitted pheromones that attracted and disoriented their prey. They were warm and had a pulse.

The undead were a different story. Unlike their living brethren who seemed to rely on their physical attributes to attract prey, the undead relied on magic. The undead died during their transformations and it was at that moment of death that a demon entered their body and took residence.

Most of the person's previous life and human connection were instantly forgotten. They were also strong and fast, but they didn't spread a virus from their bite. Their powers included telepathy, mind-control, telekinesis and flying, depending on how strong the demon that inhabited their body was. The undead were very clannish, too. The oldest vampire maker was usually the strongest, with the most connection to the demon within. Those created further down the line deferred to their matriarch or patriarch. Living vampires seemed to be more...democratic. They were free-spirited loners who answered only to themselves.

The doorman handed the license back. "Birthday boys get a free drink at the bar."

"Isn't that illegal?"

The doorman smiled even wider. His eyes held and reflected the light the way a wolf in the road would in the dead of night. "I'm not talking about alcohol, Grayson."

A group of five or six girls, probably CCU undergrads stumbled up the walkway, laughing and calling out to the doorman. "Oli! Is Liam here tonight?"

"Yeah, somewhere." Oli, the doorman, offered Grayson his license between two fingers. "Be careful in there, birthday boy."

Grayson took his license and stepped across the threshold.

The music swallowed him whole. The crush of bodies was overwhelming but not complete. With a few polite words, he could navigate fine. People stepped aside for him. A few eyes lingered on his, which surprised him. But what surprised him most was how easy it was to tell the humans from the vampires.

The humans dismissed him almost immediately. It was as if they knew he wasn't what they were looking for. Probably the giant black X marks on his hands. By contrast, the vampires seemed to watch him closely. Some smiled, some looked away. Grayson suspected there was a whole exchange happening here, a subtext he didn't understand.

Instead he made his rounds, getting the lay of the land so to speak. It was like a large house with rich wooden bannisters and high ceilings. Bodies filled most corners and a great deal of the throughways, but it wasn't too hard to make his way through. Eventually he found a ballroom complete with bar and a dance floor. At the head of the dance floor was a band playing some kind of dark rock music.

Since Grayson didn't drink, he moved on.

He was on the stairs when he saw a young man that looked about his age. He had soft brown hair and sharp blue eyes. His thick lips quirked into a smile when he saw Grayson. In one hand, he had a cocktail of some kind. He saw Grayson looking at it.

"Can I buy you a drink?" he asked, pausing on the stairs two steps above Grayson's.

"I'm only eighteen," he said. He held up his X-marked hands. "But the guy at the door said I could have a free drink for my birthday."

"Oh they didn't mean a cocktail. He meant blood. You can have a free shot on your birthday. House policy."

"*Oh,*" Grayson said. He wasn't sure what to do with this information.

"You're cute," the guy said. His lips quirked into another smile. "I'll open a vein if you want."

He turned over a pale wrist in offering.

Vampire blood. Grayson's stomach turned. "No, thanks."

The guy placed the hand on his hip. "Good call. It can be addicting."

Grayson leaned into the bannister.

The vampire mimicked him. "What's your name, birthday boy?"

"Grayson."

"Happy birthday, Grayson. Why did you pick The House for your birthday celebration?"

Grayson wasn't sure how to answer this question. He didn't want to talk about the cove or Landon. He didn't want to think about anything, really.

"Something new," he said.

The vampire seemed to sense his dark mood. "Are you here alone?"

"Yeah. I was with my friends earlier."

"Yeah, birthdays always depress me," he said, taking a casual drink from his red cocktail. The liquid shimmered strangely in the martini glass. "Of course, it could just be that I've had too many."

"How old are you?" Grayson asked.

The guy crossed the staircase and leaned into the bannister beside Grayson, now just one step above. "That's rude, Grayson. Didn't your mother teach you not to ask about a lady's age?"

When Grayson looked apologetic the vampire laughed harder.

"Oh you're too sullen for me, birthday boy. Lighten up. I'll be 98 this year."

The guy looked no older than 22 or 23.

"How old were you when you turned?"

"You go right for the jugular, don't you?" The vampire smiled. "You're like a puppy who has no idea how cute he is, you know that? You could've at least asked me my name first."

Grayson felt his face flush. "Sorry, I—"

This only seemed to encourage the vampire. "I'm Daniel and

to answer your question I was 26. But I've always looked young. I didn't mature much after the change, either. Some do." He gestured at a guy on the landing above them as if pointing out a friend in the crowd. "Liam was changed when he was a kid and matured through his late twenties. Now he looks like that. It can go either way, you know what I'm saying? Well, if you're a living vampire that is. You're undead, you're stuck."

Grayson recognized the name Liam. Wasn't that who the girls at the door were looking for?

"Who is he?" Grayson pointed at the vampire leaning against the wall talking to a group of girls. They were crowded in around him, cornering him and laughing at every word out he said.

"Liam?" the blue-eyed vampire asked. "He owns this place. He's kind of a big deal in town. I'm guessing you've never heard of him otherwise you'd be chasing him like half these groupies."

Liam was beautiful and Grayson felt the strange allure that seemed to emit from him, almost like an aura, if one believed in such things. But he couldn't imagine walking up to the guy and saying *hey, bite me.*

"He owns this place?" Grayson asked. He felt like there was a lot more to the story than that.

Daniel didn't seem to hear. "Oh, don't get me wrong. He'll show you a good time, but he's not on the market, if you know what I'm saying. And he's not what you want for your first time. Heartbreaker doesn't even begin to cover it. Of course, you could do worse. There are some real freaks up in here. I'm very mild by comparison, you know what I'm saying?"

Grayson couldn't say he did. There was something about this guy that made Grayson's mind fuzzy around the edges.

Living vampire, he thought. *This one is a living vampire. I'm reacting to his chemistry or something.*

"*Are* you a living vampire?" The words were out of Grayson's mouth before he had a chance to consider the propriety of his question.

The vampire didn't seem offended in the slightest. "Oh yeah. That's all you'll find around here. The undead have their own haunts."

"Like ghosts?"

The vampire laughed and leaned his body into Grayson's. His lips trailed over Grayson's neck up to the lobe of his ear. His breath was hot on the inner folds as he spoke. "Grayson, you're killing me. If you get any cuter, I'm going to lose it. You wanna go somewhere else? We could head up to the Heights—"

"No, not the Heights," Grayson said, pulling back to look into his eyes. Perhaps not the smartest thing to do with a vampire. Weren't their eyes supposed to be hypnotic or something? He couldn't remember. The closer the guy stood to him, the harder it was to think.

But he knew about the Heights. Vendetta Heights was a glorified make out spot on the edge of town where vampires and humans hooked up. But it was also where people went missing sometimes. Going there in the middle of the night was beyond stupid, especially after his run-in at the cove.

"Okay, not the Heights," the vampire said, his lips quirking. "There's also my apartment. It's three blocks from here if we walk east, toward campus. Then a block south."

"Toward Midtown? I live in Midtown."

The vampire's lips quirked again. "You want to be telling some strange vampire where you live, Gray? You know we're hunters, right?"

Grayson felt the heat in his face and throat.

The vampire's eyes seemed to dilate in tandem with Grayson's growing flush. "So what do you think? You want to get out of here or not?"

"What would we do?" he asked. "Once we got to your place?"

The vampire smile deepened until both upper fangs were visible. "Whatever you consent to, birthday boy. It's your party."

Grayson Choice 5
Go with the vampire (ES) - go to page 124
Call it a night - go to page 115

REESE: REFUSE TO GO TO CAVES

"I'm sorry, but I am not comfortable doing that. Reef sharks don't usually swim through deep open waters."

Ethan smiled. It was a mischievous grin that set Reese's teeth on edge. "Are you sure?"

"Yes," she said. "I'm sure you can find someone else in town to do that for you."

He turned his glass in the light. "In that case, I have one other task for you. If you would follow me."

Her body rose against her will. Much to her horror, she realized she could not open her mouth or speak. Like an obedient dog, she trailed behind him, through the garden away from the house. They followed on a stone path. No weeds or grass had pushed themselves up between the paving stones. The flowers and thick vines seemed to deepen here. They brushed her face and neck, tenderly as she pushed through.

No, she thought. *No, no, no.*

She was supposed to be immune to demon magic.

"I am not a demon." He said, glancing over his shoulder at her. "I am a chevalier. Do you know what that is?"

Help, she cried in her mind. She wondered if she could reach

Kristine, or any other shifter in range. She needed to send out an emergency beacon if she could. *Somebody help!*

As Reese felt her body pulled forward she was forced to accept two facts. First, Ethan's villa was on the westernmost cliffs. They were quite far from town. Whatever dark business Ethan wished to fulfill here, he wouldn't be disturbed.

Second, no one would hear her scream—even if she could.

The cloying garden broke open suddenly to reveal a small cottage. Reese wasn't sure if cottage was the right word. It had one maybe two rooms in the stone building. The front door was a carved wood with an elaborate floral design.

Ethan stepped up to the door and pushed it open with the gentle brush of his hand.

"I would take you into the house for this," he said. "But Liam would disapprove."

They stepped into the cottage, her boots scuffing the wooden floor. To the left there was a desk beneath a large picture window, offering an unobstructed view of the sea. To the right, an enormous four-poster bed.

"Lay on the bed," Ethan said.

Against her will, Reese's body moved to the bed. Her hands moved over the soft coverlet.

"I will not rape you. I don't have the taste for that," he said.

Reese didn't feel any better in the light of this confession. She wanted control of her body, her voice, all of herself.

"I know," he said, as if she'd spoken. "But you see, I am Vendetta's chevalier. I serve her without question. All my power is her power, used on her behalf to serve her will. Unfortunately, there is another in town who threatens her. Lie on the bed."

Reese's body lowered itself onto the mattress.

"Liam will be furious with me when he finds out what I've done." Ethan sat on the edge of the bed before sliding in beside her. "But I cannot take any chances with Vendetta's life."

You always have a choice, she thought, her heart hammering, terrified.

He pushed the hair away from her face. "Surely you've heard the stories of Vendetta."

She couldn't have said yes even if she wanted to.

"I have only one purpose in my life. I was created for the sole mission—to serve and protect the living goddess we call Vendetta. And she is in danger now. You must understand there is nothing I won't do to protect her."

Why me? her mind begged. *Why?*

She felt tears build in her eyes before spilling over her cheeks. Ethan wiped it away with a thumb.

"You are a powerful shifter," he said. "A barrier made of shifter magic will protect Vendetta. I will use it to cocoon her in an impenetrable shield until the danger has passed. Unfortunately, when I take your shifter magic, it will end your human life."

Reese thrashed, screamed, threw everything she had into the moment, but her body would not move. Ethan had enthralled her entirely.

"Your sacrifice will be rewarded," he said again. "I will make sure of it."

With fire in his eyes, Ethan lowered his mouth to hers and began to kiss her.

No, not kiss her, she realized. *Drink her.*

He was drinking her dry…

WHEN REESE NEXT CAME TO AWARENESS, AT FIRST SHE DIDN'T know where she was. It was dark and the shallow warm waters moved smoothly around her. Her strong, lithe form cut a trail through the reef, weaving in and out of the coral gardens. Small, trembling creatures dove into the coral and rock crevices, escaping her path.

She didn't give chase. She wasn't hungry. In fact, she didn't want for anything. She enjoyed the steady rhythm of her strong body in the water and the way the underwater forest gleamed in the moonlight.

She couldn't remember where she had been before this moment, or what she had been doing.

It didn't matter. She had no destination in mind. No ambition to fulfill. She simply wanted to enjoy these moments, at home on the ocean floor, as her fins cut through moonlit waters.

It was a good life, she thought.

And she was grateful to have it.

The End
Create a new story - go back to the beginning

REESE: SACRIFICE YOURSELF

"Will it really protect Vendetta? And keep Castle Cove safe?" she asked him.

He regarded her with hellfire eyes. "Yes."

"Then I'll do it."

"Really?" Ethan seemed genuinely surprised.

"Yes. I'll do it." It wasn't like she was doing anything special with her life. She had no one here that really needed her. She thought of her ex, Violet, but Violet was fine. She didn't need Reese any more than the ocean needed a grain of sand.

"Come here." Ethan leaned across the seat as if to kiss her. But before he touched her lips with his, he said, "Your sacrifice will be rewarded. I will make sure of it."

With fire in his eyes, Ethan lowered his mouth to hers and began to kiss her.

No, not kiss *her*, she realized. *Drink her.*

He was drinking her dry...

WHEN REESE NEXT CAME TO AWARENESS, AT FIRST SHE DIDN'T know where she was. It was dark and the shallow warm waters moved smoothly around her. Her strong, lithe form cut a trail through the reef, weaving in and out of the coral gardens. Small, trembling creatures dove into the coral and rock crevices, escaping her path.

She didn't give chase. She wasn't hungry. In fact, she didn't want for anything. She enjoyed the steady rhythm of her strong body in the water and the way the underwater forest gleamed in the moonlight.

She couldn't remember where she had been before this moment, or what she had been doing.

It didn't matter. She had no destination in mind. No ambition to fulfill. She simply wanted to enjoy these moments, at home on the ocean floor, as her fins cut through moonlit waters.

It was a good life, she thought.

And she was grateful to have it.

The End
Create a new story - go back to the beginning

GRAYSON: CALL IT A NIGHT

Daniel shrugged and offered a friendly smile. "No worries. Have a good birthday."

He continued down the stairs and disappeared into the crowd. Grayson turned back, looking up to see if Liam was still there, but he was gone and so had his entourage.

With a shiver, Grayson decided it was time to go home. The night was catching up to him. He was tired and suddenly wanted his bed more than anything in the world.

He stepped out into the night and took a deep breath. His mind began to clear.

Pheromones, he realized. Like the sirens, vampires had their own pheromones that clouded the mind.

It's a wonder that any human is able to accomplish anything in this town, he thought. *All these freaking pheromones floating around.*

But the pheromones had also suppressed that sad part of him, the part that was grieving the loss of Landon.

Now that he was alone walking the streets, reality pressed in on him again. His sadness felt too heavy in the moonlight. By the time he was at his front door, he was nearly in tears.

He slipped into the quiet house and mounted the stairs as

slowly as possible to avoid creaks. He found Abby asleep in his bed and climbed in beside her.

She stirred but didn't wake. That was just as well. Grayson didn't know what he could've possibly said to her if she had.

He woke to a soft knock on his bedroom door. He opened his eyes and found his mother standing in the frame, one hand on the handle, another on the jamb.

If his mother had any thoughts about the way Abigail was wrapped around his shoulder, sleeping soundly on his chest, she didn't say anything. She didn't even look directly at Abby.

And Grayson was too exhausted to care. He felt like his eyes were on fire. He couldn't have slept for more than two or three hours.

"Abigail's mom is going to be here in twenty minutes. I thought she might want a bagel or coffee before she goes."

"Abby." He shook her gently. "Abby, wake up."

At first, her hold tightened on him.

"Abby, your mom is on her way."

She raised her head, auburn hair covering her face. She pushed it back with her hand.

"Morning," his mother said from the doorway. She came to the side of the bed and put Abby's clean clothes on a pile. "I washed your clothes. Or you can just wear those." She seemed to read Abby's hesitation. "I can get them back some other time."

"Thank you," Abby said, sitting up. "I appreciate that."

"Would you like a bagel and coffee?

"Yes and yes." She smoothed her abundant hair out of her face.

"Blueberry or Everything?"

"Everything. Do you have any of that garlic spread?"

His mother smiled, but Grayson saw how it didn't reach her eyes. "I do."

"I'll take that, please. Thank you."

His mother gave him a look.

"I'll make mine," Grayson told her, before she shut the door with a nod.

"I love your mother," Abby said, stretching her arms overhead.

"Do you need a washcloth or anything?" he asked. He knew Abby liked to wash her face in the morning.

"I still have one from yesterday."

For a long time they both sat there, not moving, not speaking.

"It really happened, didn't it? He's really dead." She pressed the heels of her hands into her eyes. "There was a moment when I was just coming awake and I thought—"

"I know," he said. The last twelve hours of his life seemed like a crazy blur.

She took her clothes and disappeared into the bathroom without saying anything else.

Grayson went downstairs and found the bagels by the toaster. The smell of coffee filled the kitchen. It was some sort of mocha blend. He could smell the chocolate.

He cut a blueberry bagel in half with a knife and forced it into the slots of the toaster. He stood there while the elements glowed red.

Landon.

God, *Landon*. Was he really dead? Could he really be gone?

His mind kept bucking against the idea with disbelief.

Before he considered what he was doing, he had his cell phone out of his pocket. He dialed Landon's cell—he was the last one to call Grayson—and listened to the empty static on the line.

It went straight to voicemail.

"If you're looking for Landon, you found him! What's up?"

It beeped and Grayson considered leaving a message. His mouth was half open. The breath was there between his lips.

"Who are you calling?" his mom asked. She came through the swinging doors and crossed to the fridge. She pulled out a pitcher of OJ and stood there looking at him.

"No one," Grayson said, slipping the phone back into his pocket. "I was checking my messages."

It was a meaningless lie, but easier than opening himself up to have a conversation he wasn't ready to have.

The toaster spit out his bagel and he took it into the dining room. He sat down at the table beside his father. That left a space between him and his mother for Abby, which already had a steaming cup of coffee and hot bagel waiting.

"What are you going to do today?" his father asked.

"I think you should stay home and rest," his mother interjected. Her fierce blue eyes seemed to challenge his father to argue against her. "You clearly didn't get enough sleep."

His father seemed oblivious to any such challenge as he shoved the last bite of a bagel into his mouth and continued to scroll through his phone, catching up on the morning news.

"I'm supposed to be at work at two," Grayson said. "But I could call in."

"You should," his mother said. "What will Tabitha do? Fire you?"

It was true that Grayson didn't need his job at Curiosity Books. But he liked working there. There was something about the cramped rows and precariously perched stacks that comforted him. And it wasn't like spending his afternoons in a used bookstore was a hard job. Usually he spent it reading behind the register and saying hello to the customers who meandered in.

Every hour or so, there might be a purchase or two, but overall it was quiet.

The most exciting part of the gig was the ghost upstairs who liked to move around Ms. Monroe's dining room furniture when she was away. And sometimes, if the ghost was particularly restless, she would pull a book from the shelves just to hear it hit the dusty carpet.

"Are you guys going to be here?" Grayson asked, forcing down a bite of his bagel. Thinking of Landon was making his throat tight again, but if he didn't eat his mother would only come down harder on him. She was militant about self-care.

"No, I have to go into the lab for a few hours, but I'll be home in the afternoon," his father said.

"And I have office hours and two meetings," his mother said. "But I'd be happy to cancel those if you want me to stay with you."

"No," he said and hoped he didn't sound too eager. "I want to be alone."

"Okay," his mother said, but her face was contradicting her. It was clear she didn't really think it was okay. "There's still Chinese in the fridge and I also made a salad."

"Thanks."

"You'll let us know where you're going to be though," his mother said. It wasn't a question, even if it did tilt up at the end. "Work or here?"

Grayson Choice 6
Go to work - go to page 178
Stay home - go to page 319

REESE: FOLLOW STRANGE WOMAN

Reese ran as fast as she could down the beach. She was faster than a human, given her shifter status, so she managed to make it back to her pile of clothes and up the steep sandy slope in moments.

She was still naked when she ran across the street toward her red pickup. She'd only just thrown the door shut when twin taillights sparked to life in front of her. A car parked several meters away, farther up Canyon Road hooked a U-turn on the road. Its engine revved as it sped back toward town. Reese ducked down, pressing her face to her warm fabric seats as the car passed.

She waited a few breaths and inched up just enough to check her side mirror. The car was speeding away. The coast was clear.

Once the taillights were small enough that she thought she could also turn around and not get caught, she keyed the ignition and threw the truck into drive. She U-turned in the middle of Canyon Road. Her tires spit rock and sand along the pavement as she wrenched her wheel left then right.

She dressed as she drove, getting her bra and shirt down over her head first. She pulled her wet hair out of her shirt and let it fall down her back, knowing it would have to be washed and detangled later and what a job that would be.

The pants were harder to get on. She managed only to get one leg inside them before giving up.

Reese kept the taillights in her line of sight, but didn't get too close to the car. Again, she didn't want the woman to realize she was being followed. As they passed Vendetta Heights, Reese vaguely noted the cluster of cars parked in the wild, open fields. No one would dare go into the Western Woods that bordered the Heights, but the Heights themselves were free game for vampires who wanted to hook-up with vamp-loving humans.

The field-turned-parking lot looked like any other make-out spot for teens. Laughter rippled through her open window as she passed and also caught the metallic tang of blood. And sex.

Reese slammed on her brakes and downshifted as a woman stepped off the shoulder into her headlights. She disappeared before the red pickup could connect with her.

Reese sat in the middle of the road, heart rabbiting in her throat.

"Fucking ghosts." Reese shifted her truck back into first gear. "*Fucking* ghosts."

She stepped on the gas again, rushing to recover some of the lost distance.

The car up ahead had stopped at the four-way and turned left, creeping slowly into the adjacent parking lot.

"Damn," Reese said, knowing where the woman was headed.

Reese gave her a wide berth before pulling into the gravel lot herself.

She looked at the old-timey saloon sitting in front of her.

The Crossroads.

A demon bar posted at the last four-way stop out of town.

Patroned almost entirely by demons, shifters and humans only went into the bar if they had business. Like soul-selling business.

Reese hadn't detected any demonic energy from the woman as she'd watched her calling down her magic from the ocean and sky. So was the woman a human playing with magic or a full-blown witch? Maybe she'd made some deal with a demon for a certain power and was pissed that all it had gotten her was a stormy sky?

Surely she wouldn't like it when she found out there was a no-returns policy on souls…

The dark wave music seeping out into the night didn't match the look of the bar. It really did look like a saloon straight out of an old western. The wooden porch. The windows with worn shutters. Those windows looked possessed themselves, like twin glowing eyes watching Reese contemplate her next move in the solemn darkness of her truck.

There were half a dozen cars and three motorcycles in the lot.

She weighed her options.

Reese could hold her own in a fight, but demons never played fair. Besides, she just wanted to know what that woman was up to. It was up to the long-time residents of Castle Cove—people like Reese, Kristine, Cole—to keep their eyes open for trouble like this.

"I could pretend to be looking for Cole," she murmured to herself. Cole was a demon but also her friend and neighbor. Maybe no one would question why she came to a demon bar looking for her demon friend then. "I can just peek in there and see what she's up to."

Realizing the only person she was trying to convince was herself, she gripped the steering wheel.

Reese Choice 7

Go into the bar - go to page 338

Call it a night - go to page 156

GRAYSON: GO WITH THE VAMPIRE

"Let's go to your place," Grayson said. His face flushed hotter as he forced the words from his lips.

Daniel smiled. "Let's."

When he stepped around Grayson to take the lead, Liam stepped up to the head of the stairs. Liam held Grayson's gaze with dark, curious eyes. Looking into those eyes, Grayson suspected he understood what Daniel had meant by heartbreaker.

Liam spoke, but his eyes remained fixed on Grayson. "Daniel."

The vampire froze, his hand stiffening on Grayson's. "Yeah?"

"Be careful tonight." And with that he broke the gaze and turned away. Grayson felt all the heat in his body leave in a single *whoosh*. His knees nearly buckled underneath him.

What is it with that guy?

"Of course," Daniel said, and Grayson heard the hollow click in his throat.

Daniel pulled him down the staircase and across the foyer. They stepped out into the night together.

"You can't take the glass," the doorman said, snatching it

from Daniel's hand before he was even off the porch. He moved so fast that Grayson had barely seen the man's hand move.

Daniel forced a pouty face. "Let me finish it at least."

He snatched it back with a triumphant grin and threw back the alcohol. That's when Oli, the doorman seemed to register Grayson's appearance.

He looked from Grayson to Daniel and nodded. "Not bad. You could've done worse."

Daniel snorted. "Thank you for the endorsement, Oliver."

He reached for Grayson. "Come on."

Grayson followed him off the porch onto the sidewalk. His sneakers scuffed pavement as they headed east toward the university.

"Does the birthday boy have a wish?" Daniel asked. He was walking close to Grayson, their shoulders brushing every few steps. "Everyone gets a birthday wish."

Grayson shrugged. "I don't know." *For my friend to not be dead.*

Daniel pointed at the adjacent street and they cut across after a baby blue Prius passed.

"Gentle, rough, role play, I mean I can do just about anything."

Grayson's face flushed. "It's my first time."

Daniel stopped walking. "*Ever?*"

Grayson laughed. It was a high, nervous sound. "No. I mean with a vampire. And a man."

Daniel placed a hand over his chest. "I'm honored, Grayson. What do you usually go for?"

He thought of Abby. "Human girls."

Daniel snorted as if Grayson made a joke. Grayson wasn't sure it was. It was true he'd never slept with a man before, but he had found a few attractive. He'd wondered if it was the supernatural element. When it came to humans, it was mostly women he noticed. But when they weren't human, he seemed more...fluid in his choices.

"Then perhaps I should take the lead on this one?" Daniel suggested. He stopped outside a brick apartment building and removed a key from his pocket. It jingled on the ring. He was watching Grayson's face carefully. "Assuming you still want to come up?"

Grayson nodded.

"Just checking." Daniel pushed open the door and hit the light switch. "I'm on the top floor, 303."

Grayson followed the carpeted stairs up to the top floor. There were two doors on the large level, one on each side. Number 303 was on the left.

He waited at the red door for Daniel to fish out another key.

The apartment door opened with a creak revealing a wide, open floor plan. The kitchen was modern and nicely updated. The appliances were gleaming stainless steel and the counter a dark granite. Daniel seemed to follow his gaze. "Yeah, it's a tragedy that this place has such a nice kitchen and I'll never cook in it."

He went to the fridge. "But I do have some drinks if you want something. Coffee, tea, OJ and vodka. I can make you a screwdriver if you want."

"Isn't giving alcohol to minors illegal?" Grayson asked. He realized he was hovering in the doorway and Daniel was waiting for him to move so he could shut the door.

Grayson stepped into the apartment.

"No to the drink then?"

"Water is fine," he said.

Opposite the kitchen was an open living room with a large TV and teal couch. Between them, on the far wall were sliding doors to the balcony. He crossed and looked out on the courtyard below.

"You have a nice place," Grayson said. He listened to Daniel pull a glass from the cabinet and fill it from the tap.

He slid the cold glass into Grayson's hands. "Thank you. Do you live by yourself? I'm guessing not since you turned eighteen today."

"I live with my parents," he replied. "And my little brother."

"Going to college in the fall?"

"I was accepted to UCLA and CCU. I haven't decided which one I'm going to attend. I told UCLA yes, but..."

Daniel nodded once as if conceding a point. "Castle Cove is a special place. There's nowhere else like it. I should know. I've done quite a bit of globetrotting."

Daniel settled onto the sofa, reclining back against the pillows. His eyes seemed to beckon Grayson to join him.

He took a sip of water and placed it on the coffee table before settling down beside the vampire. Their knees brushed.

"I'd heard that there were other towns like Castle Cove," Grayson said, draping an arm along the back of the sofa. His fingers brushed Daniel's arm. He felt pretty safe here, comfortable. He wasn't sure that was how one was supposed to feel in a vampire's apartment.

"There are," Daniel admitted. "Let's see. There's the one near Kyoto, and the one outside Prague. There's another in Spain and France and the London underground. Hmmm... Two in Canada. Mexico. Brazil. South Africa. Morocco. I know I'm forgetting some of them."

"If there's so many then how can you say Castle Cove is special?" Grayson felt his mind coming alive again. It was his curiosity about Castle Cove and its true nature, but also Daniel. He was easy to talk to. Maybe it was how relaxed he looked there, reclining on his sofa.

"I don't know," Daniel said, looking at the ceiling as if the answer were written there. "There's just something this place has that the others don't. Maybe it's Vendetta."

"Who?"

For the first time Daniel hesitated.

Grayson sat back on the sofa. "You don't have to tell me if—"

"Oh damn. Not those puppy dog eyes." Daniel tilted his head. "Okay, I'll tell you, but keep this to yourself. It's not the sort of thing you're supposed to be whispering among the humans, all right?"

Grayson scooted closer. And Daniel smiled.

"I'm being rewarded. I like this," he said. He opened his arms so that Grayson could move in as close as he wanted. Grayson did scoot closer until he was in the crook of Daniel's arm.

"Vendetta is the woman who started it all, or so it's said. She was the first vampire, first demon, the first witch."

"I don't understand. How could she be all of that?" He liked watching Daniel's jaw move as he spoke.

"She was given her powers by an ancient goddess, one who existed before time was time. Hell, before day was cleaved from night, if you want to get biblical about it. One moment night ruled the universe. Then when it was halved by day, she was imprisoned here on earth. She dwelled inside an ancient tree that's supposed to be here in the Western Woods. And Vendetta is supposed to be here too, somewhere, in stasis. She sleeps, waiting until the ancient goddess wakes up. So you see, according to the stories, Vendetta serves her mistress, this tree, this night goddess. And all supernaturals came from Vendetta."

Grayson felt warm in the crook of Daniel's arm. Ease washed over him. Despite being in the den of a killer, a hunter, he wanted to be here.

"You think that her presence here—her and the tree—that's what makes it special? That's why it feels different than the other supernatural cities you've visited?" Grayson asked.

"You're a quick study. It only makes you cuter. I like them smart. " Daniel turned so that he could look into Grayson's eyes. Grayson's stomach dropped. He touched a finger to Grayson's lips. "I'm wondering how much you can learn in one night?"

A shiver ran up Grayson's spine.

"Do you mind if I kiss you, Grayson?" Daniel asked. He was watching Grayson carefully. Because Grayson was looking into his eyes, he saw the pupils dilate. Black overtook most of the clear blue.

"I don't mind," Grayson said, licking his lips.

His tongue was still on the bottom lip when Daniel moved in. Their tongues brushed and something tightened in Grayson's stomach. Heat seemed to rush through his core and pool between his legs. Fingers trailed up the back of Grayson's neck and into his hair. A strong, firm hand fixed there, trapping him into the kiss. Grayson didn't mind. Until he couldn't breathe.

He pulled back gasping.

Daniel was smiling. "Sorry. I forget you have to breathe."

He turned his head and placed a kiss on Grayson's throat.

"Your heartbeat has the sweetest rhythm. Do you know it?"

"No, I didn't," Grayson said and he felt his voice vibrate against Daniel's lips. "Are you going to bite me?"

"Would you let me bite you?" Daniel asked. His warm tongue trailed up the side of Grayson's neck and into the notch below the ear. Grayson shivered in his arms. This seemed to delight Daniel as his embrace only tightened.

"Yes," Grayson said. "I'd let you."

Daniel let out a moan. "You're killing me, you know that?"

Grayson pulled back to look into the vampire's eyes. Seeing the vampire's excitement, only intensified Grayson's.

"How am I—?" he began.

Daniel didn't let him finish. "Living vampires have venom in their bites. If I bite you, it's very possible that you'll be infected. So I can't bite you unless I want to chance changing you. Even though I really, *really* want to."

"Oh. Right. I knew that actually." Grayson felt a little stupid.

Daniel grinned. "It's hard to remember things in the heat of the moment. And we're having a moment, aren't we?"

"Yes." Grayson shivered as more kisses traced his neck.

"If I were undead I could bite you all I like and there'd be no danger. But as a living vampire, we have to be careful."

"How can we—" Grayson wasn't sure he could finish. "How, uh—"

"Oh we can still fuck," Daniel said with a devilish grin. "And I can drink your blood, if you'll let me. But no fangs. Unfortunately, that means a bit of pain for you. How do you feel about pain?"

"How much pain?" Grayson asked. A strange, excitement fluttered inside him.

"This much," Daniel said and then there was a quick prick in the side of his throat. A second later, the prick was replaced by a burning.

Daniel held up his thumb, showing the metal cuff capped on its end. It was like a pointy thimble with a strange design on its side that Grayson couldn't make out in the low light.

Grayson forgot all the about the thumbnail ring that had opened his throat when he saw the vampire's eyes. The blue was entirely gone now.

"May I kiss it and make it better?" he asked. His voice was low. It was almost a growl.

Grayson tilted his chin slightly away, offering himself to the vampire. A warm slick tongue flicked across his collarbone, and licked upward, no doubt lapping up the spilled blood.

The throb that had been building in Grayson's groin hardened him until his erection pressed uncomfortably against the inside of his jeans. There was nowhere for it to go, but the pressure only intensified the sensation.

Daniel moaned into the side of his neck, his lips locking around the wound. It burned as the vampire sucked, but the sensation wasn't altogether unpleasant.

"You're sweet," Daniel moaned into his ears.

"Thank you?"

"It means you're healthy," the vampire replied, licking his lips. "Clean living."

Whatever he wanted to say next was swallowed up by the moan slipping between his lips as the vampire locked his lips around his throat again. Because in that instance, Daniel's hand had also undone his pants and freed his erection. Daniel had Grayson's cock in his hand before Grayson had a chance to think about what was happening.

He stroked him in languid strokes, building a lazy, teasing rhythm, all the while never removing his mouth from Grayson's throat.

He's mimicking my heartbeat, Grayson realized. Because as soon as his heart sped up, responding to the mounting desire, so did Daniel's rhythm.

"Don't come on me yet," Daniel said, pulling back. His lips were red with Grayson's blood. "Your blood isn't the only thing I want to taste."

The vampire slid off the couch, between Grayson's legs so fast that Grayson hadn't been able to track the movement with his eyes. One minute they were entwined on the couch and the next, Daniel was between Grayson's legs. He had his mouth around Grayson's erection, pulling a long, deep moan from his throat.

The suction was unbelievable. The iron-clad pressure sent him over the edge. The vampire swallowed and didn't seem to want to let go. Grayson fisted the cushions around him, writhing.

Then when he thought he could take no more and would surely die if he wasn't given a break, the vampire released him.

"Too sweet," he said again, rolling his eyes up to meet Grayson's. The blue had returned, but the pupils were still dilated with desire.

Grayson felt lazy with pleasure. He was heavy on the couch, somewhere between spent and wanting more.

Daniel bit the tip of his finger and pressed it to Grayson's throat. "Just to seal this up," he said, as if that explained everything. His eyes roved Grayson. "I've made a bit of a mess of you. Do you want a shower? Your hair is still a bit wet. I'm guessing you showered before you came to The House."

"I did."

"The only danger of getting in the shower with me, is that I will want more. Of you," the vampire said, his smile once again wicked. "Would you mind that?"

Grayson found himself shaking his head before he thought better of it.

"Well," Daniel said, standing. "Let me start the shower then."

Before he left he put the glass of water in Grayson's hand. "Drink this first."

Grayson obeyed as the vampire disappeared through the door. It stood open, revealing the end of a bed. So the shower was adjacent. How easy it would be to end up in the shower and then fall into the bed together, he wondered.

And did he want that? Yes, he did. In fact, the longer he laid on the couch, sipping the cool water in his hand, the more desire built inside him.

He was bouncing back rather quickly.

Daniel appeared in the doorway and beckoned Grayson forward. "You ready?"

Grayson stood, holding the front of his jeans up with both hands. He crossed the moonlit bedroom, past the queen-sized bed that looked soft and inviting. The bathroom was bigger than he'd expected. The shower was a stand-in stall rolling with steam.

The vampire pulled him into the hot water the second his last piece of clothing hit the floor.

"You okay?" Daniel asked, pushing his head back under the

hot water. There were two showerheads, Grayson realized, once from each direction.

"Yeah. It's just a little disorienting when you move fast."

"Right," Daniel said. "Sorry about that. I'm just a little desperate for this."

This turned out to be another prick on his chest. Grayson looked down in time to see the metallic thumb drag across his chest and the blood that welled there. Daniel's tongue lapped at the cut. The sensation sent Grayson's casually building desire into overdrive. His erection was rock hard again.

"Why does that keep happening?" he murmured.

Daniel looked up with bloody lips, a soft laughter rumbling in his throat. "It's my pheromones. Living vampires create arousal in their prey. It keeps you around. For feeding."

"I'm the prey?" Grayson asked. His head rested against the tile as hot water beat down from above.

"Do you mind?" Daniel asked. The humor was gone.

Grayson didn't like this touch of seriousness. "No. I like it." He pulled Daniel into a kiss.

Daniel's hand found his erection before he broke the kiss. He moaned into Daniel's mouth, but he wouldn't let him go. He worked Grayson until he came again. Then he was lapping up the blood from his chest and sealing his wound.

The actual showering seemed like an afterthought.

"Do you want to move this to the bed?" Daniel asked. "I have about two hours left before sunrise."

"Yeah."

Daniel had them in the bed in a heartbeat.

Grayson's back hit the pillows with a gasp of surprise.

Daniel hovered above him, holding himself above Grayson. The vampire searched his face. "Listen, if you don't want something, or you want me to stop at any point, you have to tell me. I'm not a mind reader."

"Okay," Grayson said.

"No matter how into it I am, I *will* stop, all right?"

Grayson softened into the bedding. "All right."

He was dragging his thumb across Grayson's neck again.

"Why did we shower again?" Grayson laughed.

Daniel grinned. "Maybe I wanted an excuse to get your clothes off you."

Grayson laughed. "Smooth."

He rolled onto his back, pulling Grayson on top of him. Grayson looked down at the naked vampire and felt his erection stirring again. *Oh man, again?* he thought. *Really?*

"I'm sorry. You're just too cute. Do you want to do this?" Daniel was saying. His words barely penetrated the fog of Grayson's mind. "I've got a condom."

The borderline pain of his erection said yes, he wanted to. He took the condom and tore open the wrapping.

"How many times is this going to happen?" Grayson asked, grasping his own erection as if it were an alien creature. He slipped the condom on it.

"We've got two hours," Daniel said, "before I'll be too tired."

"But I'm insatiable. What if it doesn't stop?"

"Then we'll keep going." Daniel was beautiful with the moonlight falling across his cheeks and bright eyes. "Come here, Grayson."

Grayson obeyed, lowering himself down, finding that he was the same height as Daniel and that made it easier. He entered him, slowly, carefully. Perhaps he was going too slowly because Daniel grabbed his hips and thrust him in deep. Grayson moaned in surprise.

"You won't hurt me," Daniel said, hoarse. Then Grayson felt a fresh cut spring up on his arm just before Daniel wrapped his lips around it.

Grayson found that he could in fact go as hard and fast as he wanted and Daniel only seemed to enjoy it more. Daniel moaned, his lips vibrating against Grayson's skin where he fed. He almost came too quickly.

"Don't," Daniel growled. "Come on."

Grayson obeyed continuing until he couldn't hold back any longer. His rhythm faltered and his head swam. Daniel flipped him onto his back before he could collapse.

"Oh Gray," the vampire said, continuing to stroke his own erection as he leaned over him. "I like you."

"Let me," Grayson said. He took the vampire in his hand. It was strange, holding a dick that wasn't his own. But he knew what he liked, so he started there. Daniel didn't seem to mind. His soft growling indicated he was enjoying it.

When the vampire came, he collapsed on top of Grayson, squeezing the younger man in his arms.

Four times, it turned out. Four erections was the limit of vampire-pheromone-induced erections.

"Are you okay?" Daniel asked when they both seemed spent. He was looking into Grayson's eyes and pressing his fingers to his neck as if checking for a pulse. "How do you feel?"

"A little light headed, but good. Really good."

Daniel grinned. "Yeah, me too. I hope I didn't take too much."

"I'm not sure if it was the sex or the blood drinking—"

"Both," Daniel said. "But you've got quite a bit of stamina, you know that?"

Grayson blushed. After everything, he shouldn't have. They'd gone a bit too far to be embarrassed.

"I didn't do nearly as much for you as you did to me," Grayson said. "Do you want me to—"

Daniel grinned. "I'm more of a giver, actually. And I took plenty, don't worry."

Grayson wasn't sure if he was referring to the blood or something else. "I want you to be satisfied."

"*Gray*." Daniel grabbed him and kissed his lips. "Keep going like this and I'm going to want to keep you."

Grayson rolled onto his side, smiling.

Daniel glanced toward the window. There was still time before dawn. "Will you drink some juice if I get it for you? It'll help."

"Okay." Grayson relented. And Daniel was back with the juice before Grayson even had a chance to sit up against the headboard. He took a few sips gingerly. "So…" He searched for the words. "Were we safe enough?"

He wasn't sure if the vampire virus could be transferred in other ways, like sex.

"Actually, I think I'm pregnant," Daniel said, taking the empty juice glass and setting it on the side table. "And I'm keeping it."

Grayson laughed. "Be serious."

"There's nothing you can catch from me except vampirism," Daniel explained. He crawled in between the sheets and placed his warm body against Grayson's. "The condom was just for your peace of mind."

"Oh," he said.

"I figured it would be like a security blanket for you." Daniel reached up and brushed his hair out of his face.

"And I didn't catch vampirism?" Grayson asked.

Daniel's lips quirked to the side. "No. Your blood would taste different. I'd know instantly. But maybe I should check one more time just to be sure?"

Grayson loved that devilish glint in his eyes. "Just to be sure."

A quick prick on his shoulder and then Daniel's tongue was lapping at his skin. The shivers were instant, and Grayson began to worry he would get another erection. Fortunately, Daniel stopped before arousal could take root.

"You're safe," Daniel said with a grin. "Did you enjoy yourself?"

Grayson thought his stupid, flushed and grinning face was

answer enough. "Did you?"

Daniel laughed. "You were the best surprise I've had in a long time."

Grayson noticed the vampire's eyes fluttering closed with the lazy satisfied look in them. "It's close to sunrise, isn't it?"

"You *are* a clever boy," Daniel said. "But I've got enough in me to walk you home if you want."

"No, it's okay," Grayson said. "I don't live far from here."

"Tsk, *tsk*," Daniel said, his eyes closed. But the playful smile was still in place. "I've told you. You shouldn't tell vampires where you live."

Grayson couldn't imagine having to be afraid of this guy.

"I'll take my chances," Grayson said and bent to kiss his lips again. They were soft and full. But that delirious passion had faded. Maybe vampires didn't have their pheromones during the day. It seemed that way. Because while Daniel was still very attractive, it wasn't driving Grayson out of his mind anymore.

He brushed the hair off Daniel's face, regarding him one last time. "I'm going to head out. Thanks for everything."

Daniel snorted. "Any time."

Grayson stood and dressed as quietly as he could.

"Hey, Grayson?" Daniel called, rolling over in his bed to give Grayson one more gracious smile.

Grayson hesitated in the doorway. "Yeah?"

"Happy birthday."

"Thanks." Mirroring the smile, Grayson closed the bedroom door.

Grayson walked home in a delicious haze. The morning sun gave everything a dewy glow and warm shine. He felt exhausted but deliriously happy. Too happy. It was a borderline a crime to be this content with how his night had gone in the wake of his best friend's death.

The pheromones, he realized, had also suppressed that sad part of him, the part that was grieving a terrible loss.

Now that the vampire was well out of reach, his reality pressed in on him again.

By the time he was at his front door, he was nearly in tears.

He slipped into the quiet house and found that everyone was still in bed. He mounted the stairs as slowly as possible.

He took a shower—his third tonight—and changed out of his clothes. He noted the splash of blood on the collar of his t-shirt and tried to wash it out in the sink.

He found Abby asleep in his bed, curled up in his pillows.

Clean and dressed, he climbed into bed beside her. Abby stirred but didn't wake. That was just as well. Grayson didn't know what he could've possibly have said to her if she had.

HE WOKE TO A SOFT KNOCK ON HIS BEDROOM DOOR. HE OPENED his eyes and found his mother standing in the frame, one hand on the handle, another on the jamb.

If his mother had any thoughts about the way Abigail was wrapped around his shoulder, sleeping soundly on his chest, she didn't say anything. She didn't even look directly at Abby.

And Grayson was too exhausted to care. He felt like his eyes were on fire. He couldn't have slept more than two or three hours.

"Abigail's mom is going to be here in twenty minutes. I thought she might want a bagel or coffee before she goes."

"Abby." He shook her gently. "Abby, wake up."

At first, her hold tightened on him.

"Abby, your mom is on her way."

She raised her head, auburn hair covering her face. She pushed it back with her hand.

"Morning," his mother said from the doorway. She came to the side of the bed and put Abby's clean clothes on a pile. "I washed your clothes. Or you can just wear those." She seemed to read Abby's hesitation. "I can get them back some other time."

"Thank you," Abby said, sitting up. "I appreciate that."

"Would you like a bagel and coffee?

"Yes and yes." She smoothed her abundant hair out of her face.

"Blueberry or Everything?"

"Everything. Do you have any of that garlic spread?"

His mother smiled, but Grayson saw how it didn't reach her eyes. "I do."

"I'll take that, please. Thank you."

His mother gave him a look.

"I'll make mine," Grayson told her before she shut the door with a nod.

"I love your mother," Abby said, stretching her arms overhead.

"Do you need a washcloth or anything?" he asked. He knew Abby liked to wash her face in the morning.

"I still have one from yesterday."

For a long time they both sat there, not moving, not speaking.

"It really happened, didn't it? He's really dead." She pressed the heels of her hands into her eyes. "There was a moment when I was just coming awake and I thought—"

"I know," he said. The last twelve hours of his life seemed like a crazy blur.

She took her clothes and disappeared into the bathroom without saying anything else.

Grayson went downstairs and found the bagels by the toaster. The smell of coffee filled the kitchen. It was some sort of mocha blend. He could smell the chocolate.

He cut a blueberry bagel in half with a knife and forced it into the slots of the toaster. He stood there while the elements glowed red.

Landon.

God, *Landon*. Was he really dead? Could he really be gone?

His mind kept bucking against the idea with disbelief.

Before he considered what he was doing, he had his cell phone out of his pocket. He dialed Landon's cell—he was the last one to call Grayson—and listened to the empty static on the line.

It went straight to voicemail.

"If you're looking for Landon, you found him! What's up?"

It beeped and Grayson considered leaving a message. His mouth was half open. The breath was there between his lips.

"Who are you calling?" his mom asked. She came through the swinging doors and crossed to the fridge. She pulled out a pitcher of OJ and stood there looking at him.

"No one," Grayson said, slipping the phone back into his pocket. "I was checking my messages."

It was a meaningless lie, but easier than opening himself up to have a conversation he wasn't ready to have.

The toaster spit out his bagel and he took it into the dining room. He sat down at the table beside his father. That left a space between him and his mother for Abby, which already had a steaming cup of coffee and hot bagel waiting.

"What are you going to do today?" his father asked.

"I think you should stay home and rest," his mother interjected. Her fierce blue eyes seemed to challenge his father to argue against her. "You clearly didn't get enough sleep."

His father seemed oblivious to any such challenge as he shoved the last bite of a bagel into his mouth and continued to scroll through his phone, catching up on the morning news.

"I'm supposed to be at work at two," Grayson said. "But I could call in."

"You should," his mother said. "What will Tabitha do? Fire you?"

It was true that Grayson didn't need his job at Curiosity Books. But he liked working there. There was something about the cramped rows and precariously perched stacks that comforted him. And it wasn't like spending his afternoons in a used bookstore was a hard job. Usually he spent it reading behind the register and saying hello to the customers who meandered in.

Every hour or so, there might be a purchase or two, but overall it was quiet.

The most exciting part of the gig was the ghost upstairs who liked to move around Ms. Monroe's dining room furniture when she was away. And sometimes, if the ghost was particularly restless, she would pull a book from the shelves just to hear it hit the dusty carpet.

"Are you guys going to be here?" Grayson asked, forcing down a bite of his bagel. Thinking of Landon was making his throat tight again, but if he didn't eat his mother would only come down harder on him. She was militant about self-care.

"No, I have to go into the lab for a few hours, but I'll be home in the afternoon," his father said.

"And I have office hours and two meetings," his mother said. "But I'd be happy to cancel those if you want me to stay with you."

"No," he said and hoped he didn't sound too eager. "I want to be alone."

"Okay," his mother said, but her face was contradicting her. It was clear she didn't really think it was okay. "There's still Chinese in the fridge and I also made a salad."

"Thanks."

"You'll let us know where you're going to be though," his mother said. It wasn't a question, even if it did tilt up at the end. "Work or here?"

Grayson Choice 7
Go to work - go to page 178
Stay home - go to page 319

REESE: GO UP THE STAIRS

Reese transformed into her human form and pulled herself out of the water onto the steps. Her bare feet scraped across the rough stone.

The second she straightened, water dripping down her back, a horrible screeching thrummed to life behind her.

The sirens had awakened. They thrashed on their rocks, throwing themselves into the water. Their lithe forms were torpedoing through the water toward her.

"Shit." She bounded up the stairs two and three at a time, careful not to slip on the wet surface. At the top of the stairs was a stone door.

"Please be unlocked, please be unlocked, please be unlocked."

The door opened under the hard push of her hand despite the weight of the stone. Behind her the sirens had stopped advancing. They now crowded the lower steps, but seemed unwilling to come up the stairs after her.

They can't get out of the water, she thought. At least not this far.

Heart still hammering in her chest, she breathed a sigh of relief and closed the door behind her.

She was greeted by a narrow passage. Light filtered through cracks in its crumbling walls, giving her a clear enough sense of where she was going. At the end of the passage, another set of stairs appeared. She mounted these as well.

Narrow passage, then stairs.

Another passage, then more stairs.

The labyrinth seemed to lead her higher and higher until her chest and legs were aching from the ascent.

"This is the last one," she said aloud, when she pushed open yet another stone door to find only more stairs. "If there's nothing here after this, I'm going back."

But the end of this passage opened onto what could only be described as a courtyard. Light poured through a collapsed ceiling onto the flagstones below. The stones themselves were half-eaten with moss and determined vines had pushed themselves up through the cracks.

I'm in the castle, she realized, as she turned in its center, admiring the ruined splendor. The public wasn't allowed to enter the castle ruins for fear that it would collapse and kill someone. Yet here she was, having found a secret passage inside.

A cacophony of beating wings tore a shriek from her throat. A cloud of pigeons coalesced atop a crumbling wall, cooing softly at her.

She followed the outline of the room to a small chamber. It had the air of an inner sanctum. But on the walls were ornate carvings of some kind. Clearly a stoneworker had license to embellish this stone either before or after it had been installed.

Reese crossed to the nearest carving and pressed her fingers to the etchings. A woman with long, flowing hair was extending her hand toward an enormous cobra that stood entranced before her. The next panel was the same exchange but the snake had changed. Now its form hunched over on itself. In the third and fourth panels, it was unfurling into a human form. If the woman was Vendetta, then it seemed her touch alone had transformed the snake into a human.

On the next wall, there was a small child crawling out of the sea and a woman there to welcome her with open arms.

This sparked a memory in Reese. Her first memory.

She was in the ocean—swimming? She had been following the slow, curious procession of a starfish when hands scooped her out of the water. For a moment she couldn't breathe. She couldn't see. The next she was in her aunt's arms.

"Look at you!" her aunt cried. Her shocked face was full of bright sunlight. Her hazel eyes shone like amber. "Where did you come from?"

Reese couldn't have been more than three or four years old at the time.

Could it be that Reese had simply come from the ocean? Transformed for the first time in her aunt's own embrace?

Tell me again, Reese had begged over and over again. *Tell me again about the day you found me.*

You were on the beach, Constance said, *all alone in the surf.*

Reese had no memory of her parents or her life before she was here in Castle Cove. She remembered only those bright summers and endless waves, and then her aunt taking her home, caring for her as if she was her own. Her aunt had no true blood relation to her. Reese had asked on more than one occasion why she would bother taking in a child that wasn't hers. A child with no history before her mysterious arrival in Castle Cove?

We aren't kin, Reese had said.

Of course we are kin, Constance had said. With a kind smile, she'd gather the ink-dipped ends of Reese's hair and run them through her fingers. She held it up to her own. *Look at us.*

Perhaps Ethan's words had some truth to them—was it possible that Reese didn't remember her life before Castle Cove because there had been only the ocean?

Had she been a shark first? A human second? Was this human life the dream life?

Reese fingered the stone reliefs and wondered. These were the only drawings with animals transforming under Vendetta's watchful gaze, but Vendetta herself was everywhere. Reese must've found hundreds of reliefs of the woman with the wild, flowing hair in every weed-choked chamber she explored.

Another common theme was a tree, majestic with its gnarled limbs. Could it be The Crone Tree she'd heard of from the stories? She couldn't be sure. The only question she had was whether or not these carvings existed first—validating the story —or if someone had seen the carvings later and made up the stories to match.

Perhaps she would never know.

Reese noticed a shift in the light. It was far more purple now than it had been when she'd set off this morning. And the rumble in her stomach seemed to confirm her suspicion. She'd lost track of time exploring the castle. If she didn't leave now, she would have to swim back in the dark.

In all her searching, she didn't find an exit out of the castle. How wonderful it would've been if she could've simply walked out of the ruins to her car. But she suspected that Ethan—or some other caretaker of the city—had been careful to seal the castle for the public's protection.

Reese would have to return to the underground tunnel and swim back to the beach, or she could try to climb out of here. She saw enough grooves in the rockface to know that she could probably do it. But it might be a long drop from the top if there were no handholds on the outside of the castle.

Reese Choice 8
Try to climb the outer wall - go to page 146
Use the stairs - go to page 148

REESE: TRY TO CLIMB THE OUTER WALL

Reese didn't have it in her to descend all those stairs to the underground cavern, only to swim the miles back to shore. Not after spending the whole day exploring the castle and no snacks. She could eat on the way back. Nothing was stopping her from preying on any of the fish that crossed her path. But with her car so close, and only a wall between her and the parking lot, she had to give it a try.

She chose the lowest wall she could find. It was in the north corner of the courtyard, with a swath of blue sky beckoning to her.

She worked her way carefully up the side of the wall, testing each rock before putting her whole weight on it. The stone felt quite sturdy beneath her, the moist moss rubbing against her hand.

As she reached the top of this wall, she smiled. *This is going to work*, she thought.

Her hand reached out and grabbed the top of the wall eagerly, only to find wet, loose stone. The sudden lack of resistance surprised her. As the stone slid off the top of the wall, so did she. The shift in her weight unmoored the stones beneath her as well until all of it was crashing down.

Her body hit the stone floor with a crack, something snapping in her leg. Her head slammed against the stone floor. Ringing hollowed out her ears as pain shot through her skull.

She opened her eyes only a moment before a large stone collapsed on top of her, blotting out the bright expanse of sky.

The End

Create a new story - go back to the beginning

REESE: USE THE STAIRS

As much as Reese loathed the idea of walking all the way back to the underground cavern, she thought it was much safer than trying to climb out of the castle. If it had been sealed to protect the public from getting hurt, it stood to reason that the walls were not nearly as stable as they looked. The ruins were thousands of years old. They wouldn't appreciate being climbed on.

Retracing her steps, she found the courtyard and the passage connecting it to the descending staircase. By the time she reached the underground cavern, her legs were shaking with fatigue.

Aqua waters shimmered on the stone steps, but there was no horde of sirens. Perhaps they'd gotten tired of waiting as she spent hours exploring the castle above. Or perhaps they were hoping she'd jump in so they could descend on her.

Regardless, the air had cooled, and she was still naked, tired, and hungry. She had to get back to shore with what energy she had left.

With a deep breath, she dove into the water, trying her best to transform in the air even if that meant a painful belly flop on the water's surface.

She managed it, though pain ricocheted through her abdomen on impact. She sank beneath the water, seeing the sirens stir at the commotion. But unlike before they did not chase her.

It must only be human flesh, she thought, her body easing into a steady rhythm. *Human flesh in the water is what draws them.*

The swim back felt shorter despite her fatigue. She supposed it had to do with the fact that she knew where she was going this time and how far she must travel.

When she pulled her exhausted body out of the water, Ethan and Liam stood on the shore. Ethan, she realized, was standing in full sunset. Unlike the other demons she knew, he didn't seem to die at sunrise. Demons couldn't exist in the realms of light. Did this mean he was not a demon? If so, he must be something much, *much* worse.

Liam held his black umbrella open overhead.

"Have a nice swim?" Ethan asked, his patent Italian leather shoes half sunk in sand.

"Did you wait here all day?" she asked, unable to believe their timing. She pulled herself out of the water, fully aware of her nakedness. With as much confidence as she could muster, she marched toward her clothes and found them dry where she left them. But there was also a towel that wasn't hers.

"I brought it," Liam explained. He was keeping his eyes averted respectfully. His demon boyfriend was not.

"Did you run into trouble?" Ethan asked. His eyes lingered on her legs.

"Not really," she said, toweling her body. She was afraid to mention that she'd explored the castle. But she didn't seriously believe she could keep it a secret from Ethan. *Here goes nothing,* she thought. "They perked up when I transformed into a human and went into the castle."

Ethan's eyebrows twitched. "Did you? And did you find anything interesting?"

She told him about the reliefs. "Is that where you got your story?"

"No," he said. "It's true that once Vendetta destroyed the queen she took the castle for herself and it was her stronghold for hundreds of years. I'm sure she decorated its walls however she saw fit, as queens are wont to do."

"Is it possible?" Reese asked, unable to control herself. "That I wasn't dropped here by some shifter who couldn't take care of me? That I was in fact *first* a shark?"

Ethan smiled as if he knew a secret. "What did your aunt tell you?"

"She found me on a beach when I was three or so. I didn't talk. I couldn't tell them my name or anything like that. She suspected that some supernatural dropped me off, knowing this was the best place for me."

"It's possible," Ethan said companionably. "Both that you had a mother who could not care for you or that you were born in the sea. Does it matter to you?"

Reese stared out over the horizon uncomprehendingly, as if she might find the answer there. "It doesn't change anything, does it?"

"How were the sirens?" Ethan asked, trying to recapture her attention.

She told them what she saw, doing her best to explain the black lesions.

Frowning, Ethan lifted his hand as if he meant to touch her. "May I?"

She nodded, suspecting she was agreeing to some sort of mind meld.

As his fingertips brushed her temple, the sensation of cold water running over her scalp overtook her. She shivered.

"I see," he said, letting his hand fall back to his side. His frown had deepened. All of his flirtation had disappeared.

The breeze pulled at his shirt, revealing a bare chest beneath.

"Could an illness make them more aggressive?" Liam asked, turning the umbrella in his grip.

"If they were worried about population die off, yes," he said. "Especially if several had already died."

"I didn't see any corpses," she said and immediately felt stupid. He must know that having shared her memory.

"They eat their dead," Ethan said. Now he was looking out over the ocean, a dreamy look on his face. "Which would spread a disease rather than contain it."

His trance seemed to break and he turned toward her with a bright smile. "Thank you for your help. This information is very useful. If you don't mind, I have another task."

Reese shifted, wondering just what he might ask for.

He shook his head, his seriousness lingering. "Nothing lascivious, I assure you. I'm sending Liam to investigate a situation in town and he could use a hand. Or you could go interview the children who were at the beach the night the sirens attacked. Which would you prefer?"

Reese Choice 9

Help Liam - go to page 290
Go interview the witnesses - go to page 239

GRAYSON: GO TO BED

"Yeah, it's late," he said, conceding to his parents' will. The relief was written all over their faces. "I should check on Abby anyway."

He pushed back from the table and took his plate to the kitchen. He rinsed it without really seeing the dish in his hands, nor did he see the kitchen around him. It seemed like another person was making his body move through the house, up the stairs.

In his bedroom, he found Abby in his double bed. She was facing away from him, toward his big picture window at the tulip poplar tree dancing in moonlight. He thought she was asleep until she spoke.

"Will you hold me?" she asked. She glanced over her shoulder. "I can't fall asleep."

"Okay." He slipped under the covers.

She was warm now, so much warmer than when they'd been naked on the beach just hours before. Her hair smelled like his shampoo and despite everything, a strange possessiveness rose up in him.

Stop it, he told himself. *Stop thinking about her like that.*

Not only was it wrong to think about his best friend's girlfriend like that, but Landon had just *died*. She couldn't possibly be interested in him right now.

And yet she was reaching her hands under the covers. She was twining her fingers with his.

"Please," she said, snuggling deeper into his arms. He curled one arm under her head, and slipped the other over her waist.

How many times had he dreamed about this in the last six months?

How many times had he wondered what Abby would feel like in his arms?

Countless. And if he was being honest with himself, she was the reason he couldn't decide between UCLA and CCU. Part of him wanted to go to UCLA in order to get away from her. No—

from the *temptation* of her.

He'd played a scenario in his mind that went something like this: He went away to LA for four years. Abigail and Landon broke up while he was away but became friends again. Then when Grayson returned after college one summer, or when he graduated, he and Abby would have their chance. When it came time to tell Landon, he would be cool with it because he would be over Abby and dating someone else.

The alternative fantasy had been staying in Castle Cove and going to CCU with Abby. And...

Only that wasn't how it was going to go now, was it?

Landon was never going to be a problem ever again.

"Why?" he whispered. The word was out of his mouth before he could censor it. He hadn't meant to open this conversation. If he was lucky, she would be asleep and he wouldn't have to explain himself.

But she was turning over in his arms. *Her* thighs were brushing against *his* thighs.

"Why, what?" she asked. Her breath was hot on his cheeks and nose. God, her mouth was *so* close.

He licked his lips and tried to think of any other *why* he might use. But he was too aware of her body. Too aware of the way his hand felt on the dip of her hip. Too aware of the way he'd begun to throb, his heartbeat radiating from his navel down to his knees.

"Why did I see you? With the siren?" she asked.

He gave the smallest imperceptible nod. His nose brushed hers when he did.

For a long time she said nothing.

That's what you get for trying to make her talk about it, you moron, he thought. *Landon just died. He died while she was...she was... The last thing she wants to talk about is that.*

"I'm sorry," he said. "Forget I said anything."

She ignored this apology. "I think I figured it out at junior homecoming. How I feel about you."

Grayson's stomach twitched. Junior homecoming was almost two years ago.

She licked her lips. The skin shimmered as she spoke. "When I was shopping for my dress, the—"

"Navy blue one," he interjected.

Her breath hitched. "Yeah, that one. I can't believe you remember. Landon never remembers what I wear."

Remembers. Because to her he wasn't dead yet. He understood that. Was that why this felt so wrong? Holding her like this? Wanting her even after the night they had and the awful sight of Landon's body thrown against the shore...

"When I was shopping for it, I kept picturing you. I wanted to know if you'd like it. If you would notice that I'd dressed to match you."

He had noticed. But Landon's suit hadn't been so different from his own, in either style or color, so Grayson wondered if it was all in his head. Was he only seeing what he wanted to see?

"I think I've always wanted you, but Landon asked me first. And I loved him too, but it took me a long time to realize I didn't love him like that. He was a guy I trusted and cared about, but there was no…"

I'd been too scared to show interest, he thought.

"But I wanted to be sure. I started taking more of the same classes as you. The same after-school activities as you. I wanted more so I could figure out what I really wanted."

"Did you?"

"Yes. I *want* more."

The throb in his stomach was nearly unbearable, except now it was spreading upward, through his chest and into his head. It was becoming hard to think.

"If you don't see me that way," she said, licking her lips again. "If you don't—"

"I do," he said. It wasn't a smart thing to say. This was neither the time nor the place.

Right now his best friend was zipped up in a black body bag on his way to the Castle Cove County morgue. And he was lying in his warm, safe bed with more than half an erection and best friend's girlfriend in his arms. Shame flooded him.

Before he could process what was happening, she slipped an arm around his waist and closed the remaining distance. He could feel her nipples through her shirt, rubbing against his chest. Her lips found his in the dark.

When she rocked her whole body against his, he had to swallow down the sound building in the hollow of his throat.

Grayson Choice 8

Give in and tell her how you feel (ES) - go to page 163
Now is not the time - go to page 343

REESE: CALL IT A NIGHT

I t had been a long night. All that Reese wanted now was to be in her own bed. She drove through town in a daze and parked her red pickup outside her Georgian three-story home in Cliffside. It wasn't really *her* home in the financial sense. It was her aunt who'd bought and paid for the house. On a bartender salary, Reese would've been looking for an apartment in Old Town or near Red Light at best.

And there was the matter of travel. Aunt Constance was almost never home. As an oceanographer, she spent months out on the ocean with each research expedition. At present, the scientist was studying the degradation of coral in the Indian Ocean. The fact that Constance was a shark shifter no doubt helped in that research and the fact that her crew were all supernaturals at the least meant she didn't have to hide what she was or her purpose in trying to salvage what was left of the ocean.

It's our home, Aunt Constance often said. *It's where our souls live, Reese. If it's lost, that will be the end of us.*

And though Reese didn't have scientific inclinations of her own, she agreed with her aunt. And Constance was a kind and loving aunt. She hadn't pressured Reese into doing more with her gifts—or even use them in the name of the ocean they both worshipped—and Reese was very grateful for that. Bonus that Constance had insisted that Reese live in her large, well-furnished house overlooking the ocean.

Such a large house for only one person is ridiculous, she'd insisted. *And you're doing me a favor by watching the house while I'm away.*

Ridiculously large or not, Constance couldn't ever live in a house that didn't overlook the ocean. And the only homes in Castle Cove that offered such a view, were those elegant tri-levels in Cliffside.

Reese slid out of the truck with much difficulty. As she closed the door, she saw the light on at Cole's place across the street. She knew the demon and his vampire husband were no doubt awake despite the late hour. Normally she would go say hi if the light was on. But after the night she had, her desire for a hot shower overrode her desire to be a friendly neighbor.

Reese unlocked the front door and stepped into the gorgeous foyer. A high ceiling and bright crystalline chandelier greeted her. The space was furnished in impeccable whites and ocean hues—blues and turquoise. Coral and the occasional splash of green.

Reese went straight to the first floor bath, afraid to drip water on any of the house's expensive surfaces.

Fortunately, the first-floor bath was just past the living room on the right. All the towels, soap and necessities were present and accounted for. Reese had only to strip out of her sea-soaked clothes and into the hot water.

She washed the salt from her hair. Her tired mind wandered. She replayed the evening in her mind, wondering if there was a connection between seemingly separate events. Unfortunately, her concentration wouldn't hold.

Clean, Reese stepped out of the shower and collected her

clothes from the floor. She was tidy by nature, a habit instilled in her by her orderly aunt no doubt. The clothes went in the hamper. The water she'd tracked in was cleaned up with a mop.

Once every trace of her entrance had been removed, Reese climbed into bed.

She was asleep the moment her head hit the pillow.

A phone was ringing somewhere in the house. Reese groped the sheets blindly trying to find her cell. She found the cord first, tracing it to the phone itself.

"Hello?" she groaned. Her voice broke with the effort.

"Reese?"

It was Kristine, her boss and friend.

"Yeah? What's up?"

"A kid died in the cove last night. He was torn apart by a siren."

"What?" Reese sat up, alarm rocketing her mind to full wakefulness. "I was just there."

"Were you?" Kristine said. Said, because the alpha rarely asked questions. Even her questions couldn't be mistaken for questions.

Reese recounted the night, rubbing sleep from her eyes as she spoke. By the time she finished, she felt like she'd made a terrible mistake. She shouldn't have swum toward the reef after all. She should've chanced going into deeper waters. Maybe she could've helped those kids if she had.

"I saw the kids," she finished lamely. "I should've checked on them."

"Don't beat yourself up," Kristine said. "How could you have known that would happen? The sirens aren't even supposed to be in the cove."

"Yeah," Reese agreed. But guilt was already turning her stomach and adding lead to her limbs.

"I'm calling an emergency pack meeting," Kristine said finally. Her sigh made the woman sound much older. "We need to know what's going on. I called to see if you could watch the bar until I get there. I realize it's not your shift and I'll pay you double for that. But now that I know you're a witness, maybe you should be part of the discussion. I'll leave it to you to decide."

Reese Choice 10
Go to pack meeting - go to page 51
Hold down the bar - go to page 67

REESE: SWIM BACK

The swim back felt shorter despite her fatigue. She supposed it had to do with the fact that she knew where she was going this time and how far she must travel.

When she pulled her exhausted body out of the water, Ethan and Liam stood on the shore. Ethan, she realized, was standing in full sunset. If he was truly a demon, that should be impossible. Even Cole, who was as old as Hell itself, couldn't live once the sun rose. So Ethan—despite all his demonic charm—couldn't be a demon after all. Demons could not exist in the realms of light.

"Have a nice swim?" Ethan asked.

"Did you wait here all day?" she asked, unable to believe their timing. She pulled herself out of the water, aware of her nakedness. With as much confidence as she could muster, she marched toward her clothes and found them dry where she left them. But there was also a towel that wasn't hers.

"I brought it," Liam explained, his umbrella open overhead. He was keeping his eyes averted respectfully. His demon boyfriend was not.

"Did you run into trouble?" Ethan asked.

"No," she said, toweling her body.

Dressed, she moved to stand in front of them.

"So?" Ethan asked with a quizzical brow. "How were they?"

She told them what she saw, doing her best to explain the black lesions.

Frowning, Ethan lifted his hand as if he meant to touch her. "May I?"

She nodded, suspecting she was agreeing to some sort of mind meld.

As his fingertips brushed her temple, the sensation of cold water running over her scalp overtook her. She shivered.

"I see," he said, letting his hand fall. His frown had deepened. All of his flirtation had disappeared.

"Could an illness make them more aggressive?" Liam asked, turning the umbrella in his grip.

"If they were worried about population die off, yes," he said. "Especially if several had already died."

"I didn't see any corpses," she said and immediately felt stupid. He must know that having shared her memory.

"No, they eat their dead," Ethan said. Now he was looking out over the ocean, a dreamy look on his face. "Which would spread a disease rather than contain it."

His trance seemed to break and he turned toward her with a bright smile. "Thank you for your help. This information is very useful. If you don't mind, I have another task for you."

Reese shifted, wondering just what he might ask for.

He shook his head, his seriousness lingering. "Nothing lascivious, I assure you. I'm sending Liam to investigate a situation in town and he could use a hand. Or you could go interview the children who were at the beach the night the sirens attacked. Which would you prefer?"

Reese Choice 11

Help Liam - go to page 290

Go interview the witnesses - go to page 239

GRAYSON: GIVE IN AND TELL HER HOW YOU FEEL

Don't, don't do it, his mind warned. But he was already leaning in. He was already finding her lips with his.

She sighed into his open mouth and shivers ran down his spine. He slid his hand up her back and crushed her to him.

"Here," she whispered, and pushed against his arm until his hand was on her hip. Then she grabbed that hand and slid it down the front of her pants.

His fingers traced over the rough stubble from where she'd shaved. She opened her legs wider and he found her wet.

So wet.

The last time he'd fingered a girl was Olivia Richards in the back of her Ford Mercury after rehearsal for *Oklahoma!* one night. He tried to remember what Olivia had liked best about his performance—what she'd responded best to—and started there.

Grayson trailed a finger over the soft hood of her clit, back and forth. She gripped him harder, whimpering into his ear. His erection grew so hard he thought he would burst inside his sweatpants.

When her squirms gave over to desperate mewling, he slid his fingers inside her. Her moan rose in her throat.

He clasped the back of her neck and pressed her mouth against his throat, hoping to muffle her sounds.

He froze, thinking he heard a creak on the stairs. For a long time, they lay perfectly still, his fingers inside her, listening to the dark.

"You have to be quiet," he whispered.

She nodded, her soft cheeks rubbing against his throat. Her grip on him only tightened.

He began to pull his fingers out, only to slide them in again. She whimpered in his ear, but the sounds were soft. When he bore down, letting the heel of his hand press against her clit while he kept working his fingers in and out, her moans grew loud again.

"I'm sorry," she said, breath heavy. "But please don't stop. *Please.*"

He sympathized with her. The throb in his pants was unbearable.

Then he felt her hand—in her own pants. At first he was confused.

"No, don't stop," she whispered. "You should—yes."

He pumped his fingers in and out of her while she rubbed her clit. It took almost no time at all to send her over the edge, and before he'd even established a decent rhythm, loving the slick, soft feel of her, he felt her contract. He rode the wave, not stopping until she was fully spent.

Then her hand was slipping past the waistband of his pants.

He hadn't been wearing boxers or briefs under his sweats, so her hand found his erection immediately.

Her fingers were already wet with her own juices as she cupped him and began to slide her hand gently up and down his shaft.

Now it was his turn to bite back a moan.

She sucked at his throat and ear as she rubbed him, picking up speed. It was the moisture in her hand that made the sensation euphoric.

As if reading his mind, her hand disappeared.

He was close to begging, but he was rewarded for his patience. When her hand reappeared, it was even slicker than before. She'd clearly touched herself one last time for his benefit.

"God," he moaned. Whatever he meant to say next was swallowed up by her mouth closing over his.

She probed his tongue with hers and wouldn't let go. She devoured him as her hand continued its steady, relentless rhythm.

Then he came and she held on as if she could milk every drop out of him.

"Grayson?" his father called out. He was at the end of the hallway, where the landing split between the two bedrooms.

His heart jolted. "Yeah?"

His voice was tight in his throat.

"Abby's mom isn't coming tonight. She'll be here tomorrow."

"Okay," Grayson said, hoping his voice sounded steady despite the rabbit pulse in his ears. "Thanks."

"Try to get some sleep, all right?"

"Yep," he said. And that's when he *knew* his dad knew. After all, he had called out from the landing rather than from his door. And why would he tell him to get some sleep unless he suspected he hadn't even been trying?

"Good night, son."

"Night."

Neither Abby nor Grayson moved until they heard his parents' bedroom door click closed.

Abigail seemed unperturbed by this. "I want more of you," she whispered.

"My bed squeaks," he said.

"So let's get on the floor."

Grayson had heard that male sirens emitted a potent pheromone that induced arousal in women. Was Abigail still reeling from its effects? If so, no amount of effort would placate her tonight. Only time would do that.

She saw his hesitation. "Or not."

"I want to," he said and he wasn't lying. He was certain, with enough, encouragement he could rise to the occasion.

"But you don't want your parents to hear you?"

"And…" But he wasn't sure how to finish this sentence.

"And?" She pulled back and looked him in the eyes. She leaned over the side of the bed and grabbed her towel. She used it to wipe her hands and then his. This gave him time to compose his thoughts.

"I don't have any protection," he said. "And I suspect what we just did might not be the most…hygienic."

"I'm clean," she said. "I just did my annual. You won't get anything from me."

He smiled, pushing the hair back from her face. "I want to be sure you really want this. You've been through a lot tonight."

"*We've* been through a lot," she corrected him.

Landon. Grayson kept replaying all his favorite memories of Landon. Landon over at his house, eating chips and drinking soda after school while they played *Resident Evil* on PS4. Landon with slicked hair and braces as they went to their first dance. Landon when he'd confessed that he wanted to ask Abby out and whether or not Grayson thought it was okay.

Why would I care? Grayson had asked.

Because she's your friend, too.

Abby searched his face. "I know I want this. I can't tell you how many times I've rehearsed this moment in my head. I've imagined us in just about every place I could think of—my bedroom, yours, the back of my car, in the pool at school after one of your meets. I help you change out of your swimsuit in those tiny shower stalls and—"

"That's weirdly specific."

"I've also pictured us in one of those long boats out on the water."

"You can't paddle one with less than four people. Well, you can, but it would be hell."

"On the beach…" Here she stopped talking.

She'd gotten that wish tonight at least. Or a comparable experience, if the male siren had been convincing enough.

Abby's lip quivered. "It's too soon, isn't it? Oh god, you must think I'm an awful, heartless—"

"No," he said. He wrapped his arms around her as she began to cry.

"Hey, no. I don't think that."

"I'm sorry," she said. "I'm terrible."

"You're not terrible," he said again, because he wanted to be sure she'd actually heard him. She only cried harder.

"I probably just ruined the one friendship that means anything to me. God, Grayson, I'm sorry. I shouldn't have tried to—what's wrong with me?"

He held her tighter.

"You probably don't even feel that way about me."

"I do," he admitted. "I swear I do. I just didn't figure it out as quickly as you did."

She pulled back, looking into his eyes. "How long?"

He was sure that his crush on Abby had developed in tenth grade. There was evidence at least, in the way he'd begun to notice her more. Or rather, what he began to notice changed. The way her face lit up when she smiled. The way her gym shorts sat on her hips and curved under her buttocks when she did laps around the gym. The way his heart would skip a beat when she would slide her arms around his neck and hug him bye at the end of the day.

But he didn't really know for sure until he'd started applying to schools in September. When he considered the distance of each school, or tried to imagine himself with a new life in that new place, it was Abby who kept crossing his mind—not his family or his friends or his love of Castle Cove.

It was her he didn't want to leave.

"I figured it out nine months ago, but I'd been crushing for a while before that."

"Nine months ago. At the beginning of senior year?" she asked.

A shadow fell across her face as something cut across the sky, momentarily breaking the moonlight.

"Yes," he said.

"So…you liked me all year but didn't say anything."

"You're—were—with Landon."

A cascade of emotion seized her face. She began tugging on his pants again, almost feverishly.

"No," he said. "Abby, *no.*"

She stopped, her expression caught somewhere between desperation and anger.

"I'm not going anywhere," he said.

The tears broke, spilling down her face. "Once you start to think about it, once you start to realize what this means, you'll break it off."

"No, I won't," he said again, and pulled her into his arms. "I swear."

How could he explain it to her? If he was being honest with himself, he knew only loyalty to Landon had held him back and also loyalty to Abby. He'd respected their decision to be together. In fact, he respected her desires even more than Landon's and perhaps that's one of the reasons he finally realized what his true feelings were.

"You'll think it's wrong. You'll get it in your head that it's betraying Landon somehow," she said, sniffling into the hollow of his neck. "You won't believe that I'd been trying to find the right time to break up with him for a year," she insisted. "It's not because he's dead, okay. It's not because—"

"I know," he said, squeezing her against his side. "I believe you. You don't have to prove anything to me. But there's no hurry."

She stared at him, her eyes wide and disbelieving.

He smoothed the hair off her face. "There's no hurry."

Because the truth was, he wanted to be the only guy on her mind when they made love for real.

"I'm not going anywhere." He combed her hair with his fingers. She softened against him then, giving over to the exhaustion of the night.

He held her while she cried herself to sleep.

Only when she was asleep did he finally allow his own tears to flow.

He woke to a soft knock on his bedroom door. He opened his eyes and found his mother standing in the frame, one hand on the handle, another on the jamb.

If his mother had any thoughts about the way Abigail was wrapped around his shoulder, sleeping soundly on his chest, she didn't say anything. She didn't even look directly at Abby.

And Grayson was too exhausted to care. He felt like his eyes were on fire. He couldn't have slept more than two or three hours.

"Abigail's mom is going to be here in twenty minutes. I thought she might want a bagel or coffee before she goes."

"Abby." He shook her gently. "Abby, wake up."

At first, her hold tightened on him.

"Abby, your mom is on her way."

She raised her head, auburn hair covering her face. She pushed it back with her hand.

"Morning," his mother said from the doorway. She came to the side of the bed and put Abby's clean clothes on a pile. "I washed your clothes. Or you can just wear those." She seemed to read Abby's hesitation. "I can get them back some other time."

"Thank you," Abby said, sitting up. "I appreciate that."

"Would you like a bagel and coffee?

"Yes and yes." She smoothed her abundant hair out of her face.

"Blueberry or Everything?"

"Everything. Do you have any of that garlic spread?"

His mother smiled, but Grayson saw how it didn't reach her eyes. "I do."

"I'll take that, please. Thank you."

His mother gave him a look.

"I'll make mine," Grayson told her before she shut the door with a nod.

"I love your mother," Abby said, stretching her arms overhead.

"Do you need a washcloth or anything?" he asked. He knew Abby liked to wash her face in the morning.

"I still have one from yesterday."

For a long time they both sat there, not moving, not speaking.

"It really happened, didn't it? He's really dead." She pressed the heels of her hands into her eyes. "There was a moment when I was just coming awake and I thought—"

"I know," he said. The last twelve hours of his life seemed like a crazy blur.

She took her clothes and disappeared into the bathroom without saying anything else.

Grayson went downstairs and found the bagels by the

toaster. The smell of coffee filled the kitchen. It was some sort of mocha blend. He could smell the chocolate.

He cut a blueberry bagel in half with a knife and forced it into the slots of the toaster. He stood there while the elements glowed red.

Landon.

God, *Landon*. Was he really dead? Could he really be gone?

His mind kept bucking against the idea with disbelief.

Before he considered what he was doing, he had his cell phone out of his pocket. He dialed Landon's cell—he was the last one to call Grayson—and listened to the empty static on the line.

It went straight to voicemail.

"If you're looking for Landon, you found him! What's up?"

It beeped and Grayson considered leaving a message. His mouth was half open. The breath was there between his lips.

"Who are you calling?" his mom asked. She came through the swinging doors and crossed to the fridge. She pulled out a pitcher of OJ and stood there looking at him.

"No one," Grayson said, slipping the phone back into his pocket. "I was checking my messages."

It was a meaningless lie, but easier than opening himself up to have a conversation he wasn't ready to have.

The toaster spit out his bagel and he took it into the dining room. He sat down at the table beside his father. That left a space between him and his mother for Abby, which already had a steaming cup of coffee and hot bagel waiting.

"What are you going to do today?" his father asked.

"I think you should stay home and rest," his mother interjected. Her fierce blue eyes seemed to challenge his father to argue against her. "You clearly didn't get enough sleep."

His father seemed oblivious to any such challenge as he shoved the last bite of a bagel into his mouth and continued to scroll through his phone, catching up on the morning news.

"I'm supposed to be at work at two," Grayson said. "But I could call in."

"You should," his mother said. "What will Tabitha do? Fire you?"

It was true that Grayson didn't need his job at Curiosity Books. But he liked working there. There was something about the cramped rows and precariously perched stacks that comforted him. And it wasn't like spending his afternoons in a used bookstore was a hard job. Usually he spent it reading behind the register and saying hello to the customers who meandered in.

Every hour or so, there might be a purchase or two, but overall it was quiet.

The most exciting part of the gig was the ghost upstairs who liked to move around Ms. Monroe's dining room furniture when she was away. And sometimes, if the ghost was particularly restless, she would pull a book from the shelves just to hear it hit the dusty carpet.

"Are you guys going to be here?" Grayson asked, forcing down a bite of his bagel. Thinking of Landon was making his throat tight again, but if he didn't eat his mother would only come down harder on him. She was militant about self-care.

"No, I have to go into the lab for a few hours, but I'll be home in the afternoon," his father said.

"And I have office hours and two meetings," his mother said. "But I'd be happy to cancel those if you want me to stay with you."

"No," he said and hoped he didn't sound too eager. "I want to be alone."

"Okay," his mother said, but her face was contradicting her. It was clear she didn't really think it was okay. "There's still Chinese in the fridge and I also made a salad."

"Thanks."

"You'll let us know where you're going to be though," his

mother said. It wasn't a question, even if it did tilt up at the end. "Work or here?"

Grayson Choice 9
Go to work - go to page 178
Stay home - go to page 319

REESE: GO HOME

Reese climbed the dune, her legs noodles from the long swim. Falling adrenaline and the need for sleep pressed in on her. She wanted a hot shower and her own bed. Pronto.

She drove back into town in a daze. Exhaustion pressed itself against her mind, numbing all thoughts except one. The storm had been strange. It had rolled in too quickly and disappeared just as fast.

It was more than that.

It was also the way the magic had felt along her skin. Something had happened tonight and Reese couldn't help but wonder what it was.

Reese parked her red pickup outside her Georgian three-story home in Cliffside. It wasn't really her home in the financial sense. It was her aunt who'd bought and paid for the house, which was good. On a bartender salary, Reese would've been looking for an apartment in Old Town or near Red Light at best.

Across the street, she saw the light on at Cole's place and knew the demon and his vampire husband were no doubt awake despite the late hour. Normally she would go say hi, if the light was on like that. But after the night she had, she just wanted a hot shower and her bed.

Reese unlocked the front door and stepped into the gorgeous foyer. A high ceiling and bright crystalline chandelier greeted her. The space was sparsely furnished in impeccable whites and ocean blues.

Aunt Constance was an oceanographer, currently on a research expedition. The scientist was studying the degradation of coral in the Indian Ocean. The fact that Constance was a shark shifter no doubt helped that search and the fact that her crew were all supernaturals or supernatural fans at the least meant she didn't have to hide what she was or her purpose in trying to salvage what was left of the ocean.

It's our home, Aunt Constance often said. *It's where our souls live, Reese. If it's lost, that will be the end of us.*

And though Reese didn't have scientific inclinations of her own, she didn't disagree. And Constance was a kind and loving aunt. She hadn't pressured Reese into doing more with her gifts —or even use them in the name of the ocean they both worshipped—and Reese was very grateful for that.

Reese went straight to the first floor bath, afraid to drip water on any of the house's expensive surfaces.

Fortunately, the first-floor bath was just past the living room on the right. All the towels, soap and necessities were present and accounted for. Reese had only to strip out of her sea-soaked clothes and into the hot water.

She washed the salt from her hair. Her tired mind wandered. She replayed the evening in her mind, wondering if there was a connection between seemingly separate events.

Clean, Reese stepped out of the shower and collected her clothes from the floor. She was tidy by nature, a habit instilled in her by her orderly aunt no doubt. The clothes went in the hamper. The water she'd tracked in was cleaned up with a mop.

Once every trace of her entrance had been removed, Reese changed for bed.

She was asleep before her head hit the pillow.

A phone was ringing somewhere in the house. Reese groped the sheets blindly trying to find her cell. She found the cord first, tracing it to the phone itself.

"Hello?" she groaned. Her voice broke with the effort.

"Reese?"

It was Kristine. She didn't sound so great either. Of course, running the woods all night would do that to a woman.

"Yeah, it's me. What's up?"

"I'm calling an emergency pack meeting. A kid died in the cove last night. He was torn apart by a siren."

"What?" Reese sat up, alarm rocketing her mind to full wakefulness. "When? I was just there."

"Were you?" Kristine said. Said, because the alpha rarely asked questions. Even her questions couldn't be mistaken for questions.

Reese recounted the night to her boss and friend. By the time she finished, she felt like she'd made a terrible mistake. She shouldn't have swum toward the reef after all. She should've chanced going into deeper waters. Maybe she could've helped those kids if she had.

"I saw the kids," she finished lamely. "I should've checked on them."

"Don't beat yourself up," Kristine said. "How could you have known that would happen? The sirens aren't even supposed to be in the cove."

Silence stretched on the line and Reese's guilt only thickened inside her.

"Well," Kristine said finally. Her sigh made the woman sound much older. "We need to know what's going on. I called to see if you could watch the bar until I get there. I realize it's not your shift and I'll pay you double for that. But now I wonder if you should be part of the discussion. I'll leave it to you to decide."

Reese Choice 12
Go to pack meeting - go to page 51
Hold down the bar - go to page 67

GRAYSON: GO TO WORK

"I'm going to work," he said and checked the time on his phone. He had two hours before his shift started.

"Come home if it's too much," his mother said.

"Yes," his father agreed, looking up from his phone again. "There's no shame in needing personal time."

"I know," Grayson said and he meant it. Grayson didn't know another kid at his school who could call his mother and be removed, no questions asked, because he needed a mental health day.

His mother squeezed his hand. It was warm from the coffee mug she'd been holding.

"We want to give you space and we trust you to take care of yourself," she said. "But we also worry. No one should have to go through what you went through last night. Loss is terrible, but last night…last night."

He squeezed her hand back and then let it go. "Don't worry about me."

She clucked her tongue. "As if I can turn it off."

Abby came into the dining room and took the empty seat.

She sipped the coffee, then added creamer from the carafe on the table. She also poured herself a juice.

"Mom texted me and said she's going to be a few minutes late. She got hung up on a 911 call or something."

"You're welcome to stay here as long as you need to," Grayson's father said, looking up from his phone.

"We love having you," his mother added, tapping her rings against her coffee mug. "How are you feeling today?"

"Awful," Abigail said and his mother responded by rubbing Abby's back.

"Your bagel is cold. Want me to reheat it?"

"No, this is fine."

The front door slammed open. "I'm home! Grayson! How was your birthday?"

Tanner, his ten-year-old brother, burst into the dining room. His hair was blown back from his face and he had his backpack slung over his shoulder. He dropped it with a *clunk* onto the floor.

He took one look at his family and his eyes widened. "Whoa. Who died?"

Grayson snorted. His brother had an uncanny ability to hit the truth spot on. His father often said he was fairly certain Tanner—because he'd been born in this creepy town—was some kind of psychic. Grayson had been born in LA, and while he might have a knack for surviving, he didn't seem to know things out of the blue like Tanner did.

Grayson's mother was standing at the dining room window, waving to Will's mother in the driveway.

"Landon died," Abby said. She took a bite of her bagel as if to stop herself from saying more.

"Shit."

"Tanner!" his father cried.

"Language," his mother said, releasing the curtain.

"You're one to talk," Tanner shot back and he had a point.

Everyone at that table knew his mother said words that would make a sailor blush.

"Please put your shoes and bag where they go," his father said pointing at the pile Tanner made upon his arrival.

Tanner didn't seem to hear him. "Did he really die?" He was looking to Grayson for confirmation.

Grayson found his voice. "There was an accident when we were swimming."

Both his parents shot him warning looks. Grayson understood that he was supposed to omit the details of Landon's death. Tanner knew Castle Cove was different. He knew about the vampires, werewolves, and witches—even the sirens in the cove. As with Grayson, his parents took great care to raise a curious but cautious boy.

But just because Tanner knew there were monsters in Castle Cove didn't mean that Tanner fully understood what those monsters could do to a person.

Grayson thought that Tanner comprehended more than he let on. Perhaps it was his gift for knowing that kept him safe. This gift worked as well as, if not better than, their parents' diligent training.

"He drowned?" Tanner asked. His eyes were wide. Too wide.

"Yeah," Abby said, lifting her coffee from the table. Grayson saw the tremble in her hand.

"Your best friend *drowned* on your freaking birthday?" Tanner asked. Now he was hanging off Grayson's chair, looking him in the eye. "I'm sorry, dude."

Dude was his favorite word the last few weeks and to hear it uttered with such sincerity undid Grayson inside. Tears formed and spilled over onto his cheeks. He pulled his little brother into a tight hug. "Thanks, man."

His parents let the moment unravel between them. No one spoke. Breakfast continued as if nothing was happening. Tanner pulled back first.

"Shoes, bag," his mother said.

Tanner dutifully obeyed, putting his backpack on the hook and slipping his shoes into their cubby.

The doorbell rang.

Because he hadn't closed the door behind him, it stood open with a clear view of Officer O'Reilly on the porch. She didn't have the officer uniform on. She wore pressed black dress pants and a deep burgundy dress shirt tucked into the waistband. Her badge was clipped to one hip and her gun was visible in its holster.

"Abby, it's your mom," Tanner said, and opened the screen door. "Hi, Miss Una."

"Hey, buddy." She sounded as exhausted as she looked. Deep pillows of purple had formed under each of her eyes.

Abby started to clear up her plate, but Grayson's mother gently tugged her hands away. "Leave it. I'll take care of it."

Officer O'Reilly stepped into the hallway, ushered in by Tanner.

"Are you ready?" she asked, when she saw Abigail.

Abigail patted her pockets as if she'd forgotten something. "I guess so. I didn't really have anything on the beach, did I?"

"We might've left things in Landon's car," Grayson said. It had been Landon who'd driven them to the beach.

"I'll see what I can do," Una said with another tight smile. To his parents she said, "Thanks for letting Abby stay."

"Of course," his parents said in unison.

"Abby is welcome here anytime," his mother added, lifting her coffee mug to her lips again.

"I thought nothing could get into the cove because of the rocks," Tanner said. He was looking up at Officer O'Reilly with a strange expression on his face. "It's got that rock barrier, right?"

Una's lips pinched.

"Why do you think something was in the cove?" his mother asked. "We said he drowned."

Una frowned. "It was rough seas last night. A storm rolled in really quick."

Tanner's eyes lit up. "Yeah, we saw it. Will and I were in the backyard catching fireflies and then all of a sudden it was lightning and thundering."

Officer O'Reilly lifted the pile of Abby's clothes from the bench. "Where does Will live?"

"Cliffside," his father answered. "Near the east lot."

"That's North Beach. Very close to the water." Officer O'Reilly shrugged as if to say *there you go.*

"Yeah, we walk down to the beach and catch crabs. Will's dad cooks them. *Alive.*"

"Are you going back to work?" Abby asked.

"For a few hours," Una said. Then she clamped a hand on Grayson's shoulder and gave it an affectionate squeeze. "Happy belated birthday."

"Thanks."

Tanner pulled open the door, holding it open for them.

"Such a gentleman," Una said and stepped out onto the porch again. "Thank you again."

Abby hesitated in the doorway. Her gaze fixed on Grayson. "Call me later, okay?"

"I will." He'd already planned on checking on her at least a hundred times today.

With a weak smile, she descended the porch steps to the waiting unmarked car.

"Bye," Tanner said and shut the door. He met Grayson's eyes and frowned. "*That* was awkward."

Curiosity Books was on the corner of Apple Street and Magnolia Street. He parked at the curb outside the old Victorian building. The bookshop was purple with light brown windows and trim.

The sign in the yard read Curiosity Books, Treasure For Those Who Seek It. And below that, Used Books and Oddities— just in case those treasure seekers should get the wrong idea.

"Grayson!" Ms. Monroe exclaimed. She stood on the porch, her key in one hand, her mouth gaping. "What are you doing here?"

"My shift is from two until eight," he said. He hesitated on the step, wondering if he'd gotten it wrong. A lot had happened in the last 24 hours. It was very possible.

"Yes, but I didn't think you'd come in today. Not after what happened last night."

"You heard about that?" he asked, stuffing his hands down in his pocket.

She pulled at her tangle of necklaces around her neck. "Yes, well. It might've come on over the scanner."

Grayson had never asked his boss why she had a police scanner in her upstairs apartment, or more specifically, why she thought she needed one. It was possible that she was only nosy. But sometimes he liked to imagine that she'd come to Castle Cove to escape a life of crime. The idea was so ridiculous that it amused him to no end.

Ms. Monroe's hair was crimped, and stood out from her head in all directions. She wore a scarf across her head and coke bottle glasses so large that her eyes gave the impression of really drinking someone in. Her clothes were bright, flowing fabrics of wild designs and her neck always had at least five or six necklaces hanging around it. Despite their tendency to tangle, she seemed committed to wearing them.

She looked like the garden variety cat lady, though she had no cats. Well, if one didn't count Pumpkin—an orange tabby who strolled Midtown at her leisure. But it was as much a patron of the other shops as she was of Curiosity Books.

Since Grayson had received strict instruction to always let Pumpkin in, should she come calling, he often had the chore of vacuuming the cat hair that seemed to accumulate in her wake.

"I thought work might take my mind off things," he said. "But if you're closing—"

He looked at the key in the door and her hand still on the handle.

"Oh, yes, well I'm meeting someone for tea and so I thought I'd just close early. But if you really want to be here…?"

"I do," he insisted, adjusting his messenger bag on his shoulder. "If it's okay with you."

"Of course, of course." She unlocked the door, pushing it open with her hand.

"I just want to keep busy," he said.

"Yes, I like to rearrange my spice rack when my mind gives me trouble." She checked her watch one more time and then stepped into the shop after him. "There's a big pile here that needs to be reshelved. You could also vacuum. Pumpkin was here earlier."

"Okay," he said, removing his jacket and throwing it over the wooden chair behind the register.

"Oh, and you could call about these books." She pulled a piece of paper from her pocket. She smoothed it against the table top so he could better read it.

He reviewed the list, seeing the description of each and the ISBN and telephone numbers beside it.

"We had a lot of special orders this week," she said, gesturing to the list. "Just find out if the stores I've listed are carrying any copies and at what price we can get it for. Then you can call the buyer and ask them to commit."

"All right."

Ms. Monroe seemed to hover for a moment. "Are you sure you're going to be all right here alone?"

He forced himself to smile. "I'll have Gladys."

Ms. Monroe arched her eyebrows instead of laughing at his joke. "Dear, the dead aren't good company."

"I'll be fine." If he didn't say it, he was sure she wouldn't leave.

With an awkward pat on the counter, she turned to the door. "I'll be back around seven or so, but if I'm not, just lock up when you leave."

When she pulled the door closed after her, the overhead bell rang. The air vibrated with the twang, then fell silent.

For a long time, he only sat there, feeling the chair against his back, his fingers picking at a hole in his jeans.

Then when the silence began to feel alive, almost as if it were breathing down the back of his neck, he got to work.

He started with vacuuming, angling the ancient contraption through the narrow stacks. More than once he clipped a pile of books and sent it tumbling. He restacked them the best he could and kept on.

After he reshelved the pile by the register, he dusted. There were limitations to what one could accomplish in this old shop in terms of dusting. Running a light feather duster over the exposed spines was about as much as one could do.

Cleaning had only taken him about two hours, so he decided it was time to make the phone calls. He called the listed book sellers and dutifully recorded the prices. Then he called the customers who'd requested those items and confirmed that they would pay. When he was finished he sent an update text to Ms. Monroe. She instructed him to buy them all.

He did so using her business credit card, locked away in the register for exactly such purchases.

He'd just written out the total and put it in the register when table legs scraped overhead. He smiled. There was something comforting about Gladys the ghost being her usual restless self. Then for the first time he wondered if he might see Landon again.

How would it feel to see ghost-Landon?

And what if something did develop between him and Abby? Would ghost Landon be okay with it? Or would he haunt them for the rest of their lives—breaking their dishes or windows and shaking their bed whenever they tried to have sex?

Grayson listened to the legs catch on the wood floor above. Then nothing. When it seemed she'd completed her task, he called out to her.

"Gladys? I could use a book recommendation."

For a moment, he sat perched on the chair, listening to the ringing silence in the shop.

Then he heard the soft shuffle of a book sliding from the shelf, followed by the hollow thump of it hitting the floor.

Grayson stood from the chair and followed the narrow aisle, searching the floors for the fallen book.

He'd made it almost to the biographies section when he turned a corner and saw it.

He bent and picked the book up, brushing a hand over its cover. Maybe the book had been red once, but now it had faded to a burnt orange. The binding was frayed and the exposed pages were stained yellow with age.

"A Siren Song," he read aloud. "The history of Atlantis' survivors."

Grayson's heart rocketed in his chest. His pulse built to the point of painfulness. It pounded like a war drum in his temples.

He saw movement in the corner of his eye and turned. Farther up the row, another book was sliding out of its place on the shelf. It inched forward once, twice, and then tumbled onto the floor.

Grayson crossed to the fallen book and picked it up off the floor.

"The Dark Mother and Her Children," he said. He opened the cover and was surprised to see it was published by the Castle Cove University Press over a hundred years ago. He flipped page after page until he found an old pencil etching of a young woman about to enter a dark wood. The woman had long black hair and wide dark eyes.

Eyes peered at her from the darkness, yet she didn't seem deterred. She was about to enter the woods anyway.

He closed the book and ran his hand over the cover. His fingernail caught on the embossed tree stamped into the leather. In the tree were six birds. He knew the species. Any wood scout would've been able to name them too: a crow, a heron, a hawk, an owl, a blue jay, and a swan. But the swan was black, not white, as evidenced by its inked-in body.

A shiver ran up his spine.

Of all these books in the entire shop, what were the chances that Gladys would pick a book about sirens at random?

Grayson returned to the desk and opened the inventory file on the computer. There were only six books on sirens in the whole shop. Six out of nearly seventy thousand titles. The chances seemed small indeed.

"So if it isn't random," he said, aloud. "Then what is the connection between the sirens and The Dark Mother?"

He spoke aloud but there was no answer. No more books slipped from the shelves to the floor. He strained, listening intently to the hum as if expecting an answer.

His phone buzzed suddenly and he yelped, squeezing the books to his chest.

"Come on," he muttered. He lifted his phone from the desk and saw Abby's name above the incoming text.

He opened the text and read: *Hey, how are you?*

He took a breath, and tried to steady the wild hammer of his heart. *Same. You?*

Same. This sucks, she wrote.

Yeah.

What are you doing?

At work. You?

Lying in bed staring at the ceiling like a weirdo

He looked at the books on the desk. He opened the cover again and stared at the woman entering the menacing woods. He counted those eyes watching her.

It made him think of the stories he'd heard about the Western Woods. West of the territory line, the forest was supposed to be full of old, ancient creatures. Dryads for starters, who craved human flesh and who would eat a person while they were still alive. Wendigos did much the same, but also dragged people to their underground dens. Then they overwintered, snacking on their captives until they went aboveground again.

As a tenured professor at CCU, his mother would know more about this book and its stories. He would ask her later what she thought the connection between The Dark Mother and the sirens might be.

He typed, *we should find out what happened.*

We know what happened.

I don't think we do, he replied.

?

There was the storm and the sirens came into the cove. What if there's a reason for that?

?????

They're not supposed to be in the cove. What made them come in like that?

You think there's a reason?

Yes, he wrote. *Not just a reason but probably someone to blame.*

Abby didn't seem to have a response for that.

Don't you want to know? What if it saves someone's life?

Not Landon's life. Landon was dead and even in Castle Cove, he would probably stay that way. But Grayson was thinking about the next time someone was in the cove and the sirens broke the boundary of Heart's Rock. What then?

He typed out, *For next time.*

It seemed like she wouldn't write back. For minutes he

stared at the screen. He put the phone down and searched the computer for the other book, The Dark Mother and Her Children. There was no listing in the computer. He checked his spelling twice, but nothing.

How many secret treasures—like a hundred-year-old book —were hidden in this old dusty shop? Grayson couldn't help but wonder.

His phone buzzed.

Sure, she wrote back. *I'd want to know. But my mother will shit a brick if we start "investigating." She's already on the case.*

Do they have a lead?

He traced the embossed tree with his fingers. His hand kept going to the blue heron.

Not yet, she wrote. *Promise you'll take me with you if you plan on "investigating."*

He smiled at her incessant use of quotation marks. What her mother did was no doubt investigating without quotation marks. Whatever sleuthing they would undertake—tomorrow or next week—certainly merited that distinction. They were not professionals.

His phone buzzed again but it wasn't a text message. It was an alarm for closing time. He powered down the computer and checked all the windows and back door to make sure they were locked up. He saw a book sitting open on a stool. A page turned.

"Don't stay up too late reading, Gladys," he said and smiled to himself. "You'll be *dead tired* tomorrow." That was the one problem about making jokes with ghosts. One could never tell if they were appreciated.

At the register, he wrote a note for Ms. Monroe, officially "checking out" the two books that Gladys had recommended. This was the shop's policy, that he was allowed to borrow any book from the shelves that he liked, as long as he brought it back in the same condition he'd found it and made sure he recorded what he took.

He always did.

He flipped the open sign to closed, and with the two books under his arm, he stepped out onto the porch. His keys clanked against the wood as he locked up. He drove home in silence with the radio off, the two books sitting in the passenger seat beside him.

When he got home, he found a note from his parents on the kitchen table.

Gray,
Took Tanner to his game. Might be back late, especially if they win. Pizza! Pizza! Leftovers in the fridge. Text us when you get home so we know you're okay. Someone came by the house looking for you. See the note. Call us if something comes up.
Mom and Dad

A twinge of disappointment tightened his chest. He'd forgotten about the baseball game and he never missed Tanner's games. Even when his parents couldn't make it, Grayson was always there. He hadn't even thought about the game. It wasn't like him to have something so completely slip his mind.

That's what happens when your best friend dies, he thought. The mind vacillates between forgetting it happened—pretending nothing had changed—to being slammed with the reality of it again and again.

Like a body tumbling in the moonlit surf.

He sank into the dining room chair with tears in the corner of his eyes. He felt the image pressing in on him again. He bit his lip so hard that it bled. But at least the image was gone and he was in his body again.

He texted his parents.

I'm home. Tell T I'm sorry I missed the game.

His mother wrote back almost instantly, as if she'd been holding the phone at the ready exactly for this moment.

He understands. Are you staying in tonight?

He practically heard the plea in her voice.

I'm home for the night, he wrote as if throwing her a bone. He slid the books onto the table. *I'll be reading.*

Eat something. Call me if you need something. ANYTHING, she instructed.

OK. And that was the end of it.

Grayson left the books on the table and went into the kitchen. He made himself a plate of leftover Chinese, wanting to eat it cold this time, and added a heap of salad too.

He didn't look at the second note until he sat down at the table again.

"Reese," he read aloud, forking noodles into his mouth.

Neither the number nor the name were in his parents' handwriting, both of which he knew by heart. That meant the note must've been tacked to the door or stuffed in their mailbox while they were at work.

So who was this mystery person? He didn't know anyone by the name of Reese. If it was a cop or someone wanting to follow up on Landon's death, wouldn't they just have called him? Or maybe this was a reporter. There were two newspapers in Castle Cove.

Unlike the rest of the country where the newspaper was dying a slow, bloody death, they were doing just fine in Castle Cove—both the respectable paper, *The Cove Chronicle*, and the gossip rag, *The Daily Bite*.

The only problem was that Grayson detested speaking on the phone. He certainly wasn't going to call some stranger for a chat.

"Here's hoping this is a cell phone," he said. He typed in the number and opened a new text message.

This is Grayson H. You came by my house?

No answer.

He finished his dinner, rinsed his plate in the sink and when he opened the dishwasher to slide the plate into the rack, he heard the phone buzz on the kitchen table.

hi grayson. i'm reese. i have some questions about what happened last night. can you talk?

Grayson looked at the text for a long time. Reese was probably not a reporter, given the shorthand text speak. Hell, maybe they weren't even out of high school. Was this about sports or graduation or something?

He wrote back, *I can talk.*

He carried his books into the living room and collapsed onto the sofa. No sooner did he get the pillow under his head did the phone ring.

He sighed and accepted the call. "Hello?"

"Hi," a woman said. That answered the first mystery. Reese was a woman, not a man. And she sounded like a young woman from what he could tell, but not as young as he was imagining. Maybe her twenties? "Is this Grayson?"

"Yeah. And you're Reese?"

"You got it," she said.

He could hear the smile in her voice. He wasn't sure where to go from here. His silence probably conveyed as much.

"I'm calling because I've got questions about what happened last night."

"Are you with the police?" He knew well enough to know that he shouldn't give details to just anyone. After all, this woman could be a reporter or just a nosy—

"Let's call me a liaison. I already spoke to Detective O'Reilly. You can call her and confirm that it's okay to talk to me if you're worried. If you're smart, you would."

"Are you a reporter?"

"No. I've been asked to look into what happened so that's what I'm doing."

Asked to look into it by whom? he wondered. And he

wondered what it was about Reese that made her qualified for this job.

Was she calling his bluff? She sounded so young.

He said, "Can I call you right back?"

"Sure. I'll be here. My shift doesn't start for another hour."

"Shift where?"

"Alpha's. I'm a bartender."

Grayson thought he might have seen the name *Alpha's* above one of the bars near campus, but he couldn't be sure.

"Okay, just a minute." He hung up and called the police station's non-emergency line.

"Castle Cove PD."

He recognized Yvonne Jenkins voice immediately. "Hi Officer Jenkins. This is Grayson Helmson. Is Detective O'Reilly around?"

"Sure, honey. One second."

He flinched at the use of honey, but couldn't remember a time that Yvonne hadn't called everyone that. Honey. Sugar. Sometimes she added the word bear to the end of the affectionate title: Honey bear. Sugar bear. Though she'd seemed to drop the latter once he'd turned sixteen.

"Here she is."

The phone clicked and Grayson heard the intake of breath. "Grayson, you there?"

"Yeah."

"You okay?"

He realized that was concern in her voice. The sort of knee jerk reactive fear that crept in when he called his own mother when she wasn't expecting it.

"I'm fine," he said, knowing she'd hear nothing else he said until he assured her. "I'm calling about Reese." Here he realized he hadn't gotten her last name. "The bartender from Alpha's."

"Oh, yeah." All the breath left her at once. "She's all right."

"She wants to ask me about what happened and I wanted to make sure that was okay before I said anything."

"Yes, it's fine. She's not officially with the police department, but she is investigating on behalf..." She seemed to search for the right word. "She's investigating on our behalf."

Grayson had a sense that it was likely far more complicated than that. "So I can tell her what happened to Landon?"

What happened to Landon... His chest tightened.

"As long as you aren't going to tell her something you haven't already told me."

The question hung in the air between them.

"No, there's nothing else," he said, wondering when he would be old enough that he no longer needed to constantly reassure the adults around him. Or maybe it was just the human parents in Castle Cove who were having such a hard time.

"Then tell her what you know. She's a good person. Clean record. She's just trying to get us some answers."

Me too, he thought, feeling the weight of the books against his chest.

"If that's all—" she began.

"Yes, that's it. Thanks for taking my call."

"Sure thing."

Then the line clicked and his cell phone returned to the home screen. It was a picture of the three of them—Abby in the middle with their arms thrown over her shoulders. They were all smiling and laughing. He remembered his father taking that photo before they went to senior prom.

He dialed Reese back.

"We good?" she asked by way of hello.

"We're good," he said. "What do you want to know?"

"Actually I'd like to talk in person, if that's okay," she said.

He was about to offer that she come by his house, but remembered what she'd said about work. "When?"

"I can come by your place tomorrow if you'll be home or you could come to Alpha's tonight. It's up to you."

"Is Alpha's 21 and up?" he asked.

"Oh, right. You're eighteen." She covered the phone with her hand. He heard her ask someone a question and he thought heard the gruff voice of a man responding. "You can come by if you want. Nick is working the door and he'll let you in. Just give him your name and say you're here to talk to me."

Grayson Choice 10
Spend the night reading - go to page 205
Go to Alpha's - go to page 196

GRAYSON: GO TO ALPHA'S

"I'll come to Alpha's," he said. "Give me twenty minutes."

"Great, I'll tell Nick to keep an eye out for you."

When they hung up, Grayson leapt up from the couch in search of a pen. He had to leave his parents a note or they would panic to come home and find him gone.

There was a blue ink pen with no cap in the kitchen junk drawer. Despite the loss of cap, it wrote fine. Grayson told his parents where he'd gone and about the conversation with Detective O'Reilly, just in case they thought his sudden trip to a bar might have another motive.

He backed out of the driveway, pausing to let the orange tabby, Pumpkin, cross safely. He drove north-northeast, toward part of the city where the CCU campus ended and the strip began.

The cloudy night meant little moonlight reached the road. Instead, the orange glow of street lamps prevailed, casting long shadows along the street and adjacent walkways.

Grayson was surprised to see so many people out on the streets despite the hour. Castle Cove didn't really sleep, not with so many supernaturals in town. But they tended to flock in certain areas. The people he saw meandering through town now looked human and young. Then he remembered it was the weekend during summer break. Of course people were out. The good weather and warm night air beckoned them to enjoy it.

Grayson had a hard time finding street parking outside Alpha's so he chose to canvass the parking garage a block away. He found a space on the third level and locked up his little sedan, pocketing the key.

On the street he almost collided with a group of giggling girls. One was laughing so hard she was wheezing.

He flashed a polite smile and stood aside for them to pass. He spotted Nick as soon as Alpha's was in view. The man at the door was large and beefy. He had tattoos covering his forearms. A hint of ink peeked out from under his collar, suggesting he had full sleeves. His shaved head was specked with black stubble from regrowth. Grayson wondered if he intended to grow it out or shave it again. It didn't seem like something he could ask as he stood in front of the man.

"Are you Nick?" he asked. His mouth was dry.

"Yeah."

"I'm Grayson," he said. He thought about extending his hand to shake, but that seemed inappropriate.

Nick nodded toward the door. "Go on, then."

The rough wooden door opened easily under the push of his hand, revealing a bustling bar inside. In fact, it looked more like a pub than a bar to Grayson, who had in fact gone to London for a week for a crew tournament. It was the booths and casual atmosphere. There was no dance floor or electro-pop blasting.

Behind the bar there was a woman with blond hair pulled up into twin ponytails. The black-tipped end of the ponytails brushed her shoulders. She seemed to feel his eyes on her because she looked up and waved him over.

He slid onto the only open stool. "I'm Grayson."

"Reese." And she did extend her hand with a wide, friendly

grin. "Thanks for coming down. I couldn't really leave. Kristine needed the help."

As if reading his mind she pointed at the woman emerging from the back with a case of beer.

"That's Kristine," Reese said. "She owns the place."

As soon as Grayson saw her, he knew she was a werewolf. The glowing, golden eyes gave her away. She regarded him with a polite, but reserved smile.

"Hey," she said, before opening the cooler and beginning the restock.

Reese was speaking again. "Like I said on the phone, I've been asked to investigate what happened in the cove the night you were attacked. We're worried about the sirens' behavior."

"They aren't supposed to come into the cove," Grayson said, placing his laced hands on the cool, wooden bar. There was something sticky there. "At least that's what we thought. The closest they were supposed to get was Heart's Rock."

"Bingo," she said, tipping over a tequila bottle to make four quick shots. She slid the shots across the bar and gave the tall guy with glasses waiting for them his bill. Turning back to him, she said, "So what can you tell me?"

Grayson recounted the night to her, starting with the birthday swim out to the rock and ending at the moment they saw Landon's body thrashing on the shore.

"Did you—" the woman began. Grayson thought he knew what she was asking. Did they mate with the sirens? Was that why they were spared?

Grayson met her eye without looking away. "I don't think that's relevant."

Reese held up her hands in mock surrender. She picked up a silver container and shook it. Then she poured it into a martini glass and added two olives. The woman with pink streaks in her hair thanked her before moving away from the bar.

She saw Grayson's eyes following her. "Can I get you something? I make a mean Shirley Temple or a cherry soda."

"Sure," he said. "Whichever you think is best."

She looked at him for a moment before snapping her fingers. He watched her dance behind the bar, pouring grenadine, ginger ale and some juices into a glass. Then she threw in a cherry for good measure.

She placed the drink on a napkin for him. "A virgin millionaire sour."

He sipped and smiled, surprised. "Refreshing."

This seemed to please her. "I wasn't trying to pry or be a pervert. I just wanted to know if they seemed interested in sex or were they just being violent. I thought that might help the investigation, to get a report on their behavior."

"They were interested," Grayson said evasively.

Reese let it slide. "Do you remember anything else about the night? Some people reported a couple of interesting details."

When she didn't go on, Grayson assumed she didn't want to lead her witness.

"There was the storm," he said, gauging her reaction to see if that was one of them. "It rolled in fast. It was pretty weird."

"Which direction did it come from?" she asked, betraying her emotion.

"From the south, from the ocean."

Reese nodded. "Anything else?"

Grayson gripped the cold drink in his hand and thought. "No," he said finally. "Sorry."

"Hey, it's okay." She flashed a bright smile. "You've been a big help."

He pulled out his wallet, intending to pay for the drink but she waved him off. "It's on me. Thanks for coming down."

"Thanks." He slipped his wallet back into his pocket.

The bar door opened, sending a wave of fresh air wafting

over Grayson's face and neck. It was welcome given the building heat in the bar. He turned to see who'd come in.

Abby appeared in the doorway of the bar. Her hair had been pulled up in a high ponytail making her collarbones look particularly inviting. He suddenly had a desperate urge to kiss them and maybe her throat also.

She smiled when she saw him.

"That's Abby," he said.

"Yeah, I called her," Reese said by means of explanation.

Abby stepped up to the bar and introduced herself.

"Thanks for coming. Can I offer you something to drink?"

Abby who was still smiling at Grayson, pointed at his drink. "I'll have what he's having."

"One virgin sour coming right up."

Abby slid onto the open bar stool beside him. Her knees bumped his and she apologized.

"Don't be stupid," he said, grinning. It felt like one of those goofy grins. He hadn't expected to see her here. And they were in a bar on the weekend. The absurd adultness of it was throwing him.

Abby tried to decipher the confused look on his face. "My mom knows I'm here. She told me to cooperate."

"Great," Reese said, placing the drink on a fresh napkin in front of her. "Then please tell me what happened."

Abby looked at Grayson as if seeking his approval. Grayson smiled reflexively. In truth, the unexpected eye contact made his stomach drop. "I already told my part. It's all yours."

Abby recounted the night slowly with even more detail than Grayson had been able to recall. When she finished, Abby flicked her eyes to meet Reese's. "Someone was using magic. A lot of it."

Grayson's heart kicked. He turned toward her, unable to hide his surprise. "How do you know that?"

Abby looked suddenly shy. That was another shock because the Abby Grayson knew was never shy about anything.

"I'm apprenticed to the coven," Abigail said plainly. "I can feel it."

Grayson began free-falling. "You're a witch?"

Reflexively, both Abby and Grayson cast awkward glances at the patrons nearest them.

"No need to worry," Reese told them with a gentle smile. "This is a werewolf bar, kids. Not everyone is a werewolf. In fact, we have a pretty good mix tonight. But bottom line, they don't give a damn if you're a witch."

Abby seemed not to hear her. Her eyes were fixed on Grayson, desperately trying to read his face. "I didn't tell you because I wasn't sure you'd be okay with it." Color rose in her cheeks. "Your parents are sort of—purists."

"No, they're not. Tanner's best friend is a werewolf!" Grayson felt like he'd been kicked in the gut.

"Who's a werewolf?" Kristine asked, reappearing with a steaming wet rag.

"My little brother's best friend, Will."

Kristine smiled. "Oh yeah, I think I've met him. He can't be more than twelve—"

"Ten," Grayson interjected.

"—and he curses like a sailor."

Reese crinkled her nose. "Now I'm sorry I didn't come to your house."

Abby's face tried to convey humor, but he saw her tense shoulders. "Yeah, he's pretty funny."

Don't screw this up, Grayson's mind screamed. Some older, wiser part realized this was an incredibly important moment. And the absolute last thing he should do was make Abby's confession about him.

He reached over and squeezed her knee. "Abby, I don't care

if you're a witch. And I don't think one person in my family would give a damn that you're a witch either."

Abby wouldn't look at him. She grabbed the cherry by the stem and dragged it along the surface of her drink. It hurt Grayson more to see it. He wanted to reach over and grab her. He'd pull her into his arms and kiss her until she believed him. But Reese and Kristine were both looking at them.

"So you could feel the magic?" Reese asked, clearly trying to break back into the conversation.

Abby looked up from her drink "Yeah, and there was a surge of it right before the sirens showed up. I knew something was up, but I was halfway to shore when I felt it so I couldn't do anything in the water. Then once I did get to shore—" She licked her lips. "Everything happened so fast after that."

Grayson could agree with that. It seemed the swim to shore and Landon's death had happened in the same breath.

Reese rubbed her knees. "Could you tell where the magic was coming from?"

"West," Abby said without hesitation. "Somewhere along Canyon Road. But I can't more specific than that. Sorry."

"But the storm came from the south," Grayson said.

"Yeah," Abby agreed before plucking the cherry from the drink and popping it into her mouth. "But the person who conjured it was in the west. I'm guessing they were parked somewhere along Canyon Road. You should see if anyone saw any cars parked along the road that night."

Reese snapped her fingers. "Good idea. It's like you have a detective for a mom or something."

Abby gave a weak, half-hearted grin. "I have my moments."

"You've been a huge help," Reese said. "I don't have any other questions now, but would either of you mind talking to me again if I think of more?"

They both shook their heads.

"Cool. I need to do some bartender things now. You going to

be okay? You can stay and hang out of if you want. Drinks on me."

"Thanks." They said in unison. Once Reese had moved away, turning her attention to two women at the end of the bar, Abby turned on her stool. She pointed her chin at a booth that was opening up along the wall. "Let's take that."

"Okay." He grabbed his drink off the bar and followed her through the tightly packed crowd. Despite the bodies, no one sprang to take the booth from them before they reached it. Grayson found himself wondering if that was Abby's doing. Did she magically reserve it somehow? God, everything Abby did would make him wonder now.

They slid into the booth opposite each other, their drinks between them. Neither of them spoke for several moments.

"You didn't tell Landon about the coven?" Grayson asked.

She shrugged. "No. I think he would've been okay with it but..."

She never finished her thought.

Grayson sighed, trying to give himself room in the face of all these emotions. He was disappointed that she hadn't told him sooner, but relieved to know now. He was also honored that he now knew a secret that Landon hadn't. But this honor was quickly blotted out by a rising tide of guilt.

"Why didn't you tell me? Did you really think I'd freak out?" He felt the heat rising in his cheeks.

"No," she said with another lopsided smile. "I was looking for the right time to tell you. I've been waiting for the right time to tell you a lot of things, actually."

His heart hammered in his chest. He wanted her to know he was here for her. That he was in her corner. He stretched his hand across the table. "Now would be a good time. You can tell me everything you want to tell me. Right now."

She placed her cool hand in his. It was slightly moist from her sweating glass. "You sure about that?"

He noticed the color building in her cheeks and the way her eyes shone. He brushed his thumb across her knuckles. "I'm sure."

For a long moment she just looked at her hand in his. Then she sighed as if she'd been holding her breath for years.

"I was accepted to CCU. And UCLA for engineering." She searched his face for a reaction. "Actually I was accepted into about a dozen other schools too, but these are the two that matter."

"Why?" he asked.

"You know why," she said, squeezing his hands. "Grayson, you know why."

His heart hammered in his chest.

"I love you," she said. Her eyes were wide, fearful. "I'm happiest when I'm with you. I like to know you're near and you're safe. I don't care if we are in LA or if we're here at CCU, but I want to be with you. And after what happened to Landon —" Her breath hitched and she squeezed his hand even harder. "I don't want to mess around anymore. I want to spend every moment I have left knowing you're mine. I just need to know if you feel the same way?"

Grayson Choice 11

Yes, Grayson Feels the Same Way - go to page 317
No, Grayson Met Daniel Has Feelings for Him Instead - go to page 312

GRAYSON: SPEND THE NIGHT READING

"I can't tonight, sorry," he said. Dragging his introverted self to a bar sounded like an awful idea for many reasons. Not only would it make his parents' anxiety spike, but he was dead tired. He hadn't slept worth a damn the night before and he wasn't entirely sure sleep would come tonight either.

"No problem," Reese said, the bar noise rising behind her. "I'll come by your place tomorrow afternoon if you'll be home?"

Grayson didn't have work tomorrow and didn't think his family had plans. He'd wanted to go check on Abby but that could be done anytime.

"I'm thinking four or five," she added.

"That's fine," he said, switching the phone to the other ear. "I should be home."

"Cool. We'll talk then. Night."

Grayson thanked her and ended the call. Then he opened the text message thread he had going with Abby and wrote, *you OK?*

The texting bubble appeared and disappeared for a long time. He braced himself.

No, she texted.

Then, *I miss him.*

Me too, he wrote.

Do you think we could've done anything differently? she asked. *He wasn't a great swimmer. We shouldn't have made him go out there.*

Grayson called her. "Hey."

"Hey."

He knew immediately that she'd been crying. Her voice was thick. He wondered if the throat, like the eyes swelled when one cried. He would have to ask his dad. His dad wasn't a doctor, but he understood basic anatomy pretty well.

"And no," Grayson said firmly. "No we couldn't have done anything differently."

"I feel like we did something wrong," she said. She sniffed. "I keep feeling like maybe if I wasn't fucking around with a siren I could've gone into the water and saved him."

"You couldn't have," he insisted.

"How do you know?"

"Because female sirens are territorial. If you'd come into the water and tried to…" He searched for a word. "*Interrupt* they would've attacked you."

"What?" she sounded genuinely surprised. "I thought they only drowned people accidentally."

"They're not violent except during mating and self-defense. My mom said they're pretty desperate to conceive so—"

Abby didn't seem willing to let go of her guilt yet. "When that storm rolled in we should've kept him on the rock. He was already having a hard time. If he'd stayed—"

"There's no guarantee that the sirens wouldn't have come onto the rock with us. And if they'd planned on going into the cove anyway, maybe they would've just hopped in after us. Then we would've been even farther from shore."

A rock orgy or dead in the water. Not great choices, he thought but had the good sense not to say.

"So he was going to die. No matter what we did," she whispered.

"We can't blame ourselves for this. He should've tried to get to the shallows before—"

"God, Grayson we can't blame *him* either," she huffed into the phone. "He's dead!"

"Right. You're right. There's no blame. Period."

For a long time they said nothing. He listened to her soft breathing through the phone and found comfort in it.

Then she said, "You said you thought someone caused the storm."

He looked at the book in his hand.

"I didn't say someone caused the storm. I said that I think there's a reason they came into the cove even though it's out of bounds."

"My mom thinks they got confused."

His heart sped up. "What do you mean?"

The rustle of fabric, either Abby sitting up or turning over in her covers, rustled in the phone. "Because of the attack on South Beach."

"But we were on Hunter's Beach." It was Grayson's turn to sit up, leaning back against the sofa's throw pillows.

"Right. But the attack from last week was on South Beach."

Grayson visualized the geography of Castle Cove in his mind.

Castle Cove city was bordered by wild forests in the north and west and oceanfront on the east and south. On the far east was the first of three beaches: North Beach. No sirens, sharks or even jellyfish had ever been seen on that beach so it was considered the most family friendly. That's also why it was crowded as hell. There was never parking in the east lot. It was also the most desirable because it was the only beach of the three that had a gentle wooden walkway to take beachgoers down to the shore. Both Hunter's Beach and South Beach just had dunes and a sandy, trodden path from the upper ridge down to the water.

It made getting back to one's car hell after a long day of sun and swimming.

Hunter's Beach was the name for the u-shaped strip of beach surrounding the cove. It ended on each side where it met the sharp cliff faces and deep water.

Swimming in the cove, Hunter's Beach, was the second best choice—for those who could stand the trek up and down the sandy ledge. Its waters were considered the calmest, being the most protected from wind from the open sea. And as long as swimmers stayed close to shore, the risk of predators or injury were low.

The third beach, South Beach, followed Canyon Road out of town toward the interstate. Few people went to South Beach. The strip of sandy shore didn't even have an official parking lot. People just parked their cars along the side of the road and walked down to the water.

The waters were rougher here, and sirens came to South Beach all the time, especially after dark. In fact, people went to South Beach *hoping* to run into the sirens.

"What happened on South Beach?" he asked. Because if someone was at South Beach after dark, they must've known what they were in for.

"They were new," she said. "So it's possible they were fodder."

It was a known fact to long-time residents of Castle Cove that one didn't find this place on a map. It couldn't be found in an internet search or on a satellite view. Residents only heard about Castle Cove when they received mysterious job offers or acceptances to an interesting university, with full funding. But usually it was someone inside the town who brought new people in.

But not everyone invited into the town was invited so that they could be a member of this strange little community. Others were invited for *dinner*.

Grayson often wondered if he'd only survived until adult-hood because his parents had been so useful to the town. Maybe it wasn't his street smarts at all. Maybe it was pure luck. After all, his mother was the premier folklorist at the university. She protected and cultivated its long, dark—and utterly unique—history.

His father worked as a head biochemist at EB labs. They'd worked on everything from blood substitutes to studying the metamorphic changes in werewolves and shifters. His father seemed particularly interested in the metabolic differences between those who had been born with the ability to shift and those who'd acquired it through infection.

The bottom line was their work here was important. It supported Castle Cove's wellbeing. Grayson—with his love of nature and the water—wasn't. Would he be on his own now that he was eighteen?

Grayson realized Abby was speaking again. "They'd gone down to the water but hadn't got in it. I think the sirens only come if you touch the water. That's how they know you're there, right?"

Before Grayson could affirm that he also thought this was true, she was barreling on.

"So these people weren't in the water. They were on the ledge. And another freak storm rolled in and they'd started to walk back to their cars and that's when four sirens had come out of the water after them."

"But they can't leave the water."

"Well, no one has seen them out of the water. But these people said they did and practically chased them up the embankment."

"No way." He couldn't believe it.

He could practically hear her shrug. "That's what they said, but my mom thinks they were exaggerating. She says that they were pretty drunk when they gave their statements. Anyway, she suspects that there's some connection between the weird storms that keep rolling in and the sirens' strange behavior."

It wasn't much to go on, this connection between freak thunderstorms and agitated sirens.

"Anyway, enough about that. What were you doing before you called?"

He looked at the two books on his lap. Then he told her about the books and Gladys's recommendation.

"Send a pic," she said.

He dutifully snapped two pics of the books in his lap and texted them to her while she waited. There was a pause as she looked at the pics, then her voice returned, though a bit farther away. Grayson suspected he was on speaker phone now. But if her mom was at the station, then she was home alone.

"I can't read the title on the leather one. Is that a tree?"

"Yeah," he replied. "It's called The Dark Mother and Her Children."

"Creepy."

He laughed.

"What does it have to do with sirens?"

"I don't know. I'll have to read to find out."

Finally, she said, "About last night."

"I meant what I said." He wanted to get that out there before she had a chance to do anything ridiculous like apologize again. "I'm not going anywhere."

She sighed. "Does this mean I can go to bed?"

He smiled. "Get some rest. I'll talk to you tomorrow."

Once the call ended and he was once again sitting in his dark quiet house, he turned his attention to the books.

He decided to begin with the first book. It told a story about a woman named Vendetta, who lived in a small barony with her six brothers and a little sister. The sister died of starvation shortly after her mother did. The family had been wealthy when her parents had first married, but had lost their wealth with time because of a demanding and greedy queen who brought ruin to the people through extensive (read: expensive) military campaigns. In one way or another, the queen became responsible for her whole family's deaths, events picking off her father and brothers one at a time.

While she was still alive, Vendetta's mother had been a woman who worshipped the old gods. It was her mother who told her the story of The Crone Tree, which Grayson learned, was the tree depicted on the front of the cover.

This tree had many names—The Tree of Knowledge, The Tree of Life and so on. But inside this tree that could not be torn down or destroyed was the soul of a goddess.

Vendetta's mother believed that this goddess would help anyone, but particularly women, who prayed to her in their time of need. They need only be willing to give her a sacrifice.

When Vendetta had only one brother left, she and her brother walked into the wilderness to find this tree. At this point they were on the brink of starvation themselves, so they were willing to believe in old gods. They walked through the woods in the dead of winter for many miles.

They had just found the tree when some of the queen's soldiers found the pair. They killed her last brother and raped her. It is said that these two sacrifices were more than enough to awaken the sympathy of The Crone.

After Vendetta buried him beneath the tree and made her way home alone with only her grief as company, she had no life left in her. She died from cold and hunger that night in her bed. The following morning, just before the sun rose, she was visited by her six brothers, who were now demons.

They asked her if she wanted to be a demon too, with immense power, so that she could vanquish the evil queen. Vendetta agreed and with her six demon brothers, they rode to the castle, killed the queen's soldiers and slayed her court. Lastly, Vendetta killed the queen herself, finally avenging her family. After they killed her, they razed the castle. The castle ruins that now overlook the sea just east of the cove were supposed to be what was left of that very castle.

It was said that the goddess was so impressed with Vendetta's strength and will, that she offered Vendetta immortality in exchange for hunting down and destroying The Crone's enemies.

The front door burst open. "WE ARE THE CHAMPIONS MY FRIENDS!"

Heart hammering, Grayson slammed the book closed just as his brother Tanner ran in, covered head to toe in dust and tossing his glove dramatically on the couch.

"Off!" his mother cried. "That's *filthy*."

Tanner dragged his glove off the couch. "Gray, we won!"

"Whoa! High-five!" Grayson put his hand up and the kid gave it a hearty slap, his grin at full-wattage.

"Go take a shower. Now," his father begged, swatting at the glove-shaped outline of dirt now stuck to his sofa.

"You can tell me all about it later," Grayson assured his brother, when he looked ready to refuse. "Go on."

He kept singing the Queen song long after the bathroom door shut and the water came on. His father sighed, knocking the last bit of the dust off the cushion. "I don't understand why he slides across home plate when he can run across it just fine."

Grayson smiled. "Good game?"

"They won by ten points," his mother beamed. Then she saw the books. "Oh, what are you reading?"

Grayson almost laughed. She'd shown immense interest in her family's reading choices for as long as he could remember.

"The Dark Mother and Her Children. I found it at Curiosity. It was published by Castle Cove's University Press over a hundred years ago. I think it's a collection of fairytales."

Having ticked all her boxes, his mother came to the sofa and squeezed in beside him. "Let me see."

She took the large volume in her hand. "This is amazing. Can I read it when you're done?"

"Sure."

"What've you learned so far?"

He recited the tale of Vendetta to her. Instead of looking delighted, she looked worried.

"What?" he asked, not understanding the worry on her face. "What's wrong?"

"Why did you pick this book?" she asked. He couldn't understand the strange, searching expression on her face.

"I didn't," he said. "Gladys picked it. Why?"

"They're just fairytales," she said. She was staring at the embossed cover, the creases between her eyes deeper than he'd ever seen them.

"I know." It was so unlike his mother to say such a thing. She *lived* for fairytales. She believed they were keys to hidden truths and untold magic. There was no such thing as *just* fairytales. "What's wrong?"

She handed the book back, but her scowl had deepened.

He thought of the returned demon brothers. Of what it had cost Vendetta to achieve her revenge.

His mind also caught on the words *Druid's Hollow*.

"Promise me you're not planning to do anything crazy," his mother said. She clutched the book, looking as if she wouldn't return it to him. "Like look for The Crone Tree so you can make a sacrifice and bring Landon back."

When he didn't answer quick enough, she yelled his name. "Grayson!"

"What?"

"Promise me!"

"I don't even know what I'm promising not to do!" he admitted.

"Don't go into the Western Woods and try to bring Landon back. It wouldn't be Landon you brought back anyway."

"It would be demon Landon," he said.

"That isn't funny," his mother replied. Color had risen in her cheeks. "Don't even joke about it."

His father was regarding them both in a way as if he realized what danger they were all in. "It's about time for bed, isn't it?" he asked. When no one moved, his father added, "Honey, Grayson is a smart kid. He isn't going to go into the Western Woods to resurrect demons. Right?"

It never occurred to Grayson that he *could* take it back. That maybe this was his chance to undo what had been done. With Landon alive, he wouldn't have to live with this awful, terrible guilt.

With Landon alive…

His mother looked ready to explode. He forced a smile, "You worry too much, Mom."

"Do I?" she asked.

Druid's Hollow.

He thought he knew where it was.

As a wood scout, he'd done a report on the woods for his explorer badge. This meant that he'd crafted a detailed (and enormous) map of the woods for his project. It was his scout leader—a werewolf named Thomas—who'd corrected the map and made it to scale for him.

"Now you'll never get lost, buddy," he'd said.

Once his parents' bedroom door clicked shut, Grayson crept up the stairs to his room. He eased open the closet. He pulled down a box of old photo albums and a box of trophies. Behind that was the mail canister. He popped the white plastic lid off one side and found the map rolled up inside. He took the map to his bed and unrolled it on top of his comforter.

It showed the city in the center and the outline of ocean on two sides—east and south. Then it showed the woods. North of the city stretching off into nowhere was the Wayward Woods. Sunset Park, the lake and lupine trails, Black Water River, even the Witch's Backbone, a steep 8-mile hike. All of it was there. His scout master had even penciled in Howler's Hollow, the meeting place of the resident werewolf packs.

In case you ever want to visit, he'd said with a wink.

But then there were the woods west of the territory line bisecting the Wayward Woods.

A marker read 23 miles from the territory line to Druid's Hollow. So that's where the tree was supposed to be.

Of course, 23 miles through a treacherous forest full of maneaters would be one hell of a trek. However, it was only about nine miles from Vendetta Heights to Druid's Hollow. If he parked on Canyon Road and walked across the field known as Vendetta Heights, his journey would be shorter. There was the fact that Vendetta Heights was the make-out and feeding spot for local vampires and that these woods—even if only nine miles—were still crawling with monsters.

Was bringing Landon back really worth risking his own life?

He could never go in at night. It would be a massacre. But tomorrow, with daylight on his side, maybe, just *maybe* he could pull it off.

Grayson Choice 12
Go into the Western Woods - go to page 227
Do not go into the Western Woods - go to page 302

REESE: GO HOME WITH VIOLET

Reese considered the offer. It was an excuse to get her out of the bar and away from the other demons. Even when they'd been together, Violet had a way of angling Reese away from her demonic companions. Reese had once asked why, and Violet had laughed. *We're a bunch of bastards. I thought that'd be obvious to you.*

Reese drank down the last of her beer and nodded toward the door. "Let's go then."

Violet rose from the table and led the way. As they passed the bar, Bathory flashed a wink. "Have a good night, you two."

Reese stepped out into the cool night air and descended the wooden steps.

"I'll follow you to your place," Violet said, throwing her leg over her Honda Rebel. "That okay?"

"Sure."

Violet lifted the bike, and kicked back its stand. Reese watched her walk it backwards out of its parking spot before turning the key in her ignition. Her pickup rumbled to life.

Heading toward her place in Cliffside, Reese kept looking in her rearview, half-believing the demon might ditch her. But the single headlight of her Honda stayed with her as she drove through the dark streets.

Reese's mind wandered back to Violet's protective measures and her tendency to buffer her from the demons in town. She suspected the real answer lay in the confession Violet gave her one night about eight months into their relationship. They'd been lying in Violet's bed in her Old Town apartment. Dawn had been approaching, the moment when Violet would go unconscious for the day. Maybe that's why she'd been speaking so freely, delirious with the approaching sunlight.

"You know why demons are so attracted to shifters?" she'd mumbled. She'd been curled into her pillows and blankets, looking deceptively angelic.

"Because we fuck like animals?"

"*That.*" Violet snorted. "And your magic."

"What do you mean?" Reese had asked, reaching over to run her hand through Violet's hair.

"In low-level demons like me, it neutralizes us. But in stronger demons, in the old ones—they like to eat it."

A shiver had run down Reese's spine.

"It gets them high as hell on the power of it," she said. "You smell like magic."

The sleepy demon had rubbed her nose.

"Not like that diluted shit we can find anywhere. *Pure* magic. *Source* magic. You have no idea how intoxicating that is. It's like being starved for a thousand years and here you come, smelling like the best Bolognese I've never had."

Reese laughed. "Bolognese is your favorite."

Violet smiled. "It is."

But just as quick the smile was gone.

"But stay away from the old demons, okay? You can't fully neutralize them. And the moment they see a chance to—"

She'd kissed Violet then. "You worry too much. I'm safe."

"No one is safe in Castle Cove."

Reese laughed. "Then why are we here?"

Violet had opened her eyes in sudden clarity then. "Where else can we be what we are?"

That's when the rising sun had taken her.

A rough knock on her pickup window startled her out of her thoughts. The sound brought her back to her surroundings. She was sitting in her driveway, staring at the three-story oceanview house without really seeing it.

It was Violet.

She opened the door and climbed out. "Sorry. It's been a long night."

Violet wore her usual smirk. The tension surrounding her in the bar had dissipated. "Then let's put you to bed, princess."

Reese leaned against the driver's side door. "Why did you really want me out of there?"

"I told you. Channery was about to gobble you up."

"And what about the other two—the woman in the back and whoever she was talking to."

"The woman," Violet said, her eyebrows arching. "So that's who you followed in?"

"How do you know I followed her?"

Violet snorted. "She arrives and then a couple of minutes later, so do you, looking for someone. Then you directly refer to her while interrogating me about her. How in the world did I ever figure it out?"

Violet crossed her arms.

"At least you weren't looking for the other one. Of course *the woman* isn't much better."

"Who is she?"

Violet shook her head. "Invite me inside, Ree. Make me a drink. Maybe I'll tell you."

Reese knew that if Violet came inside and they started drinking, very little conversation would be had. Of course. Maybe Violet would surprise her.

"Would you like to come in?" Reese said. "I can make you a Jager bomb if you want."

Violet wrinkled her nose. "I'm not trying to get trashed. A G&T will do."

Reese unlocked the door and led them both inside. They kicked their shoes off at the door and crossed into the living room on the right. On the far wall, past the soft pale blue rug and glass coffee table was the bar. Reese made the G&T, but needed lime from the kitchen. When she came back with one, she found Violet on the white leather sofa. She'd removed her jacket and had thrown it over the arm of the couch. She'd pulled her hair up into a ponytail, revealing a luscious line of neck that Reese instantly wanted to kiss.

Violet knew the effect she had and blinked her long lashes. "Smell that lust. You *did* miss me."

Reese wasn't masking her scent, so no doubt her pheromones were betraying her. No matter how calmly she put her own gin and tonic on the ceramic coaster and sat down beside the demon, body language never lied.

"Don't distract me," Reese said. She found her voice thick in her throat. "That woman was doing something down in the cove. If she's here to cause trouble—"

Violet laughed. "No doubt she's here to cause trouble. But you need to stay out of it. She could wipe Alpha's floor with both of us. Let Ethan handle her. He's probably the only one in town who can."

"How can I tell him—"

She wrinkled her nose in disgust. "Don't be a tattletale, Ree. Besides, I can think of a better way to spend the morning with you."

Her eyes had filled with soft, flickering hellfire. Of course, they did that when Violet was pissed off too. But Reese had the strong impression Violet wasn't angry at the moment.

Before she could set her drink down, Violet had moved

across the couch and pressed the full length of her body against Reese's. This shoved her back into the cluster of blue, green, and gold throw pillows clotting the corner of the sofa.

The demon's mouth was hot, sparking electric across Reese's lips. Muscles low in her body filled with heat. When Violet slid down the length of her body, making Reese hyper aware of every curve, every patch of exposed flesh, Reese moaned.

Violet pulled back with a Cheshire cat grin. "Already? I haven't even started."

Reese finally got her gin and tonic onto the table, freeing her other hand. She entwined the demon in her arms, slipping her fingers under the hem of her black tank top. There was no bra to unfasten so Reese enjoyed the freedom to trace her skin without hindrance.

They kissed until their mouths were raw with it and the heat between Reese's legs was so intense, she thought one movement of her legs might spark a fire.

Violet pulled back, her face flushed. "Meet me in your bed."

The demon dematerialized, leaving Reese cold and panting on the sofa. Alone. "Freaking demons."

While it was true that Violet could not use any of her demon powers *on* the shifter, it didn't mean she couldn't torture her by proxy.

She grabbed her drink, downed it in one go and ran up the stairs to her bedroom, crunching ice between her teeth as she climbed.

When she threw open the door, panting with loss of breath, she found Violet reclining on the bed, a gleam in her eye.

Violet had taken the liberty of killing the lights and filling the room with candlelight. Soft music played from an unseen speaker. She ran a hand over the coverlet. "Took you long enough."

Reese regarded the candlelit room. "You're really trying here."

"It's been a while since I've fucked you," Violet said. "I want to remind you how good I am."

Reese was across the bedroom in two strides, slamming the demon back against the pillows. "I haven't forgotten."

Violet's eyes danced with fire. Though whether it was her own demonic hellfire or the candles in the room, Reese couldn't be sure.

Violet flipped her easily, sliding her legs down on either side of Reese's body. "Take off my shirt."

Reese obeyed, grabbing the bottom of the thin fabric and pulling it up over Violet's head. She stole several kisses while their mouths were aligned. And while Reese's mouth was greedily sucking on full lips, Violet was relieving her of her own shirt, then the black sports bra beneath it.

Then their breasts touched, nipples lightly grazing one another. Violet pushed her back against the bed. "Do you still have a strap-on?"

"Pretty sure they're all at your place," Reese said.

Violet pouted. "Disappointing. I wanted to see you on your hands and knees." A wicked grin covered her face. "I can still get you there."

Violet laid down alongside Reese, aligning her body as if she were the big spoon. She slid her arm down between her legs.

"Already so wet," Violet purred in her ears. "Was I the last person to fuck you?"

"Yes," Reese admitted. No point in lying about it.

"That was a while ago."

"I'm aware," Reese groaned. As Violet found her clitoris, gently rubbing it between two fingers, she bit down on Violet's arm.

"Careful," Violet said, hissing. "You know how much I like pain. I'll get carried away."

Reese pretended not to hear, biting harder as Violet slipped two fingers inside her.

She teased Reese toward her first orgasm with slow, steady strokes. As her desire built, obliterating all thought from her mind, Violet pulled her up onto her hands and knees. Her hand stayed between her legs, ruthlessly building speed. Reese buried her face in the pillow, crying out as white and red sparks danced behind her eyelids.

"That's it, baby," Violet cooed. "Just for me, okay?"

A second surprise climax echoed through her. Reese fisted the pillows around her.

"You're cheating," Reese said. "You're using lust magic or something."

Violet snorted. "I wish. Then I could *really* blow your mind."

Violet forced her legs farther apart, sliding between them. She turned, so that she was lying on her back between Reese's spread legs. She pulled Reese down onto her chest.

The first brush of her tongue so soon after two orgasms rocked Reese. Her legs shook with the force of keeping her weight aloft.

But Violet had already wrapped her hands around the shifter's legs, refusing to let go. It didn't matter that Reese's legs were shaking. It didn't matter when she collapsed onto her side, unable to hold herself above the demon's mouth anymore. The demon wouldn't let go. She rolled with her, continuing her tongue's assault until Reese was on her back, orgasming for a third time.

"Enough," Reese begged. She grabbed a fistful of Violet's hair. "Enough. My turn."

Violet let herself be hauled up between her legs and into a sloppy kiss.

Reese sat up, pulling Violet into her lap before laying her down the other way, her head now at the foot of the bed. She began work on removing her pants.

"You can barely keep your eyes open," Violet teased. "I'm pretty good, huh?"

"Shut up," Reese said, but there was no malice in it. She was enjoying the bright flush in Violet's face and the cat-like grin on her face.

"I bet I could—" Violet's words were swallowed by a moan.

Reese slid her fingers into the demon. *"Hushhh."*

Reese was delighted to find that Violet was just as wet as she'd been. "Am I the last one who fucked you?" Reese asked, teasingly.

"Yes," Violet said, bearing down on her hand.

Reese's emotions swelled.

"I'm not lying, Ree." Violet pulled her forward, looking into her eyes. "You are."

Of course, this said nothing about how many pants Violet may have dropped since their breakup. Reese pushed back against the swell of emotion threatening to rise like a tide and destroy this nice little oblivion they'd formed around them.

They were running out of time. Reese could already see the first hint of purple behind the bedroom curtains. It would be sunrise within the hour.

Violet grabbed Reese's free hand and pulled it up to her throat. She squeezed until Reese took over, adding the pressure of her own. Violet liked being choked as she came. Reese hadn't forgotten. So she let Violet writhe against her hand until the last waves of her climax fell away.

Reese waited, trying to read Violet's body to see if she wanted more, or if the approaching sun was going to win.

She thought the demon had fallen asleep when she said, "We could pick this up again, you know."

Reese lay down beside her. "Could we?"

Reese knew she wasn't talking about the sex. She was talking about their failed relationship. They'd been together for two years and apart for almost one. Reese still liked her. There was no point in lying to herself about that. But she'd had her reasons for ending it.

Seeing Violet make out with people in the bars, or invite people into dark corners hadn't been easy, even if it was only to feed off their baser emotions—jealousy, lust, envy.

"Eating isn't cheating," Reese said. "That's what you said."

"That's why you ended it, wasn't it?"

Reese didn't answer.

"I've never lied to you," Violet said. She grabbed the ends of Reese's hair, playing with the inky black tips. "But a girl's got to eat and I won't feed on you."

I've never lied to you.

Violet must have sensed the dark shift in her mind.

"Forget I said anything. I've ruined the moment."

"You didn't," Reese said. She ran a hand through her hair. If she was being honest with herself, she'd missed Violet. She'd seen her around, but that wasn't the same.

She'd missed the intimacy. Even if the jealousy had also been tearing her apart.

"I know it doesn't feel like it to you," Violet said with uncharacteristic tenderness. "But it really is like watching you get emotional over my cheeseburger. I don't feel anything for the people I eat. That's exactly *why* I eat them and why I can't do that to you."

Reese was nodding, but she didn't know what to say.

"If I don't eat I'll get weak. In a place like Castle Cove, I can't be weak. It'd get me killed."

Reese rolled onto her back, staring up at the ceiling. "I get it. I really do."

Violet dragged herself from the bed. With one movement of her hands, the candles in the room extinguished, leaving dozens of trails of thin gray smoke to rise toward the ceiling.

"Where are you going?" Reese asked. She turned on her side, watching the demon dress herself.

"I want to get home before sunrise."

"You can stay," Reese said. "You'll be safe here."

Violet considered her for a long time. She spared a small smile. "Only because it might change your mind."

Reese pulled back the covers, sliding over to let Violet slip in beside her.

The moment before the sun rose, Violet spoke. "Tell me you'll think about it."

"I will." As if Reese could actually stop herself. She pulled Violet close. "I promise."

A PHONE WAS RINGING SOMEWHERE IN THE HOUSE. REESE GROPED the sheets blindly trying to find her cell phone. She found the charging cord first, and traced it to the phone itself.

"Hello?" she groaned. Her voice broke with the effort.

"Reese?"

It was Kristine. She didn't sound so great either. Of course, running the woods all night would do that to a woman.

Violet slept like the dead beside her. Reese wasn't worried about waking her. The demon couldn't rise before sunset. So she turned her attention to the alpha werewolf.

"Yeah, it's me. What's up?"

"I'm calling an emergency pack meeting. A kid died in the cove last night. He was torn apart by a siren."

"What?" Reese sat up on her elbow, alarm rocketing her mind to full wakefulness. "I was there."

"Were you?" Kristine said. Said, because the alpha rarely asked questions. Even her questions weren't really questions.

Reese recounted the night to her boss and friend. By the time she finished, she felt like she'd made a terrible mistake. She shouldn't have swum toward the reef.

"I saw the kids," she finished lamely. "I should've checked on them."

"How could you have known that would happen? The sirens aren't even supposed to be in the cove."

"There was a woman there," Reese explained. She told her what she saw of the strange magic on the beach and the storm that had come rolling in. "I followed her to the Crossroads bar, and saw her meet someone, but that's it. I didn't learn anything else."

"Maybe it's not connected," Kristine said finally. Her sigh made the woman sound much older. "Or maybe she caused it. Either way, I called to see if you could watch the bar until I can come in. I realize it's not your shift and I'll pay you double for that. But maybe you should be part of the discussion. You are a witness. I'll leave it to you to decide."

Reese looked at Violet again. If she went, she'd be sure to leave a note so the demon wouldn't wake up alone and wonder where she'd gone.

Reese Choice 13
Go to pack meeting - go to page 51
Hold down the bar - go to page 67

GRAYSON: GO INTO THE WESTERN WOODS

Sunday morning passed quickly with Nutella pancakes and cups of coffee. But then his parents went to the Farmer's market in Cliffside, which met on Sunday from May through October. Unlike the market that met in Old Town on Saturdays, Sunday's market focused on street food and live music. There were more dogs and a playground. It wasn't a bad way to spend a Sunday. On any other day, Grayson would've been thrilled to go too.

But he was tired. He'd kept trying to go to sleep and yet kept finding himself waking up, wanting to read The Dark Mother and Her Children. He reached for the book the way he usually reached for his phone.

He told his parents he wasn't feeling well, hoping they'd let him stay home. He saw the conflict on their faces as they tried to decide whether or not to force him along or to give him space.

They left without him.

No sooner did his father's sedan back out of the driveway, nearly hitting an orange tabby, did Grayson bound up the stairs.

Grayson seized the book and read it again. Before he knew what he was doing, he'd closed the book and began to pack a bag as he would for any day-long hike.

Water. Three protein bars and his knives. He took a length of rope for good measure and a mostly used roll of duct tape. One could never be sure when they might need duct tape.

He looked into his bag and felt there wasn't much else he could bring.

On second thought, he pulled an onyx pendant from his bedside table. It had been Ms. Monroe who'd given it to him for his sixteenth birthday. She'd said that onyx protected a person from magic. He hoped that would guard him against any magical creatures in the Western Woods.

He clasped the necklace around his neck, feeling its weight settle against his chest.

As he sat on the bench by the front door, pulling on his shoes, he texted Abby. *Heading out for a hike.*

Where? she asked him.

He considered lying. Then he thought of her in his bed, and lying felt like a dirty trick.

Western Woods.

Haha. When he didn't respond quick enough she added, *WTF??? Are you serious???*

I think there's a way to bring Landon back.

The text bubble rose and disappeared for several minutes. Grayson managed to write Reese a note—*Something came up. We'll have to reschedule*—and tape it to the front door. He was already in his car before Abby's response finally came through.

As what? Zombie? Vampire?

Not sure.

Demon?

I honestly don't know, he replied.

You want to bring someone back from the dead and you don't know as what? Awesome idea.

If I died wouldn't you want to bring me back? he asked.

That's different.

Why should it be different? he asked. *He's our bff.*

She didn't seem to have an answer for that.

Finally, *I'm coming with you.*

No.

Why?

It's too dangerous.

If it's too dangerous for me, it's too dangerous for you, she replied.

He wasn't sure how to respond to that.

What are you trying to prove? she asked.

That question stung. Somehow it had cut beneath the surface of the urgency. It burned. Worse, it slowed him down. It made him think.

What *was* he trying to prove?

That he was a good friend to Landon? That Abby really would've wanted him if Landon were still alive? That Grayson wasn't a consolation prize?

No. He didn't believe any of that. If he was being honest with himself, he'd known since September. The way she'd looked at him spoke volumes for the connection between them.

If he needed to prove anything, it was that he wasn't happy his friend was dead. He needed to prove that Landon's death hadn't been like a gift from above.

That was closer to the truth.

Bringing Landon back would prove that he wasn't glad to have Landon removed from the picture. He wasn't glad that he had the chance to steal the girl he always wanted for himself.

Grayson shifted uncomfortably in the driver's seat. He wrung the steering wheel.

Take me with you, Abby texted again. *Gray, please. You can't go in there by yourself.*

Grayson Choice 13

Bring Abby - go to page 231
Don't bring Abby - go to page 284

GRAYSON: BRING ABBY

I'll be there in five minutes, he wrote and reversed the car out of the driveway. It was almost eleven in the morning. If they got into the woods by noon, they'd have about nine hours before sunset. That meant they needed to cover at least two miles an hour. Doable.

His phone remained silent for the entire drive. Maybe Abby was saving her energy for a counterargument in person. Maybe she was forming a plan to detain him at her house so he couldn't go into the woods at all.

Grayson drove the perimeter of Hyde Park, driving past the large, imposing mansions that faced the park. He'd always wondered who lived there. Abigail said it was the wealthy undead vampires of Castle Cove. That each grand house was owned by one of the clans.

Apparently, there were two kinds of vampires in Castle Cove—and as far as Grayson knew—the world. There were living vampires and undead vampires. The living vampires were those who had not died as a result of their attack and transformation. Their hearts never stopped. Therefore, the virus living inside them had more of a symbiotic relationship with its host. It gave them strength and eternal youth. They detested, but were not allergic to, sunlight. They were simply creatures of the night. Their bodies emitted pheromones that attracted and disoriented their prey. They were warm and had a pulse. Mostly they were apex predators rather than supernatural creatures.

The undead were a different story. Unlike their living brethren who seemed to rely on their physical attributes to attract prey, the undead relied on magic. The undead had died during their transformations and it was at that moment of death that a demon entered their body and took up residence.

Most of the person's previous life and human connection were instantly forgotten. These vampires were reborn, strong and fast. Their powers included telepathy, mind-control, telekinesis and flying, depending on how strong the demon that inhabited their body was.

According to Abigail—or Abigail's mother, who knew almost every citizen in their town—it was actually only *one* demon per clan. The demon—and its power—was strongest in the oldest clan member, and weakest in the newest recruits. That was why they adhered to a hierarchy. Like all demons, they were unable to go into sunlight and died when the sun rose each day. They were cold to the touch, because they were essentially reanimated corpses. There was no life left in them.

As Grayson drove past the large, looming mansions, he wondered if such creatures really dwelled within. The revival architecture and old live oaks thick with moss seemed to say, *old beings dwell here.* With homes so massive, he imagined there was plenty of room for an entire clan and all their attendants to live comfortably.

Just east of Hyde Park, before Castle Cove University began, was a small neighborhood called Hummingbird Hollow. It had small, quaint ranch-style homes and postage stamp yards. He turned off Ruby Road onto Violetear Drive and found Abby sitting on her porch with a camo backpack between her knees on the step below her.

She stood when she saw him pulling into the drive and slung the sack over her shoulder.

He hadn't even fully come to a stop before she threw the passenger side door open and climbed inside.

"My mom's shift ends in ten minutes so you better step on it if you want to miss her," she said, and pulled the seatbelt across her chest.

He was back on Ruby Road moments later.

He was struck with the smell of her. Her hair looked damp and freshly washed. Her clothes reeked of fabric softener.

"So what do you know?" she asked, adjusting the pack between her legs.

"About the Western Woods?"

"No," she said then she cocked her head. "Well yeah, that too. But I meant Landon. You said you had a book about how to bring him back from the dead?"

"Not exactly," he admitted.

He could see her looking at him from the corner of his eye.

"I read a story about Vendetta and The Crone Tree. Have you heard of it?"

"No."

He recounted the story for her, from Vendetta's hard life until she was turned into a demon and took on the ruthless queen.

"What does this have to do with Landon?" she asked, when he was done.

His thighs had begun to stick to his seat. He leaned forward and adjusted the A/C. "According to the story and my mother, The Crone Tree will bring him back to life if we make a sacrifice."

"Is there a dead body in the trunk?" she asked. "Because I don't see a sacrifice."

"I was hoping my blood would be enough."

"You expect to cut your hand and resurrect Landon?" she asked. "Grayson, you didn't think this through. Which is…really unlike you."

Was he that obvious? Of course, he hadn't told her the truth. He couldn't tell her that he'd intended to cut himself—*really* cut himself. That he'd hoped his own blood would attract a dryad or some other monster and that he would kill it beneath the tree —offering *that* in exchange for Landon's life.

"What aren't you telling me?" she asked.

He shifted in his seat.

"Do you think I'm stupid?" she asked.

"No," he said. He turned and looked at her, trying to gauge how angry she was. She was irritated, but not furious. He didn't want to see how far she would push him.

"Don't you think it would be a good idea that I know what the actual plan is before we go into the big, dark woods?"

He sighed. "I was going to cut myself."

"Again, I don't think a bit of blood counts as a sacrifice."

"I was hoping the blood would attract…something."

Her lips pursed in question. "Any *particular* something? Or will any monster work for you?"

"First come, first served," he said.

"What if it is a dryad?"

His heart faltered. "What if it is?"

"Dryads are supposed to be sacred to The Crone. If you kill one maybe you'll piss her off and she'll smite you."

"Or we spare it in exchange for what we want."

"Or we get swarmed and eaten by a dozen of them. Or maybe she won't be impressed at all and tears us apart herself."

"Vendetta—" he began.

"Vendetta was turned into a demon so she could murder someone." Abigail spoke the words as if it answered everything. "That's some dark shit. I don't think the tree is into *oh-*

please-save-my-best-friend type of requests. And all the things I've ever heard about The Crone Tree or She Who Sleeps is about her loyalty to her creations—demons, sirens, dryads. I don't think slaughtering one of her children is going to win her over."

He understood what she was saying. They had no proof that this would work. And the idea that they were going to walk over eight miles into the most dangerous woods on just a hope seemed…

It'll be fine, he thought.

Grayson pulled to a stop at the four-way in front of Crossroads.

"You'd have better odds going in there," Abby said. She pointed at the demon bar across the street.

Even though it was the middle of the day, several cars sat in the gravel lot outside the old timey saloon. The Crossroads bar was a demon bar. Every long-time resident of Castle Cove knew that. One only went in there to make dangerous deals.

Abby gestured to the slouching porch and batwing doors. "At least you know what you're getting when dealing with those guys."

Grayson sat at the four-way stop, considering his options. "You don't have to come. You can wait in the car."

"Because you're going in there no matter what I say, aren't you?"

South Beach bloomed on his left, revealing sandy beaches and blue-grey water today. On his right was the open fields known as Vendetta Heights. Grayson drove until he thought he was about parallel to the place known as Druid's Hollow.

"Christ," Abby swore. "This is really happening."

"Then don't come!" he said. "I don't know why I even brought you!"

Her face reddened as if slapped. She remained silent for the remainder of the drive, all the way to Vendetta Heights.

"I'm coming," she announced. "Now give me a kiss. For good luck."

She licked her lips.

He pulled off the road and parked the car, the nose pointing at the looming woods ahead of them.

"No, you're just trying to distract me."

"Come on," she said, leaning over the console. "We might die in here."

Heart hammering in his chest, he leaned across the console toward her. She met him halfway. Her lips were warm and sticky as they slid against his. She threaded her fingers through his hair, sending shivers down the back of his neck. A strange prickling raised the hairs along his skin.

Just when he thought he might burst with the desire building in his chest—because god, if it was her plan to make out with him in this car to prevent him from going, it just might work—she pulled back, frowning.

"What are you wearing?" she asked. She was looking him over as if she'd never seen him before.

"What do you mean?"

"I mean, what are you wearing? Do you have any oils on or maybe jewelry or a rock in your pocket?"

He reached inside his shirt and pulled out the onyx. "You mean this? How did you—"

She took it between her fingers, frowning at the black stone. "At least I'm not losing my mind."

"What are you saying?"

"Why not? It's a good a time as any." She sighed and searched his eyes. "I'm a witch."

For a moment, he sat there looking at her. It sounded like a punchline to an incomplete joke. Like someone had told it poorly, skipping important information.

Finally he managed, "What?"

"I'm a witch. I joined the Castle Cove coven when I turned

eighteen. I'd wanted to join since junior year but you have to be of age. Then it's a ten-year apprenticeship until you're a full member."

"And they just let you join?" he asked. It sounded like a stupid question once it left his lips. It was funny how some questions sounded very smart inside his head, but less so once spoken.

"I have an aptitude for magic."

"Wait," he said, straightening and running a hand over his face. "What does this have to do with the onyx?"

But then he remembered Ms. Monroe's words.

"Were you trying to cast a spell on me?"

"A protection spell before we go in there half-cocked. But to be honest, I don't even know if it's going to work. There's a saying in the coven: There's not enough magic in the world to protect against stupidity."

"Is this why you wanted to come?" he asked her. "You thought you could protect me?"

"I'm trying," she said. She bit her lip, her anxiety showing. "I wanted to cast protection spells and stealth spells on us both. I was hoping that it would get us further into the woods without being detected. Or if we run into something, we'll have a bit of luck on our sides. But Grayson—"

He snapped himself out of the mental spiral that was sucking him down.

Abby is a witch. Abby is a witch. Abby—

"Grayson—the Western Woods is old magic. Old as Hell itself, do you understand? I have zero belief that my wimpy spells are going to get us through this alive. That's why I called Miriam."

"Who?" Every time his heart slowed down, Abby said something to send it kicking again.

"My coven leader. I told her where we are. I asked for her help."

Grayson dragged his hands down his face. "What if they stop us?"

Abby snorted. "If only we were so lucky. Do you really want to go in there?"

She pointed at the woods.

He looked at the darkness pooling beneath the trees. "Yes."

"And if you don't go now, you'll just sneak in by yourself some other time, won't you?"

"How did you—"

"Right. So I'm going in with you then." Abby pinched the bridge of her nose. "And I'm doing what I can to keep us safe, but I can't cast any spells on us if you have that necklace on."

He looked down at the onyx pendant resting against his chest. He lifted it, gazing into its black face. He saw his own, puzzled reflection staring back at him.

Grayson Choice 14

Trust Abby and take off the necklace - go to page 252

Leave the onyx on - go to page 275

REESE: INTERVIEW THE WITNESSES

Reese decided the best use of her time would be to interview the kids that were at the beach on the night of the attack. Perhaps they had seen or heard something that could be of use, anything that might crack the mystery.

Reese drove her rattling red truck through town. First she would—on Ethan's authority—talk to the detective who'd first arrived at the scene. She needed the contact information if she hoped to find the witnesses.

The precinct was quiet when she swung her truck into the nearby vacant lot. Reese frowned, wondering if there was some public holiday she didn't know about. Only two cars, two dark sedans, sat in the lot. The adjacent park was also deserted. An empty park swing swung lightly in the breeze.

Reese climbed out of the truck onto the hot June pavement.

She could feel the heat through her boots as she crossed the blacktop and marched up the sidewalk into the building. A wall of welcomed air conditioning hit her full in the face.

A man behind the desk answering phones cast her a look as she walked in. "Can I help you?"

"I'm looking for Detective O'Reilly," she said. From what she could see, this officer was the only one in the building.

"Detective O'Reilly is very—"

"Ethan Benedict sent me," Reese said, crossing her arms over her chest. "So if she isn't here, please tell me where she is."

Ethan's name sent red rushing into the officer's face. "O'Reilly!"

The name was thrown over his shoulder the way one might throw a ball.

A head popped out of an adjacent office. Reese could see the woman's other ear was pressed to a phone.

"She said Benedict sent her," the officer said with an arched brow. Then he muttered something under his breath that sounded to Reese like *better you than me*.

O'Reilly's face crumpled from irritation to resignation. She waved Reese forward. "Come on in."

Reese snaked around the desks and moved toward the glass office. O'Reilly, a tall woman with auburn hair and large nose held the door open for her until she entered. Then she closed it quietly behind her with a click.

She held up her hand, asking for a moment to finish her call. "Yes, I understand that. That's correct. All right, well, call me back when you figure out what's been taken."

She ended the call with a huff.

"Hello, detective." Reese extended her hand. She hadn't always felt comfortable around cops. A plain-clothes detective was apparently cop enough to make her palms sweat. "I'm Reese Cook."

O'Reilly, who'd been heading to her desk, faltered. "Any relationship to Dr. Cook?"

"She's my aunt," Reese said with a gentle smile.

O'Reilly arched her brows appreciatively. "If you're like your aunt, then that explains why Benedict has recruited you."

Reese knew just what the detective meant by *like her*. Not

brilliant, educated, adventurous, or rich. But a shark shifter. She decided to neither confirm nor deny her condition. Instead, she kept her smile bright and friendly. One benefit of being a bartender was such a smile was usually within reach.

"Ethan asked me to interview the kids that were at the beach during the attack." Reese sat in the stiff chair opposite the detective's desk. "I was hoping you could give me their contact information."

The detective made a big show of moving papers around on her desk. "They're both eighteen—Grayson and Abigail. I couldn't rightfully stop you unless they complain about harassment." She finally looked up, frowning. "Benedict is trying to solve this?"

"He is."

She leaned back in her chair. "Good. Because I'll be honest, I'm not making much progress. We don't have a means for communicating with the sirens. And we can't simply go out there—" Here the detective gestured suggestively toward the ocean. "—and euthanize them the way we might a rogue wildcat or a bear who's attacked someone."

"I know," Reese said, companionably. She was trying to settle into the chair but it was a stiff, unwelcoming sort of chair with a rigid plastic back. Reese wondered it was uncomfortable on purpose, to discourage anyone from lingering in the office and wasting the detective's precious time.

"But you must understand I have reservations about you speaking to her."

Reese felt like she'd missed something. She frowned. "Who?"

"Abigail. She's my daughter."

"I have no intention of harassing your kid. I know you want to protect them but I'm just asking questions." She held up her hand in a three-finger salute. "I promise."

Detective O'Reilly looked out her office window in contemplation. Reese followed her gaze instinctively. There was nothing out there but a cluster of maple trees and a row of trimmed bushes.

"I'll give you both addresses and their cell phones," the detective said finally. She reached across her desk and grabbed a stack of neon orange sticky notes.

The detective fixed her with a hard gaze. "Surely you realize it's not you I'm worried about."

Reese frowned.

"What kind of mother would I be if I didn't want to keep as much distance as possible between Abigail and Ethan Benedict?" the detective asked with arched brows. There was a hard edge to her voice that Reese had a hard time placing.

"I agreed to help Ethan because I'm good in the ocean. I'm not beholden to him or anything. I'm not going to kidnap your daughter and deliver her hogtied to Ethan or anything."

Detective O'Reilly cracked a smile. "I know your aunt is a good woman. And I've heard only good things about you. So I'll tell you what I think of Benedict."

Reese tried to seem only casually interested.

"A lot of bad things happen around Ethan Benedict. People disappear. Or they change. I know he practically owns this town —no matter what sham of a democracy elected him to mayor— but that shouldn't make him above the law. If three girls go into his bar—"

Here Reese knew the detective was referring to the Labyrinth.

"Then I should be able to search the place."

"Of course," Reese said. She didn't know how else to punctuate that intense stare.

O'Reilly continued staring out the window at the greenery bathed in dappled sunlight. "All I'm saying is, keep one eye on that guy at all times. And whatever you do, don't bring my daughter around him."

Reese spoke reflexively. "Yes, ma'am."

"All of that goes for Grayson as well," she added, and finally tore the sticky note off the pad, offering it to Reese across the desk. "He's a good kid."

Reese had no idea how she was supposed to stand between Ethan Benedict and a couple of kids should he want to—what? *Eat* them? But the intensity in the detective's eyes left no room to argue.

"I'll be careful," Reese said, glad to be rid of the ruthless plastic chair. "And I'll call you if I run into trouble."

"Please do."

Outside night was falling. Reese decided to grab a quick bite to eat before trying Grayson's place. She ordered a fish filet sandwich with tartar sauce and an extra-large water from the drive-thru. She ate it in silence as she used the GPS on her phone to locate Grayson's house. It was a charming Victorian in Midtown.

The lights were on and a small sedan maybe ten years old sat off to one side of the driveway. Reese parked behind it and mounted the wooden steps. The house looked as though it had been painted recently and the wood refinished and stained. Someone liked to take care of the home and Reese could appreciate that. She knocked on the door, then stretched her arms back behind her, trying to get a kink out of her tight shoulders.

The door opened on a young man holding a box of Chinese food. Wooden chopsticks stuck out of the top of the white carton. "Can I help you?"

"I'm Reese Cook," she said with short wave. "I'm looking for Grayson."

He straightened. "That's me."

"Cool, uh, I came by to ask you some questions about the attack."

His face tightened and for a second she thought he might shut the door in his face.

"I'm not talking to reporters."

"I'm not a reporter. You can call the police station and check. I got permission from Detective O'Reilly to talk to you."

He looked at his Chinese take-out box and then the open door.

"I'll wait here," she said.

Relief washed over his features. "Thanks."

He closed the door and Reese heard the lock slide back into place. She snorted to herself. Either the kid thought she was a vampire or just a plain crazy person. Either way, if she'd really wanted to get into his house, she could've thrown herself through the window.

Smiling, she sat down on the top step. For the first time in three years she craved a cigarette. She used to smoke. She'd worked herself up to half a pack a day before her aunt had asked her to quit. But moments like this would be great for a smoke break and she knew it.

She pulled out her phone to check her email and messages instead.

The door creaked open behind her and she turned to see Grayson in the doorway again.

"Okay," he said with an easier smile. "Sorry about that."

Reese shrugged. "Can't be too careful."

"Can we talk out here?" he asked.

She moved over on the step to make room for him. "Full disclosure, I'm not a vampire. And that you-have-to-be-invited-inside stuff only works on the undead. You know that right?"

His face didn't change. "I know. You're a shark shifter who bartends at Alpha's."

Reese's eyebrows shot up, impressed. "Now who's the detective?"

"It's nothing personal. My parents have a no-strangers-in-the-house-while-they're-gone policy. So I can't let you in, even if I trust you."

"Noted."

He took the seat beside her, leaving space between them.

"You're lucky you caught me here," he said. Reese realized he'd brought the Chinese out with him. At this angle she could see the noodles and smell the delicious scent of fish oil. "I almost went to work tonight."

"Where do you work?" she asked, casually. It had nothing to do with the attack, but it seemed a little rude to jump right into the horror part of the conversation.

"Curiosity Books. It's on the corner of Apple and Magnolia."

"Oh, Tabby's place," she said.

He forked noodles into his mouth. "How do you know Ms. Monroe?"

"Cat shifter," she said, picking at a small scab on her elbow. She couldn't remember how she'd gotten it. Maybe she'd nicked a fin on the coral or something. "She's a little skittish but very sweet."

"Cat shifter," Grayson repeated. He'd stopped chewing and was staring at her.

"News to you, huh?" she asked with a smile. "Well, forget I mentioned it then."

With arched eyebrows he let it slide. "A cat shifter living with a ghost. That's something you don't hear every day."

Reese had heard about the ghost. In their brief, passing conversations, Tabby had mentioned the ghost the way one mentions their plants.

Reese took a deep breath. "I'm sure it's hard to talk about, but can you tell me what happened in the cove? Try to be as detailed as you can. Even things that you don't think matter might really help us figure out what's going on."

And the more details you give me, the better chance I have keeping Ethan away from you.

He finished the noodles in his mouth, then balanced the carton on his knee.

"It was my birthday," he said, licking the oil off his lips.

"Shit." Reese flicked her finger ever though there was no cigarette ash to dispense. It was a habit, unlike the smoking itself, she hadn't been able to break.

"Yeah," Grayson said, looking out over the yard to the street. A couple of kids on bicycles waved at Grayson as they passed. He returned the wave.

"Friendly neighborhood you've got here."

Grayson smiled. "They're my little brother's friends."

She involuntarily flicked her fingers again. She didn't want to speak, waiting for him to fall into the easy retelling that she was expecting.

He didn't disappoint. He recounted in faithful detail the night in question. From the moment they stripped down on the beach—Grayson and his two friends, Abigail and Landon—and swam to Heart's Rock. He ended with the moment he saw Landon's body in the shallows.

Reese nodded as if to say that was enough. "A storm, you say?"

"Yeah," he said, digging into his noodles again. But she could see his heart was no longer in it. "It came in really fast from the ocean."

Reese tucked this detail into her memory.

"Do you think Abby noticed anything you didn't?" Reese asked. She would go over and question the girl regardless, but she was offering Grayson the chance to invite himself along.

She liked this kid. Not really a kid. There was only eight years difference in their ages, but he seemed older. She thought it might be how composed he was. Unlike a lot of the co-ed dude bros that she saw in the bars on the weekend, Grayson smacked of maturity. She liked him better for it.

"She might," he said. "We can go ask her."

Reese stood, smiling. "Are you going to bring the noodles?"

"No," he said with a brilliant smile. Perfect white teeth compliments of dental work no doubt. "One sec."

He disappeared in the house as Reese stood and stretched. She climbed in the truck and turned the key. When he opened the passenger side door, she reached across the bench seat to gather up some papers she'd left.

"Sorry," she said, folding them in half and putting them in the glovebox with a firm shove. "Just some notes."

Grayson put on his seatbelt. "No worries. I was just thinking how clean your car is."

She snorted. This kid was polite to a fault. She tapped the dash of her truck. "Yeah, she doesn't look like she should be in such good condition, but I love her."

Grayson smiled. "I can tell."

She turned the key and the truck rattled to life. "So where does Abby live?"

"Just east of Hyde Park," he said. "In Hummingbird Hollow."

"Okay." She put the car in reverse and checked her mirrors before backing into the street.

Reese focused on the road until she heard Grayson's breath hitch. She glanced over and saw his furrowed brow.

"What?" she asked.

"Don't be—" Grayson began, but he didn't seem to know how to finish. "Abby's having a hard time."

"I'm not going in to play bad cop or anything. I know how to talk to people."

He nodded, offering her another polite smile.

They rode in silence past large, looming mansions that lined Hyde Park. The revival architecture and old live oaks thick with moss seemed to say old creatures dwell here.

Just east of Hyde Park, before the Castle Cove University border began, was a small neighborhood called Hummingbird Hollow. It was populated by small, quaint ranch-style homes and postage stamp yards. They turned off Ruby Road onto Violetear Drive looking for the small yellow house.

The front door was open as if waiting for them.

Reese swung the red truck into the driveway. "Thanks for coming. I think it'll be easier for her to talk if someone she knows and trusts is with me."

They climbed out of the truck as Abby stepped out onto the porch. Reese saw the resemblance to the detective immediately. The same hair and stern face. Only the nose was different.

Abby visibly stiffened at the sight of Reese. Reese knew what this meant immediately, having watched thousands of jealous barroom exchanges in her day. Abby was into Grayson. And if Reese's nose was any judge, the feeling was reciprocal. If they hadn't already slept together, they would soon.

Reese tried not to grin and give the game away.

"Come in," Abby said, holding open the door for Reese.

Reese pretended not to see Grayson squeeze Abby's hand as he passed into the house.

"Thanks," Reese muttered, following in behind him.

The house was a ranch. It had a simple open floor plan and 9-foot ceilings, bright and airy.

Abby cleared her throat. "Do you want anything to drink or—?"

The girl smelled like shampoo and soap. Her face was freshly scrubbed and dewy.

"Water, if you don't mind," she said.

Abby gestured to the mustard yellow sofa in the center of the front room. "Take a seat."

Reese obeyed, tucking herself into the corner of the couch and pulling a lacey pillow into her lap. Grayson tucked himself into a navy arm chair, crossing his leg over his thigh.

"Here." A second later, Abby put the cool cylinder of water in her hand.

"Thanks." Reese took the obligatory sip before resting the glass on her leg. "I'm here to—"

"I know," Abby interrupted. She took the twin armchair opposite Grayson's. "I spoke to my mom earlier."

"Great," Reese said, hoping that would relieve some of the lingering tension. But Abby still seemed on guard. "If you could just tell me what happened."

After two false starts—as if the girl didn't seem to know which way she wanted to tell it—she began again. She recounted the night slowly with even more detail than Grayson had.

Because she's a detective's daughter, Reese thought. *She's been taught to pay attention.*

When she finished, Abby flicked her eyes to meet Reese's. "Someone was using magic. A lot of it."

Grayson turned, mouth slack. "How do you know that?"

Reese knew the answer before she spoke. It brought the situation into sharp focus then: her reluctance to lower her guard, her concern for retelling the story, and revealing this detail.

"I'm apprenticed to the coven," Abigail said plainly. "I'm a witch."

"You're a witch?" Grayson asked. Reese had the urge to gently slap his cheek and snap him out of it.

It hadn't been Reese's reaction that the girl had worried about. After all, shifters were walking magic.

"I didn't tell you because I wasn't sure you'd be okay with it." Abby's cheeks were burning red. "Your parents are sort of —purists."

This statement seemed to hurt him most of all.

"Abby. We love you. Not one person in my family would give a damn if you're a witch."

Her eyes flicked down to her lap. To Reese, she smelled like embarrassment and also relief. Reese wasn't sure if she should leave or pretend she hadn't become hostage to this intimate exchange.

"So you could feel the magic?" Reese asked, trying to regain ground.

"Yes. And there was a surge of it right before the sirens

showed up. I knew something was wrong, but I was halfway to shore when I felt it so I couldn't do anything in the water. Then once I did get to shore—" She licked her lips. "Everything happened so fast after that."

Reese rubbed her knees. "Could you tell where the magic was coming from?"

"West," Abby said without hesitation. "Somewhere along Canyon Road. But I can't be more specific than that. Sorry."

"You've been a huge help," Reese said, standing. "I don't have any other questions now, but would either of you mind talking to me again if I think of more?"

They both shook their heads.

"Thanks. Grayson do you want a ride back?"

"I'll take him," Abby said.

Reese didn't miss the involuntary way that Grayson's lips twitched in a suppressed smile.

"Cool," she said again. "Well, I'm off."

She returned to the truck, leaving the kids in the house.

As she reached the truck, a man shifted in her passenger seat. Reese screeched.

"That's unnecessary," Ethan said.

"Christ." She eased open the door and climbed into the truck, trying to slow her breath. "What are you doing here?"

"I want to know what happened," Ethan prompted. He examined his crystalline nails in the light. "So...what have we learned?"

Reese tried to relax against the seat as she recounted both stories, ending with the revelation that a burst of magic had been used that night.

Ethan's gaze darkened. "Interesting. Coupled with what we already know, that suggests something...very sinister indeed."

"So is this the end of my investigation?" Reese asked. She was aware that Ethan was sitting not twenty feet from the kids.

He surfaced from his thoughts, smiling at her. "You could

help Liam with further investigation…" He let his gaze slide down to her lips. "Unless you're willing to die in order to save us all?"

"That doesn't sound…appealing."

"That's what I thought," he said, with hellfire in his eyes. "But you see the person who has come to town is as strong as I am. I cannot stop her, not truly. Only Vendetta herself can do that. And Vendetta is…unreliable. When I think she will protect herself, she does not. When I think she wouldn't bother, she strikes. I can only be sure that she is safe…that we are *all* safe if I cocoon her in old magic. *Source* magic. Magic like what you have."

Reese Choice 14
Help Liam - go to page 290
Sacrifice Yourself - go to page 113

GRAYSON: TRUST ABBY AND TAKE OFF
THE NECKLACE

Grayson wrapped his hand around the onyx. "Can you get the clasp?"

He leaned toward her, feeling her cold fingers on the back of his neck.

The weight slid off his neck, clinking into her palm. She slid it into a cup holder.

"Thank you for trusting me," she said, her eyes shining. "It's just a small protection spell. I would never do anything that changed your will or something like that."

"I know." He smiled. "So how does it work?"

A crooked grin tugged her lips to one side. "Like this."

She leaned across the console and brushed her mouth against his. Her parting lips invited movement of his own. He opened his mouth and welcomed the brush of her tongue.

A warm tingle ran down his spine, raising the goosebumps on his arms and the back of his neck.

She pulled back from the kiss, panting. "We better get a move on."

"No," he said.

She laughed. "Yes."

She grabbed the pack between her legs and threw open the passenger side door.

"Come on."

Grayson looked at the dashboard clock. It was 12:12. She was right. They were losing daylight.

He stepped from the car into the tall grass. It scratched at his jeans as he rooted in the backseat for his pack. He hefted the pack onto his shoulders and locked up his car. With several long, loping strides he was able to catch Abigail at the edge of the woods.

A shiver ran down his spine as he recollected the illustration from *The Dark Mother and Her Children.* He didn't see any eyes watching him, waiting for him to step vulnerable into the woods. But he suspected there might be creatures here that he couldn't see. This was Castle Cove after all.

Abby took his hand and pulled him into the forest. "I want us out of here before dark. Come on."

The dense canopy overhead immediately blotted out most of the sunlight.

They hadn't even gone twenty feet before he realized he was right about the low light. He'd suspected the covering in this part of the forest was thick, dappling what little sunlight they had.

In the Wayward Woods, he could walk until nearly sunset and count upon the light. The trees weren't as crowded and the wide expanse of bright sky overhead invited hikers to linger in any of the beautiful, open fields surrounding the trails. Lake Trail, in particular, offered a gorgeous view for stargazing. And it was close enough to Sunset Park that one could linger well into the evening and feel relatively safe.

Here the trees seemed to stand almost on top of one another.

They are crowding in on us, he thought. He shivered again.

"We need to get to The Crone Tree within three hours if we can. We can make it if we keep a good pace," he said.

Her head was up. Her eyes were bright. He respected her even more for that. She'd always been smart, probably one of the most brilliant students at their school, but her seriousness—when seriousness was merited—had always impressed him. Landon had been a jokester. He'd laughed at all the wrong moments and whenever the moments had been tense, like when Abigail's father left town and never came back, he'd tried to use laughter to dispel the gloom.

"I don't think we should talk," she whispered.

Grayson agreed so they walked in silence.

First a mile. Then two. By the third mile, his mind had entered a sort of trance state as it often did when he walked. His thoughts flittered away and left him only with the sensation of the experience. His body laboring. Fresh air moving in and out of his chest. A slight sweat forming on his brow and the back of his neck. The shirt trapped between his skin and backpack had grown damp.

He kept walking.

However, it was difficult to traverse the woods with complete stealth. It looked lush and green. The forest floor was thick with spongy moss and soft clover. Their steps should be nearly muted. And yet, it seemed that every snapping twig, every shifting rock betrayed them.

Something is wrong, he thought. The forest was beautiful. Grayson might even have used the word inviting. But he found himself thinking of the story about lost children finding a house made of candy. He was sure the witch's candy house had seemed inviting, too.

The canopy shed sparkling light onto their path as if urging them further, deeper into the woods.

A wild thought visited him then.

This forest is alive. Like a single, sentient creature, it lived. Not only did it live, but it knew they were there and did everything it could to draw them deeper into its yawning maw.

He hesitated on the path.

Abby froze instantly beside him. She looked eager, almost ready to bolt and run the other way.

"Does it feel…." He searched for the right words. Now, the idea that he would come to this forest, that he would look for this damned tree seemed incredibly stupid. "Does it feel alive to you?" he whispered.

When Abby didn't answer, he was worried that perhaps he was too quiet to be heard.

Then she nodded. Her eyes had gone a fraction wider since they'd first entered.

"There's a lot of magic here," she whispered. He saw goose-bumps prickle along her skin. "I've never felt anything like it. There's magic all over Castle Cove, more in some places than others. But this…" She was unable to finish her sentence.

They were almost at the halfway mark in their journey between Vendetta Heights and Druid's Hollow. It seemed silly to turn and run back now after they'd come so far.

His phone buzzed in his bag. Unanswered, the call went to his voicemail, probably on account of the shitty signal. He pulled the phone from his bag and listened to the message.

"Grayson? It's Ms. Monroe. I'm just seeing your note about the books you took. One of those—The Dark Mother and Her Children—is, well, it shouldn't be read. If you haven't read it yet, don't. Just bring it back, please. It's not that you need to worry about the content or anything like that. It's…well…the book has a will of its own."

Grayson wondered what exactly that meant.

"Just don't open the book," she said. Fretfully, she added, "Call me as soon as you get this."

Abby nodded north, suggesting they press on. When he started walking, she seized his arm and shook it. She jabbed her finger north again and he frowned. Once he followed her gaze however, he understood.

There, not a hundred feet away, was a woman.

She was walking away from them. She wore an outfit that looked like equestrian riding breeches and black leather gloves. Her black hair was pulled into a low pony at the nape of her neck. Her boots crossed the forest floor in absolute silence.

She didn't look their way, but the idea that she could pass so close and not see them was unimaginable. Or perhaps she couldn't be bothered by two teenagers wandering the woods. Her incessant stride suggested she had a very important appointment she could not miss. She marched on.

Or it was a trick. Maybe she wasn't a woman at all.

"She doesn't look like a monster," Grayson whispered.

"Looks deceive," Abby replied. "Let's give her room."

They kept their distance, though both parties were headed in the same direction. There were times when they'd seem to lose her as if she were walking three or four times faster than they could manage. She would disappear around a bend, or a rock-face and be gone. But when they arrived, she would always appear again.

Was she adjusting her speed for them? Did she want to be followed?

Grayson ran through the list of dangerous creatures he knew roamed the Western Woods. Dryads, of course, with claws like blades. Wendigos—equally terrifying. But neither of those took the shape of a woman. Perhaps it was a fey. Fey was an umbrella term for any number of creatures who lived on the magic of nature. The nastiest ate children and stole husbands. The best simply hated humans for their part in the world's deforestation.

Perhaps the woman was fey and this game a trick.

What happened when she grew tired of playing with them?

They finished out seven miles, and Grayson checked his watch. He wanted to be mindful of the time. But in fact, in trying to keep up with the woman, they'd managed to cross seven miles before it was even three o'clock. They were making great time. But he was itching from the sweat glistening on his skin. He lifted his shirt and wiped his face.

"We're almost there," Abby said, her own breath labored. "Don't give up on me now. I want to get the hell out of here." She urged him on, setting the pace for the remainder of the hike.

Less than a mile later, the trees broke and the winding path dissolved into an enormous field. In the center of the field, The Crone Tree.

No one needed to tell Grayson this was the tree. Nor did he require any convincing that this was the subject of Castle Cove's oldest lore.

The name was apt. The tree was monstrous and with spindly black limbs. It was like the Indian goddess Kali, black limbed with a thousand twisted arms extended from her. Her branches were full of strange blood-red blossoms unlike any Grayson had seen before. And it sounded as if it were full of birds. No small creatures flittered from branch to branch and yet the chorus seemed to emanate from it.

The trunk itself was knotted in such as a way as to suggest an old, weathered face.

Grayson was pulled from his gawking by an incessant quiver against his spine.

Grayson's backpack vibrated against his back. He mistook it for another call, until he pulled his phone from the pack and found it dark.

It was the book. The *book* vibrated in his hands.

"What's that sound? Do you hear it?" She knelt down beside him and turned her ear as if listening. "God, is it singing?"

All the cautious attention that she'd kept about her as they walked through the woods left her. Her eyes were wild with curiosity now. She bordered on delight.

And Abby was right.

The book was doing something. Vibrating or singing, he couldn't be sure.

"Is it made of the same wood?" she asked. Her finger lovingly traced the cover.

That's when Grayson realized that it *was* wood that encased the pages. How could he have mistaken it for leather before?

"Let's bring them together," Abby said. She looked from the book in his hands to the tree sitting in the center of the field. "Maybe they want to be together."

Her voice had a faraway, dreamy quality to it now. Grayson himself felt as if he was dreaming as he wandered toward the large, imposing tree.

Suddenly, Grayson was knocked off his feet and thrown through the air.

It happened so quickly that he barely processed the feeling of his feet leaving the earth before his abdomen was jerked up and backward. He tumbled to the ground. All his breath left him in a single gush. His pack had hit the earth ten feet away, spraying its contents into the dirt. Somehow, he still held the book.

He sat up in the tall grass, confused.

"Well," someone said. "*That* was unexpected."

It was the woman in the equestrian outfit. Her black boots shone in the sunlight. Her gloved hand went to her hip as she frowned down at Grayson.

That's when Abby stood up, knocking the dirt off her knees. When she saw the woman, she let her backpack slide off her shoulders and took a fighting stance.

The woman seemed amused by this, smiling at Abby over her shoulder as she continued to stand over Grayson. "What have we here?"

Before Abigail could answer, the woman waved her arms in a furious arc as if gathering wind and hurled it in Abby's direction.

But the wind only parted around Abigail, ruffling the tall grass and eliciting groans from the trees behind her.

The gloved hand returned to her hip. "Not bad. But you reek of Miriam. Is it your power you're throwing around or is it the coven's, little girl?"

Abby didn't take the bait. "You all right?"

She spoke to Grayson but her eyes remained fixed on the woman.

"He's fine," the woman replied. "I suspect he's stunned at best. Was that your doing? A hell of a protection spell, if I do say so myself. Of course it could only be that strong if you really loved him."

Abigail's cheeks flushed.

"Oh, you two are *adorable*. But I need a sacrifice if I'm to get the Witching Blade out of this tree. Since I'm a romantic, I'll let you choose. Would you prefer to offer yourself, or watch him die? He'll only leave you anyway. Men are like that. That's what your father did, didn't he? To your mother?"

With a battle scream, Abigail ran at the other woman.

Grayson couldn't be sure what he was seeing. Flames seemed to rip from the woman's hands and sail toward Abigail. But then they only evaporated into thick plumes of smoke before Abigail threw a knee into the woman's chest.

Figures emerged from the trees at full speed.

Dryads, Grayson thought, heart hammering. Or wendigos. Or maybe the mouth of Hell had opened and all manner of creatures were now going to rise up and consume them.

But it wasn't dryads or wendigos.

It was only two women and a man. A lightning crack of energy zipped through the air and the woman in riding gear was thrown off Abigail. She tumbled across the earth and hit the dirt twenty feet from Grayson's left, closer to the tree than anyone.

The woman was on her feet almost instantly, snarling. The

curled lips and animalistic sneer turned her beautiful face into a hideous parody of itself.

Then she saw the woman responsible and her face harnessed a disturbing calm.

"Oh, Miriam, it's just you. I thought it might be an actual threat."

Miriam, a tall woman with wavy brunette hair stood beside Abigail. No, she stood *over* her as if guarding a precious charge.

Where the hell did she come from? Grayson wondered. He'd never seen the woman before.

"Can you get up?" Miriam was looking at the woman, but Abigail was the one who answered.

"Yes." She pulled herself to standing and dusted off her knees.

"And is he all right?" Miriam asked, her eyes flicking toward Grayson for only a moment.

"I think so. Just stunned. He flew pretty far."

Grayson found his voice at last. "I'm okay."

"Good. Get up. We are leaving the forest," Miriam said. Her voice was calm, almost pleasant, but it left no room for argument. "Now."

"No, they aren't," the woman replied, batting dirt from her riding breeches and gloves.

"Do you think you can stop all of us, Hope?" Miriam asked.

Miriam balled her hands and swept them into another beautiful arc. The man beside her did the same. Their hands glowed with soft light.

But before they could attack, the woman named Hope had a trick of her own.

Black smoke poured from her hands, pooling around her feet. It rose up like a blanket and encircled the woman completely.

When it dissipated, she was gone.

A hand seized him and he looked up, surprised to find Ms. Monroe of all people, her hand tightly clasping his arm.

"Get up!" Ms. Monroe yelled. She wrenched him onto his feet. "Run!'

The black man who'd stood guard beside Miriam a moment before grabbed Abigail's pack before trotting over and gathering Grayson's as well.

"Don't worry, mate," he said, seeing Grayson's distressed face. He was shoving the spilled contents back into the backpack. "It's safe as houses with me."

Grayson was surprised by his English accent, but he soon forgot it.

The book was gone. "But the book—"

Ms. Monroe shook it at him. "I've got it, I've got it. Come on!"

Grayson was dragged through the trees as if the Devil himself and all the hounds of Hell were on their heels. The man and Ms. Monroe flanked him, pulling him along so that his pace didn't falter. Abigail and Miriam stayed ahead of them.

We can't do this for eight and a half miles, Grayson thought. His body ached from its collision with the earth. *We can't.*

Yet they dragged on. Ms. Monroe was relentless as any mother who was scared out of her wits by a child's near brush with death.

"Why are we running?" he begged. "She disappeared."

"We aren't worried about Hope!" Ms. Monroe hissed. "Use your eyes boy!"

A terrible crashing through the trees made him wrench his head in the direction of the sound. A dryad was galloping after them. Like a tree come to life, it lumbered forward. Its limbs whipped about its head like uprooted tree branches.

"Dante!" Ms. Monroe yelled.

"I see it!" Dante cursed. Light sparked from his hands. "It's like stunning a stone wall. It only knocks them back for a second!"

"Lift and throw!" Ms. Monroe cried. "Lift and throw. Give us distance."

With another furious flick of his hand, the dryad was tossed through the trees away from them.

"Keep moving!" Miriam called from up ahead. "We've still a long way to go."

And to Grayson it seemed true. He felt like they'd walked for days, not hours. There was no sign of Hope, and the dryads would not give up. At one point they'd collected an entourage of five. No matter how many times they were tossed out of sight by magic they lumbered back.

It seemed enough for the three witches—not including Abigail—to handle.

Or was it two witches.

Grayson had not yet seen Ms. Monroe—who the others kept calling Tabby or Tabitha—cast a single spell.

At long last, the light broke ahead. Grayson was so relieved to see the woods part and the large expanse of Vendetta Heights before him that he collapsed to his knees.

"Not here!" Ms. Monroe hissed again, dragging him forward. "Get in the sunlight."

He obeyed, exiting the woods and falling against the hood of his car. A cherry red hybrid sat beside it.

There was a black woman leaning against the hood of the red Prius. She sighed, visibly relieved at the sight of them. "What happened?"

"Hope Duvani," Miriam said. "Naomi, did you see her?"

"*What?* No," Naomi said. "I thought it was just the book! I should've come with you!"

"No, it was good you were here," Miriam said. She was trying to catch her breath, chest heaving. "The cloaking helped.

I think we would've been found out by more than a few dryads if you hadn't stayed behind to cover us."

"I'm so sorry," Abigail said, chest heaving. She hadn't yet caught her breath. None of them had. "I put everyone in danger. I accept full responsibility for whatever punishment you want to give me. I deserve it."

"Oh my life. Do you hear this?" Dante cut his eyes to Miriam. "What do you have this girl thinkin'?"

"We're your coven, not a tribunal," Naomi said gently. She was smiling at Abigail the way one might regard a small child who has said something funny.

"She's right." Miriam gave Abigail a small smile. "You used your power in service of someone you love. That's exactly how you're supposed to use it, Abigail. There's no blame here."

Abigail's face flushed red. That was twice today someone had informed Grayson that Abigail loved him.

"I don't want to disappoint you or let you think I don't take being a witch seriously. You must think I'm the kind of person who runs into danger like—"

"We don't," Dante said, interrupting.

"I blame the book," Naomi said, fingering her braids.

"Me too," Ms. Monroe said. She was the only one who seemed to be breathing fine again so quickly.

"What's wrong with it?" Grayson asked, realizing that Ms. Monroe still had the book. He reached for it but she pulled back.

"Sorry, but we've got to keep it wrapped up. It's safer that way."

Grayson let his hands fall. "Why?"

"It's a cursed object," Ms. Monroe said, pulling her glasses off her face and cleaning them with the bottom of her shirt. There was a smudge of dirt on the side of her nose. "A cursed object with one objective, to lure human sacrifices to The Crone Tree."

"Certainly looked that way from what I saw. The moment I

looked at it, all I wanted to do was go to the tree," Abigail said. "But how could a book do that?"

Ms. Monroe pushed the glasses back up on her nose. "The printer, Bentley Yorkshire, believed that the demons might've tampered with his printing press as a joke. He recorded in his ledger that he found shards of strange tree bark in the press's gears and leftover sheets of paper that 'could absorb blood.'"

"I wonder how he discovered that trick," Dante said with a snort.

"Either way, the press made seven copies of that damned book before it was shut down. Most were gathered up and disposed of before they could get into human hands."

Grayson didn't miss the way she said human hands, as if that didn't include her.

Miriam lifted her hair off her neck, welcoming the breeze that rolled across the Heights. "Four copies have been found over the centuries—this one is the fifth. They were all disposed of properly, but there is a fear that the others might've made it out into the world."

"Maybe this is good news then," Dante said. "Maybe they're here in Castle Cove somewhere."

"I wish you'd been wearing the onyx I gave you." Ms. Monroe turned to Grayson. "Perhaps it would've protected you from the book's sway."

"No," Grayson piped up. He was beginning to feel better now that they were out of the woods and the book was away from him. "I was wearing it before we went into the forest. It didn't protect me from the stupid idea in the first place."

He thought of the night before, of the way he'd felt when he'd opened the book and began reading the story. Who knew a book could possess a person?

"I'm glad he didn't wear it," Naomi countered. "If he had, we would've never found you."

"You'd both be dead," Miriam agreed. She gave Grayson a disapproving look as if he was to blame.

"Thank you," he said, finding his manners at last. "Thank you for helping us."

They shrugged him off.

"What I want to know is why Hope is here. And by The Crone Tree of all places. There's no reason," Naomi said.

"Yes, it would help to know what she was after," Miriam said, her eyes looking across the road to the ocean beyond. "No doubt the trouble around town with the sirens and graveyard can be blamed on her."

"The Witching Blade," Abby said. She was looking at her arm, inspecting a scratch she'd received from a tree branch during their escape. "She said she wanted The Witching Blade."

The witches exchanged furtive glances, before Miriam fixed her with a hard gaze. "Are you sure?"

"Of course she's sure," Naomi said. "How would she even know that name unless she'd heard it?"

"This is bad," Ms. Monroe said. She squeezed the book tighter against her chest. "Really bad."

Miriam turned and considered the ocean for a long time. No one moved or spoke. Grayson wondered what that must be like, to have so much authority that people literally just stood around, waiting for you to give orders.

"We need to speak to Ethan," Miriam said finally.

"When?" Dante asked.

"Now." Miriam moved toward the cars. "Come on."

When Abby and Grayson hesitated, she jerked her head.

"You too," she said, throwing open her car door. "He might need to speak to you."

They departed, with Grayson driving his car. Abby rode shotgun as they followed Miriam's Prius onto Canyon Road then Midnight Pass.

He thought they might make it all the way to the interstate

when the Prius suddenly slowed and its blinker came on. It flashed, signaling a turn.

"There's nothing here," he said, incredulously.

"You can't see it?" Abby asked. She gave him a curious look. When he shook his head, she added. "There's a road there. On the left. It must be concealed with magic."

Again he was confronted with the idea that Abby was a witch. That Abby, unbeknownst to him, had crossed that line without his knowing.

Had they been heading for this shift even before the horrible night in the cove? Had it always been only a matter of time before they crossed the line between worlds?

Abby was fully on the other side of that line now. But where was he?

Maybe that's what his question about college—about what kind of life he saw his future self in—was really about. What kind of life did he want? Which world did he want to live in?

"What are you thinking about so hard?" Abby asked.

"Nothing," he said. He turned onto the dirt road.

The smell of salty ocean air filled the car.

The road was clogged with thick foliage from overgrown brush on both sides of the road. Grayson hissed as branches scraped at the sides of his car. He expected dips and ruts, but the road was smooth.

"He probably forces the branches back," Abby said.

"What do you mean?"

She makes a motion with her hands. "Like with his mind. Ethan is really powerful, probably the most powerful demon in town, from what I hear."

"We are driving to a demon's house?" he asked. He wasn't sure how he should feel about that.

"Honestly, no one can be sure of what he is. He walks in daylight, and demons can't do that." The trees broke open and a two-story Spanish villa sprang into view. The dirt road turned to beautiful paving stones that circled in front of the house. In the center of the roundabout was a fountain bubbling softly with turquoise water.

Miriam parked her car in front of the cream-colored steps. Grayson parked behind her and got out of the car. With his dirty clothes he felt wholly underdressed for a place like this. He was sure someone who'd just run more than half a marathon through the woods to save their lives didn't look or smell too great. But his self-consciousness was obliterated by the gorgeous ocean view. It sparkled like champagne in the late afternoon sun.

"Somethin' is wrong," Dante said behind him, breaking the spell.

"Yes, I see that," Miriam answered.

Grayson followed their gaze and found the front door to Ethan's house had a giant hole blasted out of it. It hung on its hinges.

"What in the world could do that?" Abby asked.

"Hope," said Naomi and Ms. Monroe at the same time.

"They should stay in the car," Miriam said and Grayson realized that she meant him and Abby.

"What if she finds 'im there and kills 'im?" Dante asked.

"I could stay with them," Ms. Monroe offered, a hand resting on top of her bristly orange hair. The hope was evident in her tone.

"No, Tabby, I want you to be my eyes." Miriam sighed. "We'd better stay together then."

Ms. Monroe visibly deflated as Miriam nodded toward the door. "You first."

"I was afraid you'd say that." Ms. Monroe sighed. "All right."

Then the woman who'd been Grayson's boss for the last two years did something he'd never expected. She transformed.

Into a cat.

The stark orange hair that always jutted uncontrollably from her head smoothed itself onto the sleek, lithe body of a house cat. And not just any cat. But the cat that he'd known as Pumpkin.

"She—" he began but could only point at the cat. "Shit."

Abby grinned. "You didn't know? At least I'm not the only one."

Ms. Monroe stepped out of her human clothes and trotted up the cream-colored steps into the house. The five of them—Miriam, Dante, Naomi, Abigail and himself—lingered on the steps, looking around at the approaching night darkening the distant horizon.

It was nearly fifteen minutes before Ms. Monroe returned. By then the cricket song had swollen to a full cacophony and the ocean waves had nearly lulled Grayson into a doze.

As soon as he realized Ms. Monroe was transforming back into her human form, Grayson turned around quickly. He didn't want to see the woman whose shelves he stocked, *naked*, even in twilight.

"They're in the crypt below. There's only one way in and out. I heard voices."

"Hope?" Miriam asked.

Ms. Monroe shrugged. "Maybe. It was hard to tell."

"We need to see him," Miriam decided at last. Then she turned on Abigail and gave her a stern look. "You'll have to keep him close."

Abigail nodded, stepping closer to Grayson.

They followed Ms. Monroe into the house as she led them through the labyrinth of lavish rooms. Grayson had always suspected that the mayor of the town was wealthy. Not only because of his position but because he was one of the oldest residents in town. It was likely he'd had centuries to acquire and stockpile his wealth.

But seeing it with his own eyes was something else. He felt like he was in a museum, surrounded by paintings and tapestries. It looked like Ethan had raided the Palace of Versailles or something.

Finally they came to a study. The walls were replaced with floor-to-ceiling bookcases made of dark wood. Red fabric couches and highbacked chairs rounded out the decor. Ms. Monroe approached a fireplace with twin carved panthers of black stone flanking each side. She placed her hand on the right panther and the fireplace shifted. A passageway appeared behind the flames.

"It won't burn you," Ms. Monroe whispered. "Just step through."

She waited for someone else to take the lead and Miriam obliged. Dante crossed in after her with Naomi in third position.

Then Ms. Monroe was waving Grayson and Abby forward. "I'll be right behind you!"

Grayson crossed the threshold. The flames felt like a cool breeze on his skin, but he passed through them without feeling pain.

Ahead was a spiral staircase. Grayson was behind Abigail, following her down. The air grew colder with each step. It felt as if they were underground now, with only the cold earth pressing in against them in all directions.

When he reached the bottom of the stairs, he saw several things at once.

First, the walkway that he was forced to step out onto in order for Ms. Monroe to exit the stairs. The walkway had only one direction, straight ahead to a stone coffin. The lid of this coffin had been thrown across the room. It lay broken in three large pieces against the far wall.

It had collided with some of the stone carvings lining the walls. It gave Grayson the impression he was in an old temple, surveying ancient etchings of fallen gods.

The only two people in the room—Ethan and the woman—

each stood on one side of the stone coffin. Ethan was on the left, the woman on the right. Their gazes were locked.

Then a shadow moved and Grayson realized there was a third person. A tall, attractive man who looked vaguely familiar. He'd seen him before, but he couldn't be sure where.

"Do not mind the mess, my friends," Ethan said calmly. But he didn't take his gaze off of the woman. "Hope is a chaos demon. She can hardly help herself."

"I'm so much more than that!" the woman hissed. Her face took on a hideous snarl. "I'm her chevalier. Just as well as you! You have no more right to her than I do!"

Hope jabbed her finger into the center of the coffin each time she said the word *her*.

Grayson wasn't sure he wanted to see *her*, whoever might be entombed here.

"You weren't successful in getting the blade," Ethan said calmly. "This isn't going to work."

"It will work," Hope snarled. "It *will*."

"All that Ydril told you was untrue," Ethan said calmly. He placed one hand on the coffin's stone. "I know you spoke to him at Crossroads, but you didn't like his answer."

"He said the blade was in the ocean. That the sirens had it."

"He deceived you," Ethan said.

"Yeah, well, I didn't realize every piece of shit in this town was loyal to you," Hope hissed, her fingers gripping her edge of the coffin. "They won't be once they know what a coward you are."

"So how did you learn the blade was in the forest?" Ethan asked.

"It doesn't matter," Hope said.

"Because you didn't manage to get it. You can't do a full resurrection without it."

"I don't need to! I'm her chevalier. She *chose* me, Ethan. And you've hated me ever since."

"My queen does as she pleases. I would never question her will."

Hope snorted. "Then watch this."

"I wouldn't," Ethan warned.

But Hope's eyes had already filled with red fire. Her teeth elongated and tore open her wrist in a single vicious bite.

Ethan made the smallest movement in Miriam's direction and all hell broke loose. Three curses, thrown by three witches —Miriam, Naomi, and Dante—flew across the room at once.

A second after the red sparks flew from the end of her fingertips, Miriam shouted at them over her shoulder. "Shield, Tabby! Now!"

Before he understood what was happening, Ms. Monroe had shoved Grayson and Abby into the far corner of the room. She'd forced them both down into crouches, as if making them the smallest targets possible and with walls on their sides and back.

The only problem, was Ms. Monroe looked ridiculous with her arms thrown out in front of her, as if she would physically intercept any attack thrown their way. Until one of the dozens of curses hurled around the room did in fact sail in their direction.

"Ms. Monroe!" Grayson screamed. But he needn't have bothered. The spell hit the air inches in front of the bookshop owner and rippled the air around them. Ms. Monroe was in fact, somehow shielding them.

Dante flew across the room and slammed into the wall with a *humph.*

"Come on!" Ms. Monroe cried and the three of them crossed the rubble strewn floor toward the unconscious witch. "Abby!"

"On it!" Once she was in range and safely behind Ms. Monroe's shield, Abby began working on Dante. She rolled the man over and without a second thought, opened his shirt.

Grayson's mouth fell open

"Don't look at me like that," Abby hissed. "I need to concentrate."

"Sorry," Grayson said and did his best to school his features. But he was sure that his shock and amazement was showing through as he watched the tips of Abby's fingers begin to glow. Soft, light seeped into Dante's chest, building and brightening with each passing moment.

Abby's eyes were closed, her mouth moving in an inaudible incantation. With her face in concentration like that and her face awash in the soft, magical light, Grayson thought she'd never looked so beautiful.

I'll be with her forever, he thought. He wasn't sure if this was precognition or wishful thinking, but the words felt true either way. *From right now until the day I die.*

Dante's eyes fluttered open.

"How do you feel?" Abby asked.

Dante grinned. "All right. Thanks for stitching me up, love."

Abby grabbed his hand and squeezed.

A blood curdling scream tore through the room and all eyes went to it.

Ethan had the woman by the throat. Blood was burbling up between his fingers as her mouth opened and closed like a fish out of water.

"You shouldn't have come here," he said. The calm didn't match the violence.

And with one furious throw, he dashed the woman against the wall. Her skull cracked open and its contents sprayed across the floor.

Everyone else stood there as if unsure what to do next.

Ethan looked around the broken wreckage of the temple. He stepped on a piece of stone and crushed it under his foot, rendering it to powder on the bottom of his black dress shoe.

"That's *twice* someone has come into my house looking for

her," Ethan said, touching the edge of the stone coffin lovingly. "Liam, I will have to move her."

The tall man that Grayson recognized from somewhere, hooked his arms around the demon's waist. "We'll find somewhere safe."

Ms. Monroe tugged on Grayson's sleeve and nodded toward the stairs. "Let's get out of here."

"Before you go," Ethan called as the five of them stood crowded at the base of the stone steps.

Miriam spoke for them. "We came to tell you what we learned of Hope's plans—now that we're not needed—"

"I know." Ethan held up his hands, making it clear he didn't intend to keep them. "I only wanted to thank you, heartily, for your assistance here tonight. If your arrival had not distracted her, perhaps it would have gone quite differently."

"You're welcome," Miriam said. She seemed to be the only one with the courage to speak to the man who was soaked up to his elbows in the dead woman's blood.

They left the villa in silence. Before Grayson and Abigail climbed into his car, Miriam called out. "Abigail."

"Yes?" Abigail sounded nervous, even to Grayson.

"You did well today. Be proud of yourself."

Abigail beamed. "Thank you, Miriam."

They waved toward the departing coven and followed the car back to the road.

"Do you want me to take you straight home?" Grayson asked as Castle Cove's lights came into view. Night had arrived. The city was awake.

"No," she said. "I'm too wound up after everything. You would think I wouldn't be after the hike but—"

"I know what you mean," he said. "How about Sam's Soda and Shakes? We did cover like seventeen miles and a full-out monster battle—twice. I think that merits milkshakes."

It was a diner in Old Town a couple blocks from the First

Night Theater. They specialized in burgers, fries and had an old-fashioned soda counter. After the long and physically exhausting day, Grayson thought he could eat three burgers alone.

Abigail smiled. "Sure. And then we'll live happily ever after."

Grayson couldn't keep the grin off his face.

"After we go to UCLA for four years," she said. "Of course."

"UCLA?" he stuttered.

"I was accepted. Or we could go to CCU if you want. I got in there, too. Oh, don't look so surprised. My grades are way better than yours." Abigail smiled and twined her fingers in his.

He wanted Abby, without a doubt. The events of the last few days had made her time with him seem incredibly precious. But he was still surprised that she wanted *him*.

"Are you sure you want to be with me?" he asked. "You can have anyone."

"But I deserve to have who I want, don't I?"

"Yes. But are you sure—?"

She didn't even let him finish. "Grayson. I've never been more sure of anything."

The End

Create a new story - go back to the beginning

GRAYSON: LEAVE THE ONYX ON

Grayson wrapped his hand around the onyx. "But I don't want to take it off."

"Of course you do." She looked out the window, searching Canyon Road. No doubt she was hoping the cavalry would arrive.

"It's not that I don't trust you," he was quick to add, only that he wasn't sure how to end that statement. "I just want to wear it."

"That's fine." She grabbed the pack between her legs and threw open the passenger side door. "We better get a move on."

Grayson looked at the dashboard clock. It was 12:12. She was right. They were losing daylight.

He stepped from the car into the tall grass. He hefted the pack onto his shoulders and locked up his car. With several long, loping strides he was able to catch Abigail at the edge of the woods.

A shiver ran down his spine as he recollected the illustration from *The Dark Mother and Her Children.* He didn't see any eyes watching him, waiting for him to step vulnerable into the woods. But he suspected there might be creatures here that he couldn't see. This was Castle Cove after all.

Abby took his hand and pulled him into the forest. "I want us out of here before dark. Come on."

The dense canopy overhead immediately blotted out most of the sunlight.

They hadn't even gone twenty feet before he realized he was right about the low light. He'd suspected the covering in this part of the forest was thick, dappling what little sunlight they had.

In the Wayward Woods, he could walk until nearly sunset and count upon the light. The trees weren't as crowded and the wide expanse of bright sky overhead invited hikers to linger in any of the beautiful, open fields surrounding the trails. Lake Trail, in particular, offered a gorgeous view for stargazing. And it was close enough to Sunset Park that one could linger well into the evening and feel relatively safe.

Here the trees seemed to stand almost on top of one another. *They are crowding in on us*, he thought. He shivered again.

"We need to get to The Crone Tree within three hours if we can. We can make it if we keep a good pace," he said.

Her head was up. Her eyes were bright. He respected her even more for that. She'd always been smart, probably one of the most brilliant students at their school, but her seriousness—when seriousness was merited—is what impressed him. Landon had been a jokester. He'd laughed at all the wrong moments and whenever the moments had been tense, like when Abigail's father left town and never came back, he'd tried to use laughter to dispel the gloom.

"I don't think we should talk," she whispered.

Grayson agreed so they walked in silence.

First a mile. Then two. By the third mile, his mind had entered a sort of trance state as it often did when he walked. His thoughts flittered away and left him only with the sensation of the experience. His body laboring. Fresh air moving in and out of his chest. A slight sweat forming on his brow and the back of his neck. The shirt trapped between his skin and backpack had grown damp.

He kept walking.

However, it was difficult to traverse the woods with complete stealth. It looked lush and green. The forest floor was thick with spongy moss and soft clover. Their steps should be nearly muted. And yet, it seemed that every snapping twig, every shifting rock betrayed them.

Something is wrong, he thought. The forest was beautiful. Grayson might even have used the word inviting. But he found himself thinking of the story about lost children finding a house made of candy. He was sure the witch's candy house had seemed inviting, too.

The canopy shed sparkling light onto their path as if urging them further, deeper into the woods.

A wild thought visited him then.

This forest is alive. Like a single, sentient creature, it lived. Not only did it live, but it knew they were there and did everything it could to draw them deeper into its yawning maw.

He hesitated on the path.

Abby froze instantly beside him. She looked eager, almost ready to bolt and run the other way.

"Does it feel…." He searched for the right words. Now, the idea that he would come to this forest, that he would look for this damned tree seemed incredibly stupid. "Does it feel alive to you?" he whispered.

When Abby didn't answer, he was worried that perhaps he was too quiet to be heard.

Then she nodded. Her eyes had gone a fraction wider since when they'd first entered.

"There's a lot of magic here," she whispered. He saw goosebumps prickle along her skin. "I've never felt anything like it."

They were almost at the halfway mark in their journey between Vendetta Heights and Druid's Hollow. It seemed silly to turn and run back now after they'd come so far.

His phone buzzed in his bag. Unanswered, the call went to his voicemail, probably on account of the shitty signal. He pulled the phone from his bag and listened to the message.

"Grayson? It's Ms. Monroe. I'm just seeing your note about the books you took. One of those—The Dark Mother and Her Children—is, well, it shouldn't be read. If you haven't read it yet, don't. Just bring it back, please. It's not that you need to worry about the content or anything like that. It's…well…the book has a will of its own."

Grayson wondered what exactly that meant.

"Just don't open the book," she said. Fretfully, she added, "Call me as soon as you get this."

Abby nodded north, suggesting they press on. When he started walking, she seized his arm and shook it. She jabbed her finger north again and he frowned. Once he followed her gaze however, he understood.

There, not a hundred feet away, was a woman.

She was walking away from them. She wore an outfit that looked like equestrian riding breeches and black leather gloves. Her black hair was pulled into a low pony at the nape of her neck. Her boots crossed the forest floor in absolute silence.

She didn't look their way, but the idea that she could pass so close and not see them was unimaginable. Or perhaps she couldn't be bothered by two teenagers wandering the woods. Her incessant stride suggested she had a very important appointment she could not miss. She marched on.

Or it was a trick. Maybe she wasn't a woman at all.

"She doesn't look like a monster," Grayson whispered.

"Looks deceive," Abby replied. "Let's give her room."

They kept their distance, though both parties were headed in the same direction. There were times when they'd seem to lose her as if she were walking three or four times faster than they could manage. She would disappear around a bend, or a rockface and be gone. But when they arrived, she would always appear again.

Was she adjusting her speed for them? Did she want to be followed?

Grayson ran through the list of dangerous creatures he knew roamed the Western Woods. Dryads, of course, with claws like blades. Wendigos—equally terrifying. But neither of those took the shape of a woman. Perhaps it was a fey. Fey was an umbrella term for any number of creatures who lived on the magic of nature. The nastiest ate children and stole husbands. The best simply hated humans for their part in the world's deforestation.

Perhaps the woman was fey and this game a trick.

What happened when she grew tired of playing with them?

They finished out seven miles, and Grayson checked his watch. He wanted to be mindful of the time. But in fact, in trying to keep up with the woman, they'd managed to cross seven miles before it was even three o'clock. They were making great time. But he was itching from the sweat glistening on his skin. He lifted his shirt and wiped his face.

"We're almost there," Abby said, her own breath labored. "Don't give up on me now. I want to get the hell out of here." She urged him on, setting the pace for the remainder of the hike.

Less than a mile later, the trees broke and the winding path dissolved into an enormous field. In the center of the field, The Crone Tree.

No one needed to tell Grayson this was the tree. Nor did he require any convincing that this was the subject of Castle Cove's oldest lore.

The name was apt. The tree was monstrous and with spindly black limbs. It was like the Indian goddess Kali, black limbed with a thousand twisted arms extended about her. Her branches were full of strange blood-red blossoms unlike any Grayson had seen before. And it sounded as if it were full of birds. No small creatures flittered from branch to branch and yet the chorus seemed to emanate from it.

The trunk itself was knotted in such as a way as to suggest an old, weathered face.

Grayson was pulled from his gawking by an incessant quiver against his spine.

Grayson's backpack vibrated against his back. He mistook it for another call, until he pulled his phone from the pack and found it dark.

It was the book. The *book* vibrated in his hands.

"What's that sound? Do you hear it?" She knelt down beside him and turned her ear as if listening. "God, is it singing?"

All the cautious attention that she'd kept about her as they walked through the woods left her. Her eyes were wild with curiosity now. She bordered on delight.

And she was right.

The book was doing something. Vibrating or singing, he couldn't be sure.

"Is it made of the same wood?" she asked. Her finger lovingly traced the cover.

That's when Grayson realized that it *was* wood that encased the pages. How could he have mistaken it for leather before?

"Let's bring them together," Abby said. She looked from the book in his hands to the tree sitting in the center of the field. "Maybe they want to be together."

Her voice had a faraway, dreamy quality to it now. Her eyes had glazed. Grayson himself felt as if he had entered a dream. His body moved of its own accord toward the large, imposing tree.

They'd almost reached it when a hand shot out and snatched

the back of Abigail's neck. The fierce hand wrenched her head back, stretching Abby's pale throat.

It was the woman in the equestrian riding gear.

This close she didn't look fey. But what did Grayson know?

The woman's hand shredded Abby's clothes and slid under her rib cage as easily as a Mayan blade adept at human sacrifice. Abby's scream ripped Grayson's soul in two. He couldn't bear the sound of it. When it was cut short, it was both a blessing and curse. Abby's crumpled body fell to the ground between their feet.

I'm not seeing this, he thought. *This isn't happening. This is a terrible, terrible dream.*

But he was.

The woman was lifting a red heart to her lips and she was sucking it. No, *eating* it.

"I'll be with you in a minute," the woman said, her blood-stained teeth pulled into an awful grin as fire-filled eyes met Grayson's. "It's better warm, you see. I can barely get it down when it's cold."

Grayson fell to the ground, aware that the crumpled form before him was Abby.

Abby. Abby. Hot tears streamed from the corner of his eyes.

"Now," the woman purred. She climbed onto Grayson, straddling him. Her warm pelvis pressed into his stomach. Her eyes were dilated, her mouth and cheeks smeared with Abby's blood. "Thanks for waiting for me, lover."

She bent and kissed him full on the mouth.

Grayson wanted to scream. Grayson wanted to throw her off and kill her with his bare hands.

But he remained frozen, pinned to this earth with invisible force.

"Oh yes, this feels good," she said, running her bloody hands over Grayson's chest, shredding his clothes as she went. "Your friend had a lot of juice running through her veins. Give her ten or twenty years of decent training and she would've been a hell of a witch. She would've been running the coven for sure. Maybe she would've been running the town."

Then she laughed.

"Too late now."

"Fuck you," Grayson managed.

"We could try sex magic," she said, with a salacious grin. "But that only works if you're a virgin. So no point in raping you. Unless you'd like one more go of it before you die?" She caressed his face again. "I wouldn't mind."

Her fingers tightened on his chin. She lifted her head as if listening to something. "There's the dryads. They can smell the blood," she said, wistfully. "I better finish up here or I'll have my work cut out for me."

She lifted Grayson off the ground and hauled him to the tree. She shoved his aching body against the rough bark. From this angle, he could see Abby, her crumpled body motionless in the grass, her hollow eyes vacant. The woman's black gloves lay on the ground by her head.

"It's nothing personal," the woman said. "I hope you know that. But I need the Witching Blade. I thought the sirens had it, but that was a lie. It was always hidden in the tree."

Grayson's chest exploded with black fire. That sound was him screaming. That thump in his chest was his own wounded heart resisting the probing fingers that would crush it.

Or perhaps it was the tree's heartbeat.

It certainly felt like the branches were twining around him, pulling his body into its trunk. The woman was smiling. The bird song swelled to an ear-splitting chorus that ricocheted in his brain.

Darkness pressed in on the corners of his vision.

The woman didn't seem to notice. She only smiled. "That's a good boy."

He wondered if she would keep smiling once the galloping dryad closing in fast reached her.

Grayson didn't know.

For him, the world went black before the beasts arrived.

The End
Create a new story - go back to the beginning

GRAYSON: DON'T BRING ABBY

He didn't respond to her text. Instead, he put his cell phone on silent and slipped it into his backpack. It was easier this way. She would try to talk him out of it and he had to go. He had to.

Maybe it was the exhaustion, but Grayson felt as if he were in a dream as he drove through town. Before he knew it, he found himself at the four-way stop at the edge of town. Across the street sat The Crossroads, a demon bar where humans could make literal deals with the devil. Or devils.

South Beach bloomed on his left, revealing sandy beaches and blue-grey water. On his right was the open fields known as Vendetta Heights. It was premier make-out spot and vampire feeding ground after dark. All the more reason to make it back to the car before the sunset. Grayson drove until he thought he was about parallel to the place known as Druid's Hollow.

It was eight or nine miles deep into the woods, but no need in making the journey longer by parking too far away.

Satisfied that this was his best guess for its location, he pulled off the road and parked.

Grayson glanced at the dashboard clock. It was 11:32. Daylight was still on his side.

He stepped from the car into the tall grass. He hefted the pack onto his shoulders and locked up his car.

The forest loomed before him.

A shiver ran down his spine as he recollected the illustration from *The Dark Mother and Her Children*. He didn't see any eyes watching him, waiting for him to step vulnerable into the woods. But he suspected there might be creatures here that he couldn't see. This was Castle Cove after all.

The dense canopy overhead immediately blotted out most of the sunlight.

He hadn't even gone twenty feet before he realized he had been right about the low light. He'd suspected the covering in this part of the forest was thick, dappling what little sunlight they had.

In the Wayward Woods, he could walk until nearly sunset and count upon the light. The trees weren't as crowded and the wide expanse of bright sky invited hikers to linger in any of the beautiful, open fields surrounding the trails. Lake Trail, in particular, offered a gorgeous view for stargazing. And it was close enough to Sunset Park that one could linger well into the evening and feel relatively safe because of its proximity to town.

Here the trees seemed to stand almost on top of one another.

They are crowding in on you, he thought. He shivered again.

He needed to get to The Crone Tree within three hours. If he kept a good pace, he could do it.

He walked in silence, or as silent as was possible given the thick forest floor.

First a mile. Then two. By the third mile, his mind had entered a sort of trance state as it often did when he hiked. His thoughts flittered away and left him only with the sensation of the experience. His body labored. Fresh air moving in and out of his chest. A slight sweat formed on his brow.

However, it was difficult to traverse the woods with complete stealth. It looked lush and green. The forest floor was thick with spongy moss and soft clover. His steps should be nearly muted. And yet, it seemed that every snapping twig, every shifting rock betrayed him.

Something is wrong, he thought. The forest was beautiful. Grayson might even have used the word inviting. But he found himself thinking of the story about lost children finding a house made of candy. He was sure the witch's candy house had seemed inviting, too.

The canopy cast sparkling light onto his path as if urging him further, deeper into the woods.

A wild thought visited him then.

This forest is alive. Like a single, sentient creature, it lived. Not only did it live, but it knew he was there and did everything it could to draw him deeper into its yawning maw.

He hesitated on the path.

On the path, he realized.

Why was there a path in these unruly woods? Worse, why did he feel like it was forming before his very eyes. It could be a trick of the light, or the forest could actually be leading him deeper into its gullet.

He was almost at the halfway mark in his journey between Vendetta Heights and Druid's Hollow. It seemed silly to turn and run back now after he'd come so far. And it wasn't lost on him that the path behind wasn't nearly as inviting. It was darker. The roots and brush seemed to grow up behind him.

Why leave? a little voice in his mind asked. *Hadn't he wanted to explore these woods all his life?* And he was finally here. *There are no monsters. Have you seen even one?*

His phone buzzed in his bag but he didn't reach it before the call went to voicemail.

He listened to the message.

"Grayson? It's Ms. Monroe. I'm just seeing your note about

the books you took. One of those—The Dark Mother and Her Children—is, well, it shouldn't be read. If you haven't read it yet, don't. Just bring it back, please. It's not that you need to worry about the content or anything like that. It's…well…the book has a will of its own."

Grayson wondered what exactly that meant.

"Just don't open the book," she added, fretfully. "Call me as soon as you get this."

Grayson put his phone back in his bag and resumed hiking.

Less than an hour later, the treelined broke and the winding path dissolved into an enormous field. In the center of the field sat The Crone Tree.

No one needed to tell Grayson this was the tree. Nor did he require any convincing that this was the subject of Castle Cove's oldest lore.

The name was apt. The tree was monstrous and with spindly black limbs. It was like the Indian goddess Kali, black limbed with a thousand twisted arms extended about her. Her branches were full of strange blood-red blossoms unlike any Grayson had seen before. And it sounded as if it were full of birds, yet no small creatures flittered from branch to branch.

The trunk itself was knotted in such as a way as to suggest an old, weathered face.

Grayson was pulled from his gawking by an incessant quiver against his spine.

Grayson's backpack seemed to vibrate against his back. He mistook it for another call, until he pulled out his phone and found its screen dark.

It was the book.

The book vibrated in his hand.

Bring us together, he thought. *The book and the tree. We want to be together.*

In a dreamy haze he stumbled forward, holding the book out the way a child offers a toy to its mother. He'd almost reached the tree when a hand shot out and snatched the back of Grayson's neck. He dropped the book.

She stepped into his view, but never relinquished her hold on his neck. It was a woman in equestrian riding gear. Pants, vest and riding boots. Her hands were in black leather gloves.

Or maybe she wasn't a woman. Maybe she was a creature pretending to be a woman. How could he be sure?

I'm not seeing this, he thought. *This isn't happening.*

But it was.

Grayson wanted to throw her off, but he remained frozen, pinned by an invisible force stronger than the woman's grip.

"Hello," she said, running her hands over Grayson's chest. "What's your name, handsome?"

"Fuck you," Grayson managed.

"We could try sex magic," she said, grinning. "But that only works if you're a virgin. So no point in raping *you*, hmmm? Unless you'd like one more go of it before you die?" She caressed his face again. "I wouldn't mind."

Her fingers tightened on his chin.

She threw him against the tree. She shoved his aching body against the rough bark.

"It's nothing personal," the woman said, scraping her free hand down the front of his chest. She shredded his clothes with one swipe, exposing his skin to the cool breeze. "I hope you know that. But I need the Witching Blade. And the crone won't give me the blade without a sacrifice."

First the soft, almost tender brush of fingers. Then Grayson's chest exploded with black fire. That ear-splitting sound was him screaming. That thump in his chest was his own wounded heart resisting the probing fingers trying to grab ahold of it.

Or perhaps it was the tree's heartbeat.

It certainly felt like the branches were twining around him, pulling his body into its trunk. The woman was smiling. The bird song swelled to an overbearing cacophony that ricocheted in his brain.

Darkness pressed in on the corners of his vision until only the pain remained.

And something that smelled of ancient magic and old earth.

Then there was only the pain, a world blacker than black, and bird song that would never end.

The End
Create a new story - go back to the beginning

REESE: HELP LIAM

Reese was instructed to meet Liam at Two Doves Cemetery. Reese navigated her rumbling red pickup through the Castle Cove streets, considering the task ahead. The idea of traipsing around a cemetery with a vampire after dark was not all that appealing.

It wasn't that she was afraid of the vampire, of the dark, or all those dead people under the ground. She only hoped there would be no labor involved. She was tired. And when tired, gravedigging wasn't even in her top fifty choices for how she'd like to spend an evening.

When she pulled into the cemetery parking lot, she found Liam leaning against the trunk of his BMW, his ankles crossed and hands in his pockets. Reese thought he looked a little like Zac Efron with his hair swooped up and back and that burgundy silk scarf wrapped around his neck.

She parked beside him and climbed out. "You late for your Esquire photoshoot or something?"

She hoped his outfit meant that no digging would be involved—or he expected her to do it.

He spared her a wry half-smile. "This shouldn't take too long. Hopefully."

He began crossing the parking lot to the wood-chipped footpath ahead.

She fell into step beside him. "What are we doing here?"

"Someone reported grave vandalism."

Reese frowned. "Isn't that something the police should handle?"

Liam snorted, continuing his long, easy stride even as the path steepened. "It is. Until they call Ethan."

"So what does that make you?" she asked. "The deputy?"

His smile deepened. "I see why Kristine likes you so much."

"Thanks. I think."

As the path ended, the vampire's eyes swept the cemetery. "Over here."

She followed him in silence. Twilight purpled around them, the shadows thickening beneath the trees that bordered the cemetery. They seemed to elongate like fingers stretching toward them.

Don't, she warned. *You'll whip yourself into hysterics with thoughts like that.*

But then she saw the ghosts, rising like mist from the graves. She stiffened, her stride faltering.

Liam turned back, frowning at her. "What?"

"Are you seeing this?" Reese pointed at the mist materializing in front of the grave two rows over.

Liam followed her finger. "The ghosts? They're fine. They won't bother us. I don't think they can even see us."

He resumed his walk. As she watched the phantoms rise from their graves and then float in whichever direction suited them—Reese counted eight—she saw he was right. They were neither coming this way nor showing signs that they knew they were here.

Relief softened the rock in her stomach—until she turned

and saw Liam had gotten away from her. She took off at a run to catch up. It was hard to keep her balance over the uneven ground. Some graves seemed to be rising, others sinking. The scent of fresh earth pressed in on her.

She almost yipped with joy when she found him, crouching down in front of a crooked stone.

"Come here," he commanded pointing at the ground. "This is what I needed you for."

"What?" But as soon as the word was out of her mouth, Reese saw what he was pointing at. There was a hole where the grave should be. Someone had crudely exhumed the body. The dirt was gone, piled behind the tombstone itself. It wasn't crooked, she realized. It was half buried. In the grave was the unopened casket.

"What do you need me to do *exactly?*" Reese asked, relieved that the vandal had done the labor himself—or herself. But also terrified that he was going to ask her to climb into the grave.

"Can you feel any magic?" he asked. "I need to know if magic was used here."

"Why are you asking me?"

"I can't feel it," he said. "An undead vampire could. But living vampires can't. *I* can't."

Reese sniffed the air. "No. I don't feel anything."

Liam sighed. "Damn. I was hoping you wouldn't say that."

A cold hand clamped onto Reese's shoulder and she shrieked.

"Hell's Bells," Violet hissed. The leather clad demon took a step back. "Shut up, would you?"

Liam stood, brushing dirt from his knees. "You scared her."

"You think, bloodsucker? And she busted both my ear drums." Violet stuck a finger in her ear and twisted it. "Remind me never to take you to a haunted house. Or a scary movie for that matter."

"What are you doing here?" Reese demanded. She had one hand over her chest as if trying to hold her heart in.

Violet crossed her arms. "I *was* going to ask if it was true that you were dumb enough to help Ethan investigate what's going on in this town, but now that I see his cabana boy in tow, I have my answer."

"Hello, Violet," Liam said. He didn't look at her. He continued frowning at the open grave. "You couldn't tell me why this grave is unearthed, could you?"

"Sure," Violet said with a smirk. "I *could*. But why would I?"

"Because if we don't figure this out, Ethan is going to drink your girlfriend here dry and use her magic to put Vendetta in some kind of stasis cocoon to protect her."

"What?" Reese turned toward Liam, trying to tell if the vampire was joking. She didn't think he was.

Violet's smirk disappeared. "Excuse me?"

"You heard me."

"Fuck," Violet said and then to Reese as if this was all her fault. "This is why you stay away from them. Did you even realize they were setting you up to be dinner? Hell, he's probably going to drain you the second you report back!"

"To be fair, that was only Ethan's Plan B. I'm against it. I think it will make Kristine sad."

Reese pressed the heels of her hands against her eyes. "Could you not talk about me like I'm already dead." Then to Liam. "He was really going to—whatever the hell you just said?"

Liam shrugged, moonlight dancing on his shoulders. "It wouldn't have killed you. But it would've turned you into a shark, permanently. You wouldn't be able to return to shore anymore." Then to Violet, "So what do you know?"

Violet groaned. "You play dirty, bloodsucker. I'll remember that."

Liam nodded as if he understood.

"Hope dug up this guy because the corpse had some ancient

coin that Ydril wanted. She gave Ydril the coin as payment in order to find out where the Witching Blade was."

"Who the hell is Hope?" Reese asked.

"A chaos demon. Used to be pretty close to Ethan and Vendetta. I hear she's one of the original chevalier."

"Is that all?" Liam asked.

"No. She also wanted to know where Ethan was keeping Vendetta. She seems to be under the impression that he's keeping her in stasis against her will."

"And since this grave is clearly excavated, the transaction has already happened."

"You're so smart," Violet said, clapping her hands. "You must be his favorite *good boy*."

Liam's head snapped up.

The look in his eyes made both Reese and Violet step back.

"Hey man, I was just kidding. Take a—"

"Shut up," Liam said. He craned his head as if listening to something. He met Reese's gaze. "We have to go. *Now.*"

"Why?" Reese's heart had finally started to quiet in her chest only to now rev up again.

Liam was already running through the graves, cutting the shortest path to his car. "Hope's at the house."

"I'm coming too," Violet said, following them down the sloping hill.

"You don't have to," Reese said, secretly touched.

"That's what I thought until I just found out how much trouble you're in. I'm riding with you."

They climbed into the pickup and followed Liam's BMW out of the parking lot. As she shifted gears, Reese had a chance to realize she'd picked up dirt on her knees. And her hair was starting to stick to the back of her neck.

"Any chance I can get you to give me your soul?" Violet asked, swaying in the passenger seat as they drove west out of town.

"What? Why?" Reese asked.

"Ethan can't touch your magic if your soul is promised to someone else. Think of it as giving it to me for safe keeping," Violet gave her a grin worthy of a devil.

Reese shifted gears, laughing. "I was considering it until you smiled like that."

Violet shrugged. "At least you're smart. But seriously, you need to be on your guard here. Liam, no matter how friendly he is with your buddy Kristine, he's loyal to Ethan. He will live and die for him. You got that? He would throw you under the bus to save his beau."

"And what about you, Violet? Whose side are you on?"

Violet grinned from the passenger side of the truck. "Tonight? I'm yours."

The trees broke open and the two-story Spanish villa sprang into view. The dirt road turned to beautiful paving stones that circled in front of the house. In the center of the roundabout was a fountain bubbling softly with turquoise water.

Liam parked his BMW in front of the cream-colored steps and Reese pulled up right behind him. They were out of their vehicles and on the steps a moment later. But they hesitated.

The front door to Ethan's house had a giant hole blasted out of it. It hung on its hinges.

"Hope had to make an entrance." Violet shrugged in her leather jacket. "Not surprising. Chaos demons like to blow shit up."

"Come on," Liam said. "We need to help him."

"Do we?" Violet said with arched eyebrows. "I thought Ethan was the baddest boy in town. And what are you going to do anyway, bloodsucker? Hope can incinerate you with a thought."

If Liam heard this taunt, he gave no sign. They followed

him into the house as he led them through the labyrinth of lavish rooms straight to a study. In this room, the walls were hidden behind floor-to-ceiling bookcases made of dark wood. Red fabric couches and highbacked chairs rounded out the decor.

Liam approached a fireplace with twin carved panthers of black stone flanking each side. He placed his hand on the right panther and the fireplace shifted. A passageway appeared behind the flames.

"It won't burn you," Liam whispered, presumably so Hope would not hear them. "Just step through."

Liam went first, followed by Violet. Reese trailed behind. The flames felt like a cool breeze on her skin as she passed through.

Ahead a spiral staircase appeared. They followed it down silently. Their feet slipped over the stone without making a sound. The air grew noticeably colder with each step. Reese was certain they'd gone underground.

When they reached the bottom of the stairs, she saw several things at once.

First, the walkway stretching before them led to a stone coffin. The lid of this coffin had been removed and thrown across the room. It lay broken in three large pieces against the far wall.

It had collided with some of the stone carvings lining the walls. The impact destroyed a section, revealing jagged rock beneath.

Ethan stood on the left side of the stone coffin. Hope stood on the right. Their gazes were locked on one another. Reese could feel the magic like electricity crackling in the air.

"Do not mind the mess, my friends," Ethan said calmly. But he didn't take his gaze off of the woman. "Hope is a mere chaos demon. She can hardly help herself."

"I'm so much more than that!" Hope's face contorted in a

hideous snarl. "I'm *her* chevalier. Just as well as you! You have no more right to her than any of us!"

Hope jabbed her finger into the center of the coffin each time she said the word *her*.

"You have the Witching Blade and your blood. What do you mean to do now?" Ethan asked.

"It will work," Hope hissed. "It *will*."

"All that Ydril told you was untrue," Ethan said calmly. He placed one hand on the edge of the coffin.

"He said the blade was in the ocean. That the sirens had it. But I figured out where it really was." Hope twisted the strange knife in her hand. It looked more like a stake than a blade to Reese.

"He deceived you," Ethan said. "So that you would give him the coin he sought. He can't go on hallowed ground. Did you know that?"

"Yeah, well, I didn't realize every piece of shit in this town was loyal to you." Her free hand gripped her edge of the coffin. "They won't be once they know what a coward you are."

"So how did you learn the blade was in the forest?" Ethan asked.

And with a sudden spark of clarity, Reese understood why he was asking. He wanted to know what mistake he'd made, and how his secret had been uncovered.

"It doesn't matter," Hope said. "*I'm* her chevalier. She *chose* me. You have no right to keep her."

"My queen does as she pleases," Ethan said calmly. "Six months ago, Henry made the mistake of thinking he could also take her from this place."

Hope's lower lip began to tremble. "I've missed her. I want her back."

"This isn't the way."

But Hope had already pulled the long wooden blade above her head. Reese thought the demon meant to plunge it into the coffin, but no. She dragged the tip of the blade down her arm, splitting the skin. Blood welled up instantly, flowing over her flesh.

Hope extended her hand into the coffin.

For a moment there was only a dripping sound. *Tap, tap, tap.* Like a faucet leaking somewhere in this grand house.

Hope's pained expression gave over to pleasure. "See? You don't know her like you think you do. You think you know what she wants but—"

Hope's words were swallowed by a sudden intense scream. The volume of it echoed off the walls, colliding and overlapping with itself. Reese, Violet, and Liam all covered their ears.

Hope was yanked forward, her body slamming into the side of the stone coffin. Then the arm was wrenched entirely from her body and disappeared into the sarcophagus.

The chaos demon stumbled back, still wailing. She looked at her severed arm, now torn from her shoulder as if she couldn't believe it was gone. She opened and closed her mouth like a fish out of water.

Reese wasn't sure what she expected to crawl out of the coffin. Some creature worthy of a lifetime of nightmares.

But what she saw instead was a woman. A young woman, slowly rising. To Reese, she didn't look like the majestic living goddess Reese had always imagined Vendetta to be. Instead, she resembled like a child, no more than sixteen. Her eyes were large liquid pools of moonlight and her face cherubic. The hair flowing down her back, impossibly long, seemed to shine with a life of its own, as black as a moonless night.

Blood dribbled down her chin as she released her hold on the severed arm. It fell to the floor with a wet *splat.*

This was Vendetta. In the flesh. One moment she was standing in the coffin like a sleeping beauty just wakened. Then she was in front of Hope, wrenching the other woman into her embrace.

Vendetta tore open her throat with one ruthless bite.

"Please," Hope begged, tears streaming down her face. "Please, my queen. I only want to serve you. I only want—"

Vendetta tore her head off her shoulders the way one rips an annoying tag from the inside of a shirt. Pieces of the demon fell to the marble floor. Blood escaped the body in a red stream.

Go! A voice cried in Reese's mind. Violet startled beside her and Reese suspected she'd heard the same cry. Liam had already placed a hand on both of them, pushing them toward the stairs. *Go! Before she can—*

But Vendetta was in front of Reese. Her liquid brown eyes sparked with an internal fire. Not the hellfire Reese had come to know in the eyes of the demons around her.

Magic, she realized. *I'm seeing the golden burn of magic inside her. That's all she is in there...*

"Hello," Vendetta purred sweetly. She was almost a head shorter than Reese. She gazed lovingly up into Reese's eyes. "Did I make this one? She smells like mine."

"We are all yours," Ethan said. He was at her back now, one hand on her arm as if to pull her away. But he wasn't exerting any will over his queen.

"So beautiful," Vendetta said. She ran a blood-stained finger down Reese's cheek.

"Very beautiful. But look what you've done to your room, my lady. I will have to clean it up."

Vendetta turned and regarded the pool of blood and Hope's destroyed body.

"I called her here. I called her like I called the other ones," she purred. Her words were in their minds, Reese realized. Her lips weren't moving at all. "More will come, Ethanu."

"I know," Ethan said. "You are very clever."

"I need more. I must be strong when she wakes up."

"Who, my treasure?" Ethan asked, mimicking her tone.

"Mother." A crystalline laugh like a bell echoed through the room. It was as if the idea delighted Vendetta to no end. "Were you afraid? You never liked Hope."

Vendetta slid her arms around Ethan's neck, slicking the collar with blood. It was a strangely sexual movement. It didn't match the child-like image in Reese's mind. "Do you think I will eat you next?"

"I'm not afraid." Ethan smiled sweetly. He wiped at her chin the way a father might for his daughter. "You may do what you want with me. My body and soul are yours."

"But I smell your fear. Why are you afraid, Ethanu?" She bent and smelled his chest. She moaned as if the smell was more than pleasant. "I am *so* hungry."

"I know," he said and put a hand on the back of her head. "You may feed on me, my queen, if you wish it."

Over her head, Ethan met our gazes. *Please,* his eyes begged. *Please get Liam out of here.*

Vendetta bent forward and sank her fangs into Ethan's neck.

"Come lie down," he said, gathering her up like one would a child. She didn't remove her fangs. "Rest now."

Violet shoved Liam up the staircase and pushed Reese up behind him. They fled as if their lives depended on it—and it was possible they did. No one spoke until they were in the pickup, rushing down the road at full speed.

"Christ," Liam sighed, removing his scarf the way one loosens a tie. "I thought we were dead. I thought she was going to drain every single one of us dry."

"You and me both, bloodsucker. Holy *shit* she's terrifying. More terrifying than I imagined."

She whooped and both Liam and Reese jumped.

"Take me to a bar," Violet demanded. "I need a fucking drink."

"Go to Setting Sun," Liam said. "Drinks on me."

"Is she going to drain him?" Reese asked. The world was

beginning to solidify around her again. The blind panic seizing her left a cold chill in its wake.

"He's all right," Liam said. "But Hope is the second chevalier that Vendetta has killed."

"What the hell is a chevalier?" Reese asked, having heard that word twice tonight.

"Like her personal servants. Uh, minions maybe?" Liam tried.

"Like generals in hell," Violet said. "She created them to do her bidding. To protect and serve her."

"Why the hell would she kill her personal servants?" Reese asked.

"She's taking her power back," Liam said, darkly. His moody gaze regarded the ocean waves.

"Does this mean she'll kill Ethan too?"

"Someday," he said. "But he was her first chevalier. I have a feeling he'll also be the last one standing."

As the Castle Cove lights came back into view and a feeling of safety enveloped her once again, Reese relaxed.

"The goddess is waking up," Violet murmured from the backseat. "Any idea what that means?"

"No idea."

"What shall we do in the meantime?" Reese asked, slowing at the four-way stop outside Crossroads.

"Drink like it's the end of the world?" Liam offered.

Violet met her gaze in the rearview mirror, a wicked grin on her lips. "I can think of more than a few things to keep you busy."

The End

Create a new story - go back to the beginning

GRAYSON: DO NOT GO INTO THE WESTERN WOODS

Sunday morning passed quickly with Nutella pancakes and cups of coffee. But then his parents went to the farmer's market in Cliffside, which met on Sunday. Unlike the market that met in Old Town on Saturdays, Sunday's market focused on street food and live music. There were more dogs and a playground. It wasn't a bad way to spend a Sunday between May and October. On any other day, Grayson would've been thrilled to go to the market. He liked to buy hot kettle corn from a booth and walk around looking at the crafts for sale.

But today was different.

"I'm waiting for Reese to come by," he told his parents, and they seemed to accept their son's responsibility to the case at hand. They let him stay home without a fight.

"Want me to bring back some kettle corn for you?" his father asked. Grayson admitted that he did.

Once his family had left, Grayson spent most of the morning lying in his bed, staring at the ceiling. It felt stupid to keep his eyes open and gaping at the rough plaster like that, but every time he closed his eyes, he saw Landon's body tumbling in the surf, replaying how his moonlit flesh slapped clumsily at the shore like a beached animal.

And all the blood.

It had stained the sand, and dyed the frothy waves.

He pushed the heels of his hands into his eyes and sighed.

A robust knock on the front door made him sit up in his bed.

He went to the window and saw a red pickup in the driveway. He rushed downstairs, hand on the bannister and found a woman on the porch, giving him a short wave and polite smile. "I'm Reese. We talked on the phone."

She was pretty. Her hair was blond with the tips black. It was like she'd taken her hair and dipped the ends in an ink pot.

Her eyebrows were also black and her body was lean and muscular.

"Come on in."

Reese stepped into the house, the polite grin remaining on her face. "You have a beautiful house."

"Yeah my dad loves working on it," Grayson said. Then he did what every child over the age of five knew to do when a guest came to the house. "Can I get you anything?"

Castle Cove was full of all sorts of creatures after all. If someone—or something—came to the house, the owners had to make an offering. Even if they thought they knew the person, they should still make an offering just in case a mischievous fae was wearing the face of a friend. Giving them food or drink meant they could not harm you. Otherwise...

"A glass of water is fine," she said. She pointed at the round dining table. "Want to talk here?"

"Sure," he said. "Be right back."

He went into the kitchen and pulled a glass from the cupboard. He heard the chair scrape back in the dining room as he filled the glass from the tap.

In the dining room, he extended the cool glass toward her.

"Thanks," she said, taking it gratefully. After a long drink she said, "As I mentioned on the phone, I've been asked to investigate what happened. They're worried about the sirens' behavior and want to make sure no one else gets hurt. Anything you can tell me about that night would be very helpful."

Grayson noticed her remarkable eyes. They were metallic gray—like liquid silver.

She caught him looking and smiled. "I'm a shifter."

"Cool," he said, too quickly. He cleared his throat and tried to find his metaphoric footing. "Sirens aren't supposed to come into the cove. At least that's what we thought. The closest they were supposed to get was Heart's Rock."

"Bingo," she said. "So what happened?"

Grayson recounted the night to her, starting with the birthday swim to Landon's body thrashing on the shore. He left out the gory details.

"Did you—" the woman began.

Grayson knew what she was asking.

"I survived," he said, plainly. "So did Abby."

"Can we talk to her?"

A fierce protectiveness rose up in him at the mention of Abby. "I'm assuming you got permission from Detective O'Reilly?"

Reese flashed a patient smile, turning the water glass in her hand. "Yes, I did. She's fine with it, but you can come with me if you want."

"Yeah. Let me put on my shoes."

Reese waited on the porch, overlooking the neighborhood with relaxed shoulders.

"Okay," he said, stepping out and locking up the house behind him.

He climbed into Reese's red pickup not knowing what to expect. But the interior was remarkably clean. There weren't any traces of smoke or ash, so he guessed she wasn't a smoker.

No fast food wrappers or empty soda bottles on the floorboard. The dashboard didn't even have dust on it.

In the middle of the bench seat there were some papers though, which she gathered up quickly before he sat down.

"Sorry," she said, folding them in half and putting them in the glovebox with a firm shove.

Grayson put on his seatbelt. "I was just thinking how clean your car is."

She snorted. "Yeah, she doesn't look like she should be in such good condition, but I take care of her."

Grayson pat the dash affectionately. "I can tell."

"So where does Abby live?"

"Just east of Hyde Park," he said. "In Hummingbird Hollow."

"Got it." She keyed the ignition and the car rattled to life.

Grayson texted Abby to make sure she was home. She responded quickly. He wondered if she'd been lying in her bed on her phone all day as he'd been tempted to. After all, she didn't have an affectionate family forcing her to breakfast and dress. And he had a feeling that Landon's loss might be hitting her even harder than it was hitting him—as difficult as that was for him to imagine.

"Don't be—" Grayson began, but then he wasn't sure how to finish. "Abby's having a hard time." He finished lamely.

"I won't be an asshole," Reese said with a smile. "I'm a bartender. I know how to talk to people."

And how to listen probably.

They rode in silence past large, looming mansions that lined Hyde Park. The revival architecture and old live oaks thick with moss seemed to say old creatures dwell here.

The Hyde Park mansions were supposedly owned by the undead vampire clans. And with homes so massive, he imagined there was plenty of room for an entire clan and all their attendants to dwell within. Many of them even had second dwellings, what Grayson thought might be called a carriage house, set further back from the road.

Just east of Hyde Park, before the Castle Cove University border began, was a small neighborhood called Hummingbird Hollow. It had small, quaint ranch-style homes and postage stamp size yards. The pickup turned off Ruby Road onto Violetear Drive.

The front door was open as if waiting for them.

Reese swung the red truck into the driveway. "Thanks for coming. I think it'll be easier for her to talk if someone she knows is with me."

Grayson climbed out of the truck as Abby stepped out onto the porch. He saw her visibly stiffen at the sight of Reese. He wasn't sure if it was because the woman was beautiful or if it was just seeing Grayson riding around with another woman but he recognized jealousy when he saw it.

"Come in," Abby said, holding open the door.

Grayson squeezed her hand as he passed. The ranch-style house had a single floor with three bedrooms: one for Abby, one for her Mom and one for guests.

"Do you want anything to drink?" Abby's question hung in the air.

Grayson noticed that the end of her hair was still wet from a shower. Her face was freshly scrubbed and dewy but it didn't hide the puffiness surrounding her eyes. She'd been crying.

"Water, if you don't mind," Reese said as if she hadn't just sucked down an entire glass at Grayson's. Grayson began to wonder what kind of shifter she might be.

Abby gestured to the mustard yellow sofa in the center of the front room. "Take a seat."

Reese tucked herself into the corner of the sofa and pulled a lacey pillow into her lap. Grayson sat in the navy armchair, crossing his leg over his thigh. The room felt a little hot, or perhaps he was wearing too much clothing. His long shirt was likely too much for the June heat.

Abby reappeared with a glass of water, extending it toward Reese. "Here."

"Thanks." Reese sipped the water then balanced the glass on her knee. "I'm here to—"

"I know," Abby interrupted. She sat in the armchair beside Grayson instead of sharing the couch with Reese. Something about this made Grayson's pulse quicken. He found himself looking toward her, tracing the line of her jaw and throat. "I spoke to my mom earlier. She told me who you are and what's going on."

"Great," Reese said, visibly relieved. "If you could just run me through what happened that would really help."

Abby looked at Grayson as if seeking his approval. Grayson smiled reflexively. In truth, the unexpected eye contact made his stomach drop. "I already told my part. It's all yours."

Abby recounted the night slowly with even more detail than Grayson had been able to recall. When she finished, Abby flicked her eyes to meet Reese's. "Someone was using magic. A lot of it."

Grayson's heart kicked. He turned toward her, unable to hide his surprise. "How do you know that?"

Abby looked suddenly shy. That was another shock because the Abby Grayson knew was never shy, about anything.

"I'm apprenticed to the coven," Abigail said plainly.

He began free-falling. "You're a witch?"

"I didn't tell you because I wasn't sure you'd be okay with it." Her cheeks burned red. "Your parents are sort of—purists."

Grayson felt like he'd been kicked in the gut.

Don't screw this up, some part of his mind screamed. Some older, wiser part realized this was an incredibly important moment. The absolute last thing he should do now was make it about him.

"Abby." He took a breath and tried to clear away any emotion that clouded his mind. "Not one person in my family would give a damn if you're a witch."

Abby wouldn't look at him. Her eyes remained fixed on her lap. It hurt Grayson to see it. He wanted to reach over and grab her hand. He'd pull her into his arms and kiss her until she believed him. But Reese was sitting right here, looking at them with thinly veiled curiosity.

"So you could feel the magic?" Reese asked, clearly trying to break back into the conversation.

Abby found her voice. "Yes. There was a surge of it right before the sirens showed up. I knew something was up, but I was halfway to shore when I felt it so I couldn't do anything in the water. Then once I got to shore—"

She licked her lips.

"Everything happened so fast after that."

Grayson agreed. It seemed the swim to shore and Landon's death had happened in the same breath.

Reese rubbed her knees. "Could you tell where the magic was coming from?"

"West," Abby said without hesitation. "Somewhere along Canyon Road. But I can't be more specific than that. Sorry."

"You've been a huge help," Reese said, standing. She finished the glass of water in a few gulps and set the glass down on a coaster. "I don't have any other questions now, but would either of you mind talking to me again if I think of more?"

They both shook their heads.

"Cool. I need to go, but I'll be in touch if I need you." She turned her gray eyes on Grayson. "Do you want a ride back to your house?"

"I'll take him," Abby said.

Grayson tried not to break into an enormous grin at the offer.

"Okay then." Reese gave them both polite smiles. "I'm off."

They watched her exit the house and descend the steps. Once she reached her truck, they turned and faced each other.

"You didn't tell Landon about the coven." Grayson wanted to give her a chance to speak for herself, truthfully, now that they were alone.

"No." Abby covered her face and sighed. "I didn't tell him a lot of things."

Grayson tried to give himself room in the face of all these emotions. He was disappointed that she hadn't told him sooner, but relieved to know. He was also honored that he now knew a secret that Landon hadn't. But this honor was quickly blotted out by a rising tide of guilt.

"He would've freaked out."

"You thought I'd freak out too." He felt the heat rising in his cheeks.

"No," she said. "I was looking for the right time to tell you. I've been waiting for the right time to tell you a lot of things, actually."

"What about now?" he asked. He rubbed his hands on his jeans, trying to dry the damp palms. "Put it all on me now."

She stood and gestured for him to take her hand. "Come with me."

"Your mom—" Detective O'Reilly had a strict rule about no boys in the bedroom. Grayson had been adhering to that rule since he started coming over five years ago.

"She won't be home for hours. There's a lot going on in town at the moment, so she wants me here. I don't mind being homebound as long as you stay with me." She beckoned him forward, smiling. "Come on."

He took her hand, noticing how cool it felt in his, and let himself be dragged into the back of the house.

Abby's bedroom was an assault of purple. Her bed, an elevated twin mattress pushed into the corner against the left wall, had a fluffy bedspread and more pillows than the bed could comfortably hold. At the foot of the bed, running along the wall until the bed stopped it, was an enormous bookcase overflowing with books. A pile had been made on the floor in front of it. The subjects ran from travel guides to design tomes and book after book about architecture and engineering. Beneath the window beside the head of the bed was the drafting desk, with a half-finished design for a garden sketched in pencil.

The floor was clean, the books were neatly arranged on the shelves, and the closet took up the right wall of the room.

From the stack of papers on her drafting desk, Abby pulled out two sheets and offered them to Grayson.

He took them, reading the top line several times before understanding what he was seeing. Then he turned the page and read the other.

"You were accepted to CCU. And UCLA," he managed finally. He was searching her face for comprehension. "For engineering."

She beamed. "Yeah. And a half dozen other schools too, but these are the only two I'm seriously considering."

"Why?" he asked.

"You know why," she said. She stepped toward him. "Grayson."

She took the papers from him before tossing them onto the desk again. She laced her fingers into his.

"Grayson, I love you. I've loved you for a long time but I didn't know how to tell you. First there was Landon and now that he's dead the timing feels even worse. But it doesn't change how I feel."

His heart knocked in his throat. "How you feel?" he whispered.

"I want to be with you. I don't care if we're in LA or if we're here, but I want to be with you. After what happened to Landon —" Her breath hitched. She swallowed. "No one knows how long they have. I can't keep waiting for the right time. I want every minute I can get with you. I just need to know if you feel the same way about me?"

Grayson Choice 15
Yes, Grayson Chooses Abby - go to page 317
No, Grayson Met Daniel Has Feelings for Him Instead - go to page 312

GRAYSON: HAS FEELINGS FOR DANIEL

Grayson stood outside the three-story apartment building trying to slow his heartbeat. At this rate, he was going to work himself into a frenzy. He wanted to handle this right. He really did. And yet he found a small handful of gravel on the sidewalk and scooped it up into his hand. Chalk residue stuck to his sweaty palms as he paced the sidewalk, trying to find the right window.

"Here goes nothing."

He took a deep breath and threw the smallest pebble at the third-floor window, the one he knew overlooked Daniel's bed. As soon as the rock clipped the window, he felt incredibly stupid. *What am I even doing?*

He could've gone to the bar. He could've hung out at the House of the Setting Sun and tried to run into Daniel that way. He could've been *cool* about it. He didn't need to be standing here just after dark throwing rocks at someone's window like a total creeper.

He dropped the remaining pebbles and turned.

That's when the window creaked open and a familiar face appeared.

"Grayson?"

"Hey." Grayson wiped his sweaty palms on his jeans. "How are you?"

Daniel laughed. "I'm fine. How are you, Romeo?" He gestured at the window. "You going to recite some poetry now or something?"

Grayson laughed. "No."

"You better come up then. Go to the front door. I'll buzz you in."

Grayson walked around to the front of the building and stood nervously outside the glass entrance. Several excruciatingly long heartbeats later, a buzzer sounded and Grayson pulled the door open.

Daniel stood on the third floor landing, bare chested and barefoot with only black silk pants on. He smiled when Grayson appeared on the landing below.

"Come on in," he pushed open the door.

Grayson stepped into the apartment and found it was the same as it had been on his first visit. The impeccable kitchen. The inviting sofa. The soft glow of lamps well placed in the corners of the room.

"Can I get my hopes up that you're here for my company alone?"

Grayson slid onto the kitchen barstool. "Yes."

Daniel smiled, leaning one hip into the counter. "Can I get you something to drink? I don't have any food in the house, but I'll take you out for dinner if you want."

"I imagine it would be pretty boring to watch me eat," he said.

"You'd be surprised." He went to the fridge and pulled out two see-through packs. Grayson recognized it as a blood pack, which he'd seen many of in his father's lab.

Daniel misunderstood his gaze. "Does blood gross you out? I get it from a blood stand near Hyde's Park."

"I know," Grayson said. When Daniel frowned, he added, "My father's lab harvests and manufactures a lot of the blood in town."

"Really?" Daniel looked genuinely surprised as he cut the corner off the blood pack and poured the contents into a pot on the stove. "So your father is a scientist."

"Biochemist."

"And your mother?"

"She teaches folklore at CCU."

"Both human?"

"Yep."

"Good genes," he said with a smile, pulling a metal spoon from the drawer. "That explains you."

Blush spread across Grayson's cheeks.

"Forgive my frankness, but I never thought I was going to see you again, Grayson. I'm more than a little surprised you're here."

"If you want me to go—"

"No," he said, turning away from the stove. "I didn't say that. I just said I'm surprised."

Grayson bit his lip, unsure of how to answer.

"I was under the impression that I was a hookup for a curious guy. Are you telling me that I'm mistaken?"

Grayson picked at his sleeve. "Maybe."

"Maybe?" With steam rising from the pot, the vampire reached for a ceramic mug in the counter and poured the blood from the pot into the mug. He set the mug on the counter, untouched and turned off the stove. He came to stand in front of Grayson. "*Maybe?*"

Grayson could only smile.

"How about we play a game? Do you know Hot or Cold?"

"My little brother loves that game."

"I hope he doesn't play it like this." Daniel stepped forward and grabbed Grayson's hand. He pulled him from the chair, forcing him to stand in front of the vampire. Then he placed a hand on Grayson's hip. "Is this what you came for? Hot or cold?"

"Warm."

Daniel stepped forward so that the entire length of his body was flushed against Grayson's. "Now?"

"Warm*er*."

The vampire enveloped Grayson in his arms and pressed his lips to his throat. "And now?"

"Hot." Daniel's smile spread against his skin.

He kissed Grayson's throat, placing several sweet kisses along the exposed skin.

"So you came back for some kisses?" Daniel asked.

Be brave, Grayson thought. *You didn't come all this way just to chicken out now.*

"No," he said, his heart knocking in his chest. "I came back for you."

Daniel stepped back, regarding him with an amused expression. "For *me*? Are you sure that's not the pheromones talking?"

"Yes."

"I know that vampires have this mysterious, sexual vibe going on, but you should know that I'm the monogamous type," Daniel said. "So be clear. When you say you came for *me*, are you saying you want to keep hooking up with a vampire or are you saying you want more?"

Grayson managed to breathe despite the pulse in his throat. "More."

"I-want-to-be-a-vampire more or I-want-a-boyfriend more?"

Grayson rubbed the back of his head. "If you're already with someone—"

"I'm not."

"Donors or—"

Daniel smiled. "No donors. Or boyfriends."

"Okay. Then would you be open to..." He searched for the words. "Seeing where this goes?"

"Seeing where this goes," Daniel repeated. He looked ready to burst with laughter. "You want to date me?"

"Yeah," Grayson said. He stepped forward and wrapped his arms around Daniel. He placed a kiss on the vampire's bare throat. "But only if you want to. I mean I—"

Daniel pulled him up into a deep kiss. His cool mouth nearly devoured Grayson's as he forced his tongue past his lips. Grayson felt his feet leave the floor, followed by the collision of soft pillows at his back. When he opened his eyes, the ceiling above the sofa came into view.

"*If* I'm interested?" Daniel ran his fingers down Grayson's chest. He bent and placed a kiss on Grayson's throat, where the jaw and ear met. "What do you think?"

The End
Create a new story - go back to the beginning

GRAYSON: YES, HE FEELS THE SAME WAY

His mind raced. "What about the coven? You've apprenticed—"

"I don't have to be here until I'm a full member," she said. "And I can't become a full member for several years. College won't interfere with that. Assuming you wouldn't mind being with a witch. Or living in Castle Cove someday. Would that be a problem?"

No, he realized. Because in reality, he wanted to spend whatever time he had left with this beautiful, smart woman.

"If it's a problem," she began, misreading his silence.

"No, it's not," he said. He broke into a smile. "I think witches are sexy."

"It's going to take us a while to figure this out. How to make room for us and Landon," she said. "But we'll figure it out."

He squeezed her hand. "We will."

She squeezed him back, hard. Then reaching up and clasping the back of his head, she pulled him into a kiss, a deep lingering kiss that sent the room spinning.

Her breath was hot on his lips. "Just tell me you want this."

"I want this," he said, his whole body alive with electricity.

"Good." She pulled back smiling. "Because I'm going to make you stupidly happy, Grayson Helmson. Just you wait."

The End
Create a new story - go back to the beginning

GRAYSON: STAY HOME

"I'll stay home," he said and checked the time on his phone. He had two hours before his shift started. "It's short notice, but I think Ms. Monroe would understand."

"If she doesn't I'll talk to her," his mother said.

"Yes," his father agreed, looking up from his phone again. "There's no shame in needing personal time."

"I know," he said and he did. While his parents did worship at the altar of work and productivity, they were also into self-care. *Really* into self-care. Grayson didn't know another kid at his school who could call his mother and be removed, no questions asked, because he needed a mental health day.

His mother squeezed his hand. It was warm from the coffee mug she'd been holding.

"We want to give you space and we trust you to take care of yourself," she said. "But we also worry. No one should have to go through what you went through last night. Loss is terrible, but last night…last night."

He squeezed her hand back and then let it go. "Don't worry about me. I'm just going to read or maybe I'll go for a walk."

Abby came into the dining room and took the empty seat.

She smelled like soap and her face was a little red from being scrubbed. She sipped the coffee first, then added creamer from the carafe on the table. She also poured herself a juice.

"Mom texted me and said she's going to be a few minutes late. She got hung up on a 911 call or something."

"You're welcome to stay here as long as you need to," Grayson's father said.

"We love having you," his mother added. "How are you feeling today?"

"Awful," Abigail said and his mother responded by rubbing Abby's back.

"Eat your breakfast. Your bagel is already cold. Want me to reheat it?"

"No, this is fine."

Abby and Grayson shared a meaningful look. They both knew the breakfast would have to be choked down regardless. No amount of spread or toastedness was going to make it taste like anything other than ash in their mouths.

The front door slammed open. "I'm home! Grayson! How was your birthday?"

Tanner, ten years old burst into the dining room. His sandy blond hair was blown back from his face and he had his back-pack slung over his shoulder. He dropped it with a clunk on the floor.

He took one look at his family and his brown eyes widened. "Whoa. Who died?"

Grayson snorted before he could stop himself. His brother had an uncanny ability to hit the truth spot on. His father often said he was fairly certain Tanner—because he'd been born in this creepy town—was some kind of psychic. Grayson had been born in LA and while he might have a knack for surviving, he didn't seem to know things out of the blue.

Grayson's mother was standing at the dining room window, waving to Will's mother in the driveway.

"Landon died," Abby said. She took a bite of her bagel as if to stop herself from saying anything more.

"Shit."

"Tanner!" his father cried.

"Language," his mother said, which was very funny because everyone at that table knew his mother knew words that would make a sailor blush.

"Please put your shoes and bag where they go," his father said.

Tanner didn't seem to hear him. "Did he really die?" He was looking to Grayson for confirmation.

Grayson found his voice. "There was an accident when we were swimming."

Both his parents shot him warning looks. Lucky for them, Grayson understood that he was supposed to omit the details of Landon's death. Tanner understood Castle Cove was different. He knew about the vampires, werewolves, and witches—even the sirens in the cove. As with Grayson, his parents took great care to raise a curious but cautious boy.

Tanner knew there were monsters in Castle Cove. But this didn't mean that Tanner fully understood what those monsters could do to a person if caught unaware.

However, Grayson thought that Tanner understood more than he let on. Perhaps it was his gift for knowing that seemed to protect him from saying too much. This gift worked as well as, if not better than, their parents' diligent training.

"He drowned?" Tanner asked. His eyes were wide. Too wide.

"Yeah," Abby said, lifting her coffee from the table. Grayson saw the tremble in her hand.

"On your birthday?" Tanner asked. Now he was hanging off Grayson's chair, looking him in the eye. He began to cry. "I'm sorry, dude."

Dude was his favorite word the last few weeks and to hear it uttered with such sincerity undid Grayson inside. Tears formed and spilled over onto his cheeks. He pulled his little brother in to a tight hug. "Thanks, man."

His parents let the moment unravel between them. No one spoke. Breakfast continued until Tanner pulled away.

"Shoes. Bag," his mother said.

He returned dutifully to the bag he'd dumped upon arriving and removed his shoes. The backpack went on its wall hook and the shoes in their designated cubby.

The front doorbell rang.

Because he hadn't closed the door behind him after his arrival, it stood open with a clear view of Officer O'Reilly on the porch. She wore pressed black dress pants and a deep burgundy dress shirt tucked into the waistband. Her badge was clipped to one hip and her gun was visible in its holster.

"Abby, it's your mom," Tanner said, and opened the door. "Hi, Una."

"Hey, buddy." She sounded as exhausted as she looked. Deep pillows of purple had formed under each of her eyes.

Abby started to clear up her plate, but his mother gently tugged her hands away. "Leave it. I'll get it."

Officer O'Reilly stepped into the hallway, ushered in by Tanner.

"Are you ready?" she asked, when she saw Abigail.

Abigail patted her pockets as if she'd forgotten something. "I guess so. I feel like I don't have enough stuff, but I didn't really have anything before…"

"Thanks for letting Abby stay," Una interjected.

"Of course," his parents said in unison.

"Abby is welcome here anytime," his mother added, lifting her coffee mug to her lips again.

"I thought Landon was a good swimmer," Tanner said. He was looking up at Officer O'Reilly with a strange expression on his face.

Una's lips pinched. "It was rough seas last night. A storm rolled in really quick."

His eyes lit up. "Yeah, we saw it. Will and I were in the backyard catching fireflies and then all of a sudden it was lightning and thundering."

Officer O'Reilly frowned at him. "Where does Will live?"

"Cliffside," his father answered. "Near the east parking lot."

"North Beach?"

"Yeah. We go down there sometimes and look for crabs. Will's dad will cook them. *Alive.*"

"That's very close to the water." Officer O'Reilly shrugged as if to say *there you go.* "No surprise you saw the storm."

"Are you going back to work after you take me home?" Abby asked.

"For a few hours," Una said. Then to Grayson. "Okay, well we have to go." She clamped a hand on his shoulder and gave it an affectionate squeeze.

Tanner pulled open the door, holding it open for them.

"Such a gentleman," Una said and stepped out onto the porch again. "Thank you."

Abby hesitated in the doorway. Her gaze fixed on Grayson. "Call me later, okay?"

"I will." He'd already planned on checking on her at least a hundred times today.

With a weak smile, she descended the porch steps to the waiting unmarked car.

"Bye," Tanner said and shut the door. "Well *that* was awkward."

GRAYSON SPENT MOST OF THE MORNING LYING IN HIS BED, staring at the ceiling. It felt stupid to keep his eyes open and gaping at the popcorn plaster, but every time he closed his eyes, he saw Landon's body slapping against the dark, sandy shore.

And all the blood.

He should've gone to work. At least then, he could've kept his mind busy.

A soft knock on the door made him look up.

It was Tanner. He stood in the doorway with his baseball glove. It was fitted to his right hand, his left hand punching the worn leather gently. "You wanna play catch with me?"

He looked ready for rejection.

"Mom told me not to bother you," he went on, blowing his bangs out of his face. "But I thought you might want to get out of this shithole."

"Language," Grayson said, but he couldn't help smiling. His little brother discovering swear words had been the highlight of his year. "This place isn't a shithole. You'll really hurt Dad's feelings if he hears you say that."

Their father took a lot of pride in their restored home. From the renovations to the décor, he'd put a lot of time and money into this place.

Tanner frowned. "I didn't mean it. I was just trying to make you smile."

"And what do I say about that?"

Tanner sighed. "The joke's not worth it if it's at someone else's expense."

Grayson spared him a wan smile. "I'll play with you. Go get me a mitt."

Tanner's sneakered feet bounded down the hall, squeaking as he cut the corner toward his own room at the opposite side of the landing.

Grayson sat up, dragging a hand down his face. He took deep breaths, trying to compose himself. Some fresh air would do him some good. A crash in Tanner's room echoed through the floor, rumbling under Grayson's feet.

"I'm fine," Tanner called out. "It was just stuck under some of my bullshit."

Grayson snorted. Correction: Tanner's *misuse* of swear words was the highlight of his year.

Tanner reappeared in the bedroom doorway and tossed a worn glove to Grayson. It was their father's. He recognized the initials on the thumb and the fact that it was right-handed. Tanner was a lefty.

"I've got a game tonight," Tanner said.

Grayson felt like he'd been kicked in the stomach. "I'd totally forgot."

"You don't have to come. It's against Plainsville. They're not very good, so it'll be a landslide. It won't even be fun to watch. It's only fun when the games are too close to tell who's gonna win."

Grayson had to agree.

At the door, Tanner grabbed his father's Red Sox hat off the hook and put it on his head backwards. Grayson had to adjust the strap for him so that it would fit his head, and then he reached around and opened the front door.

Tanner bounded down the steps, hitting the ground at full speed.

Since they would be in the yard, it didn't make any sense to lock their door. Grayson left it open and wiggled his hand into the worn glove.

It fit fine and because it was nice and broken in, it moved well with each flex of his hand.

"I'll come to your game," Grayson said.

"Someone *died*," Tanner said, stopping in the middle of the yard. The dogwood tree behind him was thick with fat pink blossoms. Tanner seemed oblivious. His eyes were on the battered baseball in his hand which he worked in his grip as if getting a feel for it.

"Yeah, but if I don't go I'll just be here thinking about it," Grayson admitted. "That isn't healthy either. The least I can do is show up and support you."

"I know you love me, dude," Tanner said and threw the ball straight into Grayson's open mitt. The kid had great aim, which is probably why he was shifted between the pitcher and short-stop positions. "You don't have anything to prove to me."

Grayson smiled. He loved this kid. But his grown-up atti-tude was shocking at times. Every time he was reminded that Tanner was growing up it went against the firm image of him as his kid brother. The baby his mother had brought home from the hospital when Grayson was eight.

"I know," Grayson said. "But I want to be there."

They threw the ball for five minutes in blessed silence. It was a gift from Tanner who could be chatty as hell. Grayson knew his brother was intentionally trying not to overwhelm him with questions. Maybe their parents had said something. Or maybe in that uncanny way of his he knew what Grayson needed better than Grayson himself did.

But Grayson could tell he wanted to talk. Tanner was waiting for permission.

"How's Will?" Grayson asked, opening the door to conversation.

"He's okay. Well, he's sort of okay." Tanner shrugged before tossing the ball again. This one went a little to the right.

"Watch those hitching shoulders," Grayson told him. "What's going on with Will?"

"He's worried about the change," Tanner said. His voice was low and dramatic.

Grayson hesitated, his fingers tightening around the leather ball. The stitches pressed into his hands. "Puberty?"

"No, dude. Will is a werewolf. He's going to wolf out any day now and he's freaking out about it."

"Why were you over there last night if he's a werewolf? It was a full-moon." He didn't ask the obvious *do our parents know he's a werewolf?*

"His parents weren't home," Tanner asked as if reading his

mind. "They go out running with their pack in the Wayward Woods or something. "We were home with his cousin, Josh. He's cool, but not a werewolf. I think he's something though. He's got these eyes."

Tanner made his impression of crazy eyes.

Grayson laughed. "Guess it would be rude to ask."

"Anyway, Will isn't going to change into a werewolf until he's like twelve. Maybe even fourteen. He's just anxious."

That was one of their mother's words.

"He was trying to tell me last night that he could feel his hair growing. He made me look at his arms and back with a flashlight and everything. There wasn't anything."

Grayson smiled. "You're a good friend. But don't be around when he wolfs out for the first time, okay? You could get hurt."

Tanner shrugged and the action made the ball go wide again. Grayson had to reach high to grab it. "I'm not scared of Will. Besides, I'm not going to be a werewolf. I'm going to be something else."

A chill ran up Grayson's neck. "Why do you think that?"

Tanner shrugged, looking a little self-conscious for the first time.

Grayson wanted to push him on this and figure out what he'd meant by it. Did he have a dream or something? Sometimes Tanner's dreams came true. Or was it just a feeling or—

A car pulling into the driveway cut off his chance to interrogate Tanner more. The red pickup wasn't new by any stretch of the imagination. It rumbled like an ancient beast awakened from the grave to do its master's bidding.

A woman stepped out and shut the heavy door. The whole truck rattled as it slammed closed. She was pretty. Her hair was blond with the tips black. It was like she'd taken her hair and dipped the ends in an ink pot.

Her eyebrows were also black and her body was lean and muscular.

"She's a shark," Tanner whispered.

She crossed the yard toward the boys.

"Can I help you?" Grayson asked. Without meaning to, he'd squeezed the ball in his fist so hard that it made his palm ache.

"I'm looking for Grayson," she said with a 100-watt smile. "Is he home?"

"I'm Grayson."

"Hi Grayson. I'm Reese." She extended her hand and he held up the glove with an apologetic smile.

"I heard you were in the cove last night. I have some questions for you," she said.

Grayson looked at Tanner. He wasn't sure why. It wasn't like he needed to defer to a ten-year-old kid.

"I'll heat up lunch. You want some Chinese?" Tanner asked her. That was as close to a *she's okay* as Grayson was probably going to get.

The woman smiled. "Sure, but I only eat seafood."

"We've got some crab rangoon. And some fried rice I think."

"Perfect." She watched Tanner mount the stairs and disappear into the house. "Cute kid."

"That's my little brother, Tanner."

She turned and faced him. He was startled by her silver eyes. Like liquid moonlight.

"You with the police?"

"No," she said. "I've been asked to investigate what happened by someone else. They're worried about the sirens' behavior."

"They aren't supposed to come into the cove," Grayson said. "At least that's what we thought. The closest they were supposed to come was Heart's Rock."

"Bingo," she said. "So what can you tell me?"

Grayson recounted the night to her, starting with the birthday swim to Landon's body thrashing on the shore. He left out the gory details.

"Did you—" the woman began.

Grayson knew what she was asking.

"I survived," he said, plainly. "So did Abby."

"Can we talk to her?"

A fierce protectiveness rose up in him at the mention of Abby. "Her mom is a detective at the Castle Cove PD. You're going to have to ask her."

Reese held up her hands as if in defense. "Not a problem."

This relaxed him. The screen door creaked open. "Food is warm."

Reese followed him into the house and sat down at their little table. Grayson smiled when he saw that he'd put a proper place setting down for her. Their mother would be stoked.

"What do you want to drink? Coke?" Tanner asked.

"Just water is fine," she said, taking the seat to Grayson's left. "After we eat, do you think we can ride over to Abby's?"

Grayson took his seat. "I need to call the station first."

"Please do."

Grayson accepted the fork his little brother offered before putting a glass of water down in front of Reese. "Thanks."

Tanner climbed into his seat and dug into the lo mein while casting curious glances at their guest. He was burning with questions, Grayson could tell. Anyone's guess how long he could hold out.

Grayson pulled his cell phone from his pocket and dialed the police station. He used the non-emergency number.

"Castle Cove PD."

He recognized Yvonne Jenkins voice immediately. "Hi Officer Jenkins. This is Grayson Helmson. Is Detective O'Reilly around?"

"Sure, honey. One second."

He flinched at the use of honey, but couldn't remember a time that Yvonne hadn't called everyone that. Honey. Sugar. Sometimes she added the word bear to the end of the affectionate title: Honey bear. Sugar bear. Though she'd seemed to drop the latter once he'd turned sixteen.

"Here she is."

The phone clicked and Grayson heard the intake of breath. "Grayson, you there?"

"Yeah."

"You okay?"

He realized that was concern in her voice. The sort of knee jerk reactive fear that crept in when he called his own mother when she wasn't expecting it.

"I'm fine," he said, knowing she'd hear nothing else he said until he assured her. "I'm calling about Reese." Here he realized he didn't get her last name. "She said she's been asked to investigate what happened last night."

"Oh, yeah." All the breath left her at once. "I spoke with her earlier. She's all right."

"She wants to talk to Abby. I thought it would be best if we had your permission first."

"That's real considerate of you, Gray. Yes, it's fine. She's not officially with the police department, but she is investigating on behalf…" She seemed to search for the right word. "She's investigating on our behalf."

Grayson had a sense that it was likely far more complicated than that. "So you don't mind if we go over and talk to Abby about what happened to Landon?"

What happened to Landon… His chest tightened.

"Sure. As long as neither of you are going to tell her something you haven't already told me."

The question hung in the air between them.

"No, there's nothing else," he said, wondering when he would be old enough that he no longer needed to constantly reassure the adults around him. Or maybe it was just the human parents in Castle Cove who were having such a hard time.

"She's fine. She's a good person. Clean record. She's just trying to get us some answers. If that's all—" she began.

"Yes, that's it. Thanks for taking my call."

"Sure thing."

Then the line clicked and his cell phone returned to the home screen. It was a picture of the three of them—Abby in the middle with their arms thrown over her shoulders. They were all smiling and laughing. He remembered his father taking that photo before they went to senior prom.

He saw Reese looking at him. "Detective O'Reilly said it's fine. We'll go over there after we eat. But if my parents aren't back, I'll have to bring Tanner. I can't leave him here alone."

"I'm not a baby," Tanner said around a mouth of noodles. "You can leave me here."

Reese snorted.

"Mom would murder me."

But his parents did roll up twenty minutes later and while they gave Reese curious glances and polite hellos, they had let Grayson go without question.

He climbed into Reese's red pickup not knowing what to expect. But the interior was remarkably clean.

There weren't any traces of smoke or ash, so he guessed she wasn't a smoker. No fast food wrappers or empty soda bottles on the floorboard. The dashboard didn't even have dust on it.

In the middle of the bench seat there were some papers though, which she gathered up quickly before he sat down.

"Sorry," she said, folding them in half and putting them in the glovebox with a firm shove.

Grayson put on his seatbelt. "No worries. I was just thinking how clean your car is."

The half, non-committal laugh seemed to be a favorite of hers. "Yeah, she doesn't look like she should be in such good condition, but I love her."

Grayson smiled. "I can tell."

"So where does Abby live?"

"Just east of Hyde Park," he said. "In Hummingbird Hollow."

"Okay." She keyed the ignition and the car rattled to life.

Grayson texted Abby to make sure she was home and to tell her to expect them. She responded quickly and he wondered if she'd been lying in her bed on her phone all day as he'd been tempted to. After all, she didn't have a little brother to force her into interaction. And he had a feeling that Landon's loss might be hitting her even harder than it was hitting him—as difficult as that was for him to imagine.

"Don't be—" Grayson began, but then he wasn't sure how to finish. "Abby's having a hard time." He finished lamely.

"I won't be an asshole," Reese said with a smile. "I'm a bartender. I know how to talk to people."

And how to listen, he suspected.

They rode in silence past the large, looming mansions that lined Hyde Park. The revival architecture and old live oaks thick with moss seemed to say old creatures dwell here.

The Hyde Park mansions were supposedly owned by the undead vampire clans. And with homes so massive, he imagined there was plenty of room for an entire clan and all their attendants to dwell within. Many of them even had second dwellings, what Grayson thought might be called a carriage house, set further back from the road.

Just east of Hyde Park, before the Castle Cove University border began, was a small neighborhood called Hummingbird Hollow. It had small, quaint ranch-style homes and postage stamp size yards. They turned off Ruby Road onto Violetear Drive.

The front door was open as if waiting for them.

Reese swung the red truck into the driveway. "Thanks for coming. I think it'll be easier for her to talk if someone she knows and trusts is with me."

Grayson climbed out of the truck as Abby stepped out onto

the porch. He saw her visibly stiffen at the sight of Reese. He wasn't sure if it was because the woman was beautiful or if it was just seeing Grayson riding around with another, older woman.

"Come in," Abby said, holding open the door.

They obeyed, and Grayson squeezed her hand as he passed. The ranch-style house had a single floor with three bedrooms: one for Abby, one for her Mom and one for guests.

"Do you want anything to drink or—?" Abby's question hung in the air.

Grayson noticed that the end of her hair was still wet from a shower. Her face was freshly scrubbed and dewy.

"Water, if you don't mind," Reese said.

Abby gestured to the mustard yellow sofa in the center of the front room. "Take a seat."

Reese obeyed, tucking herself into the corner of the couch and pulling a lacey pillow into her lap. Grayson tucked himself into a navy arm chair, crossing his leg over his thigh. The room felt a little hot, or perhaps he was wearing too much clothing. His long shirt was likely too much for the June heat.

Abby reappeared with a glass of water, extending it toward Reese. "Here."

"Thanks." Reese sipped the water then balanced the glass on her knee. "I'm here to—"

"I know," Abby interrupted. She sat in the armchair beside Grayson instead of sharing the couch with Reese. Something about this made Grayson's pulse quicken. He found himself looking toward her, tracing the line of her jaw and throat like a man possessed. "I spoke to my mom earlier. She told me who you are and what's going on."

"Great," Reese said, visibly relieved. "If you could just tell me what happened."

Abby looked at Grayson as if seeking his approval. Grayson

smiled reflexively. In truth, the unexpected eye contact made his stomach drop. "I already told my part. It's all yours."

Abby recounted the night slowly with even more detail than Grayson had been able to recall. When she finished, Abby flicked her eyes to meet Reese's. "Someone was using magic. A lot of it."

Grayson's heart kicked. He turned toward her, unable to hide his surprise. "How do you know that?"

Abby looked suddenly shy. That was another shock because the Abby Grayson knew was never shy, about anything.

"I'm apprenticed to the coven," Abigail said plainly.

He began free-falling. "You're a witch?"

"I didn't tell you because I wasn't sure you'd be okay with it," Abby said. Her cheeks were burning red. "Your parents are sort of—purists."

Grayson felt like he'd been kicked in the gut.

Don't screw this up, some part of his mind screamed. Some older, wiser part realized this was an incredibly important moment. And the absolute last thing he should do was make it about him.

He took a breath and tried to clear away any emotion that clouded his mind. "Abby. We love you. Not one person in my family would give a damn if you're a witch."

Abby wouldn't look at him. Her eyes remained fixed on her lap. It hurt Grayson more to see it. He wanted to reach over and grab her. He'd pull her into his arms and kiss her until she believed him. But Reese was sitting right here, looking at them with thinly veiled curiosity.

"So you could feel the magic?" Reese asked, clearly trying to break back into the conversation.

Abby found her voice. "Yes. And there was a surge of it right before the sirens showed up. I knew something was up, but I was halfway to shore when I felt it so I couldn't do anything in the water. Then once I did get to shore—"

She licked her lips.

"Everything happened so fast after that."

Grayson could agree with that. It seemed the swim to shore and Landon's death had happened in the same breath.

Reese rubbed her knees. "Could you tell where the magic was coming from?"

"West," Abby said without hesitation. "Somewhere along Canyon Road. But I can't be more specific than that. Sorry."

"You've been a huge help," Reese said, standing. She finished the glass of water in a few gulps and set the glass down on a coaster. "I don't have any other questions now, but would either of you mind talking to me again if I think of more?"

They both shook their heads.

"Cool. I need to go now, but I'll be in touch if I need you." She turned her gray eyes on Grayson. "Do you want a ride back to your house?"

"I'll take him," Abby said.

Grayson tried not to break into an enormous grin at the offer.

"Okay then." Reese gave them both polite smiles. "I'm off."

They watched her exit the house and descend the steps to the walk. Once she reached her truck, they turned and faced each other.

"You didn't tell Landon about the coven." Grayson said again, giving her a chance to speak for herself, truthfully, now that they were alone.

Abby reached out and took his hand. She squeezed it hard. "No, I didn't."

Grayson sighed, trying to give himself room in the face of all these emotions. He was disappointed that she hadn't told him sooner, but relieved to know now. He was also honored that he now knew a secret that Landon hadn't. But this honor was quickly blotted out by a rising tide of guilt.

"He would've freaked out," she said.

"You thought I'd freak out too?" he asked. He felt the heat rising in his cheeks.

"No," she said with a mischievous smile. "I was looking for the right time to tell you. I've been waiting for the right time to tell you a lot of things, actually."

"Will you come with me?" she asked.

He noticed the high color in her cheeks and the way her eyes shone. In that moment he didn't think he could deny her anything.

"Your mom—" he began lamely.

She grinned. "She won't be home for hours. There's a lot going on in town at the moment, so she wants me right here. I don't mind as long as you stay."

She stood and beckoned him forward.

He took her hand, noticing how cool it felt in his, and let himself be dragged into the back of the ranch house.

Abby's bedroom was an assault of purple. Her bed, a twin pushed into the corner against the left wall, had a fluffy bedspread and more pillows than the bed could comfortably hold. At the foot of the bed, running along the wall until the wall stopped it, was an enormous bookcase overflowing with books. So much in fact, that a pile had been made on the floor in front of it. The subjects ran from travel guides to design tomes and titles about architecture and engineering. Beneath the window beside the head of the bed was the drafting desk, with a half-finished design for a garden sketched in pencil.

The floor was clean, the books were neatly arranged on the shelves, and the closet took up the right wall of the room.

From the stack of papers, Abby pulled out two sheets and offered them to Grayson.

He took them, reading the top line several times before understanding what he was seeing. Then he turned the page and read the other.

"You were accepted to CCU. And UCLA," he managed

finally. He was searching her face for comprehension. "For engineering."

She beamed. "Yeah. And a half dozen other schools too, but these are the two that matter.

"Why?" he asked.

"You know why," she said. She stepped toward him. "Grayson."

She took the papers from him before tossing them onto the desk again. She laced her fingers into his.

"Grayson, I love you. I've loved you for a long time but I didn't know how to tell you. I want to be with you. I don't care if we are in LA or if we're here, I want to be with you. And after what happened to Landon—" Her breath hitched. "No one knows how long they have. I can't keep waiting for someday to happen. I just need to know if you feel the same way."

Grayson Choice 16

Yes, Grayson Feels the Same Way - go to page 317

No, Grayson Met Daniel Has Feelings for Him Instead - go to page 312

REESE: GO INTO THE BAR

Her bare butt stuck to her seat, reminding her that she still needed to finish pulling up her pants. She did, and slid out of her truck. Gravel shifted under her boots as she shut and locked her door. She ran a hand through her wet hair and pulled her shoulders back. She did what she could to mask her scent, knowing it would betray her uneasiness.

Pushing against the rough, bat-wing door, Reese stepped into the bar.

The wooden floor creaked under her boots as she crossed the threshold slowly. She made a show of looking around, as if searching for someone.

She *was* searching for someone.

The interior of the bar was a crude outline of Alpha's. Tables running along the left wall were squat, unstable-looking things. There was a jukebox somewhere. The song had changed to the 99 problems cover by Hugo.

Behind the bar was the owner, Bathory, a tall woman with black hair, black eyes, and inhuman porcelain skin. She regarded Reese with a curious expression.

Crossroads stood out from the other bars in Castle Cove for one other reason—apart from the fact it was teeming with demons—patrons could smoke. A thin gray cloud of smoke hung in the air, giving it a cloudy look that Reese hadn't seen in a long time—since the ban on indoor smoking had gone into effect fifteen years ago.

Reese felt eyes on her. Hungry, greedy eyes followed her as she moved through the room toward the bar.

"What brings you to The Crossroads, Reese?" Bathory said. She put one hand on her hip and regarded Reese with an expression that was half curiosity, half suspicion. "Kristine send you?"

"No," Reese said, knowing that her lie could be detected easily by a demon. They did specialize in them. "I'm looking for someone."

Bathory arched her eyebrows. "You have business here?"

Reese settled on a half-truth. If there was a woman using dark magic in Castle Cove, wasn't it her good Samaritan business to find out what was going on? *See something, say something.* "Maybe."

She saw Bathory trying to detect the lie. Her face hardened in confusion. Then her eyes searched the bar. "Do you see who you're looking for?"

This gave Reese a full invitation to search the bar.

Once Bathory had pulled her into conversation, most eyes had slid away, returning to the whispered conversation they'd nurtured before her arrival—except for one man. He leaned against the wall, a cigar balanced between his fingers. He regarded her with his one milk-white eye from beneath the rim of his felt fedora.

"That's Cole's brother," Bathory said in warning. "He can't be the one you came for."

"She came for me," a voice piped up.

Reese turned to see Violet climbing onto the barstool beside her. She wore a grin, masking whatever emotions she felt beneath. Like any demon, she hid her emotions perfectly. "Miss me already, baby?"

A gentle knock echoed on the door of her mind. *Open up.*

Reese cracked the door just enough to allow unspoken communication with Violet. When they'd broken up, she'd revoked the demon's free pass to play in the recesses of her mind.

Come get a table with me, before these guys eat you alive, Violet said. Even in Reese's head, she sounded just as she did aloud. Bossy.

"I thought you two broke up," Bathory said, wringing a hot washcloth into the sink behind the bar before wiping down the bar top.

"We did." Violet gave Bathory a suggestive grin. "Maybe it's my lucky night. Maybe she wants me back. Tell me you missed me."

Reese smiled, trying to play along. "I did."

And Reese realized she didn't have to lie. Surprise flickered on Violet's face as she registered the truth as well.

"Can I get you a drink?" Violet asked, tapping her black nails on the wood. She was searching Reese's face earnestly now.

"A beer," Reese said.

"Two Surly Darkness, Bath." Violet cut her eyes to the barkeep who was already opening the cooler. To Reese she said, "Why don't you wait for me at that table?" The demon pointed at the empty table against the wall. "I'll be right over."

Reese didn't miss the fact that this table was about as far from the other demons as possible. But she dutifully crossed the room and took a seat. From here, she was able to see the part of the room that had been blocked by the bar.

The back of the room was cloaked in shadows, actual cloaking magic to be sure. She suspected to most eyes they saw only darkness. But Reese caught the outline of two people talking at a table. One was the woman she'd followed.

Reese took her seat with her back to the couple. She wouldn't be able to see them from the other seat. At least this way, maybe she could hear their words.

"It didn't work!" the woman hissed between song changes.

Reese glanced over her shoulder and saw the woman from the beach tucked into a deep pocket of shadow. The demon she spoke to remained hidden. He—or she—was wrapped in deliberate shadows with the exception of a pale, bloodless mouth. Reese knew that demons exploited darkness, but she'd never seen one so adept at it. She was more than curious to know who was controlling the dark. Did she know them? If not, from what rock did the creature crawl out from under?

The chair across from Reese scraped across the floor and Violet settled into it. She rotated her shoulders, shifting the leather jacket she wore. She slid the bottle across the table toward Reese.

"You didn't have to," Reese said, referring to both the drink and the intervention at the bar.

"Sure I did." Then directly into Reese's mind, she added, *Channery was about to fuck your soul three ways to church.*

Reese saw that she'd made a small, nearly imperceptible motion toward Cole's brother.

In my opinion, he's the worst demon in town. I wouldn't spit in his drink for a billion dollars, Violet added. *So you're welcome.*

Reese was honestly touched by the demon's protectiveness, but she wasn't stupid. *I can't thank you, Vi. Or you might get the idea that I owe you something.* Being indebted to a demon—however chivalrous—invited trouble.

The demon offered a cocky half-smile. *It was worth a try.*

Reese was trying to hear the conversation going on at the table behind her, but nothing was coming through. The next tune—a blue grass remix of another Top 40 hit—now filtered through unseen speakers.

So what's really going on? Violet asked, taking a long drink on her own beer. *If Kristine didn't send you for bartender shit, why are you here?*

Reese tried to decide what she could and couldn't tell Violet.

"You have your thinking face on," Violet said, taking another sip. "Last time I saw it, you broke up with me. Should I be worried?"

Reese flashed an apologetic smile. *I'm trying to hear this conversation behind me.*

Violet's eyebrows arched. *Why?*

Reese quickly recounted what she saw on the beach.

When she finished, Violet turned up her beer, finishing it off in several strong gulps. *My advice to you would be to stay out of it.*

Reese had the distinct impression that Violet knew exactly who was in the shadows, making deals with the would-be witch. *Why?* Reese asked in the same mocking tone.

Violet laughed. *I don't remember you being stupid about these things. You tend to have a nose for danger. That's why you broke up with me, right?*

That stung. Violet seemed to realize this and sighed.

Aloud, she said, "If you're so bored, Reese, you should come home with me for the night. I'll keep you busy."

Reese Choice 15
Go home with Violet (ES) - go to page 216
Call it a night - go to page 156

GRAYSON: NOW IS NOT THE TIME

"Abby." Grayson grabbed her shoulders gently and pushed her back so that she was forced to look at him. "We can't."

She stiffened beside him. The rhythm she'd been trying to build evaporated. "Sorry."

Oh god, he thought. *She's going to cry.*

Then the tears were there, standing out in her eyes. Moonlight from the window made her tears sparkle like liquid silver.

"I don't know what's wrong with me," she said.

He suspected he knew.

Sirens produced powerful sexual pheromones. They aroused their targets so they could keep mating with them. This was supposed to be particularly true for male sirens.

And while Grayson felt very stupid most of the time, he knew well enough not to say that her feelings were pheromone-induced.

"It's been a hard night," he said, squeezing her against him. He didn't want to watch her cry. This was easier. Maybe it was easier for her too, as she softened against him immediately.

"I'm making a fool of myself," she cried. "You must think I'm an idiot. I mean he isn't even buried!"

"I don't think you're an idiot," he said, stroking her hair.

She pulled back to look into his face. "Who confesses their feelings to their best friend hours after their boyfriend dies? I'm so embarrassed."

"Don't be," he said. "Nothing has changed."

"Everything has changed," she said.

"I meant between us," he said. Then he realized how that must sound. "I mean, we are still best friends."

"Is that all we are?" It was such a small, desperate voice that it hurt Grayson's chest.

"No," he admitted. "No, but..." He wasn't sure how to finish. "Just not now, okay."

He wasn't sure she understood. Hell, he wasn't sure he was making sense. But she nodded, curling against him.

Slowly her breath evened out and grew steady. Then she was asleep in his arms.

I do want more, he thought. He'd wanted more for a long time. But he couldn't do it like this. Not on the back of Landon's death.

He woke to a soft knock on his bedroom door. He opened his eyes and found his mother standing in the frame, one hand on the handle, another on the jamb.

If his mother had any thoughts about the way Abigail was wrapped around his shoulder, sleeping soundly on his chest, she didn't say anything. She didn't even look directly at Abby.

And Grayson was too exhausted to care. He felt like his eyes were on fire. He couldn't have slept more than two or three hours.

"Abigail's mom is going to be here in twenty minutes. I thought she might want a bagel or coffee before she goes."

"Abby." He shook her gently. "Abby, wake up."

At first, her hold tightened on him.

"Abby, your mom is on her way."

She raised her head, auburn hair covering her face. She pushed it back with her hand.

"Morning," his mother said from the doorway. She came to the side of the bed and put Abby's clean clothes on a pile. "I washed your clothes. Or you can just wear those." She seemed to read Abby's hesitation. "I can get them back some other time."

"Thank you," Abby said, sitting up. "I appreciate that."

"Would you like a bagel and coffee?

"Yes and yes." She smoothed her abundant hair out of her face.

"Blueberry or Everything?"

"Everything. Do you have any of that garlic spread?"

His mother smiled, but Grayson saw how it didn't reach her eyes. "I do."

"I'll take that, please. Thank you."

His mother gave him a look.

"I'll make mine," Grayson told her before she shut the door with a nod.

"I love your mother," Abby said, stretching her arms overhead.

"Do you need a washcloth or anything?" he asked. He knew Abby liked to wash her face in the morning.

"I still have one from yesterday."

For a long time they both sat there, not moving, not speaking.

"It really happened, didn't it? He's really dead." She pressed the heels of her hands into her eyes. "There was a moment when I was just coming awake and I thought—"

"I know," he said. The last twelve hours of his life seemed like a crazy blur.

She took her clothes and disappeared into the bathroom without saying anything else.

Grayson went downstairs and found the bagels by the toaster. The smell of coffee filled the kitchen. It was some sort of mocha blend. He could smell the chocolate.

He cut a blueberry bagel in half with a knife and forced it into the slots of the toaster. He stood there while the elements glowed red.

Landon.

God, *Landon*. Was he really dead? Could he really be gone?

His mind kept bucking against the idea with disbelief.

Before he considered what he was doing, he had his cell phone out of his pocket. He dialed Landon's cell—he was the last one to call Grayson—and listened to the empty static on the line.

It went straight to voicemail.

"If you're looking for Landon, you found him! What's up?"

It beeped and Grayson considered leaving a message. His mouth was half open. The breath was there between his lips.

"Who are you calling?" his mom asked. She came through the swinging doors and crossed to the fridge. She pulled out a pitcher of OJ and stood there looking at him.

"No one," Grayson said, slipping the phone back into his pocket. "I was checking my messages."

It was a meaningless lie, but easier than opening himself up to have a conversation he wasn't ready to have.

The toaster spit out his bagel and he took it into the dining room. He sat down at the table beside his father. That left a space between him and his mother for Abby, which already had a steaming cup of coffee and hot bagel waiting.

"What are you going to do today?" his father asked.

"I think you should stay home and rest," his mother interjected. Her fierce blue eyes seemed to challenge his father to argue against her. "You clearly didn't get enough sleep."

His father seemed oblivious to any such challenge as he shoved the last bite of a bagel into his mouth and continued to scroll through his phone, catching up on the morning news.

"I'm supposed to be at work at two," Grayson said. "But I could call in."

"You should," his mother said. "What will Tabitha do? Fire you?"

It was true that Grayson didn't need his job at Curiosity Books. But he liked working there. There was something about the cramped rows and precariously perched stacks that comforted him. And it wasn't like spending his afternoons in a used bookstore was a hard job. Usually he spent it reading behind the register and saying hello to the customers who meandered in.

Every hour or so, there might be a purchase or two, but overall it was quiet.

The most exciting part of the gig was the ghost upstairs who liked to move around Ms. Monroe's dining room furniture when she was away. And sometimes, if the ghost was particularly restless, she would pull a book from the shelves just to hear it hit the dusty carpet.

"Are you guys going to be here?" Grayson asked, forcing down a bite of his bagel. Thinking of Landon was making his throat tight again, but if he didn't eat his mother would only come down harder on him. She was militant about self-care.

"No, I have to go into the lab for a few hours, but I'll be home in the afternoon," his father said.

"And I have office hours and two meetings," his mother said. "But I'd be happy to cancel those if you want me to stay with you."

"No," he said and hoped he didn't sound too eager. "I want to be alone."

"Okay," his mother said, but her face was contradicting her.

It was clear she didn't really think it was okay. "There's still Chinese in the fridge, and I also made a salad."

"Thanks."

"You'll let us know where you're going to be though," his mother said. It wasn't a question, even if it did tilt up at the end. "Work or here?"

Grayson Choice 17
Go to work - go to page 178
Stay home - go to page 319

AUTHOR'S CHOICE – NIGHT TIDE (ES)

Reese

Reese's feet hurt and the muscles between her shoulder blades were beginning to knot into a single, dull throb. The bar room around her was in full roar as patrons laughed with their friends. Balls clanked along the surface of the pool tables before bouncing into soft pockets. The bitter tang of alcohol was softened by the smell of fresh popcorn, oil slicked and salty, blooming behind her. The latest batch was almost ready. And a good thing because they were running low.

Despite her sore feet and aching back, Reese had to keep an eye on the room. Her best friend, and the owner of Alpha's bar, Kristine, was counting on her.

Tonight was the full moon. That meant Kristine and all members of her pack were in the Wayward Woods tonight. On nights like this when the moon held her sway, they would run the forests until dawn.

That meant that tonight the bar was full of humans. Vulnerable as they were, it was up to Reese and Nick to keep them safe. Nick—the bouncer guarding the door—was a shifter, like she was. They were physically stronger than humans and impervious to magic of all kinds. That meant that demons and witches weren't much competition. The oldest creatures in town obeyed the treaty set forth by Ethan Benedict. Benedict, whatever corner of hell he crawled out of, was the peacekeeper, mayor, and co-founder of Castle Cove. It was rumored that he served Vendetta herself as her direct attendant.

Reese wasn't sure how true all of that was. But she'd felt the magic rolling off Ethan herself, and it had been enough to let her know that she had no desire to see how deep his power trenches were.

Once in a while, something truly ancient and terrible would roll through town and Ethan would handle it. Everything else was usually some low-level menace too stupid to play by the rules. So while there were a handful of demons in the bar and even a couple of living vamps and a table of shifters, Reese wasn't worried. There wasn't anything here she couldn't handle.

Except maybe her ex.

A woman with bright purple eyeshadow and dark red lips stumbled up to the bar and placed her empty martini glass on the bar top. The clatter broke Reese's concentration, pulling her out of the overheard conversation.

"Can I have another dirty martini, please?" the woman hiccupped.

"You sure?" Reese asked, taking the empty glass and putting it in the plastic bin out of sight. It was about time for Bethany to come up and do a round of bussing.

Reese watched the drunk girl's gaze shift to a couple in the corner, on the wall behind the nearest pool table. A man and woman were kissing like there wouldn't be another sunrise for either of them. The girl's face pulled into a sneer.

"Actually," she began. "Can I add two shots of Cuervo to my order?"

She slapped a twenty on the bar top.

With a sympathetic smile, Reese poured three shots, including one for herself. The woman kissing her face off was her ex, Violet. That merited a drink.

Reese clinked glasses with the girl and threw back the shot. "Cheers."

Reese made the martini and slid it toward the customer. Then, with a sigh, she stepped out from behind the bar and moved toward the couple on the wall.

There was no protecting humans from humans, but she had to do something about the demon.

"Oh god, no." The girl with the martini grabbed Reese's arm in a panic. "Don't say anything."

"I have to," Reese said, gently removing the red lacquered nails from her flesh. They left a ring of tiny crescent moons in their wake, but Reese didn't mind. "Nothing will happen to you. Don't worry."

She wasn't sure if the message was getting through those glassy eyes and slack jaw, but the girl let Reese go without further protest.

The pool players, all of whom knew Reese, parted for her like water. Several gave friendly smiles. No doubt, they thought it couldn't hurt being friends with the bartender. They weren't wrong.

Reese stopped in front of the couple on the wall. "Violet."

The girl pulled back. For a moment, hellfire danced in her eyes before they softened to a sweet, caramel brown. "Reese. What is it? Want some kisses too?"

The demon named Violet sounded almost hopeful.

"You know the rules," Reese said, slapping away the flirtation. She had a lot of practice as bartender—and with Violet in particular. "No feeding on pack grounds."

"I don't know what you're talking about." Violet batted her

eyes as the guy moved from Violet's mouth to her neck without pause. He hadn't even registered Reese's arrival.

Violet raised her chin to accommodate him.

"You *absolutely* know," Reese said and grabbed her arm. "Stop it or I'll stop *you*."

The hellfire returned to Violet's eyes. She pinned Reese with that menacing gaze. But her magic had no effect. Shifters were immune to demonic guile.

"Last time I'm saying this. Let him go, or I'll walk you outside," Reese said calmly. And she would have to. She couldn't let a demon enthrall humans without consequence. If rumor got around that Alpha's was lax on the full moon while the pack was out running the woods, then it would only invite more trouble. And to be clear, Violet was just being greedy. Not only had she enthralled the guy and fed on his lust, but she was milking the girl's jealousy as well. Reese could feel it.

"You're no fun anymore, Reese," Violet said with a deep eyeroll.

Reese felt the magic shift around them and the man stumbled back as if shoved. He stared at them, frowning.

"Go see your friends," Violet commanded.

The man stumbled away, on unsteady legs.

"Now what am I supposed to do with the rest of my night?" Violet crossed her leather boots and then her arms, leaning against the wall. She pouted up at Reese. "Were you even jealous? I was trying to make *you* jealous."

Reese wasn't and Violet knew it. Violet couldn't drink a shifter's jealousy as well as she could a human's anyway.

"Because if you were jealous," Violet said, leaning forward with a devil's smile. "You know I can kiss that and make it better."

She flicked her eyes down Reese's body suggestively.

Reese turned back toward the bar.

"Ouch." Violet laughed behind her back. "Rejected."

"You better cut it out," one of the demon boys said, giving Reese a wink as she passed him. "Or she'll stop making your Jager bombs."

"Hey," Violet said. Her smile was sweet again. "You going to tell your precious Kristine about this?"

Here Reese heard the tone of bitterness loud and clear.

"Behave and I won't have to," Reese said with an equally sweet smile before stepping back behind the bar.

The demons had a reason to be scared of Kristine. It wasn't just that she had more power and magic than Reese had seen in an alpha in a long time, nor that she was fiercely loved by her pack members in a way that made her seem untouchable. It was also Cole.

Cole was the oldest demon that Reese had ever met and he considered Kristine a dear friend. If he found out that the demons were giving her a hard time, they would be very, *very* sorry.

The rest of the night passed without further incidents. Reese threw a few furtive looks in Violet's direction, but from what she could tell, the demon had turned her attention to her friends and their pool game. Then they left thirty minutes before close.

"Good night, Reese." Violet had winked on her way out. Minutes later, Reese heard the chorus of motorcycle engines rev to life outside.

Only then did the rope of muscle in her back relax.

They closed quickly. All the tabs were settled. The drawer was counted out and bagged. Bethany—a single-mother and witch with the local coven—bussed the room and Nick locked up.

Reese bid her coworkers good night and stepped out onto the cobblestone sidewalk.

She considered going home, putting on the television and taking a long, hot bath before falling into bed.

But despite her aching feet and back, her mind was too restless.

"A swim," she said to no one in particular. "That would be perfect right now."

It would do wonders for unfurling the tight coil of her mind too, which kept circling back to her demon ex-girlfriend and the drunken hellfire in her eyes when she'd been kissing that guy.

If she swam for a couple hours now, by the time she fell into her bed at four or five in the morning, she would sleep like the dead.

Reese walked three blocks to her red pickup parked in front of the closed froyo station. The truck still had some of the evening heat inside it as she climbed in and turned the key.

It rattled to life, grumbling like an old man who'd been awakened from a deep slumber.

She drove east until it connected with the main strip outlining Castle Cove University campus. Then she turned right, heading south. She'd drive out of town and take Canyon Road. There she could pull off and walk down to the water.

Following the ridge, Reese enjoyed the view of the white, frothy waves and luminous moon. It hung in the sky, bright with milk-white light. The waves crashing against the shore seemed violent. Then she remembered the scrap of conversation she'd heard from the booth in Alpha's.

"A guy died, Trace. Fuck." She'd tracked the voice to a booth against the far wall. Two guys and two girls had sat in it, nursing the long-necked bottles between them.

"I'm just saying it's weird. Why wouldn't they announce it? Why do they have to act like it's a secret?"

"Maybe they don't want to freak people out," the woman had said. She'd turned her beer in her hands, her thumbnail picking at the label.

"If sirens were killing people, I'd want to know," the other guy had agreed.

A guy died.

She hadn't heard about anyone drowning or getting hurt in the water. Could they have been mistaken? Or had something happened that Ethan or the others were keeping quiet for the time being? Usually if true danger cropped up in Castle Cove, the police would issue a city-wide alert. There were too many humans living in Castle Cove not to put them on their guard. It was easy for drifters or new arrivals to miss these important updates, simply because they didn't know where to look. However, long-time residents were savvy. They knew what dwelled within the city limits—let alone the ocean and woods bordering on all sides.

Reese pulled off Canyon Road and parked her car on the gravel shoulder.

Looking both ways, and seeing only moonlit pavement as far as the eye could see, she crossed the street to the beach. Carefully, she slid down the sandy dune to the wet-packed sand below.

The sharp smell of salt overtook her. Her skin prickled in anticipation. Each crashing wave against the shore seemed to call her magic to the surface of her skin. It danced as if alive.

Ocean spray misted against her skin.

"Just a minute," she told herself as she shed her clothes. She folded them up neatly and put them on a jagged boulder at the base of the dune. They should stay dry there until she returned.

She waded naked into the surf. Cool water slapped against her calves and then her thighs. She shivered.

A trill of laughter caught her ears and she turned toward the sound of it. Her eyes adjusted to the dark and the distance. Even so, she could just make out three kids sitting on Heart's Rock. They were playing chicken with the sirens no doubt.

Reese thought the rite of passage—the tradition of swimming from Hunter's Beach to Heart's Rock—was too dangerous. But who was she to say?

The water rose to her chest and she almost couldn't contain it anymore. She gave herself over to the magic thrashing beneath her skin. Slipping beneath the wave, she transformed.

Her body softened and elongated. Her limbs merged with her torso, becoming a single lithe form of muscle. Two blinks and her eyes adjusted to the watery depths. Sensations radiated along her skin, taken in by her flesh in a way that her human skin could never manage.

Reese was a black-tipped reef shark.

She was a fixed shifter, meaning she took only one form, unlike the doorman Nick who was a chimera.

And in moments like this, when she was in her shark form and one with the water, she wondered if she'd ever really been human at all. Her life on the land slipped away, becoming little more than a dream in her mind.

She felt powerful here. Strong not only in body and speed but in spirit. She often wondered if there may come a day when she simply wouldn't want to change back. What if she stayed in the ocean and lived here forever? She knew she could.

But that decision was for another day.

Reef sharks like herself preferred to trace the drop off, patrolling the place where the life-rich shallows met the deep expanse of sea. That had been her original aim when she'd driven to this stretch of beach after the exhausting night tending bar.

But now that she was here, she also had the option of swimming through the cove toward the kids. That was deeper water, and held some danger. But maybe the kids needed someone looking after them. After what the patrons had said about the sirens, maybe the kids were in danger.

Reese decided to stick with her original plan. She longed to patrol the moonlit waters along the drop.

So she swam south through the reef. She swam in a hypnotic rhythm as she slid along the ocean floor. Her body enjoyed the slow steady drag of the water over her skin. She felt weightless, becoming one with the currents.

The tips of her fins registered the moment the reef dropped away and only an expanse of ocean stretched out before her. She hooked right around the reef, tracing the outline of its slumbering form. Ethereal moonlight cut through the surface, ghostly beams illuminating the coral. Nighttime feeders darted into available nooks and crannies as she passed. No one wanted to be the evening meal for a reef shark.

She might be a predator in these waters, but reef sharks were small, comparatively. She was a little large for a reef shark, reaching six feet. But that was nothing for a tiger or bull shark that might come toward shore.

Castle Cove waters had the usual flora and fauna of a shallow reef ecosystem—and then also creatures that did not exist in other parts of the world. Apart from the shapeshifting sirens they also had a resident *Bake-kujira*, a skeletal ghost whale. Reese felt it in her electromagnetic field and could hear its long, mournful song. But she had not seen it with her own eyes. It was far out in the deep blue sea. Reese wasn't interested in becoming someone's meal just to satisfy her curiosity.

Apart from sirens and *Bake-kujira*, there were also undines who swam these waters. Undines were tricky little water demons. Playfully luring a human into a riptide, causing them to drown, was their idea of a good time.

But the ocean was quiet tonight. Reese saw nothing out of the ordinary as she swam the reef.

Until magic rippled across the water, and her sensors shifted into high alert.

A massive burst of magic ejected from somewhere overhead. She darted west, tracing the reef until it opened up, giving her a path to the shore.

Thunder rolled across the sky, intensifying the strange electric feelings cascading over Reese's skin. The pressure in the ocean changed.

As inconspicuously as possible, she transformed from shark to human in the warm shallows.

Slowly, she stood up in the water, dripping. There, crouched beside a large boulder, was a dark-haired woman. Reese kept low, using another boulder to hide her position as she inspected the scene. Despite the heat, she wore black gloves, boots, and equestrian pants. She looked ready to ride a horse, not go for a swim.

Open on the sand in front of her was an enormous book. Something glinted, sparking with reflected moonlight.

A knife, Reese thought.

The storm raged stronger. A bolt of lightning tore across the sky, illuminating the woman's pale face and black eyes. She was whispering something to the dark, waiting.

Except nothing happened.

The woman cursed and threw the blade into the sand.

She stood and kicked the earth, sending a spray of sand arcing into the water. She gathered up her book, shook the sand from it and started to march away.

After a few feet, she returned and grudgingly picked up the knife again. Obviously displeased with its performance. She looked ready to throw it into the ocean.

Performance, she repeated in her mind. Maybe it wasn't a knife then, but an athame, a ceremonial tool for magic. Reese could certainly feel the magic still dancing along her skin, though now it seemed to be dissipating. The storm overhead was quieting, too. The wind eased its assault on her hair and ears. The woman was halfway up the dune, sand shifting under her boots. Had she caused the storm? The surge in magic? What the hell had just happened?

What was Reese going to do about it?

Reese ran as fast as she could down the beach. She was faster than a human, given her shifter status so she managed to make it back to her pile of clothes and up the steep sandy slope in moments.

She was still naked when she ran across the street toward her red pickup. She'd only just thrown the door shut when twin taillights sparked to life in front of her. A car parked several meters away, farther up Canyon Road hooked a U-turn on the road. Its engine revved as it sped back toward town. Reese ducked down, pressing her face to her warm fabric seats as the car passed.

She waited a few breaths and inched up just enough to check her side mirror. The car was speeding away. The coast was clear.

Once the taillights were small enough that she thought she could also turn around and not get caught, she keyed the ignition and threw the truck into drive. She U-turned in the middle of Canyon Road. Her tires spit rock and sand along the pavement as she wrenched her wheel left then right.

She dressed as she drove, getting her bra and shirt down over her head first. She pulled her wet hair out of her shirt and let it fall down her back, knowing it would have to be washed and detangled later and what a job that would be.

The pants were harder to get on. She managed only to get one leg inside them before giving up.

Reese kept the taillights in her line of sight, but didn't get too close to the car. Again, she didn't want the woman to realize she was being followed. As they passed Vendetta Heights, Reese vaguely noted the cluster of cars parked in the wild, open fields. No one would dare go into the Western Woods that bordered the Heights, but the Heights themselves were free game for vampires who wanted to hook-up with vamp-loving humans.

The field-turned-parking lot looked like any other make-out

spot for teens. Laughter rippled through her open window as she passed and also caught the metallic tang of blood. And sex.

Reese slammed on her brakes and downshifted as a woman stepped off the shoulder into her headlights. She disappeared before the red pickup could connect with her.

Reese sat in the middle of the road, heart rabbiting in her throat.

"Fucking ghosts." Reese shifted her truck back into first gear. "*Fucking* ghosts."

She stepped on the gas again, rushing to recover some of the lost distance.

The car up ahead had stopped at the four-way and turned left, creeping slowly into the adjacent parking lot.

"Damn," Reese said, knowing where the woman was headed.

Reese gave her a wide berth before pulling into the gravel lot herself.

She looked at the old-timey saloon sitting in front of her.

The Crossroads.

A demon bar posted at the last four-way stop out of town. Patroned almost entirely by demons, shifters and humans only went into the bar if they had business. Like soul-selling business.

Reese hadn't detected any demonic energy at all from the woman as she'd watched her calling down her magic from the ocean and sky. So was the woman a human or a witch? Maybe she'd made some deal with a demon for a certain power and was pissed that all it had gotten her was a stormy sky?

Surely she wouldn't like it when she found out there was a no-returns policy on souls...

The dark wave music seeping out into the night didn't match the look of the bar. It really did look like a saloon straight out of an old western. The wooden porch. The windows with worn shutters. Those windows looked possessed themselves, like twin glowing eyes watching Reese contemplate her next move in the solemn darkness of her truck.

There were half a dozen cars and three motorcycles in the lot.

She weighed her options.

Reese could hold her own in a fight, but demons never played fair. Besides, she just wanted to know what that woman was up to. It was up to the long-time residents of Castle Cove—people like Reese, Kristine, Cole—to keep their eyes open for trouble like this.

"I could pretend to be looking for Cole," she murmured to herself. Cole was a demon but also her friend and neighbor. Maybe no one would question why she came to a demon bar looking for her demon friend then. "I can just peek in there and see what she's up to."

Realizing the only person she was trying to convince was herself, she gripped the steering wheel.

Her bare butt stuck to her seat, reminding her that she still needed to finish pulling up her pants. She did and slid out of her truck. Gravel shifted under her boots as she shut and locked her door. She ran a hand through her wet hair and pulled her shoulders back. She did what she could to mask her scent, knowing it would betray her uneasiness.

Pushing against the rough, bat-wing door, Reese stepped into the bar.

Grayson

He stood on the beach and stared out at the moonlit horizon. White light shone on the iridescent waves. The salt stung his nose and the wind rolling off glowing crests pulled tears from his eyes.

Someone laughed farther up the beach. He turned and saw Landon and Abigail trying to get the bonfire going. They were bent over the kindling. Abby's lighter sparked, once, twice in the dark. Both times it revealed their faces hard with concentration.

"Birthday boy!" Landon yelled. "Get your ass over here and help us."

Grayson's bare feet sank deeper in the cool sand with each step. It squished up between his toes as the sea sprayed water onto his bare calves.

"I thought the point of having a birthday was so people would do things for me," he said. But he extended his open palm toward Abby.

She handed the lighter over too willingly. "You're better at this shit than the rest of us. Weren't you a wood scout for six years or something?"

"Or something," he said. Eight years was more like it. He struck the lighter and caught the soft brush on the first try. They'd been trying to burn the sticks themselves, not the soft nest he'd made for them out of dry grass and kindling. That was where they'd gone wrong.

"I can't believe your parents let you go into the Western Woods as a kid," Landon said, dragging his hand under this nose. He sniffed. "My parents *still* forbid me from going in there."

"There's a big difference between the Western Woods and the Wayward Woods." Grayson fanned the sparks. "Even scouts don't go in the Western Woods."

In truth, the entire forest spanning Castle Cove County was called the Wayward Woods. But there was a clear distinction to all who knew better.

"Here we go," Abby said with a teasing smile. He elbowed Landon in the ribs. "We're about to get a lesson from Professor Richt."

Landon snorted, settling down onto the sand beside her. The fire grew, illuminating both their faces with the warm orange glow.

Grayson affected a prim English accent and smoked an invisible pipe for comedic effect. "Yes, children, well, it is all about the territory line. If you go *west* of the territory line you will find yourself in the *Western Woods*. If you stay east of the territory line, and I highly suggest that you *always* stay east of the territory line, then you remain in the Wayward Woods. During the right times, and with the right company, the Wayward Woods are safe enough. You can't be foolish out there, but you'll likely be all right. However!" He pointed his finger into the air. "Under no circumstances should *anyone* cross the territory line into the Western Woods. Do you understand, children?"

"Yes, Professor Richt," they both chimed. They always loved his impressions of their junior year history teacher. All Grayson was missing was a shock of wild gray hair and a mustache Mark Twain would be proud of.

"There are creatures in those woods. Old, ancient and *hungry* creatures. They will devour you alive. Or drag you screaming to their lairs, where they will eat you. Slowly."

Landon shivered.

Then all three laughed.

Grayson dropped the act and sank down onto the sand beside them.

It was true he'd spent his summers scouting the Wayward Woods. He learned more about the flora and fauna of those woods than he thought possible. More about the seasons and cycles of the earth and what it meant to work in harmony with the land. But this education wasn't the result of generous parents. Rather, they fully understood the dangers of living in a place like Castle Cove and they wanted their children well-equipped against any danger that might arise.

We can't always be there to protect you, they'd said as they kissed his cheeks and sent him off into the woods. *The people who get hurt are the people who aren't prepared or who don't under-*

stand what is going on around them. We want to raise you strong, Grayson.

Grayson knew that most parents kept their kids out of the darkest corners of Castle Cove. Abigail's mom hadn't even let her outside after sunset until she was sixteen. Landon's parents still never let him go anywhere alone without at least two or three friends in tow.

By comparison, Grayson's parents must seem like free-range hippies.

Maybe it was because both of his parents were from Los Angeles. To them, anywhere in the world could be dangerous. It didn't matter if it was drugs or violence in LA or monsters in Castle Cove. Living required intelligent precautions.

Grayson watched the flames dance on the pyre, the wood crackling. His mind wandered. Eighteen. Tonight he was eighteen and he had to decide what he would do next.

He'd told UCLA that he would attend in the fall. He spoke of his love of nature in his admissions essay and was granted a scholarship to their conservation program. However, he also had an open invitation at Castle Cove University where his mother taught folklore.

Two paths were laid out before him. Two worlds offered him a place.

He had to decide which road he wanted to take.

His family had moved to Castle Cove when he was eight. He'd been in this town for ten years. He could stay here, and keep living this extraordinary life full of mystery and surprise, a life where unimaginable creatures and magic were very real. Or, he could leave and see what it was like to live in the outside world, a world he barely remembered.

Abigail pressed the bottom of her foot against his. The sand rubbed between their toes. "You trying to think of a way out of this? Because you're going in the water, birthday boy."

Grayson smiled. "I was thinking about school."

"You excited about UCLA?" Landon asked.

"Maybe."

"We'll miss you," Abby added. She'd pulled her bottom lip into her mouth when she said it. The look in her firelit eyes made Grayson's heart hitch. She wasn't supposed to look at him like that. Not with her boyfriend sitting beside her. But it was also the way she worked her lower lip. It was her *I have something to tell you* face, and yet she wasn't speaking.

Grayson managed a smile. "I'll be back before you know I'm gone."

"Doubt it," she said, looking out over the dark water.

"You'll be busy at CCU," he said. "Engineering is a rigorous program."

She shrugged, trying for nonchalance. But Grayson saw the tightness in her shoulders.

Landon put an arm around her. "You'll rock it, babe. Your brain is bigger than my stomach which we all know is *enormous*."

It was true. He might be rail thin, but Landon ate enough for four grown men.

"And I've got that internship with your dad this summer," Abigail said. She was looking at Grayson, searching his face as if hoping to see something there. "He's going to teach me to calibrate the machines in the lab."

"I think he's more excited than you are." Grayson was careful to keep his smile neutral. Perhaps if Landon wasn't sitting so close to him, he would've dared a real smile. "When do you start?"

"In three weeks," she said, tucking her hair behind her ear. "Will you be working there too?"

"Maybe."

Grayson hadn't missed the subtle advances she'd made in the last few months. The three of them had been friends since middle school. They had classes together, ate lunch together, and hung out together after school and on the weekends when Grayson didn't have scouts. When Abigail and Landon started dating in tenth grade, he hadn't been jealous.

But now...

In the fall, she'd joined the yearbook and school mag, *The Circuit*, which Grayson had worked on since his freshman year. His love of photography was second only to his love of nature. He knew Abigail didn't care about either. At first he didn't understand why she'd want to spend an extra two hours after school every day, until he started to notice *the look*.

Then she tried out for and made the crew team during winter. She took—surprisingly, position seven, which had been vacated by a graduating senior the year before. By doing so, she'd become his able lieutenant to his position, stroke.

He'd known she was a good swimmer, and she'd always come to watch his team compete in the May races. But it was still clear why she was really there.

The only problem was Landon.

He loved Abigail even more than he loved food and had since fourth grade. If she dumped him for his best friend—for Grayson—*no*.

Just no.

Grayson knew it wasn't worth it. Even if Abigail was beautiful and smart and brave and—

Abigail stood up from the fire and pulled her shirt over her head. Firelight danced across her bare breasts.

"Come on, birthday boy" she said, meeting his eyes.

Grayson did his best to keep his gaze fixed on hers.

Don't look down, he thought. *Don't...*

But her lips had already quirked into a smile. She knew she'd won. "You're not getting any younger."

"This is going to be cold," Landon whined. He stood and shrugged off his shirt.

He slid out of his shorts and stood in boxers. He offered a

hand to help Grayson to his feet. Grayson was reluctant to leave the warm fire, but Abigail was right.

Castle Cove teens had a rite of passage.

On their eighteenth birthday, they came down to Hunter's Beach and swam the 800 feet from the shore to Heart's Rock. If they chickened out, there was Coward's Clutch, a small rock off to the left, a mere 350 feet from shore.

But the goal was to swim to Heart's Rock under the mournful gaze of the full moon. Doing so would ensure that Castle Cove would always be your home. You could leave town and never worry that it would disappear on you, as it was wont to do for outsiders.

It just so happened that Grayson's eighteen birthday was a full moon.

It wasn't the swim itself.

It wasn't the sharks, or jellyfish, or even drowning that he worried him. It wasn't the idea of floating out there in the dark waves alone—because Abigail and Landon had both wanted to come with him. That was *their* tradition.

Landon was the first one to turn eighteen last October. After standing on the shore for fifteen minutes, it was clear he'd been afraid to get in the water. So they'd each taken one of his hands and pulled him in. Then the three of them swam to Heart's Rock together.

He had wanted to take the detour to Coward's Clutch, but they'd urged him on, staying beside him until he'd reached Heart's Rock.

When Abigail turned eighteen in April, they'd done the swim again. Abby hadn't been afraid, but they'd entered the water with her anyway.

Now it was June and Grayson's turn. The waters would be warm and the swim pleasant.

So why was his throat thick with fear?

In a word: sirens.

Abigail seemed to read his face as she stood naked in the surf. "They don't come into the cove. They might come onto the rock, but that's when we jump off. No problem."

That's what they had done on Abigail's birthday. A male siren had come onto the rock and sang to her until Landon got his fingers into her ears and pulled her back into the water.

Grayson kept his eyes on hers, but was hyperaware of her bare breasts glowing in the moonlight.

Landon wasn't even trying to hide his gaze.

"Babe, real talk." Landon cracked his neck to one side. "Are you going to be pissed if I fuck a mermaid?"

"Are *you* going to be pissed if I fuck a mer*man*?" she retorted.

Landon frowned.

"Sirens just want love too." Grayson tried to break up the tension forming between them.

Abigail snorted and walked out into the water. She beckoned Grayson forward. "You first birthday boy. This is your party."

It was true that they were likely safe. This inlet was supposed to be off-limits. It was supposed to be safe. But sirens did come to the beach and there was a real danger of being raped or drowned by them.

Abigail was staring at him. He looked down, and saw the blade.

"Why do you always bring that?" she asked him. "This is the third time we've done this swim. Nothing happens."

He looked at the six-inch blade strapped to his left forearm. He could see how it seemed paranoid. They'd completed the first two birthday swims with no need of a weapon. However, just because they hadn't run into trouble before didn't mean they wouldn't find some tonight.

"Better safe than sorry," he said, and stepped through the first wave. Cool water slapped his torso and he bent over protectively as if that would spare him.

"It's June," Landon whimpered, wading into the surf after him. "I thought it'd be warmer."

Once it rose above Grayson's thighs, he dove in.

He found a rhythm quickly. His freestyle crawl helped him stay on top of the waves as they buoyed and dropped him.

Salt stung his eyes, but it was bearable. The deeper the water got, the cooler it felt beneath him. He tried not to think about that. He tried not to think about sharks hunting the inlet for their nighttime meals. He tried not to think about what might be circling below.

He kept swimming.

A splash on his right made his heart lurch. But it was only Abby. She had caught up to him and was gaining.

He swam after her and tried to remember why they were doing this. It was a silly superstition. Or it would be, if this was any other town in the world. And the story was given credibility because it had been his mother—the head folklorist at CCU, who'd told him the story of Heart's Rock.

Castle Cove is a unique town with its own history, she's said. *And all myths stem from fact.*

Two myths centered on the large bolder jutting from the dark sea ahead.

First, there was a belief that Castle Cove only invited certain citizens. One had to be chosen in order to even find the town on the map, to even see the exit from the highway. Both his mother and father had been offered jobs here, though they hadn't applied for them. The head-hunting scout had worked hard to sell the town to them. And once they'd arrived, they quickly realized why this town was…*unique.*

The second myth that made swimming 1600 feet beneath a full moon remotely tempting, was the idea that in order for children to remain in the town, in order to *remain* chosen, they needed the cove's blessing—and that was only achieved by touching Heart's Rock, the metaphorical and perhaps literal, heart of Castle Cove.

And while Grayson wasn't sure he wanted to stay in this town, he also wasn't sure he wanted to chance being cast out of it either.

His knee scraped something rough the same time he slapped the granite surface of the rock. He pulled, hefting himself out of the water.

His arms burned. His chest ached. The swim felt harder than it should have been. The waves were doubling in size now. Or perhaps the tide had turned against them. He looked up at the sky and saw thick gray clouds rolling in. It masked the moon like a shroud.

Abigail hauled herself out of the water a minute later, coughing. He offered an arm and she took it. Her skin was cold to the touch.

"Whew," she said, laughing. "Refreshing."

"Where the hell did that storm come from?" he asked, wiping water from his face. He looked out toward the horizon and saw the spiderweb of lightning spread across the sky.

"Right? Those waves are crazy."

He checked his arm and found the blade snug in its sheath. Maybe he would look stupid for bringing it after all.

"Gray—" Abby said. "I need to talk to you, okay?"

His heart crept up his throat. "About what?"

"Something important. Not tonight, but we need to talk."

"Okay."

"Without Landon," she said. She searched his face. "So don't say anything."

"Okay," he said, feeling like a parrot.

He looked out over the water, searching for Landon almost guiltily. He was struggling with the last ten feet.

"Come on," Grayson said, clapping as if to cheer him on. "You can do it, buddy."

When he got close enough, they heaved him out of the water.

"Man," he said, coughing. "Was it me or did it feel like swimming upstream there at the end?"

Grayson pointed at the sky. "A storm is coming in."

"We'll rest before swimming back," Abby said, dragging a hand down her face to clear the water. "But not for too long. My nipples are going to freeze off."

"I can help with that," Landon said. But his teeth were chattering.

Abby snorted. "Worry about yourself, Jack Frost."

Grayson looked north over his shoulder at the cliff face. There sat the castle ruins for which the town was named. It was a dilapidated structure cutting the sky. Something flew above the highest remaining spire.

Bats, he thought, but whatever it was looked too large to be a bat, even if it was flying like one. Perhaps a nightjar then.

A deep ache formed in his chest.

He would miss Castle Cove. As strange as this place might be and perhaps as unsafe for a human like him, it still felt like home.

A cold hand brushed his arm and he looked down, half expecting to see a siren pulling itself out of the water onto the rock that marked neutral territory.

But it was Abigail. She squeezed harder and gave him a smile. "Happy birthday, Gracie."

Instinctively, his eyes darted toward Landon, but the other boy was trying to blow something out of his nose.

"God, I hate salt water," Landon grumbled, hacking into the sea.

"We have a lake," Abigail said. Her voice was perfectly calm as if she wasn't holding Grayson's hand at all.

Landon laughed. "With water demons in it. No, thanks. I'll stick to the city pool."

"The pool's haunted," Grayson said. He marveled at how calm his voice was—as if his heart wasn't knocking wildly in his throat.

"I'll take my chances."

His hand was warming in hers. He was about to withdraw when she let go and stood.

"Okay boys, let's go get some slices at CC Pizza after this. Last one back pays."

She dove into the water. Her pale skin flashed iridescent before disappearing beneath a black wave.

Landon stood, looking into the water. "Man, I'm in love with her."

"I know." Grayson felt like he'd been kicked in the gut.

The grin on Landon's face was sweet and so goofy that Grayson could only laugh. "Go get her then, man."

Landon's grin widened as he jumped off the rock. "Cannonball!"

Before Landon surfaced, a shimmer caught Grayson's eye.

A shark fin stuck three or four inches out of the water. It cut beneath the wave. It had a distinguished black tip, so it was only a reef shark. Luckily, the underwater rock barrier kept all big predators out of the cove. But it was still a shark and a bite was a bite.

The fin had been moving north across the cove and if it kept to its course, it would directly cut across Abby and Landon's paths.

But that didn't mean they were in danger. Shark attacks happened so rarely. In Castle Cove, they'd never had someone even bitten by sharks, let alone killed by one. It was vampires, werewolves and other land creatures one had to look out for.

And he had the blade.

He stood, stretched his arms overhead and readied to take the plunge.

That's when he saw the real danger.

Three shimmering forms darted around Heart's Rock. They glimmered and twirled beneath the water. The three bioluminescent forms swam in tight formation toward Abby and Landon. Then they split. Two followed Landon, one rushed toward Abby who was more than halfway to shore.

She might make it before it reached her. Or not.

Landon definitely wouldn't make it.

Sirens. Inside the territory line. Inside *the cove*. That wasn't supposed to happen.

And what was Grayson supposed to do? Stay on the rock and wait for a better moment to swim to shore? Or jump into the water and try to reach Landon before the sirens did?

Grayson spotted Landon swimming toward shore. His strokes were wild and uneven. No wonder he wasn't even halfway there. It wasn't until this moment, when Grayson was terrified for his life, that he realized how terrible of a swimmer Landon was. It didn't matter. He had to reach him as quickly as possible.

Grayson fixed the path in his mind and dove. The objective was to reach Landon on the heels of the sirens. Perhaps they were only curious. Hopefully they would swim around or tug playfully on their legs.

Of course, Grayson knew better.

Sirens had one objective when it came to humans. They wanted to mate.

As Grayson swam furiously toward his friend, he tried to remember everything his mother had taught him about sirens.

"The males are more aggressive than the females. They are more likely to accidentally drown their human mates than the females, though they are also incredibly strong. You have to understand that the males are only looking for sexual gratification. The females, however, are hoping to procreate, so they must be more careful with their prey."

"Why in the world would they want to mate with humans?" Grayson had asked.

"Male sirens are sterile. Therefore, a healthy population of the sirens is entirely dependent upon females successfully mating with humans."

"But how do you fuck a fish?" his little brother Tanner had asked.

His father had slapped him gently on the back of the head. "Don't be crude."

"I'm just asking. I thought they had fish tails!"

"They are like shapeshifters," their mother explained. Her face had soured. She hated it when Tanner cursed. "They can take humanoid form long enough to mate."

"Humanoid," Grayson had repeated. Because they didn't really look human. Not without their glamour.

Cold seawater hit the back of Grayson's throat and he choked, coughing. But he'd almost reached Landon.

"Landon," he cried. "Landon!"

Landon stopped swimming, turning toward the sound of his voice. "What—oh shit."

Two streaks of bioluminescence cut beneath them leaving shimmering blue bubbles in their wave.

"Landon, listen to me." Grayson wanted to make his instructions clear before the sirens started singing. "They're probably females looking to mate."

"Oh man." Landon couldn't suppress his goofy grin. "I hear they turn into—"

"Listen!" Grayson spat. "You need to get to shallow water. Don't stay here or she will drown you. Do you understand?"

Landon was watching one of the sirens rise from the depths to the surface.

"Landon!"

"Shallow water. Got it!" He began to paddle to shore half-heartedly.

That's when Grayson saw he had his own problem. A young woman surfaced six feet between him and the shore. He began to paddle toward her. It wouldn't be smart to try to flee into deeper water, nor could he tread the waves all night.

But she didn't look ready to move aside either.

He closed the distance—four feet, three, just two—

He cut to the right, giving himself room. She moved into his path. It looked like Abigail. It *wasn't* Abigail. He *knew* that.

"I'll do it," he said, hoping she understood. "But not here. Okay? Not here."

If the sirens could get into his head well enough to find his perfect image of a mate, surely, it could understand these thoughts too.

But she didn't look like she was going to let him pass.

She began to cut a circle around him, not unlike a shark.

A shark. He'd forgotten all about it and it hardly mattered now. They wouldn't come near the sirens or anything else that smelled of magic.

He dared to look away long enough to check on Landon. He was closer to shore. That was good, though his siren was already practically on top of him.

Grayson felt a hand on his penis and froze in the water.

When he glanced away, the siren had seized the opportunity. She stroked him. Slow and gentle, trying to conjure an erection. So these sirens really did know how it worked.

It was Abigail. It was Abigail touching him.

"No," he said. "No, *not* her."

The anger in his voice startled her. Her grip faltered. She moved back a little as if afraid of him. Of course, her advantages far outweighed his. But she was obviously confused about her failing glamour.

He was in waist deep water now. The silty bottom met his toes and relief rushed through his body. Abigail's red hair and deep blue eyes fell away. It was replaced with luscious blond locks, pouty lips and green eyes.

He almost laughed, but he kept backing toward shore.

"All right, Mrs. Miller," he said. "You'll do."

It was ridiculous. Mrs. Miller had been his ninth grade geometry teacher and he'd dreamt about her nearly every night that year.

The siren, smiling again, wrapped her body around his. Her grip was so strong, it pulled him under the waves. But the hand was on his penis again, furiously working.

When that didn't seem to have the desired effect, her head dipped below the surface. Lips fastened onto his penis with a suction so intense a moan was pulled from his throat.

He tried to elbow crawl toward the shore. He needed to be in the shallows or he was going to die getting blown by a fish girl with baby fever.

By the time he got his head above water, his erection was fully formed. Her mouth released him the same moment that hands grabbed onto his hips, pulling him toward her.

He realized she was trying to mount him.

Not here. God, not here.

Three or four feet of water was plenty to drown in, especially if his back was ground into the sandy ocean floor.

This was his chance. He could scramble for shore and hope he made it onto the sand before she caught him, or he could pull his knife and cut her. Cutting her would buy him more time to clear the shallows, but it might escalate the situation. His mother had said sirens could be violent when afraid.

Instead of pulling his knife, Grayson committed to getting to shore. There was no escaping really, and if he struggled, it would only cost him.

So he wrapped his arms around Mrs. Miller, knowing Mrs. Miller smelled like Clinique and not ocean water.

He stood up. Her legs wrapped around his torso, welcoming his embrace. She sighed into the hollow of his throat.

He kept one hand on her back, as he waded through the shallows toward the shore. This was difficult to do with her relentless enthusiastic hand, but at least she wasn't heavy.

When she finally managed to slide his erection inside of her, his step faltered.

He fell forward into the surf. A wave crashed over them, pummeling his back.

But when he rolled, body aching, it was dry sand under his head. The pounding waves were only covering his legs and groin. At least he wouldn't drown.

For a moment, it was only the strange storm clouds above, sparking with heat lightning. Then she mounted him.

Her body glistened with ocean water. Sand clinging to her breast and arms looked like crystals in the diffused moonlight.

She stayed astride him, grinding her hips into his. The sand scraped his back and buttocks. There was a rock or shell of some kind pushing into his tailbone. But he knew the best option was to lie still and indulge in his ninth grade fantasy come to life.

He turned his head, looking up the beach. He hoped he would spot Abby and Landon both safe on the shore. But the bonfire had died down and with only momentary bursts of lightning, shadows prevailed.

It looked like there was something happening at the other end of the beach—bodies moving. But it was too far to see.

Mrs. Miller picked up her pace. As she bent forward, and her cool breasts brushed his face, all thoughts were shoved out of his mind. Everything disappeared but the stormy night sky and Mrs. Miller's dripping, hard nipples.

He came and for a moment he was the one holding onto her hips, rocking against her.

But before he even caught his breath, the weight lifted and she was gone.

Two splashes and a bright flash of blue bioluminescence beneath a wave—and she was gone.

It wasn't his best sexual experience. It had been too quick, and the shells under his back had no doubt scraped his skin to hell. He also preferred his partners warm rather than as cold as a sea slug.

He tried not to think of what she must've looked like in her true form. He'd heard sirens resembled the fish monster from the Black Lagoon. If that was true, then the telepathic glamour was a blessing—even if he would find it hard to look Mrs. Miller in the eye again. *Ever.*

Grayson wanted to rinse himself in the ocean, but decided against it. The ocean water would burn like hell with the cuts stinging his back. Plus, now that he knew the sirens had breached the Cove's rock barrier, it was entirely possible that a second female could approach him and he—*no*. He couldn't do it again.

He'd have to put his clothes on as he was and worry about cleaning himself later.

Screaming tore the night in two.

Grayson's heart rocketed into his chest and before he knew what he was doing, he was running down the beach as fast as his unsteady legs would carry him.

It was Abigail. Abigail was screaming.

He pulled the knife from his forearm sheath, afraid he would have to fight a siren after all.

Abigail was still naked on the sand, her hands and knees sinking into the wet shoreline. Her face was contorted. Her mouth hung open, before another wave of sound tore through her.

"Abby—Abby!" He bent to pull her away from the water. But he saw no siren. A flash of bioluminescence sparked a hundred feet away, swimming in the direction of the ruined castle and the cliff it rested on. If it was the male siren, he was swimming away from them.

That wasn't what she was looking at.

Her eyes were fixed on a strange tangle of limbs tumbling in the ocean surf.

"Landon." Grayson's voice cracked.

It was Landon's body tossing in the white waves. Wave after wave pummeled him into the sand.

Grayson forgotten about his plan to stay out of the ocean and went into the water. He grabbed a slick limb and dragged Landon onto beach.

He wanted to turn him over, do CPR, or pound on his chest until water spurted from his mouth the way it did in the movies.

But Grayson knew his friend was dead the moment he touched his skin. There was something unnatural in its weight. The living had a lightness to their being. Landon's lightness was gone.

Yet Grayson turned him over on the shore anyway, aware that Abigail was still screaming though the sound had become a distant annoyance. It was a fly buzzing in the other room.

Grayson was shoving the heel of his hand into Landon's sternum. He was tilting back the chin so he could pinch the nose closed and blow into the mouth. But the lips were cold. The chest wasn't moving. The heart wasn't beating.

Landon was dead.

Reese

The wooden floor creaked under her boots as she crossed the threshold slowly. She made a show of looking around, as if searching for someone.

She *was* searching for someone.

The interior of the bar was a crude outline of Alpha's. Tables running along the left wall were squat, unstable-looking things. There was a jukebox somewhere. The song had changed to the 99 problems cover by Hugo.

Behind the bar was the owner, Bathory, a tall woman with black hair, black eyes, and inhuman porcelain skin. She regarded Reese with a curious expression.

Crossroads stood out from the other bars in Castle Cove for one other reason—apart from the fact it was teeming with demons—patrons could smoke. A thin gray cloud of smoke hung in the air, giving it a cloudy look that Reese hadn't seen in a long time—since the ban on indoor smoking had gone into effect fifteen years ago.

Reese felt eyes on her. Hungry, greedy eyes followed her as she moved through the room toward the bar.

"What brings you to The Crossroads, Reese?" Bathory said. She put one hand on her hip and regarded Reese with an expression that was half curiosity, half suspicion. "Kristine send you?"

"No," Reese said, knowing that her lie could be detected easily by a demon. They did specialize in them. "I'm looking for someone."

Bathory arched her eyebrows. "You have business here?"

Reese settled on a half-truth. If there was a woman using dark magic in Castle Cove, wasn't it her good Samaritan business to find out what was going on? *See something, say something.* "Maybe."

She saw Bathory trying to detect the lie. Her face hardened in confusion. Then her eyes searched the bar. "Do you see who you're looking for?"

This gave Reese a full invitation to search the bar.

Once Bathory had pulled her into conversation, most eyes had slid away, returning to the whispered conversation they'd nurtured before her arrival—except for one man. He leaned against the wall, a cigar balanced between his fingers. He regarded her with his one milk-white eye from beneath the rim of his felt fedora.

"That's Cole's brother," Bathory said in warning. "He can't be the one you came for."

"She came for me," a voice piped up.

Reese turned to see Violet climbing onto the barstool beside her. She wore a grin, masking whatever emotions she felt beneath. Like any demon, she hid her emotions perfectly. "Miss me already, baby?"

A gentle knock echoed on the door of her mind. *Open up.*

Reese cracked the door just enough to allow unspoken communication with Violet. When they'd broken up, she'd revoked the demon's free pass to play in the recesses of her mind.

Come get a table with me, before these guys eat you alive, Violet said. Even in Reese's head, she sounded just as she did aloud. Bossy.

"I thought you two broke up," Bathory said, wringing a hot washcloth into the sink behind the bar before wiping down the bar top.

"We did." Violet gave Bathory a suggestive grin. "Maybe it's my lucky night. Maybe she wants me back. Tell me you missed me."

Reese smiled, trying to play along. "I did."

And Reese realized she didn't have to lie. Surprise flickered on Violet's face as she registered the truth as well.

"Can I get you a drink?" Violet asked, tapping her black nails on the wood. She was searching Reese's face earnestly now.

"A beer," Reese said.

"Two Surly Darkness, Bath." Violet cut her eyes to the barkeep who was already opening the cooler. To Reese she said, "Why don't you wait for me at that table?" The demon pointed at the empty table against the wall. "I'll be right over."

Reese didn't miss the fact that this table was about as far

from the other demons as possible. But she dutifully crossed the room and took a seat. From here, she was able to see the part of the room that had been blocked by the bar.

The back of the room was cloaked in shadows, actual cloaking magic to be sure. She suspected to most eyes they saw only darkness. But Reese caught the outline of two people talking at a table. One was the woman she'd followed.

Reese took her seat with her back to the couple. She wouldn't be able to see them from the other seat. At least this way, maybe she could hear their words.

"It didn't work!" the woman hissed between song changes.

Reese glanced over her shoulder and saw the woman from the beach tucked into a deep pocket of shadow. The demon she spoke to remained hidden. He—or she—was wrapped in deliberate shadows with the exception of a pale, bloodless mouth. Reese knew that demons exploited darkness, but she'd never seen one so adept at it. She was more than curious to know who was controlling the dark. Did she know them? If not, from what rock did the creature crawl out from under?

The chair across from Reese scraped across the floor and Violet settled into it. She rotated her shoulders, shifting the leather jacket she wore. She slid the bottle across the table toward Reese.

"You didn't have to," Reese said, referring to both the drink and the intervention at the bar.

"Sure I did." Then directly into Reese's mind, she added, *Channery was about to fuck your soul three ways to church.*

Reese saw that she'd made a small, nearly imperceptible motion toward Cole's brother.

In my opinion, he's the worst demon in town. I wouldn't spit in his drink for a billion dollars, Violet added. *So you're welcome.*

Reese was honestly touched by the demon's protectiveness, but she wasn't stupid. *I can't thank you, Vi. Or you might get the idea that I owe you something.* Being indebted to a demon—however chivalrous—invited trouble.

The demon offered a cocky half-smile. *It was worth a try.*

Reese was trying to hear the conversation going on at the table behind her, but nothing was coming through. The next tune—a blue grass remix of another Top 40 hit—now filtered through unseen speakers.

So what's really going on? Violet asked, taking a long drink on her own beer. *If Kristine didn't send you for bartender shit, why are you here?*

Reese tried to decide what she could and couldn't tell Violet.

"You have your thinking face on," Violet said, taking another sip. "Last time I saw it, you broke up with me. Should I be worried?"

Reese flashed an apologetic smile. *I'm trying to hear this conversation behind me.*

Violet's eyebrows arched. *Why?*

Reese quickly recounted what she saw on the beach.

When she finished, Violet turned up her beer, finishing it off in several strong gulps. *My advice to you would be to stay out of it.*

Reese had the distinct impression that Violet knew exactly who was in the shadows, making deals with the would-be witch. *Why?* Reese asked in the same mocking tone.

Violet laughed. *I don't remember you being stupid about these things. You tend to have a nose for danger. That's why you broke up with me, right?*

That stung. Violet seemed to realize this and sighed.

Aloud, she said, "If you're so bored, Reese, you should come home with me for the night. I'll keep you busy."

Reese considered the offer. It was an excuse to get Reese out of the bar and away from the other demons. Even when they'd been together, Violet had a way of angling Reese away from her demonic companions. Reese had once asked why, and Violet had laughed. *We're a bunch of bastards. I thought that'd be obvious to you.*

Reese drank down the last of her beer and nodded toward the door. "Let's go then."

Violet rose from the table and led the way. As they passed the bar, Bathory flashed a wink. "Have a good night, you two."

Reese stepped out into the cool night air and descended the wooden steps.

"I'll follow you to your place," Violet said, throwing her leg over her Honda Rebel. "That okay?"

"Sure."

Violet lifted the bike off its stand and walked it backwards out of its parking spot. Reese was already in her pickup when it rumbled to life.

Heading toward her place in Cliffside, Reese kept looking in her rearview, half-believing the demon might ditch her. But the single headlight of her Honda stayed with her as she drove through the dark streets.

Reese's mind wandered back to Violet's protective measures and her tendency to buffer her from the demons in town. She suspected the real answer lay in the confession Violet gave her one night about eight months into their relationship. They'd been lying in Violet's bed in her Old Town apartment. Dawn had been approaching, the moment when Violet would go unconscious for the day. Maybe that's why she'd been speaking so freely, delirious with the approaching sunlight.

"You know why demons are so attracted to shifters?" she'd mumbled. She'd been curled into her pillows and blankets, looking deceptively angelic.

"Because we fuck like animals?"

"*That.*" Violet snorted. "And your magic."

"What do you mean?" Reese had asked, reaching over to run her hand through Violet's hair.

"In low-level demons like me, it neutralizes us. But in stronger demons, in the old ones—they like to eat it."

A shiver had run down Reese's spine.

"It gets them high as hell on the power of it," she said. "You smell like magic."

The sleepy demon had rubbed her nose.

"Not like that diluted shit we can find anywhere. *Pure* magic. *Source* magic. You have no idea how intoxicating that is. It's like being starved for a thousand years and here you come, smelling like the best Bolognese I've never had."

Reese laughed. "Bolognese is your favorite."

Violet smiled. "It is."

But just as quick the smile was gone.

"But stay away from the old demons, okay? You can't fully neutralize them. And the moment they see a chance to—"

She'd kissed Violet then. "You worry too much. I'm safe."

"No one is safe in Castle Cove."

Reese laughed. "Then why are we here?"

Violet had opened her eyes in sudden clarity then. "Where else can we be what we are?"

That's when the rising sun had taken her.

A rough knock on her pickup window startled her out of her thoughts. The sound brought her back to her surroundings. She was sitting in her driveway, staring at the three-story oceanview house without really seeing it.

It was Violet.

She opened the door and climbed out. "Sorry. It's been a long night."

Violet wore her usual smirk. The tension surrounding her in the bar had dissipated. "Then let's put you to bed, princess."

Reese leaned against the driver's side door. "Why did you really want me out of there?"

"I told you. Channery was about to gobble you up."

"And what about the other two—the woman in the back and whoever she was talking to."

"The woman," Violet said, her eyebrows arching. "So that's who you followed in?"

"How do you know I followed her?"

Violet snorted. "She arrives and then a couple of minutes later, so do you, looking for someone. Then you directly refer to her while interrogating me about her. How in the world did I ever figure it out?"

Violet crossed her arms.

"At least you weren't looking for the other one. Of course *the woman* isn't much better."

"Who is she?"

Violet shook her head. "Invite me inside, Ree. Make me a drink. Maybe I'll tell you."

Reese knew that if Violet came inside and they started drinking, very little conversation would be had. Of course. Maybe Violet would surprise her.

"Would you like to come in?" Reese said. "I can make you a Jager bomb if you want."

Violet wrinkled her nose. "I'm not trying to get trashed. A G&T will do."

Reese unlocked the door and led them both inside. They kicked their shoes off at the door and crossed into the living room on the right. On the far wall, past the soft pale blue rug and glass coffee table was the bar. Reese made the G&T, but needed lime from the kitchen. When she came back with one, she found Violet on the white leather sofa. She'd removed her jacket and had thrown it over the arm of the couch. She'd pulled her hair up into a ponytail, revealing a luscious line of neck that Reese instantly wanted to kiss.

Violet knew the effect she had and blinked her long lashes. "Smell that lust. You *did* miss me."

Reese wasn't masking her scent, so no doubt her

pheromones were betraying her. No matter how calmly she put her own gin and tonic on the ceramic coaster and sat down beside the demon, body language never lied.

"Don't distract me," Reese said. She found her voice thick in her throat. "That woman was doing something down in the cove. If she's here to cause trouble—"

Violet laughed. "No doubt she's here to cause trouble. But you need to stay out of it. She could wipe Alpha's floor with both of us. Let Ethan handle her. He's probably the only one in town who can."

"How can I tell him—"

She wrinkled her nose in disgust. "Don't be a tattletale, Ree. Besides, I can think of a better way to spend the morning with you."

Her eyes had filled with soft, flickering hellfire. Of course, they did that when Violet was pissed off too. But Reese had the strong impression Violet wasn't angry at the moment.

Before she could set her drink down, Violet had moved across the couch and pressed the full length of her body against Reese's. This shoved her back into the cluster of blue, green, and gold throw pillows clotting the corner of the sofa.

The demon's mouth was hot, sparking electric across Reese's lips. Muscles low in her body filled with heat. When Violet slid down the length of her body, making Reese hyper aware of every curve, every patch of exposed flesh, Reese moaned.

Violet pulled back with a Cheshire cat grin. "Already? I haven't started."

Reese finally got her gin and tonic onto the table, freeing her other hand. She entwined the demon in her arms, slipping her fingers under the hem of her black tank top. There was no bra to unfasten so Reese enjoyed the freedom to trace her skin without hindrance.

They kissed until their mouths were raw with it and the heat between Reese's legs was so intense, she thought one movement of her legs might spark a fire.

Violet pulled back, her face flushed. "Meet me in your bed."

The demon dematerialized, leaving Reese cold and panting on the sofa. Alone. "Freaking demons."

While it was true that Violet could not use any of her demon powers *on* the shifter, it didn't mean she couldn't torture her by proxy.

She grabbed her drink, downed it in one go and ran up the stairs to her bedroom, crunching ice between her teeth as she climbed.

When she threw open the door, panting with loss of breath, she found Violet reclining on the bed, a gleam in her eye.

Violet had taken the liberty of killing the lights and filling the room with candlelight. Soft music played from an unseen speaker. She ran a hand over the coverlet. "Took you long enough."

Reese regarded the candlelit room. "You're really trying here."

"It's been a while since I've fucked you," Violet said. "I want to remind you how good I am."

Reese was across the bedroom in two strides, slamming the demon back against the pillows. "I haven't forgotten."

Violet's eyes danced with fire. Though whether it was her own demonic hellfire or the candles in the room, Reese couldn't be sure.

Violet flipped her easily, sliding her legs down on either side of Reese's body. "Take off my shirt."

Reese obeyed, grabbing the bottom of the thin fabric and pulling it up over Violet's head. She stole several kisses while their mouths were aligned. And while Reese's mouth was greedily sucking on full lips, Violet was relieving her of her own shirt, then the black sports bra beneath it.

Then their breasts touched, nipples lightly grazing one

another. Violet pushed her back against the bed. "Do you still have a strap-on?"

"Pretty sure they're all at your place," Reese said.

Violet pouted. "Disappointing. I wanted to see you on your hands and knees." A wicked grin covered her face. "I can still get you there."

Violet laid down alongside Reese, aligning her body as if she were the big spoon. She slid her arm down between her legs.

"Already so wet," Violet purred in her ears. "Was I the last person to fuck you?"

"Yes," Reese admitted. No point in lying about it.

"That was a while ago."

"I'm aware," Reese groaned. As Violet found her clitoris, gently rubbing it between two fingers, she bit down on Violet's arm.

"Careful," Violet said, hissing. "You know how much I like pain. I'll get carried away."

Reese pretended not to hear, biting harder as Violet slipped two fingers inside her.

She teased Reese toward her first orgasm with slow, steady strokes. As her desire built, obliterating all thought from her mind, Violet pulled her up onto her hands and knees. Her hand stayed between her legs, ruthlessly building speed. Reese buried her face in the pillow, crying out as white and red sparks danced behind her eyelids.

"That's it, baby," Violet cooed. "Just for me, okay?"

A second surprise climax echoed through her. Reese fisted the pillows around her.

"You're cheating," Reese said. "You're using lust magic or something."

Violet snorted. "I wish. Then I could *really* blow your mind."

Violet forced her legs farther apart, sliding between them. She turned, so that she was lying on her back between Reese's spread legs. She pulled Reese down onto her chest.

The first brush of her tongue so soon after two orgasms rocked Reese. Her legs shook with the force of keeping her weight aloft.

But Violet had already wrapped her hands around the shifter's legs, refusing to let go. It didn't matter that Reese's legs were shaking. It didn't matter when she collapsed onto her side, unable to hold herself above the demon's mouth anymore. The demon wouldn't let go. She rolled with her, continuing her tongue's assault until Reese was on her back, orgasming for a third time.

"Enough," Reese begged. She grabbed a fistful of Violet's hair. "Enough. My turn."

Violet let herself be hauled up between her legs and into a sloppy kiss.

Reese sat up, pulling Violet into her lap before laying her down the other way, her head now at the foot of the bed. She began work on removing her pants.

"You can barely keep your eyes open," Violet teased. "I'm pretty good, huh?"

"Shut up," Reese said, but there was no malice in it. She was enjoying the bright flush in Violet's face and the cat-like grin on her face.

"I bet I could—" Violet's words were swallowed by a moan.

Reese slid her fingers into the demon. *"Hushhh."*

Reese was delighted to find that Violet was just as wet as she'd been. "Am I the last one who fucked you?" Reese asked, teasingly.

"Yes," Violet said, bearing down on her hand.

Reese's emotions swelled.

"I'm not lying, Ree." Violet pulled her forward, looking into her eyes. "You are."

Of course, this said nothing about how many pants Violet may have dropped since their breakup. Reese pushed back against the swell of emotion threatening to rise like a tide and destroy this nice little oblivion they'd formed around them.

They were running out of time. Reese could already see the first hint of purple behind the bedroom curtains. It would be sunrise within the hour.

Violet grabbed Reese's free hand and pulled it up to her throat. She squeezed until Reese took over, adding the pressure of her own. Violet liked being choked as she came. Reese hadn't forgotten. So she let Violet writhe against her hand until the last waves of her climax fell away.

Reese waited, trying to read Violet's body to see if she wanted more, or if the approaching sun was going to win.

She thought the demon had fallen asleep when she said, "We could pick this up again, you know."

Reese lay down beside her. "Could we?"

Reese knew she wasn't talking about the sex. She was talking about their failed relationship. They'd been together for two years and apart for almost one. Reese still liked her. There was no point in lying to herself about that. But she'd had her reasons for ending it.

Seeing Violet make out with people in the bars, or invite people into dark corners hadn't been easy, even if it was only to feed off their baser emotions—jealousy, lust, envy.

"Eating isn't cheating," Reese said. "That's what you said."

"That's why you ended it, wasn't it?"

Reese didn't answer.

"I've never lied to you," Violet said. She grabbed the ends of Reese's hair, playing with the inky black tips. "But a girl's got to eat and I won't feed on you."

I've never lied to you.

Violet must have sensed the dark shift in her mind.

"Forget I said anything. I've ruined the moment."

"You didn't," Reese said. She ran a hand through her hair. If she was being honest with herself, she'd missed Violet. She'd seen her around, but that wasn't the same.

She'd missed the intimacy. Even if the jealousy had also been tearing her apart.

"I know it doesn't feel like it to you," Violet said with uncharacteristic tenderness. "But it really is like watching you get emotional over my cheeseburger. I don't feel anything for the people I eat. That's exactly *why* I eat them and why I can't do that to you."

Reese was nodding, but she didn't know what to say.

"If I don't eat I'll get weak. In a place like Castle Cove, I can't be weak. It'd get me killed."

Reese rolled onto her back, staring up at the ceiling. "I get it. I really do."

Violet dragged herself from the bed. With one movement of her hands, the candles in the room extinguished, leaving dozens of trails of thin gray smoke to rise toward the ceiling.

"Where are you going?" Reese asked. She turned on her side, watching the demon dress herself.

"I want to get home before sunrise."

"You can stay," Reese said. "You'll be safe here."

Violet considered her for a long time. She spared a small smile. "Only because it might change your mind."

Reese pulled back the covers, sliding over to let Violet slip in beside her.

The moment before the sun rose, Violet spoke. "Tell me you'll think about it."

"I will." As if Reese could actually stop herself. She pulled Violet close. "I promise."

Grayson

They dressed before the police arrived. They'd had about fifteen minutes between the moment he'd pulled his cell phone from his pocket until he saw the flashlights first sweep the sandy dunes.

Then the police were calling out their names and Grayson found a way to call back, though his throat was raw and burning.

Abigail's mother was first on the scene. As an officer at Castle Cove PD, she would've heard the call come into the station and would've taken it upon herself to drive straight to Hunter's Beach.

What he hadn't expected was that his own parents would be a close second.

It was his father who threw a gray wool blanket over his shoulders. It was his mother who squeezed him so hard he couldn't breathe.

"Are you all right?" she asked. "Are you—Christ, you're trembling."

"I'm fine," he managed, yet his teeth were chattering. "But Landon—Landon."

His voice broke and his father pulled him into his embrace. He wasn't sure how long they held him, cocooned by his parents on either side. Someone was stroking his wet hair.

When they finally released him, dozens more had arrived. There were officers in jackets, but also paramedics. They wanted to give both Abigail and Grayson full physicals.

One shone a penlight into Grayson's eyes.

"I'm fine," Grayson insisted. But they still sat him and Abigail down against a rock. She hadn't stopped crying. "Forget about me. Check on Abby."

"We need to know what happened," Officer Una O'Reilly said. Una was Abigail's mom.

"Grayson," his father said. It was the one-word command he'd heard often in his life, but never delivered with such tenderness.

Grayson told the story. He began with their plan to swim to Heart's Rock and then go get pizza.

"It's his eighteenth birthday," his mother interjected as if defending him.

"Then they came around the rock," he said. "Three sirens."

"Onto the rock?" Officer O'Reilly corrected.

"No," Grayson shook his head and cold water fell from his hair on to his cheek. "Around the rock. They passed me and swam straight into the cove. They were chasing Abigail and Landon. The females split off for Landon and the male went after Abby."

Officer O'Reilly stiffened. Her face pinched.

"I thought the inlet was safe," his father said, searching the detective's face. "I thought this tradition was harmless."

"If you call the threat of rape harmless," his mother Lillian countered.

Officer O'Reilly seemed to struggle, but finally found her words. "There was also a siren attack last Saturday." She pointed south, down the beach. "While they do visit the southern beaches from time to time, they've never crossed into the inlet before. We will have to investigate what would drive them this far into the cove."

"If there was another attack, why haven't we heard about it? Why didn't you issue a warning?" his mother demanded.

"There hasn't been time," the detective replied.

"It happened last weekend. Why didn't you let us know they were agitated? The community deserves to know if our children—"

"Lillian," his father said. He squeezed her arm, and to her credit, she seemed to regain control of herself.

"We thought last weekend's attack was an isolated incident. We did report it to…the proper authorities. But we haven't heard any new information on the situation. Frankly, we didn't know what was going on and therefore weren't sure what to report."

"Tell that to *them!*" Grayson's mother pointed at the couple further down the beach. Landon's parents were surrounded by police. It looked like they wanted to come over and talk, but the authorities weren't allowing them to come any closer.

"You could have reported that there was an attack," Lillian said stiffly. "At least tell people to stay off the beach."

"You're right. We will have to now," Officer O'Reilly conceded.

"Landon is dead." It was Abigail speaking. "Landon is dead."

"I know, sweetie." Una stooped and wrapped her arms around her daughter. "I'm so sorry."

Grayson heard the unspoken relief in her voice. *At least it wasn't you.* That must be what she was thinking. Someone's child had died tonight. But it hadn't been her child. And though both of their parents knew who Landon was to Abby and Grayson, they couldn't hide their own gratitude. They might have seen Landon grow into a young man, they might've had him over for dinners and playdates, but none of that meant they would sacrifice their own children in his place.

A man in a dark blue jacket stood awkwardly to one side, waiting to get Officer O'Reilly's attention.

She spotted him. "What is it?"

"We just wanted to let you know that the markings on the body and the water in the respiratory system are consistent with a siren attack. There was no ejaculate present—"

"Christ," Grayson's mother swore.

"—it was likely washed away in the surf."

Una held up one hand. The other remained on Abby's shoulder. "That's enough for now, Darryl. Thank you."

"Lillian, Wade, I hate to ask but could you take Abigail home, please. I will need to stay here until the scene is processed. The kids are both cold and—"

"I don't want to be alone," Abigail said. She lifted her head and dragged her nose across the blanket draping her arm.

"You can come to our house," Lillian said, tugging the blanket tighter around her. Then turning her face up to Una she said, "We'll be with them."

"Thank you." Una helped Abby to her feet. "I'll come get you as soon as I leave here. If it's too late, I'll wait until the morning. I'm sure you're all exhausted. Don't wait up for me."

"Text me either way," his mother told Officer O'Reilly. "I'll be awake."

In silence the four of them climbed the steep ledge to the parking lot above. Grayson and Abby followed his parents, shoulder to shoulder, to the parking lot beside the castle ruins. No one spoke as his father unlocked the car and they climbed in. In the dark back seat, Abigail snuggled close to Grayson's side, crying quietly.

"Are you hungry?" his father asked.

Grayson met his eyes in the rearview. "I don't know if I can eat now."

"We will pick up something anyway," his mother said, regarding him with one of her stern faces. "You don't have to eat it. But it will be there if you want it."

"Not pizza," Abby said softly from her corner of the car. Her voice was thick with tears. "Anything but pizza."

They picked up Chinese from the Moodle Noodle shop on the west side of campus. His father went in and paid while his mother stayed in the car.

No one spoke. The radio remained off. But distant music from a closing bar reached them.

It was Abigail who broke the silence first. "When I get to your house, can I please take a shower?"

"Of course," his mother said, turning in her seat to gaze at her. "Of course you can."

"Where's Tanner?" Grayson asked. His parents wouldn't

have brought him to a murder scene, but it couldn't have been easy finding a sitter at two in the morning.

"He had a sleepover with Will." It was like her face was drinking him in. "We will tell him what happened later."

Don't say it, he thought. He could practically see the *I'm just so glad you're okay* written on her face. But if she said it, Abby would begin to cry again and she'd finally started to quiet down.

"All right," his father said, climbing into the car and handing a brown sack to his mother. "We have enough chicken and lo mien to feed an army. Anything else?"

"A shower," Abby begged.

His father favored her with a weak smile. "Coming right up."

His father waited for a trio of drunk coeds to cross the street before he pulled away from the curb into the post-bar traffic.

Grayson's parents had bought a house in historic Midtown. This was a vintage neighborhood with beautiful restored Victorian homes and small shops. There was a coffeeshop and bookstore and it had the feel of a small antiquated town, complete with a local grocer and old-fashioned video store, where people could still rent DVDs and video games.

This neighborhood's insular seclusion was one of the reasons Grayson had been allowed to roam so freely as a child. Everything he could have wanted—candy or ice cream, a park or playground, his friends—were within a few blocks of his house.

The porchlight was on when they pulled into the drive, illuminating freshly stained steps and the railing. The house itself was a deep cherry red. He and his father had just repainted it the previous summer. It had taken them all three months, and it wasn't like his family didn't have the money to hire a team to do it faster. It was simply one of his father's "bonding" projects—of which there had been many over the years.

But seeing the house had the effect Grayson suspected his father wanted.

Every time Grayson saw it, he felt proud. Proud of what a good job the four of them had done together, and proud of his family.

This was home. He was safe here.

When he threw open the car door, he had tears in his eyes. His father saw them as he was closing his own door.

"I know," his father murmured quietly. "I know."

He squeezed Grayson's shoulder hard, and pulled him toward the house.

His mother got the door open, ushering Abigail over the threshold.

"Honey, get some towels," she said, tossing her keys and purse on the bench beside the stairs. "When you get out of the shower, Abigail, I'll have something clean for you to wear. It'll be a little big on you."

The shirt would be fine, but Abigail wasn't as tall as his mother. The pants would have to be rolled up and perhaps belted at the waist.

"It's fine," Abigail managed, looking small and worn under the gray wool blanket. "Thank you."

His mother carried the food into the kitchen and disappeared through the swinging door.

"Grayson, show her how the taps work," his father instructed, putting two fresh towels in his hand. He took the blanket off Grayson's shoulder. "And make sure there's enough soap and all that."

"Come on." Grayson took the lead on the stairs even though Abby had been visiting his house since the fourth grade. Of course, she'd never stayed the night before.

The wooden staircase creaked under their weight. When they reached the top of the stairs, he turned left and then left again to his own bathroom at the end of the hall.

He placed the towels on the sink, aware of Abigail standing beside him.

"It's backwards. You turn the handle this way for hot, and this way for cold. If it sputters, it's just air in the pipes. It'll kick back up in a second. Don't let the rattle scare you."

He left the tap on hot and pulled up the stop. The water was diverted from the spout to the showerhead, spraying the basin in a gentle rain.

Abigail handed him the blanket and began to undress.

He shouldn't care. He'd seen her naked before. But he still backed toward the door.

"I'll put the clothes outside the door," he said.

He thought it best to look her in the eyes, rather than chance staring at anything else.

But when he looked into her eyes, she was crying.

"It was you," she said, standing there naked in his bathroom, with the hot water running into a cream-colored tub.

His heart hammered in his chest.

"When the siren—I wanted it because—" She bit her quivering lip. Her hand fisted on the burgundy shower curtain. "When he was—he looked like you."

Then Grayson understood what she was trying to say. The male siren *had* caught up to her and she hadn't resisted him.

It was Grayson she'd been making love to as her boyfriend was killed.

"I'm sorry," he said. He wasn't sure what he was apologizing for. Probably all of it. The whole shitty situation. But she'd already climbed inside the shower and had pulled the curtain closed between them.

Grayson showered in his parents' bathroom.

Then after he put the fresh clothes on the sink for Abigail— she hadn't finished yet—he went downstairs to find his parents sitting around the dining room table.

Grayson had always loved this table. It was strange and ornate and looked more like a table built for 1920s seances than for family dinners. But it was one of the many charming features of their restored home.

"Come sit with us," his mother said. She was trying not to sound desperate, which Grayson appreciated. A swell of affection filled his chest.

After his shower, he found he could eat after all. The headache building behind his eyes and the shaking in his exhausted limbs begged him to eat something. "Let me grab some food first."

He went into the kitchen and pulled a white ceramic plate from the shelf. He loaded it with pineapple fried rice, lo mien, General Tso's chicken, and three pieces of crab rangoon.

He grabbed a sparkling water from the fridge and carried it into the dining room.

He sat down between his parents, knowing that was where they wanted him.

"Your father and I talked and we decided to waive the no-girls-sleeping-in-your-room policy," his mother said.

"Good call. I don't think she'll sleep alone."

"But we want you to leave the door open," his father added.

Grayson didn't even fight them. He didn't care.

His mind kept replaying the image of Landon tossing in the surf, his pale body thrashing in the waves.

"We don't have to talk about what happened," his mother began. Her words had the practiced air about them. She was a professor, but Grayson was certain that it was also because she liked to rehearse what she would say in her mind long before saying it. He was like his mother in this way.

And when had she composed this speech? In the car on the way home? When he was in the shower? Or maybe even in the car on their way to retrieve their *almost* dead son.

"Especially if you're tired," his father added. "The swim alone must've been exhausting, not to mention—" There was a jerk under the table and Grayson was fairly sure his mother had just kicked him. His father grimaced. "We just want you to know we're proud of you."

"Landon is dead." Grayson pushed the rice around on his plate with the back of his fork.

His father reached out and squeezed his shoulder. "You couldn't do anything about that."

"I should've done more. I should've—"

"If anyone is to blame for Landon's death, it's the authorities," his mother interjected. "They should have told the town about the siren attack. There should've been a notice to stay out of the water. This town—"

"Lill," his father said and her mouth snapped shut.

"I'm just saying. How are people supposed to stay safe if they aren't properly informed?"

His father fixed him with his gaze again. "You're not to blame for what happened and we're proud of you for handling the situation the best you could."

"Please stop saying that," Grayson said. He couldn't sit at this table with his Chinese food and be congratulated by his parents as if he'd won some prize. Landon was *dead*.

Landon was dead and—

"Keeping your cool in a dangerous situation is everything." It was his mother speaking. "It's going to take a long time to get over this. Maybe you'll never completely get over this loss. But we wanted you to know that we are here and we'll do anything we can to help you. If you need something, tell us."

This loss.

They weren't even saying his name.

He understood all of the words coming out of their mouths. He even understood that the reason he was here at the table while his best friend was dead on a beach was because he'd been blessed with smart, patient parents who'd prepared him to survive.

And it was more than that. He'd gotten lucky. He'd been

damn lucky.

Then why was he so angry? Why did he feel like he shouldn't be the one in the chair? Why did it feel like it was unfair that Landon should be dead and that he should be alive? Why did he want to trade places with him?

I wanted it to be you, Abby had said.

"If you need anything—" his mother was saying again.

He exhaled and pushed away from the table. "I need some air."

"We'd rather you stay in the house," his father said.

His mother shot him another look and his father grimaced as if expecting another kick.

"But we won't tell you what to do," his mother said. "But why don't you go to bed? You've had one hell of a night."

"Yeah, it's late," he said, conceding to his parents' will. The relief was written all over their faces. "I should check on Abby anyway."

He pushed back from the table and took his plate to the kitchen. He rinsed it without really seeing the dish in his hands, nor did he see the kitchen around him. It seemed like another person was making his body move through the house, up the stairs.

In his bedroom, he found Abby in his double bed. She was facing away from him, toward his big picture window at the tulip poplar tree dancing in moonlight. He thought she was asleep until she spoke.

"Will you hold me?" she asked. She glanced over her shoulder. "I can't fall asleep."

"Okay." He slipped under the covers.

She was warm now, so much warmer than when they'd been naked on the beach just hours before. Her hair smelled like his shampoo and despite everything, a strange possessiveness rose up in him.

Stop it, he told himself. *Stop thinking about her like that.*

Not only was it wrong to think about his best friend's girl-friend like that, but Landon had just *died*. She couldn't possibly be interested in him right now.

And yet she was reaching her hands under the covers. She was twining her fingers with his.

"Please," she said, snuggling deeper into his arms. He curled one arm under her head, and slipped the other over her waist.

How many times had he dreamed about this in the last six months?

How many times had he wondered what Abby would feel like in his arms?

Countless. And if he was being honest with himself, she was the reason he couldn't decide between UCLA and CCU. Part of him wanted to go to UCLA in order to get away from her. No—

from the *temptation* of her.

He'd played a scenario in his mind that went something like this: He went away to LA for four years. Abigail and Landon broke up while he was away but became friends again. Then when Grayson returned after college one summer, or when he graduated, he and Abby would have their chance. When it came time to tell Landon, he would be cool with it because he would be over Abby and dating someone else.

The alternative fantasy had been staying in Castle Cove and going to CCU with Abby. And...

Only that wasn't how it was going to go now, was it?

Landon was never going to be a problem ever again.

"Why?" he whispered. The word was out of his mouth before he could censor it. He hadn't meant to open this conversation. If he was lucky, she would be asleep and he wouldn't have to explain himself.

But she was turning over in his arms. *Her* thighs were brushing against *his* thighs.

"Why, what?" she asked. Her breath was hot on his cheeks and nose. God, her mouth was *so* close.

He licked his lips and tried to think of any other *why* he might use. But he was too aware of her body. Too aware of the way his hand felt on the dip of her hip. Too aware of the way he'd begun to throb, his heartbeat radiating from his navel down to his knees.

"Why did I see you? With the siren?" she asked.

He gave the smallest imperceptible nod. His nose brushed hers when he did.

For a long time she said nothing.

That's what you get for trying to make her talk about it, you moron, he thought. *Landon just died. He died while she was...she was... The last thing she wants to talk about is that.*

"I'm sorry," he said. "Forget I said anything."

She ignored this apology. "I think I figured it out at junior homecoming. How I feel about you."

Grayson's stomach twitched. Junior homecoming was almost two years ago.

She licked her lips. The skin shimmered as she spoke. "When I was shopping for my dress, the—"

"Navy blue one," he interjected.

Her breath hitched. "Yeah, that one. I can't believe you remember. Landon never remembers what I wear."

Remembers. Because to her he wasn't dead yet. He understood that. Was that why this felt so wrong? Holding her like this? Wanting her even after the night they had and the awful sight of Landon's body thrown against the shore...

"When I was shopping for it, I kept picturing you. I wanted to know if you'd like it. If you would notice that I'd dressed to match you."

He had noticed. But Landon's suit hadn't been so different from his own, in either style or color, so Grayson wondered if it was all in his head. Was he only seeing what he wanted to see?

"I think I've always wanted you, but Landon asked me first. And I loved him too, but it took me a long time to realize I didn't love him like that. He was a guy I trusted and cared about, but there was no…"

I'd been too scared to show interest, he thought.

"But I wanted to be sure. I started taking more of the same classes as you. The same after-school activities as you. I wanted more so I could figure out what I really wanted."

"Did you?"

"Yes. I *want* more."

The throb in his stomach was nearly unbearable, except now it was spreading upward, through his chest and into his head. It was becoming hard to think.

"If you don't see me that way," she said, licking her lips again. "If you don't—"

"I do," he said. It wasn't a smart thing to say. This was neither the time nor the place.

Right now his best friend was zipped up in a black body bag on his way to the Castle Cove County morgue. And he was lying in his warm, safe bed with more than half an erection and best friend's girlfriend in his arms. Shame flooded him.

Before he could process what was happening, she slipped an arm around his waist and closed the remaining distance. He could feel her nipples through her shirt, rubbing against his chest. Her lips found his in the dark.

When she rocked her whole body against his, he had to swallow down the sound building in the hollow of his throat.

Don't, don't do it, his mind warned. But he was already leaning in. He was already finding her lips with his.

She sighed into his open mouth and shivers ran down his spine. He slid his hand up her back and crushed her to him.

"Here," she whispered, and pushed against his arm until his hand was on her hip. Then she grabbed that hand and slid it down the front of her pants.

His fingers traced over the rough stubble from where she'd shaved. She opened her legs wider and he found her wet.

So wet.

The last time he'd fingered a girl was Olivia Richards in the back of her Ford Mercury after rehearsal for *Oklahoma!* one night. He tried to remember what Olivia had liked best about his performance—what she'd responded best to—and started there.

Grayson trailed a finger over the soft hood of her clit, back and forth. She gripped him harder, whimpering into his ear. His erection grew so hard he thought he would burst inside his sweatpants.

When her squirms gave over to desperate mewling, he slid his fingers inside her. Her moan rose in her throat.

He clasped the back of her neck and pressed her mouth against his throat, hoping to muffle her sounds.

He froze, thinking he heard a creak on the stairs. For a long time, they lay perfectly still, his fingers inside her, listening to the dark.

"You have to be quiet," he whispered.

She nodded, her soft cheeks rubbing against his throat. Her grip on him only tightened.

He began to pull his fingers out, only to slide them in again. She whimpered in his ear, but the sounds were soft. When he bore down, letting the heel of his hand press against her clit while he kept working his fingers in and out, her moans grew loud again.

"I'm sorry," she said, breath heavy. "But please don't stop. *Please.*"

He sympathized with her. The throb in his pants was unbearable.

Then he felt her hand—in her own pants. At first he was confused.

"No, don't stop," she whispered. "You should—yes."

He pumped his fingers in and out of her while she rubbed her clit. It took almost no time at all to send her over the edge, and before he'd even established a decent rhythm, loving the slick, soft feel of her, he felt her contract. He rode the wave, not stopping until she was fully spent.

Then her hand was slipping past the waistband of his pants.

He hadn't been wearing boxers or briefs under his sweats, so her hand found his erection immediately.

Her fingers were already wet with her own juices as she cupped him and began to slide her hand gently up and down his shaft.

Now it was his turn to bite back a moan.

She sucked at his throat and ear as she rubbed him, picking up speed. It was the moisture in her hand that made the sensation euphoric.

As if reading his mind, her hand disappeared.

He was close to begging, but he was rewarded for his patience. When her hand reappeared, it was even slicker than before. She'd clearly touched herself one last time for his benefit.

"God," he moaned. Whatever he meant to say next was swallowed up by her mouth closing over his.

She probed his tongue with hers and wouldn't let go. She devoured him as her hand continued its steady, relentless rhythm.

Then he came and she held on as if she could milk every drop out of him.

"Grayson?" his father called out. He was at the end of the hallway, where the landing split between the two bedrooms.

His heart jolted. "Yeah?"

His voice was tight in his throat.

"Abby's mom isn't coming tonight. She'll be here tomorrow."

"Okay," Grayson said, hoping his voice sounded steady despite the rabbit pulse in his ears. "Thanks."

"Try to get some sleep, all right?"

"Yep," he said. And that's when he *knew* his dad knew. After all, he had called out from the landing rather than from his door. And why would he tell him to get some sleep unless he suspected he hadn't even been trying?

"Good night, son."

"Night."

Neither Abby nor Grayson moved until they heard his parents' bedroom door click closed.

Abigail seemed unperturbed by this. "I want more of you," she whispered.

"My bed squeaks," he said.

"So let's get on the floor."

Grayson had heard that male sirens emitted a potent pheromone that induced arousal in women. Was Abigail still reeling from its effects? If so, no amount of effort would placate her tonight. Only time would do that.

She saw his hesitation. "Or not."

"I want to," he said and he wasn't lying. He was certain, with enough, encouragement he could rise to the occasion.

"But you don't want your parents to hear you?"

"And…" But he wasn't sure how to finish this sentence.

"And?" She pulled back and looked him in the eyes. She leaned over the side of the bed and grabbed her towel. She used it to wipe her hands and then his. This gave him time to compose his thoughts.

"I don't have any protection," he said. "And I suspect what we just did might not be the most…hygienic."

"I'm clean," she said. "I just did my annual. You won't get anything from me."

He smiled, pushing the hair back from her face. "I want to be sure you really want this. You've been through a lot tonight."

"*We've* been through a lot," she corrected him.

Landon. Grayson kept replaying all his favorite memories of Landon. Landon over at his house, eating chips and drinking soda after school while they played *Resident Evil* on PS4. Landon with slicked hair and braces as they went to their first dance. Landon when he'd confessed that he wanted to ask Abby out and whether or not Grayson thought it was okay.

Why would I care? Grayson had asked.

Because she's your friend, too.

Abby searched his face. "I know I want this. I can't tell you how many times I've rehearsed this moment in my head. I've imagined us in just about every place I could think of—my bedroom, yours, the back of my car, in the pool at school after one of your meets. I help you change out of your swimsuit in those tiny shower stalls and—"

"That's weirdly specific."

"I've also pictured us in one of those long boats out on the water."

"You can't paddle one with less than four people. Well, you can, but it would be hell."

"On the beach…" Here she stopped talking.

She'd gotten that wish tonight at least. Or a comparable experience, if the male siren had been convincing enough.

Abby's lip quivered. "It's too soon, isn't it? Oh god, you must think I'm an awful, heartless—"

"No," he said. He wrapped his arms around her as she began to cry.

"Hey, no. I don't think that."

"I'm sorry," she said. "I'm terrible."

"You're not terrible," he said again, because he wanted to be sure she'd actually heard him. She only cried harder.

"I probably just ruined the one friendship that means anything to me. God, Grayson, I'm sorry. I shouldn't have tried to—god, what's wrong with me?"

He held her tighter.

"You probably don't even feel that way about me."

"I do," he admitted. "I swear I do. I just didn't figure it out as quickly as you did."

She pulled back, looking into his eyes. "How long?"

He was sure that his crush on Abby had developed in tenth grade. There was evidence at least, in the way he'd begun to notice her more. Or rather, what he began to notice changed. The way her face lit up when she smiled. The way her gym shorts sat on her hips and curved under her buttocks when she did laps around the gym. The way his heart would skip a beat when she would slide her arms around his neck and hug him bye at the end of the day.

But he didn't really know for sure until he'd started applying to schools in September. When he considered the distance of each school, or tried to imagine himself with a new life in that new place, it was Abby who kept crossing his mind—not his family or his friends or his love of Castle Cove.

It was her he didn't want to leave.

"I figured it out nine months ago, but I'd been crushing for a while before that."

"Nine months ago. At the beginning of senior year?" she asked.

A shadow fell across her face as something cut across the sky, momentarily breaking the moonlight.

"Yes," he said.

"So…you liked me all year but didn't say anything."

"You're—were—with Landon."

A cascade of emotion seized her face. She began tugging on his pants again, almost feverishly.

"No," he said. "Abby, *no*."

She stopped, her expression caught somewhere between desperation and anger.

"I'm not going anywhere," he said.

The tears broke, spilling down her face. "Once you start to think about it, once you start to realize what this means, you'll break it off."

"No, I won't," he said again, and pulled her into his arms. "I swear."

How could he explain it to her? If he was being honest with himself, he knew only loyalty to Landon had held him back and also loyalty to Abby. He'd respected their decision to be together. In fact, he respected her desires even more than Landon's and perhaps that's one of the reasons he finally realized what his true feelings were.

"You'll think it's wrong. You'll get it in your head that it's betraying Landon somehow," she said, sniffling into the hollow of his neck. "You won't believe that I'd been trying to find the right time to break up with him for a year," she insisted. "It's not because he's dead, okay. It's not because—"

"I know," he said, squeezing her against his side. "I believe you. You don't have to prove anything to me. But there's no hurry."

She stared at him, her eyes wide and disbelieving.

He smoothed the hair off her face. "There's no hurry."

Because the truth was, he wanted to be the only guy on her mind when they made love for real.

"I'm not going anywhere." He combed her hair with his fingers. She softened against him then, giving over to the exhaustion of the night.

He held her while she cried herself to sleep.

Only when she was asleep did he finally allow his own tears to flow.

Reese

A phone was ringing somewhere in the house. Reese groped the sheets blindly trying to find her cell phone. She found the charging cord first, and traced it to the phone itself.

"Hello?" she groaned. Her voice broke with the effort.

"Reese?"

It was Kristine. She didn't sound so great either. Of course, running the woods all night would do that to a woman.

Violet slept like the dead beside her. Reese wasn't worried about waking her. The demon couldn't rise before sunset. So she turned her attention to the alpha werewolf.

"Yeah, it's me. What's up?"

"I'm calling an emergency pack meeting. A kid died in the cove last night. He was torn apart by a siren."

"What?" Reese sat up on her elbow, alarm rocketing her mind to full wakefulness. "I was there."

"Were you?" Kristine said. Said, because the alpha rarely asked questions. Even her questions weren't really questions.

Reese recounted the night to her boss and friend. By the time she finished, she felt like she'd made a terrible mistake. She shouldn't have swum toward the reef.

"I saw the kids," she finished lamely. "I should've checked on them."

"How could you have known that would happen? The sirens aren't even supposed to be in the cove."

"There was a woman there," Reese explained. She told her what she saw of the strange magic on the beach and the storm that had come rolling in. "I followed her to the Crossroads bar, and saw her meet someone, but that's it. I didn't learn anything else."

"Maybe it's not connected," Kristine said finally. Her sigh made the woman sound much older. "Or maybe she caused it. Either way, I called to see if you could watch the bar until I can come in. I realize it's not your shift and I'll pay you double for that. But maybe you should be at the meeting too. As a witness you might have something to contribute to the discussion. I'll leave it to you to decide."

Reese looked at Violet again. If she went, she'd be sure to leave a note so the demon wouldn't wake up alone and wonder where she'd gone.

"I'll hold down the bar for you," Reese said. She didn't believe she could be much help at the pack meeting, but she did know that she could keep Kristine's business running smoothly while the alpha helped the community. It seemed like a better use of her time.

"Great," Kristine said. The relief in her voice was clear. "I'll be there as soon as I can."

"Will you fill me in later?" Reese asked.

"Of course." A short rustle of fabric made Reese suspect that Kristine was moving the phone to her other ear. "When can you get to the bar?"

Reese glanced at the clock. It was shaped like a great white shark, the white belly shining in the afternoon sun. And it really was afternoon. She'd slept most of the day away. "Within the hour."

"Perfect. We'll talk later."

They exchanged their goodbyes and terminated the call.

Reese considered her needs in order of importance.

Food and shower were at the top of the list. She decided on the shower first. Under the hot jets, she gently slapped her face, trying to spark some alertness in her.

She dressed in freshly laundered clothes that still reeked of fabric softener.

Breakfast, she decided, was a can of tuna on dry toast. After finishing her toast and throwing the rinsed can in the recycle bin, she brushed her teeth for a second time. She unwrapped two sticks of mint gum and washed her hands just to be sure. She hoped the fish smell wouldn't linger.

The drive to Alpha's was quiet. It was that calm hour between afternoon and evening. Most of the daytimers hadn't left work yet, and the evening crowd hadn't yet woken. The streets were nearly empty. In Cliffside, a few people were walking their dogs, their earphones in as they strolled down the white-washed sidewalk.

When Cliffside gave way to downtown, she saw more

students. Kids that were enjoying their summer break by hanging out in clusters in front of their favorite haunts. The Magic Bean coffeeshop seemed particularly busy, but there was also a cluster outside the burrito shop on the corner.

Reese parked her rattling red pickup in the parking lot across from Alpha's and crossed the street to the bar. She was the first one to the bar, using her key to open the door and begin prep work for the night.

She'd just restocked the pint glasses when Nick showed up to bounce the door. Early bird patrons requesting beer and popcorn arrived a few minutes later. After that, it seemed her shift passed quickly.

Reese looked up the moment the vampire crossed the threshold and entered the bar entrance. Not just any vampire, but Liam, one of the oldest residents in town and a good buddy of Kristine's.

Reese motioned the vampire forward. He obliged, stopping at the bar. He placed a black umbrella on the wooden top.

"Want a drink?" Reese asked. Alpha's carried blood packs that could be heated or mixed into certain cocktails.

Liam's piercing blue eyes considered her for a moment.

"No," he said finally. "I can't stay long."

"Oh. Well Kristine is down at the park. I'm not sure when she's coming in."

It was strange to see the living vampire before sunset. Unlike their undead brethren, living vampires could move around in the day. They would not explode into dust if sunlight touched them. However, they were nocturnal. Being up during the day taxed their bodies and strength. Whatever Liam wanted, it must've been important enough to disregard the nausea for. "Is it important?"

"I went to the park first," he said. "She said you were here."

She paused in the middle of the tequila sunrise she was making. "What do you want me for?"

Reese liked Liam, but they weren't exactly friends.

His ocean blue eyes fixed on hers. "Ethan heard you were in the cove last night. He wants to talk to you."

"When?" The idea of refusing Ethan Benedict was incomprehensible. Not only because he had built this town with his own two hands and a hell of a lot of magic, but because of every creature in this town, he was by far the strongest. If he wanted something, he would have it. And Reese could see no reason to make enemies with a man like that.

"He wants you to come by the house." His pale hand adjusted itself on the umbrella handle. "When can you leave?"

"I can't leave before Kristine gets back," she said, topping off the glass and sliding it across the bar to a werewolf who looked like she needed it.

Liam pushed back from the bar and brushed his hands over the front of his jacket. "I'll be outside when you're ready."

Once the vampire stepped out into the late afternoon, Reese's mind went into overdrive. In fact, her brain was so busy building up scenarios for how the Ethan Benedict conversation might go that by the time Kristine walked into the bar an hour later, she was in a proper state.

"Calm down," Kristine told her, taking the broom from her hand and the rag from her shoulder. "He just wants to ask about last night. We need eyewitnesses."

This changed nothing.

"Go on," Kristine said, nodding toward the bar door. "Liam's waiting out there for you."

And he was. Reese found him on the sidewalk, leaning against the brick face of Alpha's.

"I wanted to give you directions. It isn't easy to find his house," Liam said by means of explanation. Full twilight was upon them. The umbrella was closed, hanging from his wrist. "Where did you park?"

Reese pointed across the street. "The red pickup is mine."

They looked both ways and crossed when the light turned red.

"Have you been out in the sun this whole time?" She frowned at him. "You okay?"

"I've felt better. But we need to get on top of these killings."

She unlocked the truck and reached across the seat to do the same for the passenger door.

Liam slid onto the bench seat and tucked the umbrella between his legs. Then he pulled the heavy door shut with a clank.

"Take Canyon Road towards the interstate," he instructed, pulling the seatbelt across his chest.

Reese turned over the engine and reversed the truck. The street population had tripled since she'd started her shift hours before. Humans were wrapping up dinner and the night creatures were taking to the street for their nightly hunts. She waved to the supernaturals she knew as she passed them.

Liam said nothing on their drive through town. She didn't press him for conversation. Instead she rolled down her window to let in the warm ocean breeze. She hoped the fresh air would calm her.

At the stop sign across from The Crossroads bar, Liam lifted his right hand and pointed straight ahead. "Follow this up to Midnight Pass."

She did, casting longing looks out over the water. The waves were purple with early evening light. A faint waning moon sat above the horizon.

"There should be a road up here on your left. Do you see it?"

It was another twenty or thirty feet before the road materialized in her view. It seemed to not be there one minute, then appeared the next. Reese wasn't sure if that was magic, or simply a tricky shape of road that had hidden the drive well.

Either way, she turned onto the road per Liam's instruction.

She maneuvered the truck slowly through the dense brush.

Then something remarkable happened. The branches that were overtaking the road, at first scratching at the sides of her red pickup, suddenly pulled back, offering her a clear path.

They bent away from the truck as if held by an invisible force.

"What the—"

"Ethan," Liam said, matter-of-factly. "He knows it's us."

Reese didn't want to ask how Ethan knew who was a quarter of a mile away from the house, or how the demon had the power to bend back tree limbs thicker than her body.

She suspected that if they were a mated pair, Liam and Ethan would share a telepathic bond. She knew that demons did that from time to time—took mates. Hadn't Violet been the one to hint that such a thing was possible—if Reese was interested.

She'd seen Ethan and Liam together often and knew they were *together* in some capacity.

But Ethan was also a known playboy. In fact, many thought it was a badge of honor to have slept with Ethan Benedict and a few people claimed to have done so. He owned a bar in Red Light too, the Labyrinth and it wasn't uncommon for humans or supernaturals to disappear for a few hours in his care.

Like most demons, he probably fed on lust or sexual desire in some way. Or worse, their souls. Most humans seemed to think this was a small price to pay for such an encounter.

How Liam felt about these dalliances, Reese could only guess.

Either their relationship was open or Liam was the confident and forgiving kind.

While she shouldn't care—none of this was her business after all—Reese would've been lying to herself if she said she wasn't curious.

The trees broke open and a two-story Spanish villa sprang into view. The dirt road turned to beautiful paving stones that circled in front of the house. In the center of the roundabout was a fountain bubbling softly with turquoise water. The fountain was lit with submerged lights, changing the water from purple to a rose pink to turquoise again.

Reese parked her truck in front of the marble steps. Ethan was standing on the porch as if ready to receive them.

"Welcome to my home," he said as she stepped down from the truck.

He regarded Liam and his face pulled into a distasteful frown.

"Get inside and rest, my love," Ethan said. "And eat something."

Liam gave a dismissive wave and went inside

Reese stood on the steps looking up into the demon's face. Kristine had once called Ethan's looks *smoldering*. And this close to him, Reese had to agree. It was the sensual pout of his lips to be sure. The strong, square jaw and cat-like eyes. His dark hair had fallen forward, drawing attention to those eyes.

"Come in," he said with a mischievous grin. "Let's see if I can't make your visit...pleasurable."

With heat building in her guts, she followed him across the threshold into the house. Liam was nowhere in sight as Reese was led through the foyer to the door nestled between the twin staircases.

"Can I offer you something to eat? Drink?" He threw a mischievous grin over his shoulder. "I can accommodate any taste, I assure you."

He pushed open the door to reveal a massive kitchen.

"No, thank you." No one needed to tell her that getting drunk with this guy was a bad idea. And though she could *drink like a fish,* as she often joked, she didn't want to take any chances. Not with Ethan Benedict so close at hand.

Ethan pulled a bottle of red wine from the counter, uncorked it and poured himself a glass. He flicked his eyes up to meet hers.

"You're sure?"

"Positive."

Wine glass full, he motioned toward the adjacent door. "It's my understanding that your true form is a shark." He held the door open for her, forcing her to brush her body past his as they moved into the next room. "Is that correct?"

"I can change into a shark, yes."

He flashed a wry smile. "It is said that Vendetta herself created shifters. She so loved nature and its beauty, that she bestowed many animals the ability to take human form, so they could walk amongst them as she pleased. If we believe this tale, it would mean truly you are a shark who takes a human form, not a human who takes shark form."

The room around them could've been a library or a study. It had a desk with a laptop and folders on it. The walls were replaced with floor-to-ceiling bookcases and given how high these ceilings were, Reese was certain she was looking at tens of thousands of titles. At least.

In front of the large window, she saw the sea, reminding her of the window in her aunt's own library at home. If Constance saw this room she would be in love. Likely with Ethan as much as the room itself. Her aunt had no sexual qualms about bedding whomever she wanted.

"What kind of shark?" Ethan inquired. His gaze was intense.

"A black-tip reef shark."

He grinned. "Yes, I can see it. One might think your hair was dyed."

"Most people do." She'd heard her hair described as blond pigtails dipped in ink. But it wasn't ink or even dye, only her natural coloring betraying her true form. It hadn't mattered when she'd bleached her hair. The black tips remained. It was the same for her Aunt Constance, though her hair wasn't blond, rather a deep auburn.

Ethan placed a hand on the handle of the French doors

behind him. "Would you like to come out into the garden with me?"

He didn't wait for her to answer. He pushed opened the French doors and motioned for her to follow.

They stepped out into an assault of freesia. The high, heady fragrance of a thousand flowers assaulted her. She felt paralyzed by them, her mind unraveling like a pulled string. The cloying sweetness had a narcotic affect, dulling her mind.

They followed a small lit path to twin benches.

"I love sitting in the garden in the evenings," Ethan confessed. "Beneath the moon, it's lovely.

Ethan sat on a wooden bench nestled into a grove of roses. He settled down into it, pointing to the padded chair opposite. Reese took her seat, enjoying the last of the day's heat on her skin as well as the peach garden rose hanging inches from her face.

She'd bent forward to sniff it before considering if that was all right.

But Ethan was smiling at her. "Can you tell me what happened last night?"

"I did my closing shift at Alpha's and then drove to the beach for a swim."

"Yes," he said, in agreement, turning the glass in the fading light. It sparkled in his hand. "And then?"

She recounted all that occurred as she swam the waters the night before.

When she finished, he was regarding a blush rose and nodding as if it had spoken to him.

"Yes," he said finally. "It's clear that the sirens are unwell. Unfortunately, this could be for any number of reasons."

He turned those dark eyes on hers. A shiver crawled its way up and down her spine. Had his eyes been that color earlier? She couldn't be sure.

His smile widened as he watched the emotions dance across her face.

"I wonder if you would do something for me?" he asked sweetly. He wet his lips. "It is a task well-suited to your abilities."

She sat up straighter, trying to gather the reins of her mind and the strange electricity rippling along her skin.

"The sirens live in a cavern beneath the eastern cliffs. If you swim across the cove and then around the cliff itself, you will find their nest. You need only follow the rocks until you come upon the opening. The sirens will not bother you as long as they believe you are a shark. They revere and respect all sea creatures, it seems. Therefore they shouldn't react to your presence."

Her mind began to clear. "You want me to swim to the caverns and check on the sirens?"

"Yes," he said, taking another long draught from his glass. His lips were dyed red with the wine. "See if anything looks amiss and report back to me. Maybe by visiting their territory, we can get a sense of what ails them."

"I wouldn't know what to look for," she said, shifting on the bench.

Ethan smiled. His eyes were filled with soft flames now. She was certain his eyes had not been full of hellfire earlier.

"It doesn't matter. I only need you to look around." His grin turned wicked. "I have ways of extracting what I need from the mind."

"And they won't hurt me for swimming into their territory?"

"No," Ethan said, perhaps too quickly. "Of course, if for some reason they do realize you are a woman…" He took another sip of wine, his eyes never leaving hers. "My advice is to swim away. As fast as you can."

"I'll go tomorrow," Reese said, shifting against the creaking bench. "Once the sun is up."

It wasn't only the dangers of night swimming across open waters that concerned her. It was also that she was dead tired all of a sudden—she wondered if Ethan could be blamed for this immense loss of energy.

His mischievous grin betrayed him. "That is very wise. It will be best to go during the day when the sirens are tired and sluggish. They are as nocturnal as we are. Actually I suppose you are crepuscular, aren't you? My apologies." He took another sip of wine, his lips even redder than before.

Quite kissable, Reese thought. She wondered if it was the fragrant garden—or Ethan that was going to her head. Danger a little voice warned. *Danger, Reese. The voice sounded like Violet's.*

"Observe as much as you can and report back to me tomorrow evening. I will compensate you however you wish."

This stopped her in her tracks.

His grin turned wicked as if sensing her excitement. "Do you have a preference as to how you are compensated?"

Reese didn't want for money. Her aunt was generous and doting, and Reese made good money as a bartender. All of this was made easier by the fact Reese had few needs.

But this was Ethan Benedict she was speaking to.

"I would like a favor," she said.

He leaned back, his smile amused. "And *I* long to please you. What is your wish?"

"I don't know." Now she was the one grinning. "But if I ever find myself in trouble someday, it would be nice to know that I can call on you for...assistance."

Ethan considered his glass of wine for a moment before taking another slow, luxurious sip. When Reese saw the fire spring into his eyes, another chill seized her spine. Had she overstepped? Had she asked too much?

He extended his hand. "In exchange for your help with this situation, I offer my protection. No harm will come to you on my watch."

"Deal." She slid her palm into his.

Quick as lightning, his hand seized hers and pulled. She was yanked from her seat forward across the lit walkway and into Ethan's lap. Her body collided with his. He was warm, the way living vampires were warm after they'd fed. His chest didn't give as she pushed against it.

But it wasn't just his arms around her, or the press of his chest against hers.

It was his lips.

His soft, pillowy lips overtook hers. Her surprise came out as a sigh, or moan before she could stop it.

"This is how I seal my pacts," he said, his breath warm on her face.

Reese stood, stumbling back from the demon. He let her go with a lazy, triumphant grin on his face.

"You have my word, Reese. Should you ever need me, I will be happy to help you."

"T-thank you." She tugged at the bottom of her shirt which had ridden up to reveal her stomach.

He pointed at the French doors with the empty wine glass. "And now I'll lead you out."

His tone brooked no argument.

She'd made it all the way to the front door when she turned and saw Liam descending the right side staircase. His hair was wet and curling. He was buttoning the cuff on a clean white dress shirt that he'd tucked into tight, dark pants.

Reese realized she was staring.

"He's very beautiful, isn't he?" Ethan whispered into her ear. The warm breath made the hairs on her neck rise. "You should see him on his knees."

Heat shot through her body, tightening muscles low in her core.

"Don't let him get to you, Reese," Liam said. His eyes were on Ethan. "He likes to play with his food."

Ethan tsked. "I haven't fed on her, my love. Much."

Reese had become aware of how close Ethan was standing

behind her left shoulder. And with Liam standing in front of her, she was practically sandwiched between the two men.

"He likes shifter magic more than any meal in the world," Liam explained. He was giving Ethan a wary look. "It reminds him of Vendetta."

"Telling all my secrets, my love?" Ethan asked. It felt like his lips were micrometers above her skin.

"She deserves to know she's the prey. It's unfair when they think otherwise." He turned to Reese. "He'll get drunk on you if you let him. Better get out of here before he drains you dry."

"I wouldn't do that," Ethan said, in mock outrage. But he was practically purring in her ears.

Reese fumbled for the door handle, her face so warm she thought she would begin to sweat.

Liam took pity on her and threw the door wide, offering her the night. She burst out onto the porch, the fresh air hitting her with all the force of an ocean wave.

"Good night," she managed before the door closed behind her.

She breathed deep, letting the cool air beat back the magic. For a moment she turned and stared at the front door as if she expected Ethan to come after her. But the front door remained closed. In her mind, she imagined Liam leaning against it, barring the demon's path.

Why had he helped her?

Whatever the reason, she owed Liam and she knew it. Whether or not he was the sort of person to draw on such debts, she didn't know. But the tally mark had already been made in her mind. With a slight tremor in her arms, which she recognized as falling adrenaline, she climbed into her truck.

The tree limbs blocking the road pulled back reluctantly this time—or was she only imagining that? Just be glad they pulled back at all, she thought as she pressed the gas pedal a little harder.

Grayson

He woke to a soft knock on his bedroom door. He opened his eyes and found his mother standing in the frame, one hand on the handle, another on the jamb.

If his mother had any thoughts about the way Abigail was wrapped around his shoulder, sleeping soundly on his chest, she didn't say anything. She didn't even look directly at Abby.

And Grayson was too exhausted to care. He felt like his eyes were on fire. He couldn't have slept more than two or three hours.

"Abigail's mom is going to be here in twenty minutes. I thought she might want a bagel or coffee before she goes."

"Abby." He shook her gently. "Abby, wake up."

At first, her hold tightened on him.

"Abby, your mom is on her way."

She raised her head, auburn hair covering her face. She pushed it back with her hand.

"Morning," his mother said from the doorway. She came to the side of the bed and put Abby's clean clothes on a pile. "I washed your clothes. Or you can just wear those." She seemed to read Abby's hesitation. "I can get them back some other time."

"Thank you," Abby said, sitting up. "I appreciate that."

"Would you like a bagel and coffee?

"Yes and yes." She smoothed her abundant hair out of her face.

"Blueberry or Everything?"

"Everything. Do you have any of that garlic spread?"

His mother smiled, but Grayson saw how it didn't reach her eyes. "I do."

"I'll take that, please. Thank you."

His mother gave him a look.

"I'll make mine," Grayson told her before she shut the door with a nod.

"I love your mother," Abby said, stretching her arms overhead.

"Do you need a washcloth or anything?" he asked. He knew Abby liked to wash her face in the morning.

"I still have one from yesterday."

For a long time they both sat there, not moving, not speaking.

"It really happened, didn't it? He's really dead." She pressed the heels of her hands into her eyes. "There was a moment when I was just coming awake and I thought—"

"I know," he said. The last twelve hours of his life seemed like a crazy blur.

She took her clothes and disappeared into the bathroom without saying anything else.

Grayson went downstairs and found the bagels by the toaster. The smell of coffee filled the kitchen. It was some sort of mocha blend. He could smell the chocolate.

He cut a blueberry bagel in half with a knife and forced it into the slots of the toaster. He stood there while the elements glowed red.

Landon.

God, *Landon*. Was he really dead? Could he really be gone?

His mind kept bucking against the idea with disbelief.

Before he considered what he was doing, he had his cell phone out of his pocket. He dialed Landon's cell—he was the last one to call Grayson—and listened to the empty static on the line.

It went straight to voicemail.

"If you're looking for Landon, you found him! What's up?"

It beeped and Grayson considered leaving a message. His mouth was half open. The breath was there between his lips.

"Who are you calling?" his mom asked. She came through the swinging doors and crossed to the fridge. She pulled out a pitcher of OJ and stood there looking at him.

"No one," Grayson said, slipping the phone back into his pocket. "I was checking my messages."

It was a meaningless lie, but easier than opening himself up to have a conversation he wasn't ready to have.

The toaster spit out his bagel and he took it into the dining room. He sat down at the table beside his father. That left a space between him and his mother for Abby, which already had a steaming cup of coffee and hot bagel waiting.

"What are you going to do today?" his father asked.

"I think you should stay home and rest," his mother interjected. Her fierce blue eyes seemed to challenge his father to argue against her. "You clearly didn't get enough sleep."

His father seemed oblivious to any such challenge as he shoved the last bite of a bagel into his mouth and continued to scroll through his phone, catching up on the morning news.

"I'm supposed to be at work at two," Grayson said. "But I could call in."

"You should," his mother said. "What will Tabitha do? Fire you?"

It was true that Grayson didn't need his job at Curiosity Books. But he liked working there. There was something about the cramped rows and precariously perched stacks that comforted him. And it wasn't like spending his afternoons in a used bookstore was a hard job. Usually he spent it reading behind the register and saying hello to the customers who meandered in.

Every hour or so, there might be a purchase or two, but overall it was quiet.

The most exciting part of the gig was the ghost upstairs who liked to move around Ms. Monroe's dining room furniture when she was away. And sometimes, if the ghost was particularly restless, she would pull a book from the shelves just to hear it hit the dusty carpet.

"Are you guys going to be here?" Grayson asked, forcing

down a bite of his bagel. Thinking of Landon was making his throat tight again, but if he didn't eat his mother would only come down harder on him. She was militant about self-care.

"No, I have to go into the lab for a few hours, but I'll be home in the afternoon," his father said.

"And I have office hours and two meetings," his mother said. "But I'd be happy to cancel those if you want me to stay with you."

"No," he said and hoped he didn't sound too eager. "I want to be alone."

"Okay," his mother said, but her face was contradicting her. It was clear she didn't really think it was okay. "There's still Chinese in the fridge and I also made a salad."

"Thanks."

"You'll let us know where you're going to be though," his mother said. It wasn't a question, even if it did tilt up at the end. "Work or here?"

"I'm going to work," he said and checked the time on his phone. He had two hours before his shift started.

"Come home if it's too much," his mother said.

"Yes," his father agreed, looking up from his phone again. "There's no shame in needing personal time."

"I know," Grayson said and he did. Grayson didn't know another kid at his school who could call his mother and be removed, no questions asked, because he needed a mental health day.

His mother squeezed his hand. It was warm from the coffee mug she'd been holding.

"We want to give you space and we trust you to take care of yourself," she said. "But we also worry. No one should have to go through what you went through last night. Loss is terrible, but last night...last night."

He squeezed her hand back and then let it go. "Don't worry about me."

She clucked her tongue. "As if I can turn it off."

Abby came into the dining room and took the empty seat. She sipped the coffee, then added creamer from the carafe on the table. She also poured herself a juice.

"Mom texted me and said she's going to be a few minutes late. She got hung up on a 911 call or something."

"You're welcome to stay here as long as you need to," Grayson's father said, looking up from his phone.

"We love having you," his mother added, tapping her rings against her coffee mug. "How are you feeling today?"

"Awful," Abigail said and his mother responded by rubbing Abby's back.

"Your bagel is cold. Want me to reheat it?"

"No, this is fine."

The front door slammed open. "I'm home! Grayson! How was your birthday?"

Tanner, his ten-year-old brother, burst into the dining room. His hair was blown back from his face and he had his backpack slung over his shoulder. He dropped it with a *clunk* onto the floor.

He took one look at his family and his eyes widened. "Whoa. Who died?"

Grayson snorted. His brother had an uncanny ability to hit the truth spot on. His father often said he was fairly certain Tanner—because he'd been born in this creepy town—was some kind of psychic. Grayson had been born in LA and while he might have a knack for surviving, he didn't seem to know things out of the blue like Tanner did.

Grayson's mother was standing at the dining room window, waving to Will's mother in the driveway.

"Landon died," Abby said. She took a bite of her bagel as if to stop herself from saying more.

"Shit."

"Tanner!" his father cried.

"Language," his mother said, releasing the curtain.

"You're one to talk," Tanner shot back and he had a point. Everyone at that table knew his mother said words that would make a sailor blush.

"Please put your shoes and bag where they go," his father said pointing at the pile Tanner made upon his arrival.

Tanner didn't seem to hear him. "Did he really die?" He was looking to Grayson for confirmation.

Grayson found his voice. "There was an accident when we were swimming."

Both his parents shot him warning looks. Grayson understood that he was supposed to omit the details of Landon's death. Tanner knew Castle Cove was different. He knew about the vampires, werewolves, and witches—even the sirens in the cove. As with Grayson, his parents took great care to raise a curious but cautious boy.

But just because Tanner knew there were monsters in Castle Cove didn't mean that Tanner fully understood what those monsters could do to a person.

Grayson thought that Tanner comprehended more than he let on. Perhaps it was his gift for knowing that kept him safe. This gift worked as well as, if not better than, their parents' diligent training.

"He drowned?" Tanner asked. His eyes were wide. Too wide.

"Yeah," Abby said, lifting her coffee from the table. Grayson saw the tremble in her hand.

"Your best friend *drowned* on your freaking birthday?" Tanner asked. Now he was hanging off Grayson's chair, looking him in the eye. "I'm sorry, dude."

Dude was his favorite word the last few weeks and to hear it uttered with such sincerity undid Grayson inside. Tears formed and spilled over onto his cheeks. He pulled his little brother into a tight hug. "Thanks, man."

His parents let the moment unravel between them. No one

spoke. Breakfast continued as if nothing was happening. Tanner pulled back first.

"Shoes, bag," his mother said.

Tanner dutifully obeyed, putting his backpack on the hook and slipping his shoes into their cubby.

The doorbell rang.

Because he hadn't closed the door behind him, it stood open with a clear view of Officer O'Reilly on the porch. She didn't have the officer uniform on. She wore pressed black dress pants and a deep burgundy dress shirt tucked into the waistband. Her badge was clipped to one hip and her gun was visible in its holster.

"Abby, it's your mom," Tanner said, and opened the screen door. "Hi, Miss Una."

"Hey, buddy." She sounded as exhausted as she looked. Deep pillows of purple had formed under each of her eyes.

Abby started to clear up her plate, but Grayson's mother gently tugged her hands away. "Leave it. I'll take care of it."

Officer O'Reilly stepped into the hallway, ushered in by Tanner.

"Are you ready?" she asked, when she saw Abigail.

Abigail patted her pockets as if she'd forgotten something. "I guess so. I didn't really have anything on the beach, did I?"

"We might've left things in Landon's car," Grayson said. It had been Landon who'd driven them to the beach.

"I'll see what I can do," Una said with another tight smile. To his parents she said, "Thanks for letting Abby stay."

"Of course," his parents said in unison.

"Abby is welcome here anytime," his mother added, lifting her coffee mug to her lips again.

"I thought nothing could get into the cove because of the rocks," Tanner said. He was looking up at Officer O'Reilly with a strange expression on his face. "It's got that rock barrier, right?"

Una's lips pinched.

"Why do you think something was in the cove?" his mother asked. "We said he drowned."

Una frowned. "It was rough seas last night. A storm rolled in really quick."

Tanner's eyes lit up. "Yeah, we saw it. Will and I were in the backyard catching fireflies and then all of a sudden it was lightning and thundering."

Officer O'Reilly lifted the pile of Abby's clothes from the bench. "Where does Will live?"

"Cliffside," his father answered. "Near the east lot."

"That's North Beach. Very close to the water." Officer O'Reilly shrugged as if to say *there you go.*

"Yeah, we walk down to the beach and catch crabs. Will's dad cooks them. *Alive.*"

"Are you going back to work?" Abby asked.

"For a few hours," Una said. Then she clamped a hand on Grayson's shoulder and gave it an affectionate squeeze. "Happy belated birthday."

"Thanks."

Tanner pulled open the door, holding it open for them.

"Such a gentleman," Una said and stepped out onto the porch again. "Thank you again."

Abby hesitated in the doorway. Her gaze fixed on Grayson. "Call me later, okay?"

"I will." He'd already planned on checking on her at least a hundred times today.

With a weak smile, she descended the porch steps to the waiting unmarked car.

"Bye," Tanner said and shut the door. He met Grayson's eyes and frowned. "*That* was awkward."

.   .   .

Curiosity Books was on the corner of Apple Street and Magnolia Street. He parked at the curb outside the old Victorian building. The bookshop was purple with light brown windows and trim.

The sign in the yard read Curiosity Books, Treasure For Those Who Seek It. And below that, Used Books and Oddities—just in case those treasure seekers should get the wrong idea.

"Grayson!" Ms. Monroe exclaimed. She stood on the porch, her key in one hand, her mouth gaping. "What are you doing here?"

"My shift is from two until eight," he said. He hesitated on the step, wondering if he'd gotten it wrong. A lot had happened in the last 24 hours. It was very possible.

"Yes, but I didn't think you'd come in today. Not after what happened last night."

"You heard about that?" he asked, stuffing his hands down in his pocket.

She pulled at her tangle of necklaces around her neck. "Yes, well. It might've come on over the scanner."

Grayson had never asked his boss why she had a police scanner in her upstairs apartment, or more specifically, why she thought she needed one. It was possible that she was only nosy. But sometimes he liked to imagine that she'd come to Castle Cove to escape a life of crime. The idea was so ridiculous that it amused him to no end.

Ms. Monroe's hair was crimped, and stood out from her head in all directions. She wore a scarf across her head and coke bottle glasses so large that her eyes gave the impression of really drinking someone in. Her clothes were bright, flowing fabrics of wild designs and her neck always had at least five or six necklaces hanging around it. Despite their tendency to tangle, she seemed committed to wearing them.

She looked like the garden variety cat lady, though she had no cats. Well, if one didn't count Pumpkin—an orange tabby who strolled Midtown at her leisure. But it was as much a patron of the other shops as she was of Curiosity Books.

Since Grayson had received strict instruction to always let Pumpkin in, should she come calling, he often had the chore of vacuuming the cat hair that seemed to accumulate in her wake.

"I thought work might take my mind off things," he said. "But if you're closing—"

He looked at the key in the door and her hand still on the handle.

"Oh, yes, well I'm meeting someone for tea and so I thought I'd just close early. But if you really want to be here...?"

"I do," he insisted, adjusting his messenger bag on his shoulder. "If it's okay with you."

"Of course, of course." She unlocked the door, pushing it open with her hand.

"I just want to keep busy," he said.

"Yes, I like to rearrange my spice rack when my mind gives me trouble." She checked her watch one more time and then stepped into the shop after him. "There's a big pile here that needs to be reshelved. You could also vacuum. Pumpkin was here earlier."

"Okay," he said, removing his jacket and throwing it over the wooden chair behind the register.

"Oh, and you could call about these books." She pulled a piece of paper from her pocket. She smoothed it against the table top so he could better read it.

He reviewed the list, seeing the description of each and the ISBN and telephone numbers beside it.

"We had a lot of special orders this week," she said, gesturing to the list. "Just find out if the stores I've listed are carrying any copies and at what price we can get it for. Then you can call the buyer and ask them to commit."

"All right."

Ms. Monroe seemed to hover for a moment. "Are you sure you're going to be all right here alone?"

He forced himself to smile. "I'll have Gladys."

Ms. Monroe arched her eyebrows instead of laughing at his joke. "Dear, the dead aren't good company."

"I'll be fine." If he didn't say it, he was sure she wouldn't leave.

With an awkward pat on the counter, she turned to the door. "I'll be back around seven or so, but if I'm not, just lock up when you leave."

When she pulled the door closed after her, the overhead bell rang. The air vibrated with the twang, then fell silent.

For a long time, he only sat there, feeling the chair against his back, his fingers picking at a hole in his jeans.

Then when the silence began to feel alive, almost as if it were breathing down the back of his neck, he got to work.

He started with vacuuming, angling the ancient contraption through the narrow stacks. More than once he clipped a pile of books and sent it tumbling. He restacked them the best he could and kept on.

After he reshelved the pile by the register, he dusted. There were limitations to what one could accomplish in this old shop in terms of dusting. Running a light feather duster over the exposed spines was about as much as one could do.

Cleaning had only taken him about two hours, so he decided it was time to make the phone calls. He called the listed book sellers and dutifully recorded the prices. Then he called the customers who'd requested those items and confirmed that they would pay. When he was finished he sent an update text to Ms. Monroe. She instructed him to buy them all.

He did so using her business credit card, locked away in the register for exactly such purchases.

He'd just written out the total and put it in the register when table legs scraped overhead. He smiled. There was something comforting about Gladys the ghost being her usual restless self. Then for the first time he wondered if he might see Landon again.

How would it feel to see ghost-Landon?

And what if something did develop between him and Abby? Would ghost Landon be okay with it? Or would he haunt them for the rest of their lives—breaking their dishes or windows and shaking their bed whenever they tried to have sex?

Grayson listened to the legs catch on the wood floor above. Then nothing. When it seemed she'd completed her task, he called out to her.

"Gladys? I could use a book recommendation."

For a moment, he sat perched on the chair, listening to the ringing silence in the shop.

Then he heard the soft shuffle of a book sliding from the shelf, followed by the hollow thump of it hitting the floor.

Grayson stood from the chair and followed the narrow aisle, searching the floors for the fallen book.

He'd made it almost to the biographies section when he turned a corner and saw it.

He bent and picked the book up, brushing a hand over its cover. Maybe the book had been red once, but now it had faded to a burnt orange. The binding was frayed and the exposed pages were stained yellow with age.

"A Siren Song," he read aloud. "The history of Atlantis' survivors."

Grayson's heart rocketed in his chest. His pulse built to the point of painfulness. It pounded like a war drum in his temples.

He saw movement in the corner of his eye and turned. Farther up the row, another book was sliding out of its place on the shelf. It inched forward once, twice, and then tumbled onto the floor.

Grayson crossed to the fallen book and picked it up off the floor.

"The Dark Mother and Her Children," he said. He opened the cover and was surprised to see it was published by the Castle Cove University Press over a hundred years ago. He flipped page after page until he found an old pencil etching of a young woman about to enter a dark wood. The woman had long black hair and wide dark eyes.

Eyes peered at her from the darkness, yet she didn't seem deterred. She was about to enter the woods anyway.

He closed the book and ran his hand over the cover. His fingernail caught on the embossed tree stamped into the leather. In the tree were six birds. He knew the species. Any wood scout would've been able to name them too: a crow, a heron, a hawk, an owl, a blue jay, and a swan. But the swan was black, not white, as evidenced by its inked-in body.

A shiver ran up his spine.

Of all these books in the entire shop, what were the chances that Gladys would pick a book about sirens at random?

Grayson returned to the desk and opened the inventory file on the computer. There were only six books on sirens in the whole shop. Six out of nearly seventy thousand titles. The chances seemed small indeed.

"So if it isn't random," he said, aloud. "Then what is the connection between the sirens and The Dark Mother?"

He spoke aloud but there was no answer. No more books slipped from the shelves to the floor. He strained, listening intently to the hum as if expecting an answer.

His phone buzzed suddenly and he yelped, squeezing the books to his chest.

"Come on," he muttered. He lifted his phone from the desk and saw Abby's name above the incoming text.

He opened the text and read: *Hey, how are you?*

He took a breath, and tried to steady the wild hammer of his heart. *Same. You?*

Same. This sucks, she wrote.

Yeah.

What are you doing?

At work. You?

Lying in bed staring at the ceiling like a weirdo

He looked at the books on the desk. He opened the cover again and stared at the woman entering the menacing woods. He counted those eyes watching her.

It made him think of the stories he'd heard about the Western Woods. West of the territory line, the forest was supposed to be full of old, ancient creatures. Dryads for starters, who craved human flesh and who would eat a person while they were still alive. Wendigos did much the same, but also dragged people to their underground dens. Then they overwintered, snacking on their captives until they went aboveground again.

As a tenured professor at CCU, his mother would know more about this book and its stories. He would ask her later what she thought the connection between The Dark Mother and the sirens might be.

He typed, *we should find out what happened.*

We know what happened.

I don't think we do, he replied.

?

There was the storm and the sirens came into the cove. What if there's a reason for that?

?????

They're not supposed to be in the cove. What made them come in like that?

You think there's a reason?

Yes, he wrote. *Not just a reason but probably someone to blame.*

Abby didn't seem to have a response for that.

Don't you want to know? What if it saves someone's life?

Not Landon's life. Landon was dead and even in Castle Cove, he would probably stay that way. But Grayson was thinking about the next time someone was in the cove and the sirens broke the boundary of Heart's Rock. What then?

He typed out, *For next time.*

It seemed like she wouldn't write back. For minutes he stared at the screen. He put the phone down and searched the computer for the other book, The Dark Mother and Her Children. There was no listing in the computer. He checked his spelling twice, but nothing.

How many secret treasures—like a hundred-year-old book —were hidden in this old dusty shop? Grayson couldn't help but wonder.

His phone buzzed.

Sure, she wrote back. *I'd want to know. But my mother will shit a brick if we start "investigating." She's already on the case.*

Do they have a lead?

He traced the embossed tree with his fingers. His hand kept going to the blue heron.

Not yet, she wrote. *Promise you'll take me with you if you plan on "investigating."*

He smiled at her incessant use of quotation marks. What her mother did was no doubt investigating without quotation marks. Whatever sleuthing they would undertake—tomorrow or next week—certainly merited that distinction. They were not professionals.

His phone buzzed again but it wasn't a text message. It was an alarm for closing time. He powered down the computer and checked all the windows and back door to make sure they were locked up. He saw a book sitting open on a stool. A page turned.

"Don't stay up too late reading, Gladys," he said and smiled to himself. "You'll be *dead tired* tomorrow." That was the one problem about making jokes with ghosts. One could never tell if they were appreciated.

At the register, he wrote a note for Ms. Monroe, officially "checking out" the two books that Gladys had recommended. This was the shop's policy, that he was allowed to borrow any book from the shelves that he liked, as long as he brought it back in the same condition he'd found it and made sure he recorded what he took.

He always did.

He flipped the open sign to closed, and with the two books under his arm, he stepped out onto the porch. His keys clanked against the wood as he locked up. He drove home in silence with the radio off, the two books sitting in the passenger seat beside him.

When he got home, he found a note from his parents on the kitchen table.

Gray,
Took Tanner to his game. Might be back late, especially if they win. Pizza! Pizza! Leftovers in the fridge. Text us when you get home so we know you're okay. Someone came by the house looking for you. See the note. Call us if something comes up.
Mom and Dad

A twinge of disappointment tightened his chest. He'd forgotten about the baseball game and he never missed Tanner's games. Even when his parents couldn't make it, Grayson was always there. He hadn't even thought about the game. It wasn't like him to have something so completely slip his mind.

That's what happens when your best friend dies, he thought. The mind vacillates between forgetting it happened—pretending nothing had changed—to being slammed with the reality of it again and again.

Like a body tumbling in the moonlit surf.

He sank into the dining room chair with tears in the corner of his eyes. He felt the image pressing in on him again. He bit his lip so hard that it bled. But at least the image was gone and he was in his body again.

He texted his parents.

I'm home. Tell T I'm sorry I missed the game.

His mother wrote back almost instantly, as if she'd been holding the phone at the ready exactly for this moment.

He understands. Are you staying in tonight?

He practically heard the plea in her voice.

I'm home for the night, he wrote as if throwing her a bone. He slid the books onto the table. *I'll be reading.*

Eat something. Call me if you need something. ANYTHING, she instructed.

OK. And that was the end of it.

Grayson left the books on the table and went into the kitchen. He made himself a plate of leftover Chinese, wanting to eat it cold this time, and added a heap of salad too.

He didn't look at the second note until he sat down at the table again.

"Reese," he read aloud, forking noodles into his mouth.

Neither the number nor the name were in his parents' handwriting, both of which he knew by heart. That meant the note must've been tacked to the door or stuffed in their mailbox while they were at work.

So who was this mystery person? He didn't know anyone by the name of Reese. If it was a cop or someone wanting to follow up on Landon's death, wouldn't they just have called him? Or maybe this was a reporter. There were two newspapers in Castle Cove.

Unlike the rest of the country where the newspaper was dying a slow, bloody death, they were doing just fine in Castle Cove—both the respectable paper, *The Cove Chronicle*, and the gossip rag, *The Daily Bite*.

The only problem was that Grayson detested speaking on the phone. He certainly wasn't going to call some stranger for a chat.

"Here's hoping this is a cell phone," he said. He typed in the number and opened a new text message.

This is Grayson H. You came by my house?

No answer.

He finished his dinner, rinsed his plate in the sink and when he opened the dishwasher to slide the plate into the rack, he heard the phone buzz on the kitchen table.

hi grayson. i'm reese. i have some questions about what happened last night. can you talk?

Grayson looked at the text for a long time. Reese was probably not a reporter, given the shorthand text speak. Hell, maybe they weren't even out of high school. Was this about sports or graduation or something?

He wrote back, *I can talk.*

He carried his books into the living room and collapsed onto the sofa. No sooner did he get the pillow under his head did the phone ring.

He sighed and accepted the call. "Hello?"

"Hi," a woman said. That answered the first mystery. Reese was a woman, not a man. And she sounded like a young woman from what he could tell, but not as young as he was imagining. Maybe her twenties? "Is this Grayson?"

"Yeah. And you're Reese?"

"You got it," she said.

He could hear the smile in her voice. He wasn't sure where to go from here. His silence probably conveyed as much.

"I'm calling because I've got questions about what happened last night."

"Are you with the police?" He knew well enough to know that he shouldn't give details to just anyone. After all, this woman could be a reporter or just a nosy—

"Let's call me a liaison. I already spoke to Detective O'Reilly. You can call her and confirm that it's okay to talk to me if you're worried. If you're smart, you would."

"Are you a reporter?"

"No. I've been asked to look into what happened so that's what I'm doing."

Asked to look into it by whom? he wondered. And he wondered what it was about Reese that made her qualified for this job.

Was she calling his bluff? She sounded so young.

He said, "Can I call you right back?"

"Sure. I'll be here. My shift doesn't start for another hour."

"Shift where?"

"Alpha's. I'm a bartender."

Grayson thought he might have seen the name *Alpha's* above one of the bars near campus, but he couldn't be sure.

"Okay, just a minute." He hung up and called the police station's non-emergency line.

"Castle Cove PD."

He recognized Yvonne Jenkins voice immediately. "Hi Officer Jenkins. This is Grayson Helmson. Is Detective O'Reilly around?"

"Sure, honey. One second."

He flinched at the use of honey, but couldn't remember a time that Yvonne hadn't called everyone that. Honey. Sugar. Sometimes she added the word bear to the end of the affectionate title: Honey bear. Sugar bear. Though she'd seemed to drop the latter once he'd turned sixteen.

"Here she is."

The phone clicked and Grayson heard the intake of breath. "Grayson, you there?"

"Yeah."

"You okay?"

He realized that was concern in her voice. The sort of knee jerk reactive fear that crept in when he called his own mother when she wasn't expecting it.

"I'm fine," he said, knowing she'd hear nothing else he said until he assured her. "I'm calling about Reese." Here he realized he hadn't gotten her last name. "The bartender from Alpha's."

"Oh, yeah." All the breath left her at once. "She's all right."

"She wants to ask me about what happened and I wanted to make sure that was okay before I said anything."

"Yes, it's fine. She's not officially with the police department, but she is investigating on behalf..." She seemed to search for the right word. "She's investigating on our behalf."

Grayson had a sense that it was likely far more complicated than that. "So I can tell her what happened to Landon?"

What happened to Landon... His chest tightened.

"As long as you aren't going to tell her something you haven't already told me."

The question hung in the air between them.

"No, there's nothing else," he said, wondering when he would be old enough that he no longer needed to constantly reassure the adults around him. Or maybe it was just the human parents in Castle Cove who were having such a hard time.

"Then tell her what you know. She's a good person. Clean record. She's just trying to get us some answers."

Me too, he thought, feeling the weight of the books against his chest.

"If that's all—" she began.

"Yes, that's it. Thanks for taking my call."

"Sure thing."

Then the line clicked and his cell phone returned to the home screen. It was a picture of the three of them—Abby in the middle with their arms thrown over her shoulders. They were all smiling and laughing. He remembered his father taking that photo before they went to senior prom.

He dialed Reese back.

"We good?" she asked by way of hello.

"We're good," he said. "What do you want to know?"

"Actually I'd like to talk in person, if that's okay," she said.

He was about to offer that she come by his house, but remembered what she'd said about work. "When?"

"I can come by your place tomorrow if you'll be home or you could come to Alpha's tonight. It's up to you."

"Is Alpha's 21 and up?" he asked.

"Oh, right. You're eighteen." She covered the phone with her hand. He heard her ask someone a question and he thought heard the gruff voice of a man responding. "You can come by if you want. Nick is working the door and he'll let you in. Just give him your name and say you're here to talk to me."

"I can't tonight, sorry," he said. Dragging his introverted self to a bar sounded like an awful idea for many reasons. Not only would it make his parents' anxiety spike, but he was dead tired. He hadn't slept worth a damn the night before and he wasn't entirely sure sleep would come tonight either.

"No problem," Reese said, the bar noise rising behind her. "I'll come by your place tomorrow afternoon if you'll be home?"

Grayson didn't have work tomorrow and didn't think his family had plans. He'd wanted to go check on Abby but that could be done anytime.

"I'm thinking four or five," she added.

"That's fine," he said, switching the phone to the other ear. "I should be home."

"Cool. We'll talk then. Night."

Grayson thanked her and ended the call. Then he opened the text message thread he had going with Abby and wrote, *you OK?*

The texting bubble appeared and disappeared for a long time. He braced himself.

No, she texted.

Then, *I miss him.*

Me too, he wrote.

Do you think we could've done anything differently? she asked. *He wasn't a great swimmer. We shouldn't have made him go out there.*

Grayson called her. "Hey."

"Hey."

He knew immediately that she'd been crying. Her voice was thick. He wondered if the throat, like the eyes swelled when one cried. He would have to ask his dad. His dad wasn't a doctor, but he understood basic anatomy pretty well.

"And no," Grayson said firmly. "No we couldn't have done anything differently."

"I feel like we did something wrong," she said. She sniffed. "I keep feeling like maybe if I wasn't fucking around with a siren I could've gone into the water and saved him."

"You couldn't have," he insisted.

"How do you know?"

"Because female sirens are territorial. If you'd come into the water and tried to…" He searched for a word. "*Interrupt* they would've attacked you."

"What?" she sounded genuinely surprised. "I thought they only drowned people accidentally."

"They're not violent except during mating and self-defense. My mom said they're pretty desperate to conceive so—"

Abby didn't seem willing to let go of her guilt yet. "When that storm rolled in we should've kept him on the rock. He was already having a hard time. If he'd stayed—"

"There's no guarantee that the sirens wouldn't have come onto the rock with us. And if they'd planned on going into the cove anyway, maybe they would've just hopped in after us. Then we would've been even farther from shore."

A rock orgy or dead in the water. Not great choices, he thought but had the good sense not to say.

"So he was going to die. No matter what we did," she whispered.

"We can't blame ourselves for this. He should've tried to get to the shallows before—"

"God, Grayson! We can't blame *him* either," she huffed into the phone. "He's dead!"

"Right. You're right. There's no blame. Period."

For a long time they said nothing. He listened to her soft breathing through the phone and found comfort in it.

Then she said, "You said you thought someone caused the storm."

He looked at the book in his hand.

"I didn't say someone caused the storm. I said that I think there's a reason they came into the cove even though it's out of bounds."

"My mom thinks they got confused."

His heart sped up. "What do you mean?"

The rustle of fabric, either Abby sitting up or turning over in her covers, rustled in the phone. "Because of the attack on South Beach."

"But we were on Hunter's Beach." It was Grayson's turn to sit up, leaning back against the sofa's throw pillows.

"Right. But the attack from last week was on South Beach."

Grayson visualized the geography of Castle Cove in his mind.

Castle Cove city was bordered by wild forests in the north and west and oceanfront on the east and south. On the far east was the first of three beaches: North Beach. No sirens, sharks or even jellyfish had ever been seen on that beach so it was considered the most family friendly. That's also why it was crowded as hell. There was never parking in the east lot. It was also the most desirable because it was the only beach of the three that had a gentle wooden walkway to take beachgoers down to the shore. Both Hunter's Beach and South Beach just had dunes and a sandy, trodden path from the upper ridge down to the water. It made getting back to one's car hell after a long day of sun and swimming.

Hunter's Beach was the name for the u-shaped strip of beach surrounding the cove. It ended on each side where it met the sharp cliff faces and deep water.

Swimming in the cove, Hunter's Beach, was the second best choice—for those who could stand the trek up and down the sandy ledge. Its waters were considered the calmest, being the most protected from wind from the open sea. And as long as swimmers stayed close to shore, the risk of predators or injury were low.

The third beach, South Beach, followed Canyon Road out of town toward the interstate. Few people went to South Beach. The strip of sandy shore didn't even have an official parking lot. People just parked their cars along the side of the road and walked down to the water.

The waters were rougher here, and sirens came to South Beach all the time, especially after dark. In fact, people went to South Beach *hoping* to run into the sirens.

"What happened on South Beach?" he asked. Because if someone was at South Beach after dark, they must've known what they were in for.

"They were new," she said. "So it's possible they were fodder."

It was a known fact to long-time residents of Castle Cove that one didn't find this place on a map. It couldn't be found in an internet search or on a satellite view. Residents only heard about Castle Cove when they received mysterious job offers or acceptances to an interesting university, with full funding. But usually it was someone inside the town who brought new people in.

But not everyone invited into the town were invited so that they could be a member of this strange little community. Others were invited for *dinner*.

Grayson often wondered if he'd only survived until adulthood because his parents had been so useful to the town. Maybe it wasn't his street smarts at all. Maybe it was pure luck. After all, his mother was the premier folklorist at the university. She protected and cultivated its long, dark—and utterly unique —history.

His father worked as a head biochemist at EB labs. They'd worked on everything from blood substitutes to studying the metamorphic changes in werewolves and shifters. His father seemed particularly interested in the metabolic differences between those who had been born with the ability to shift and those who'd acquired it through infection.

The bottom line was their work here was important. It supported Castle Cove's wellbeing. Grayson—with his love of nature and the water—wasn't. Would he be on his own now that he was eighteen?

Grayson realized Abby was speaking again. "They'd gone down to the water but hadn't got in it. I think the sirens only come if you touch the water. That's how they know you're there, right?"

Before Grayson could affirm that he also thought this was true, she was barreling on.

"So these people weren't in the water. They were on the ledge. And another freak storm rolled in and they'd started to walk back to their cars and that's when four sirens had come out of the water after them."

"But they can't leave the water."

"Well, no one has seen them out of the water. But these people said they did and practically chased them up the embankment."

"No way." He couldn't believe it.

He could practically hear her shrug. "That's what they said, but my mom thinks they were exaggerating. She says that they were pretty drunk when they gave their statements. Anyway, she suspects that there's some connection between the weird storms that keep rolling in and the sirens' strange behavior."

It wasn't much to go on, this connection between freak thunderstorms and agitated sirens.

"Anyway, enough about that. What were you doing before you called?"

He looked at the two books on his lap. Then he told her about the books and Gladys's recommendation.

"Send a pic," she said.

He dutifully snapped two pics of the books in his lap and texted them to her while she waited. There was a pause as she looked at the pics, then her voice returned, though a bit farther away. Grayson suspected he was on speaker phone now. But if her mom was at the station, then she was home alone.

"I can't read the title on the leather one. Is that a tree?"

"Yeah," he replied. "It's called The Dark Mother and Her Children."

"Creepy."

He laughed.

"What does it have to do with sirens?"

"I don't know. I'll have to read to find out."

Finally, she said, "About last night."

"I meant what I said." He wanted to get that out there before she had a chance to do anything ridiculous like apologize again. "I'm not going anywhere."

She sighed. "Does this mean I can go to bed?"

He smiled. "Get some rest. I'll talk to you tomorrow."

Once the call ended and he was once again sitting in his dark quiet house, he turned his attention to the books.

He decided to begin with the first book. It told a story about a woman named Vendetta, who lived in a small barony with her six brothers and a little sister. The sister died of starvation shortly after her mother did. The family had been wealthy when her parents had first married, but had lost their wealth with time because of a demanding and greedy queen who brought ruin to the people through extensive (read: expensive) military campaigns. In one way or another, the queen became responsible for her whole family's deaths, events picking off her father and brothers one at a time.

While she was still alive, Vendetta's mother had been a woman who worshipped the old gods. It was her mother who told her the story of The Crone Tree, which Grayson learned, was the tree depicted on the front of the cover.

This tree had many names—The Tree of Knowledge, The Tree of Life and so on. But inside this tree that could not be torn down or destroyed was the soul of a goddess.

Vendetta's mother believed that this goddess would help anyone, but particularly women, who prayed to her in their time of need. They need only be willing to give her a sacrifice.

When Vendetta had only one brother left, she and her brother walked into the wilderness to find this tree. At this point they were on the brink of starvation themselves, so they were willing to believe in old gods. They walked through the woods in the dead of winter for many miles.

They had just found the tree when some of the queen's soldiers found the pair. They killed her last brother and raped her. It is said that these two sacrifices were more than enough to awaken the sympathy of The Crone.

After Vendetta buried her brother beneath the tree and made her way home alone with only her grief as company, she had no life left in her. She died from cold and hunger that night in her bed. The following morning, just before the sun rose, she was visited by her six brothers, who were now demons.

They asked her if she wanted to be a demon too, with immense power, so that she could vanquish the evil queen. Vendetta agreed and with her six demon brothers, they rode to the castle, killed the queen's soldiers and slayed her court. Lastly, Vendetta killed the queen herself, finally avenging her family. After they killed her, they razed the castle. The castle ruins that now overlook the sea just east of the cove were supposed to be what was left of that very castle.

It was said that the goddess was so impressed with Vendetta's strength and will, that she offered Vendetta immortality in exchange for hunting down and destroying The Crone's enemies.

The front door burst open. "WE ARE THE CHAMPIONS MY FRIENDS!"

Heart hammering, Grayson slammed the book closed just as his brother Tanner ran in, covered head to toe in dust and tossing his glove dramatically on the couch.

"Off!" his mother cried. "That's *filthy*."

Tanner dragged his glove off the couch. "Gray, we won!"

"Whoa! High-five!" Grayson put his hand up and the kid gave it a hearty slap, his grin at full-wattage.

"Go take a shower. Now," his father begged, swatting at the glove-shaped outline of dirt now stuck to his sofa.

"You can tell me all about it later," Grayson assured his brother, when he looked ready to refuse. "Go on."

He kept singing the Queen song long after the bathroom door shut and the water came on. His father sighed, knocking the last bit of the dust off the cushion. "I don't understand why he slides across home plate when he can run across it just fine."

Grayson smiled. "Good game?"

"They won by ten points," his mother beamed. Then she saw the books. "Oh, what are you reading?"

Grayson almost laughed. She'd shown immense interest in her family's reading choices for as long as he could remember.

"The Dark Mother and Her Children. I found it at Curiosity. It was published by Castle Cove's University Press over a hundred years ago. I think it's a collection of fairytales."

Having ticked all her boxes, his mother came to the sofa and squeezed in beside him. "Let me see."

She took the large volume in her hand. "This is amazing. Can I read it when you're done?"

"Sure."

"What've you learned so far?"

He recited the tale of Vendetta to her. Instead of looking delighted, she looked worried.

"What?" he asked, not understanding the worry on her face. "What's wrong?"

"Why did you pick this book?" she asked. He couldn't understand the strange, searching expression on her face.

"I didn't," he said. "Gladys picked it. Why?"

"They're just fairytales," she said. She was staring at the embossed cover, the creases between her eyes deeper than he'd ever seen them.

"I know." It was so unlike his mother to say such a thing. She *lived* for fairytales. She believed they were keys to hidden truths and untold magic. There was no such thing as *just* fairytales. "What's wrong?"

She handed the book back, but her scowl had deepened.

He thought of the returned demon brothers. Of what it had cost Vendetta to achieve her revenge.

His mind also caught on the words *Druid's Hollow*.

"Promise me you're not planning to do anything crazy," his mother said. She clutched the book, looking as if she wouldn't return it to him. "Like look for The Crone Tree so you can make a sacrifice and bring Landon back."

When he didn't answer quick enough, she yelled his name. "Grayson!"

"What?"

"Promise me!"

"I don't even know what I'm promising not to do!" he admitted.

"Don't go into the Western Woods and try to bring Landon back. It wouldn't be Landon you brought back anyway."

"It would be demon Landon," he said.

"That isn't funny," his mother replied. Color had risen in her cheeks. "Don't even joke about it."

His father was regarding them both in a way as if he realized what danger they were all in. "It's about time for bed, isn't it?" he asked. When no one moved, his father added, "Honey, Grayson is a smart kid. He isn't going to go into the Western Woods to resurrect demons. Right?"

It never occurred to Grayson that he *could* take it back. That maybe this was his chance to undo what had been done. With Landon alive, he wouldn't have to live with this awful, terrible guilt.

With Landon alive…

His mother looked ready to explode. He forced a smile, "You worry too much, Mom."

"Do I?" she asked.

Druid's Hollow.

He thought he knew where it was.

As a wood scout, he'd done a report on the woods for his explorer badge. This meant that he'd crafted a detailed (and enormous) map of the woods for his project. It was his scout leader—a werewolf named Thomas—who'd corrected the map and made it to scale for him.

"Now you'll never get lost, buddy," he'd said.

Once his parents' bedroom door clicked shut, Grayson crept up the stairs to his room. He eased open the closet. He pulled down a box of old photo albums and a box of trophies. Behind that was the mail canister. He popped the white plastic lid off one side and found the map rolled up inside. He took the map to his bed and unrolled it on top of his comforter.

It showed the city in the center and the outline of ocean on two sides—east and south. Then it showed the woods. North of the city stretching off into nowhere was the Wayward Woods. Sunset Park, the lake and lupine trails, Black Water River, even the Witch's Backbone, a steep 8-mile hike. All of it was there. His scout master had even penciled in Howler's Hollow, the meeting place of the resident werewolf packs.

In case you ever want to visit, he'd said with a wink.

But then there were the woods west of the territory line bisecting the Wayward Woods.

A marker read 23 miles from the territory line to Druid's Hollow. So that's where the tree was supposed to be.

Of course, 23 miles through a treacherous forest full of maneaters would be one hell of a trek. However, it was only about nine miles from Vendetta Heights to Druid's Hollow. If he parked on Canyon Road and walked across the field known as Vendetta Heights, his journey would be shorter. There was the fact that Vendetta Heights was the make-out and feeding spot for local vampires and that these woods—even if only nine miles—were still crawling with monsters.

Was bringing Landon back really worth risking his own life?

He could never go in at night. It would be a massacre. But tomorrow, with daylight on his side, maybe, just *maybe* he could pull it off.

Reese

The next day she ate and drove to the beach. Rather than park on the side of the road, she decided to park in the South Beach parking lot. This gave her a view of the dilapidated castle on the cliff. It looked like a tired, weathered beast on the edge of suicide. With its cold stone crumbling, it looked ready to throw itself into the sea.

She'd heard the story of the castle, like any other long-time resident of Castle Cove. Once it had belonged to an evil queen who had starved her people with her incessant greed and endless campaigns of war.

Vendetta alone had been granted the power to destroy the queen and bring down her queendom. Reese wasn't sure how much of that was true or embellished. But here were the ruins.

She descended to the beach carefully, doing her best to keep her footing in the sliding sands.

Once she reached the water's edge, she looked around to ensure she was alone.

She walked the eastern edge of the beach, hoping this little nook close to the cliffs would render her invisible to anyone on the ledge above. Here she stripped, placing her clothes on a large rock that seemed safe from any oncoming waves or rising tides.

She waded out into the water. It was cool, no doubt because of its depth, but not unbearable.

Once the water reached her thighs, she dove under the next wave. Her body transformed. Her muscles thickened. Organs moved. Her face elongated and her limbs condensed themselves into a single, streamlined form.

That instant calm enveloped her, a feeling she only experienced when in this form.

With gentle side-to-side motions, she propelled herself forward. She established an easy rhythm, cutting through the aquamarine waters. She would have to swim south until the rockface ended. Then the plan was to hook around it and swim north-northeast, following the cliffs as Ethan had suggested until she came upon the mouth of the underwater cave.

Her senses stretched out before her, scanning the waters for any other forms of life. She detected a school of fish feeding on even smaller fish off to her right. And also something with a slow, steady rhythm ahead. A turtle, she suspected. Nothing large, nothing dangerous loomed.

She slid through the rock wall using the gap beside Heart's Rock. Most of her dorsal fin had to break the surface to manage it, but if someone on the beach saw her shark fin, what of it? She was far enough away not to frighten any swimmers.

On this side of the rock wall, the ocean felt vast. Far more vast than she was used to. Reef sharks preferred the tight confines of the reef buffered by an ocean floor. It offered protection on most sides. They were, after all, the big fish in a little pond, so to speak.

Here, with nothing but miles and miles of deep waters on all sides, Reese knew she was exposed. She would have to keep her wits about her, or she could very well end up as lunch for a larger, more opportunistic creature.

She stayed close to the cliff face, scanning the waters around her with unease. After twenty minutes of swimming at a steady pace, the cliff face opened beside her, revealing a deep cavern.

Here, the waters were not so dark. In fact, they shone with crystalline light.

She swam into the cave, marveling at how bright the waters were and how warm as well. There was some light source coming from below.

Then she spotted the sirens. They were sleeping, half in, half out the water. Their tails stretched out behind them on the rock ledges like seals sunning in the late afternoon. Reese swam as close as she dared, trying to get a better look at them.

This close, she saw strange black markings on their skin. Rashes or growths, these patches of abnormality were embedded in the skin.

They're sick, she realized. Would a sickness make them desperate enough to aggressively seek mates on shore? Or maybe the sickness had made them confused about where they were and what they were doing?

She wasn't sure.

But they were restless even in repose, most fidgeting on their rocks as if they couldn't get comfortable. One sleepy siren picked at the open sore of another, the black pus oozing into the water like oil.

Reese circled the cave several times and took inventory of the numbers and condition of the sirens. Very few looked untouched by whatever disease this was.

On her last pass in the cavern, she spotted something at the back of the cave. A partially submerged staircase led out of the water. Where it led, she couldn't be sure from her vantage point beneath the surface. Should she go up and investigate? Maybe she would learn something about the sirens' environment that would help them. Of course, there was the danger they would see her shapeshift and know that she was no mere shark.

Reese transformed into a woman and pulled herself out of the water onto the steps. Her bare feet scraped across the rough stone.

The second she straightened, water dripping down her back, a horrible screeching thrummed to life behind her.

The sirens had awakened. They thrashed on their rocks, throwing themselves into the water. Their lithe forms were torpedoing through the water toward her.

"Shit." She bounded up the stairs two and three at a time, careful not to slip on the wet stone. At the top of the stairs was a stone door.

"Please be unlocked, please be unlocked, please be unlocked."

The door opened under the hard push of her hand despite the weight of the stone. Behind her the sirens had stopped advancing. They now crowded the lower steps, but seemed unwilling to come up the stairs after her.

They can't get out of the water, she thought. At least not this far.

Heart still hammering in her chest, she breathed a sigh of relief and closed the stone door behind her.

She was greeted by a narrow passage. Light filtered through cracks in its crumbling stone walls, giving her a clear enough sense of where she was going. At the end of the passage, another set of stairs appeared. She mounted these as well.

Stone passage, then stairs.

Another stone passage, then more stairs.

The labyrinth seemed to lead her higher and higher until her chest and legs were aching from the ascent.

"This is the last one," she said aloud, when she pushed open yet another stone door to find only more stairs. "If there's nothing here after this, I'm going back."

But the end of this passage opened onto what could only be described as a courtyard. Light poured through a collapsed ceiling onto the flagstones below. The stones themselves were half-eaten with moss and determined vines had pushed themselves up through the cracks.

I'm in the castle, she realized, as she turned in its center, admiring the ruined splendor. The public wasn't allowed to enter the castle ruins for fear that it would collapse and kill someone. Yet here she was, having found a secret passage inside.

A cacophony of beating wings tore a shriek from her throat. A cloud of pigeons coalesced atop a crumbling wall, cooing softly at her.

She followed the outline of the room to a small chamber. It had the air of an inner sanctum. But on the walls were ornate carvings of some kind. Clearly a stoneworker had license to embellish this stone either before or after it had been installed.

Reese crossed to the nearest carving and pressed her fingers to the etchings. A woman with long, flowing hair was extending her hand toward an enormous cobra that stood entranced before her. The next panel was the same exchange but the snake had changed. Now its form hunched over on itself. In the third and fourth panels, it was unfurling into a human form. If the woman was Vendetta, then it seemed her touch alone had transformed the snake into a human.

On the next wall, there was a small child crawling out of the sea and a woman there to welcome her with open arms.

This sparked a memory in Reese. Her first memory.

She was in the ocean—swimming? She had been following the slow, curious procession of a starfish when hands scooped her out of the water. For a moment she couldn't breathe. She couldn't see. The next she was in her aunt's arms.

"Look at you!" her aunt cried. Her shocked face was full of bright sunlight. Her hazel eyes shone like amber. "Where did you come from?"

Reese couldn't have been more than three or four years old at the time.

Could it be that Reese had simply come from the ocean? Transformed for the first time in her aunt's own embrace?

Tell me again, Reese had begged over and over again. *Tell me again about the day you found me.*

You were on the beach, Constance said, *all alone in the surf.*

Reese had no memory of her parents or her life before she was here in Castle Cove. She remembered only those bright summers and endless waves, and then her aunt taking her home, caring for her as if she was her own. Her aunt had no true blood relation to her. Reese had asked on more than one occasion why she would bother taking in a child that wasn't hers. A child with no history before her mysterious arrival in Castle Cove?

We aren't kin, Reese had said.

Of course we are kin, Constance had said. With a kind smile, she'd gather the ink-dipped ends of Reese's hair and run them through her fingers. She held it up to her own. *Look at us.*

Perhaps Ethan's words had some truth to them—was it possible that Reese didn't remember her life before Castle Cove because there had been only the ocean?

Had she been a shark first? A human second? Was this human life the dream life?

Reese fingered the stone reliefs and wondered. These were the only drawings with animals transforming under Vendetta's watchful gaze, but Vendetta herself was everywhere. Reese must've found hundreds of reliefs of the woman with the wild, flowing hair in every weed-choked chamber she explored.

Another common theme was a tree, majestic with its gnarled limbs. Could it be The Crone Tree she'd heard of from the stories? She couldn't be sure. The only question she had was whether or not these carvings existed first—validating the story —or if someone had seen the carvings later and made up the stories to match.

Perhaps she would never know.

Reese noticed a shift in the light. It was far more purple now than it had been when she'd set off this morning. And the rumble in her stomach seemed to confirm her suspicion. She'd lost track of time exploring the castle. If she didn't leave now, she would have to swim back in the dark.

In all her searching, she didn't find an exit out of the castle. How wonderful it would've been if she could've simply walked out of the ruins to her car. But she suspected that Ethan—or some other caretaker of the city—had been careful to seal the castle for the public's protection.

Reese would have to return to the underground tunnel and swim back to the beach, or she could try to climb out of here. She saw enough grooves in the rockface to know that she could probably do it. But it might be a long drop from the top if there were no handholds on the outside of the castle.

As much as Reese loathed the idea of walking all the way back to the underground cavern, she thought it was much safer than trying to climb out of the castle. If it had been sealed to protect the public from getting hurt, it stood to reason that the walls were not nearly as stable as they looked. The ruins were thousands of years old. They wouldn't appreciate being climbed on.

Retracing her steps, she found the courtyard and the passage connecting it to the descending staircase. By the time she reached the underground cavern, her legs were shaking with fatigue.

Aqua waters shimmered on the stone steps, but there was no

horde of sirens. Perhaps they'd gotten tired of waiting as she spent hours exploring the castle above. Or perhaps they were hoping she'd jump in so they could descend on her.

Regardless, the air had cooled, and she was still naked, tired, and hungry. She had to get back to shore with what energy she had left.

With a deep breath, she dove into the water, trying her best to transform in the air even if that meant a painful belly flop on the water's surface.

She managed it, though pain ricocheted through her abdomen on impact. She sank beneath the water, seeing the sirens stir at the commotion. But unlike before they did not chase her.

It must only be human flesh, she thought, her body easing into a steady rhythm. *Human flesh in the water is what draws them.*

The swim back felt shorter despite her fatigue. She supposed it had to do with the fact that she knew where she was going this time and how far she must travel.

When she pulled her exhausted body out of the water, Ethan and Liam stood on the shore. Ethan, she realized, was standing in full sunset. Unlike the other demons she knew, he didn't seem to die at sunrise. Demons couldn't exist in the realms of light. Did this mean he was not a demon? If so, he must be something much, *much* worse.

Liam held his black umbrella open overhead.

"Have a nice swim?" Ethan asked, his patent Italian leather shoes half sunk in sand.

"Did you wait here all day?" she asked, unable to believe their timing. She pulled herself out of the water, fully aware of her nakedness. With as much confidence as she could muster, she marched toward her clothes and found them dry where she left them. But there was also a towel that wasn't hers.

"I brought it," Liam explained. He was keeping his eyes averted respectfully. His demon boyfriend was not.

"Did you run into trouble?" Ethan asked. His eyes lingered on her legs.

"Not really," she said, toweling her body. She was afraid to mention that she'd explored the castle. But she didn't seriously believe she could keep it a secret from Ethan. *Here goes nothing,* she thought. "They perked up when I transformed into a human and went into the castle."

Ethan's eyebrows twitched. "Did you? And did you find anything interesting?"

She told him about the reliefs. "Is that where you got your story?"

"No," he said. "It's true that once Vendetta destroyed the queen she took the castle for herself and it was her stronghold for hundreds of years. I'm sure she decorated its walls however she saw fit, as queens are wont to do."

"Is it possible?" Reese asked, unable to control herself. "That I wasn't dropped here by some shifter who couldn't take care of me? That I was in fact *first* a shark?"

Ethan smiled as if he knew a secret. "What did your aunt tell you?"

"She found me on a beach when I was three or so. I didn't talk. I couldn't tell them my name or anything like that. She suspected that some supernatural dropped me off, knowing this was the best place for me."

"It's possible," Ethan said companionably. "Both that you had a mother who could not care for you or that you were born in the sea. Does it matter to you?"

Reese stared out over the horizon uncomprehendingly, as if she might find the answer there. "It doesn't change anything, does it?"

"How were the sirens?" Ethan asked, trying to recapture her attention.

She told them what she saw, doing her best to explain the black lesions.

Frowning, Ethan lifted his hand as if he meant to touch her. "May I?"

She nodded, suspecting she was agreeing to some sort of mind meld.

As his fingertips brushed her temple, the sensation of cold water running over her scalp overtook her. She shivered.

"I see," he said, letting his hand fall back to his side. His frown had deepened. All of his flirtation had disappeared.

The breeze pulled at his shirt, revealing a bare chest beneath.

"Could an illness make them more aggressive?" Liam asked, turning the umbrella in his grip.

"If they were worried about population die off, yes," he said. "Especially if several had already died."

"I didn't see any corpses," she said and immediately felt stupid. He must know that having shared her memory.

"They eat their dead," Ethan said. Now he was looking out over the ocean, a dreamy look on his face. "Which would spread a disease rather than contain it."

His trance seemed to break and he turned toward her with a bright smile. "Thank you for your help. This information is very useful. If you don't mind, I have another task."

Reese shifted, wondering just what he might ask for.

He shook his head, his seriousness lingering. "Nothing lascivious, I assure you. I'm sending Liam to investigate a situation in town and he could use a hand. Or you could go interview the children who were at the beach the night the sirens attacked. Which would you prefer?"

"I'll help Liam," she said.

Reese was instructed to meet Liam at Two Doves Cemetery. Reese navigated her rumbling red pickup through the Castle Cove streets, considering the task ahead. The idea of traipsing around a cemetery with a vampire after dark was not all that appealing.

It wasn't that she was afraid of the vampire, of the dark, or all those dead people under the ground. She only hoped there would be no labor involved. She was tired. And when tired, gravedigging wasn't even in her top fifty choices for how she'd like to spend an evening.

When she pulled into the cemetery parking lot, she found Liam leaning against the trunk of his BMW, his ankles crossed and hands in his pockets. Reese thought he looked a little like Zac Efron with his hair swooped up and back and that burgundy silk scarf wrapped around his neck.

She parked beside him and climbed out. "You late for your Esquire photoshoot or something?"

She hoped his outfit meant that no digging would be involved—or he expected her to do it.

He spared her a wry half-smile. "This shouldn't take too long. Hopefully."

He began crossing the parking lot to the wood-chipped foot-path ahead.

She fell into step beside him. "What are we doing here?"

"Someone reported grave vandalism."

Reese frowned. "Isn't that something the police should handle?"

Liam snorted, continuing his long, easy stride even as the path steepened. "It is. Until they call Ethan."

"So what does that make you?" she asked. "The deputy?"

His smile deepened. "I see why Kristine likes you so much."

"Thanks. I think."

As the path ended, the vampire's eyes swept the cemetery. "Over here."

She followed him in silence. Twilight purpled around them, the shadows thickening beneath the trees that bordered the cemetery. They seemed to elongate like fingers stretching toward them.

Don't, she warned. *You'll whip yourself into hysterics with thoughts like that.*

But then she saw the ghosts, rising like mist from the graves. She stiffened, her stride faltering.

Liam turned back, frowning at her. "What?"

"Are you seeing this?" Reese pointed at the mist materializing in front of the grave two rows over.

Liam followed her finger. "The ghosts? They're fine. They won't bother us. I don't think they can even see us."

He resumed his walk. As she watched the phantoms rise from their graves and then float in whichever direction suited them—Reese counted eight—she saw he was right. They were neither coming this way nor showing signs that they knew they were here.

Relief softened the rock in her stomach—until she turned and saw Liam had gotten away from her. She took off at a run to catch up. It was hard to keep her balance over the uneven ground. Some graves seemed to be rising, others sinking. The scent of fresh earth pressed in on her.

She almost yipped with joy when she found him, crouching down in front of a crooked stone.

"Come here," he commanded pointing at the ground. "This is what I needed you for."

"What?" But as soon as the word was out of her mouth, Reese saw what he was pointing at. There was a hole where the grave should be. Someone had crudely exhumed the body. The dirt was gone, piled behind the tombstone itself. It wasn't crooked, she realized. It was half buried. In the grave was the unopened casket.

"What do you need me to do *exactly*?" Reese asked, relieved that the vandal had done the labor himself—or herself. But also terrified that he was going to ask her to climb into the grave.

"Can you feel any magic?" he asked. "I need to know if magic was used here."

"Why are you asking me?"

"I can't feel it," he said. "An undead vampire could. But living vampires can't. *I* can't."

Reese sniffed the air. "No. I don't feel anything."

Liam sighed. "Damn. I was hoping you wouldn't say that."

A cold hand clamped onto Reese's shoulder and she shrieked.

"Hell's Bells," Violet hissed. The leather clad demon took a step back. "Shut up, would you?"

Liam stood, brushing dirt from his knees. "You scared her."

"You think, bloodsucker? And she busted both my ear drums." Violet stuck a finger in her ear and twisted it. "Remind me never to take you to a haunted house. Or a scary movie for that matter."

"What are you doing here?" Reese demanded. She had one hand over her chest as if trying to hold her heart in.

Violet crossed her arms. "I *was* going to ask if it was true that you were dumb enough to help Ethan investigate what's going on in this town, but now that I see his cabana boy in tow, I have my answer."

"Hello, Violet," Liam said. He didn't look at her. He continued frowning at the open grave. "You couldn't tell me why this grave is unearthed, could you?"

"Sure," Violet said with a smirk. "I *could*. But why would I?"

"Because if we don't figure this out, Ethan is going to drink your girlfriend here dry and use her magic to put Vendetta in some kind of stasis cocoon to protect her."

"What?" Reese turned toward Liam, trying to tell if the vampire was joking. She didn't think he was.

Violet's smirk disappeared. "Excuse me?"

"You heard me."

"Fuck," Violet said and then to Reese as if this was all her fault. "This is why you stay away from them. Did you even realize they were setting you up to be dinner? Hell, he's probably going to drain you the second you report back!"

"To be fair, that was only Ethan's Plan B. I'm against it. I think it will make Kristine sad."

Reese pressed the heels of her hands against her eyes. "Could you not talk about me like I'm already dead." Then to Liam. "He was really going to—whatever the hell you just said?"

Liam shrugged, moonlight dancing on his shoulders. "It wouldn't have killed you. But it would've turned you into a shark, permanently. You wouldn't be able to return to shore anymore." Then to Violet, "So what do you know?"

Violet groaned. "You play dirty, bloodsucker. I'll remember that."

Liam nodded as if he understood.

"Hope dug up this guy because the corpse had some ancient coin that Ydril wanted. She gave Ydril the coin as payment in order to find out where the Witching Blade was."

"Who the hell is Hope?" Reese asked.

"A chaos demon. Used to be pretty close to Ethan and Vendetta. I hear she's one of the original chevalier."

"Is that all?" Liam asked.

"No. She also wanted to know where Ethan was keeping Vendetta. She seems to be under the impression that he's keeping her in stasis against her will."

"And since this grave is clearly excavated, the transaction has already happened."

"You're so smart," Violet said, clapping her hands. "You must be his favorite *good boy*."

Liam's head snapped up.

The look in his eyes made both Reese and Violet step back.

"Hey man, I was just kidding. Take a—"

"Shut up," Liam said. He craned his head as if listening to something. He met Reese's gaze. "We have to go. *Now*."

"Why?" Reese's heart had finally started to quiet in her chest only to now rev up again.

Liam was already running through the graves, cutting the

shortest path to his car. "Hope's at the house."

"I'm coming too," Violet said, following them down the sloping hill.

"You don't have to," Reese said, secretly touched.

"That's what I thought until I just found out how much trouble you're in. I'm riding with you."

They climbed into the pickup and followed Liam's BMW out of the parking lot. As she shifted gears, Reese had a chance to realize she'd picked up dirt on her knees. And her hair was starting to stick to the back of her neck.

"Any chance I can get you to give me your soul?" Violet asked, swaying in the passenger seat as they drove west out of town.

"What? Why?" Reese asked.

"Ethan can't touch your magic if your soul is promised to someone else. Think of it as giving it to me for safe keeping," Violet gave her a grin worthy of a devil.

Reese shifted gears, laughing. "I was considering it until you smiled like that."

Violet shrugged. "At least you're smart. But seriously, you need to be on your guard here. Liam, no matter how friendly he is with your buddy Kristine, he's loyal to Ethan. He will live and die for him. You got that? He would throw you under the bus to save his beau."

"And what about you, Violet? Whose side are you on?"

Violet grinned from the passenger side of the truck. "Tonight? I'm yours."

Grayson

Sunday morning passed quickly with Nutella pancakes and cups of coffee. But then his parents went to the Farmer's market in Cliffside, which met on Sunday from May through October. Unlike the market that met in Old Town on Saturdays, Sunday's market focused on street food and live music. There were more dogs and a playground. It wasn't a bad way to spend a Sunday. On any other day, Grayson would've been thrilled to go too.

But he was tired. He'd kept trying to go to sleep and yet kept finding himself waking up, wanting to read The Dark Mother and Her Children. He reached for the book the way he usually reached for his phone.

He told his parents he wasn't feeling well, hoping they'd let him stay home. He saw the conflict on their faces as they tried to decide whether or not to force him along or to give him space.

They left without him.

No sooner did his father's sedan back out of the driveway, nearly hitting the orange tabby, Pumpkin, did Grayson bound up the stairs.

Grayson seized the book and read it again. Before he knew what he was doing, he'd closed the book and began to pack a bag as he would for any day-long hike.

Water. Three protein bars and his knives. He took a length of rope for good measure and a mostly used roll of duct tape. One could never be sure when they might need duct tape.

He looked into his bag and felt there wasn't much else he could bring.

On second thought, he pulled an onyx pendant from his bedside table. It had been Ms. Monroe who'd given it to him for his sixteenth birthday. She'd said that onyx protected a person from magic. He hoped that would guard him against any magical creatures in the Western Woods.

He clasped the necklace around his neck, feeling its weight settle against his chest.

As he sat on the bench by the front door, pulling on his shoes, he texted Abby. *Heading out for a hike.*

Where? she asked him.

He considered lying. Then he thought of her in his bed, and

lying felt like a dirty trick.

Western Woods.

Haha. When he didn't respond quick enough she added, *WTF??? Are you serious???*

I think there's a way to bring Landon back.

The text bubble rose and disappeared for several minutes. Grayson managed to write Reese a note—*Something came up. We'll have to reschedule*—and tape it to the front door. He was already in his car before Abby's response finally came through.

As what? Zombie? Vampire?

Not sure.

Demon?

I honestly don't know, he replied.

You want to bring someone back from the dead and you don't know as what? Awesome idea.

If I died wouldn't you want to bring me back? he asked.

That's different.

Why should it be different? he asked. *He's our bff.*

She didn't seem to have an answer for that.

Finally, *I'm coming with you.*

No.

Why?

It's too dangerous.

If it's too dangerous for me, it's too dangerous for you, she replied.

He wasn't sure how to respond to that.

What are you trying to prove? she asked.

That question stung. Somehow it had cut beneath the surface of the urgency. It burned. Worse, it slowed him down. It made him think.

What *was* he trying to prove?

That he was a good friend to Landon? That Abby really would've wanted him if Landon were still alive? That Grayson wasn't a consolation prize?

No. He didn't believe any of that. If he was being honest with himself, he'd known since September. The way she'd looked at him spoke volumes for the connection between them.

If he needed to prove anything, it was that he wasn't happy his friend was dead. He needed to prove that Landon's death hadn't been like a gift from above.

That was closer to the truth.

Bringing Landon back would prove that he wasn't glad to have Landon removed from the picture. He wasn't glad that he had the chance to steal the girl he always wanted for himself.

Grayson shifted uncomfortably in the driver's seat. He wrung the steering wheel.

Take me with you, Abby texted again. *Gray, please. You can't go in there by yourself.*

I'll be there in five minutes, he wrote and reversed the car out of the driveway. It was almost eleven in the morning. If they got into the woods by noon, they'd have about nine hours before sunset. That meant they needed to cover at least two miles an hour. Doable.

His phone remained silent for the entire drive. Maybe Abby was saving her energy for a counterargument in person. Maybe she was forming a plan to detain him at her house so he couldn't go into the woods at all.

Grayson drove the perimeter of Hyde Park, driving past the large, imposing mansions that faced the park. He'd always wondered who lived there. Abigail said it was the wealthy undead vampires of Castle Cove. That each grand house was owned by one of the clans.

Apparently, there were two kinds of vampires in Castle Cove—and as far as Grayson knew—the world. There were living vampires and undead vampires. The living vampires were those who had not died as a result of their attack and transformation. Their hearts never stopped. Therefore, the virus living inside them had more of a symbiotic relationship with its host. It gave them strength and eternal youth. They detested, but were not allergic to, sunlight. They were simply creatures of the night. Their bodies emitted pheromones that attracted and disoriented their prey. They were warm and had a pulse. Mostly they were apex predators rather than supernatural creatures.

The undead were a different story. Unlike their living brethren who seemed to rely on their physical attributes to attract prey, the undead relied on magic. The undead had died during their transformations and it was at that moment of death that a demon entered their body and took up residence.

Most of the person's previous life and human connection were instantly forgotten. These vampires were reborn, strong and fast. Their powers included telepathy, mind-control, telekinesis and flying, depending on how strong the demon that inhabited their body was.

According to Abigail—or Abigail's mother, who knew almost every citizen in their town—it was actually only *one* demon per clan. The demon—and its power—was strongest in the oldest clan member, and weakest in the newest recruits. That was why they adhered to a hierarchy. Like all demons, they were unable to go into sunlight and died when the sun rose each day. They were cold to the touch, because they were essentially reanimated corpses. There was no life left in them.

As Grayson drove past the large, looming mansions, he wondered if such creatures really dwelled within. The revival architecture and old live oaks thick with moss seemed to say, *old beings dwell here*. With homes so massive, he imagined there was plenty of room for an entire clan and all their attendants to live comfortably.

Just east of Hyde Park, before Castle Cove University began, was a small neighborhood called Hummingbird Hollow. It had small, quaint ranch-style homes and postage stamp yards. He turned off Ruby Road onto Violetear Drive and found Abby sitting on her porch with a camo backpack between her knees on the step below her.

She stood when she saw him pulling into the drive and slung the sack over her shoulder.

He hadn't even fully come to a stop before she threw the passenger side door open and climbed inside.

"My mom's shift ends in ten minutes so you better step on it if you want to miss her," she said, and pulled the seatbelt across her chest.

He was back on Ruby Road moments later.

He was struck with the smell of her. Her hair looked damp and freshly washed. Her clothes reeked of fabric softener.

"So what do you know?" she asked, adjusting the pack between her legs.

"About the Western Woods?"

"No," she said then she cocked her head. "Well yeah, that too. But I meant Landon. You said you had a book about how to bring him back from the dead?"

"Not exactly," he admitted.

He could see her looking at him from the corner of his eye.

"I read a story about Vendetta and The Crone Tree. Have you heard of it?"

"No."

He recounted the story for her, from Vendetta's hard life until she was turned into a demon and took on the ruthless queen.

"What does this have to do with Landon?" she asked when he was done.

His thighs had begun to stick to his seat. He leaned forward and adjusted the A/C. "According to the story and my mother, The Crone Tree will bring him back to life if we make a sacrifice."

"Is there a dead body in the trunk?" she asked. "Because I don't see a sacrifice."

"I was hoping my blood would be enough."

"You expect to cut your hand and resurrect Landon?" she

asked. "Grayson, you didn't think this through. Which is…really unlike you."

Was he that obvious? Of course, he hadn't told her the truth. He couldn't tell her that he'd intended to cut himself—*really* cut himself. That he'd hoped his own blood would attract a dryad or some other monster and that he would kill it beneath the tree —offering *that* in exchange for Landon's life.

"What aren't you telling me?" she asked.

He shifted in his seat.

"Do you think I'm stupid?" she asked.

"No," he said. He turned and looked at her, trying to gauge how angry she was. She was irritated, but not furious. He didn't want to see how far she would push him.

"Don't you think it would be a good idea that I know what the actual plan is before we go into the big, dark woods?"

He sighed. "I was going to cut myself."

"Again, I don't think a bit of blood counts as a sacrifice."

"I was hoping the blood would attract…something."

Her lips pursed in question. "Any *particular* something? Or will any monster work for you?"

"First come, first served," he said.

"What if it is a dryad?"

His heart faltered. "What if it is?"

"Dryads are supposed to be sacred to The Crone. If you kill one maybe you'll piss her off and she'll smite you."

"Or we spare it in exchange for what we want."

"Or we get swarmed and eaten by a dozen of them. Or maybe she won't be impressed at all and tears us apart herself."

"Vendetta—" he began.

"Vendetta was turned into a demon so she could murder someone." Abigail spoke the words as if it answered everything. "That's some dark shit. I don't think the tree is into *oh-please-save-my-best-friend* type of requests. And all the things I've ever heard about The Crone Tree or She Who Sleeps is about her loyalty to her creations—demons, sirens, dryads. I don't think slaughtering one of her children is going to win her over."

He understood what she was saying. They had no proof that this would work. And the idea that they were going to walk over eight miles into the most dangerous woods on just a hope seemed…fine. *It'll be fine,* he thought.

Grayson pulled to a stop at the four-way in front of Crossroads.

"You'd have better odds going in there," Abby said. She pointed at the demon bar across the street.

Even though it was the middle of the day, several cars sat in the gravel lot outside the old timey saloon. The Crossroads bar was a demon bar. Every long-time resident of Castle Cove knew that. One only went in there to make dangerous deals.

Abby gestured to the slouching porch and batwing doors. "At least you know what you're getting when dealing with those guys."

Grayson sat at the four-way stop, considering his options. "You don't have to come. You can wait in the car."

"Because you're going in there no matter what I say, aren't you?"

South Beach bloomed on his left, revealing sandy beaches and blue-grey water today. On his right was the open fields known as Vendetta Heights. Grayson drove until he thought he was about parallel to the place known as Druid's Hollow.

"Christ," Abby swore. "This is really happening."

"Then don't come!" he said. "I don't know why I even brought you!"

Her face reddened as if slapped. She remained silent for the remainder of the drive, all the way to Vendetta Heights.

"I'm coming," she announced. "Now give me a kiss. For good luck."

She licked her lips.

He pulled off the road and parked the car, the nose pointing at the looming woods ahead of them.

"No, you're just trying to distract me."

"Come on," she said, leaning over the console. "We might die in here."

Heart hammering in his chest, he leaned across the console toward her. She met him halfway. Her lips were warm and sticky as they slid against his. She threaded her fingers through his hair, sending shivers down the back of his neck. A strange prickling raised the hairs along his skin.

Just when he thought he might burst with the desire building in his chest—because god, if it was her plan to make out with him in this car to prevent him from going, it just might work—she pulled back, frowning.

"What are you wearing?" she asked. She was looking him over as if she'd never seen him before.

"What do you mean?"

"I mean, what are you wearing? Do you have any oils on or maybe jewelry or a rock in your pocket?"

He reached inside his shirt and pulled out the onyx. "You mean this? How did you—"

She took it between her fingers, frowning at the black stone. "At least I'm not losing my mind."

"What are you saying?"

"Why not? It's a good a time as any." She sighed and searched his eyes. "I'm a witch."

For a moment, he sat there looking at her. It sounded like a punchline to an incomplete joke. Like someone had told it poorly, skipping important information.

Finally he managed, "What?"

"I'm a witch. I joined the Castle Cove coven when I turned eighteen. I'd wanted to join since junior year but you have to be of age. Then it's a ten-year apprenticeship until you're a full member."

"And they just let you join?" he asked. It sounded like a

stupid question once it left his lips. It was funny how some questions sounded very smart inside his head, but less so once spoken.

"I have an aptitude for magic."

"Wait," he said, straightening and running a hand over his face. "What does this have to do with the onyx?"

But then he remembered Ms. Monroe's words.

"Were you trying to cast a spell on me?"

"A protection spell before we go in there half-cocked. But to be honest, I don't even know if it's going to work. There's a saying in the coven: There's not enough magic in the world to protect against stupidity."

"Is this why you wanted to come?" he asked her. "You thought you could protect me?"

"I'm trying," she said. She bit her lip, her anxiety showing. "I wanted to cast protection spells and stealth spells on us both. I was hoping that it would get us further into the woods without being detected. Or if we run into something, we'll have a bit of luck on our sides. But Grayson—"

He snapped himself out of the mental spiral that was sucking him down.

Abby is a witch. Abby is a witch. Abby—

"Grayson—the Western Woods is old magic. Old as Hell itself, do you understand? I have zero belief that my wimpy spells are going to get us through this alive. That's why I called Miriam."

"Who?" Every time his heart slowed down, Abby said something to send it kicking again.

"My coven leader. I told her where we are. I asked for her help."

Grayson dragged his hands down his face. "What if they stop us?"

Abby snorted. "If only we were so lucky. Do you really want to go in there?"

She pointed at the woods.

He looked at the darkness pooling beneath the trees. "Yes."

"And if you don't go now, you'll just sneak in by yourself some other time, won't you?"

"How did you—"

"Right. So I'm going in with you then." Abby pinched the bridge of her nose. "And I'm doing what I can to keep us safe, but I can't cast any spells on us if you have that necklace on."

He looked down at the onyx pendant resting against his chest. He lifted it, gazing into its black face. He saw his own, puzzled reflection staring back at him.

Grayson wrapped his hand around the onyx. "Can you get the clasp?"

He leaned toward her, feeling her cold fingers on the back of his neck.

The weight slid off his neck, clinking into her palm. She slid it into a cup holder.

"Thank you for trusting me," she said, her eyes shining. "It's just a small protection spell. I would never do anything that changed your will or something like that."

"I know." He smiled. "So how does it work?"

A crooked grin tugged her lips to one side. "Like this."

She leaned across the console and brushed her mouth against his. Her parting lips invited movement of his own. He opened his mouth and welcomed the brush of her tongue.

A warm tingle ran down his spine, raising the goosebumps on his arms and the back of his neck.

She pulled back from the kiss, panting. "We better get a move on."

"No," he said.

She laughed. "Yes."

She grabbed the pack between her legs and threw open the passenger side door.

"Come on."

Grayson looked at the dashboard clock. It was 12:12. She was right. They were losing daylight.

He stepped from the car into the tall grass. It scratched at his jeans as he rooted in the backseat for his pack. He hefted the pack onto his shoulders and locked up his car. With several long, loping strides he was able to catch Abigail at the edge of the woods.

A shiver ran down his spine as he recollected the illustration from *The Dark Mother and Her Children*. He didn't see any eyes watching him, waiting for him to step vulnerable into the woods. But he suspected there might be creatures here that he couldn't see. This was Castle Cove after all.

Abby took his hand and pulled him into the forest. "I want us out of here before dark. Come on."

The dense canopy overhead immediately blotted out most of the sunlight.

They hadn't even gone twenty feet before he realized he was right about the low light. He'd suspected the covering in this part of the forest was thick, dappling what little sunlight they had.

In the Wayward Woods, he could walk until nearly sunset and count upon the light. The trees weren't as crowded and the wide expanse of bright sky overhead invited hikers to linger in any of the beautiful, open fields surrounding the trails. Lake Trail, in particular, offered a gorgeous view for stargazing. And it was close enough to Sunset Park that one could linger well into the evening and feel relatively safe.

Here the trees seemed to stand almost on top of one another. *They are crowding in on us*, he thought. He shivered again.

"We need to get to The Crone Tree within three hours if we can. We can make it if we keep a good pace," he said.

Her head was up. Her eyes were bright. He respected her even more for that. She'd always been smart, probably one of the most brilliant students at their school, but her seriousness—

when seriousness was merited—had always impressed him. Landon had been a jokester. He'd laughed at all the wrong moments and whenever the moments had been tense, like when Abigail's father left town and never came back, he'd tried to use laughter to dispel the gloom.

"I don't think we should talk," she whispered.

Grayson agreed so they walked in silence.

First a mile. Then two. By the third mile, his mind had entered a sort of trance state as it often did when he walked. His thoughts flittered away and left him only with the sensation of the experience. His body laboring. Fresh air moving in and out of his chest. A slight sweat forming on his brow and the back of his neck. The shirt trapped between his skin and backpack had grown damp.

He kept walking.

However, it was difficult to traverse the woods with complete stealth. It looked lush and green. The forest floor was thick with spongy moss and soft clover. Their steps should be nearly muted. And yet, it seemed that every snapping twig, every shifting rock betrayed them.

Something is wrong, he thought. The forest was beautiful. Grayson might even have used the word inviting. But he found himself thinking of the story about lost children finding a house made of candy. He was sure the witch's candy house had seemed inviting, too.

The canopy shed sparkling light onto their path as if urging them further, deeper into the woods.

A wild thought visited him then.

This forest is alive. Like a single, sentient creature, it lived. Not only did it live, but it knew they were there and did every- thing it could to draw them deeper into its yawning maw.

He hesitated on the path.

Abby froze instantly beside him. She looked eager, almost ready to bolt and run the other way.

"Does it feel…." He searched for the right words. Now, the idea that he would come to this forest, that he would look for this damned tree seemed incredibly stupid. "Does it feel alive to you?" he whispered.

When Abby didn't answer, he was worried that perhaps he was too quiet to be heard.

Then she nodded. Her eyes had gone a fraction wider since they'd first entered.

"There's a lot of magic here," she whispered. He saw goosebumps prickle along her skin. "I've never felt anything like it. There's magic all over Castle Cove, more in some places than others. But this…" She was unable to finish her sentence.

They were almost at the halfway mark in their journey between Vendetta Heights and Druid's Hollow. It seemed silly to turn and run back now after they'd come so far.

His phone buzzed in his bag. Unanswered, the call went to his voicemail, probably on account of the shitty signal. He pulled the phone from his bag and listened to the message.

"Grayson? It's Ms. Monroe. I'm just seeing your note about the books you took. One of those—The Dark Mother and Her Children—is, well, it shouldn't be read. If you haven't read it yet, don't. Just bring it back, please. It's not that you need to worry about the content or anything like that. It's…well…the book has a will of its own."

Grayson wondered what exactly that meant.

"Just don't open the book," she said. Fretfully, she added, "Call me as soon as you get this."

Abby nodded north, suggesting they press on. When he started walking, she seized his arm and shook it. She jabbed her finger north again and he frowned. Once he followed her gaze however, he understood.

There, not a hundred feet away, was a woman.

She was walking away from them. She wore an outfit that looked like equestrian riding breeches and black leather gloves.

Her black hair was pulled into a low pony at the nape of her neck. Her boots crossed the forest floor in absolute silence.

She didn't look their way, but the idea that she could pass so close and not see them was unimaginable. Or perhaps she couldn't be bothered by two teenagers wandering the woods. Her incessant stride suggested she had a very important appointment she could not miss. She marched on.

Or it was a trick. Maybe she wasn't a woman at all.

"She doesn't look like a monster," Grayson whispered.

"Looks deceive," Abby replied. "Let's give her room."

They kept their distance, though both parties were headed in the same direction. There were times when they'd seem to lose her as if she were walking three or four times faster than they could manage. She would disappear around a bend, or a rock-face and be gone. But when they arrived, she would always appear again.

Was she adjusting her speed for them? Did she want to be followed?

Grayson ran through the list of dangerous creatures he knew roamed the Western Woods. Dryads, of course, with claws like blades. Wendigos—equally terrifying. But neither of those took the shape of a woman. Perhaps it was a fey. Fey was an umbrella term for any number of creatures who lived on the magic of nature. The nastiest ate children and stole husbands. The best simply hated humans for their part in the world's deforestation.

Perhaps the woman was fey and this game a trick.

What happened when she grew tired of playing with them?

They finished out seven miles, and Grayson checked his watch. He wanted to be mindful of the time. But in fact, in trying to keep up with the woman, they'd managed to cross seven miles before it was even three o'clock. They were making great time. But he was itching from the sweat glistening on his skin. He lifted his shirt and wiped his face.

"We're almost there," Abby said, her own breath labored. "Don't give up on me now. I want to get the hell out of here." She urged him on, setting the pace for the remainder of the hike.

Less than a mile later, the trees broke and the winding path dissolved into an enormous field. In the center of the field, The Crone Tree.

No one needed to tell Grayson this was the tree. Nor did he require any convincing that this was the subject of Castle Cove's oldest lore.

The name was apt. The tree was monstrous and with spindly black limbs. It was like the Indian goddess Kali, black limbed with a thousand twisted arms extended from her. Her branches were full of strange blood-red blossoms unlike any Grayson had seen before. And it sounded as if it were full of birds. No small creatures flittered from branch to branch and yet the chorus seemed to emanate from it.

The trunk itself was knotted in such as a way as to suggest an old, weathered face.

Grayson was pulled from his gawking by an incessant quiver against his spine.

Grayson's backpack vibrated against his back. He mistook it for another call, until he pulled his phone from the pack and found it dark.

It was the book. The *book* vibrated in his hands.

"What's that sound? Do you hear it?" She knelt down beside him and turned her ear as if listening. "God, is it singing?"

All the cautious attention that she'd kept about her as they walked through the woods left her. Her eyes were wild with curiosity now. She bordered on delight.

And Abby was right.

The book was doing something. Vibrating or singing, he couldn't be sure.

"Is it made of the same wood?" she asked. Her finger lovingly traced the cover.

That's when Grayson realized that it *was* wood that encased the pages. How could he have mistaken it for leather before?

"Let's bring them together," Abby said. She looked from the book in his hands to the tree sitting in the center of the field. "Maybe they want to be together."

Her voice had a faraway, dreamy quality to it now. Grayson himself felt as if he was dreaming as he wandered toward the large, imposing tree.

Suddenly, Grayson was knocked off his feet and thrown through the air.

It happened so quickly that he barely processed the feeling of his feet leaving the earth before his abdomen was jerked up and backward. He tumbled to the ground. All his breath left him in a single gush. His pack had hit the earth ten feet away, spraying its contents into the dirt. Somehow, he still held the book.

He sat up in the tall grass, confused.

"Well," someone said. "*That* was unexpected."

It was the woman in the equestrian outfit. Her black boots shone in the sunlight. Her gloved hand went to her hip as she frowned down at Grayson.

That's when Abby stood up, knocking the dirt off her knees. When she saw the woman, she let her backpack slide off her shoulders and took a fighting stance.

The woman seemed amused by this, smiling at Abby over her shoulder as she continued to stand over Grayson. "What have we here?"

Before Abigail could answer, the woman waved her arms in a furious arc as if gathering wind and hurled it in Abby's direction.

But the wind only parted around Abigail, ruffling the tall grass and eliciting groans from the trees behind her.

The gloved hand returned to her hip. "Not bad. But you reek

of Miriam. Is it your power you're throwing around or is it the coven's, little girl?"

Abby didn't take the bait. "You all right?"

She spoke to Grayson but her eyes remained fixed on the woman.

"He's fine," the woman replied. "I suspect he's stunned at best. Was that your doing? A hell of a protection spell, if I do say so myself. Of course it could only be that strong if you really loved him."

Abigail's cheeks flushed.

"Oh, you two are *adorable*. But I need a sacrifice if I'm to get the Witching Blade out of this tree. Since I'm a romantic, I'll let you choose. Would you prefer to offer yourself, or watch him die? He'll only leave you anyway. Men are like that. That's what your father did, didn't he? To your mother?"

With a battle scream, Abigail ran at the other woman.

Grayson couldn't be sure what he was seeing. Flames seemed to rip from the woman's hands and sail toward Abigail. But then they only evaporated into thick plumes of smoke before Abigail threw a knee into the woman's chest.

Figures emerged from the trees at full speed.

Dryads, Grayson thought, heart hammering. Or wendigos. Or maybe the mouth of Hell had opened and all manner of creatures were now going to rise up and consume them.

But it wasn't dryads or wendigos.

It was only two women and a man. A lightning crack of energy zipped through the air and the woman in riding gear was thrown off Abigail. She tumbled across the earth and hit the dirt twenty feet from Grayson's left, closer to the tree than anyone.

The woman was on her feet almost instantly, snarling. The curled lips and animalistic sneer turned her beautiful face into a hideous parody of itself.

Then she saw the woman responsible and her face harnessed

a disturbing calm.

"Oh, Miriam, it's just you. I thought it might be an actual threat."

Miriam, a tall woman with wavy brunette hair stood beside Abigail. No, she stood *over* her as if guarding a precious charge.

Where the hell did she come from? Grayson wondered. He'd never seen the woman before.

"Can you get up?" Miriam was looking at the woman, but Abigail was the one who answered.

"Yes." She pulled herself to standing and dusted off her knees.

"And is he all right?" Miriam asked, her eyes flicking toward Grayson for only a moment.

"I think so. Just stunned. He flew pretty far."

Grayson found his voice at last. "I'm okay."

"Good. Get up. We are leaving the forest," Miriam said. Her voice was calm, almost pleasant, but it left no room for argument. "Now."

"No, they aren't," the woman replied, batting dirt from her riding breeches and gloves.

"Do you think you can stop all of us, Hope?" Miriam asked.

Miriam balled her hands and swept them into another beautiful arc. The man beside her did the same. Their hands glowed with soft light.

But before they could attack, the woman named Hope had a trick of her own.

Black smoke poured from her hands, pooling around her feet. It rose up like a blanket and encircled the woman completely.

When it dissipated, she was gone.

A hand seized him and he looked up, surprised to find Ms. Monroe of all people, her hand tightly clasping his arm.

"Get up!" Ms. Monroe yelled. She wrenched him onto his feet. "Run!'

The black man who'd stood guard beside Miriam a moment before grabbed Abigail's pack before trotting over and gathering Grayson's as well.

"Don't worry, mate," he said, seeing Grayson's distressed face. He was shoving the spilled contents back into the backpack. "It's safe as houses with me."

His English accent surprised Grayson but he soon forgot it.

The book was gone. "But the book—"

Ms. Monroe shook it at him. "I've got it, I've got it. Come on!"

Grayson was dragged through the trees as if the Devil himself and all the hounds of Hell were on their heels. The man and Ms. Monroe flanked him, pulling him along so that his pace didn't falter. Abigail and Miriam stayed ahead of them.

We can't do this for eight and a half miles, Grayson thought. His body ached from its collision with the earth. *We can't.*

Yet they dragged on. Ms. Monroe was relentless as any mother who was scared out of her wits by a child's near brush with death.

"Why are we running?" he begged. "She disappeared."

"We aren't worried about Hope!" Ms. Monroe hissed. "Use your eyes boy!"

A terrible crashing through the trees made him wrench his head in the direction of the sound. A dryad was galloping after them. Like a tree come to life, it lumbered forward. Its limbs whipped about its head like uprooted tree branches.

"Dante!" Ms. Monroe yelled.

"I see it!" Dante cursed. Light sparked from his hands. "It's like stunning a stone wall. It only knocks them back for a second!"

"Lift and throw!" Ms. Monroe cried. "Lift and throw. Give us distance."

With another furious flick of his hand, the dryad was tossed through the trees away from them.

"Keep moving!" Miriam called from up ahead. "We've still a long way to go."

And to Grayson it seemed true. He felt like they'd walked for days, not hours. There was no sign of Hope, and the dryads would not give up. At one point they'd collected an entourage of five. No matter how many times they were tossed out of sight by magic they lumbered back.

It seemed enough for the three witches—not including Abigail—to handle.

Or was it two witches.

Grayson had not yet seen Ms. Monroe—who the others kept calling Tabby or Tabitha—cast a single spell.

At long last, the light broke ahead. Grayson was so relieved to see the woods part and the large expanse of Vendetta Heights before him that he collapsed to his knees.

"Not here!" Ms. Monroe hissed again, dragging him forward. "Get in the sunlight."

He obeyed, exiting the woods and falling against the hood of his car. A cherry red hybrid sat beside it.

There was a black woman leaning against the hood of the red Prius. She sighed, visibly relieved at the sight of them. "What happened?"

"Hope Duvani," Miriam said. "Naomi, did you see her?"

"*What*? No," Naomi said. "I thought it was just the book! I should've come with you!"

"No, it was good you were here," Miriam said. She was trying to catch her breath, chest heaving. "The cloaking helped. I think we would've been found out by more than a few dryads if you hadn't stayed behind to cover us."

"I'm so sorry," Abigail said, chest heaving. She hadn't yet caught her breath. None of them had. "I put everyone in danger. I accept full responsibility for whatever punishment you want to give me. I deserve it."

"Oh my life. Do you hear this?" Dante cut his eyes to Miriam.

"What do you have this girl thinkin'?"

"We're your coven, not a tribunal," Naomi said gently. She was smiling at Abigail the way one might regard a small child who has said something funny.

"She's right." Miriam gave Abigail a small smile. "You used your power in service of someone you love. That's exactly how you're supposed to use it, Abigail. There's no blame here."

Abigail's face flushed red. That was twice today someone had informed Grayson that Abigail loved him.

"I don't want to disappoint you or let you think I don't take being a witch seriously. You must think I'm the kind of person who runs into danger like—"

"We don't," Dante said, interrupting.

"I blame the book," Naomi said, fingering her braids.

"Me too," Ms. Monroe said. She was the only one who seemed to be breathing fine again so quickly.

"What's wrong with it?" Grayson asked, realizing that Ms. Monroe still had the book. He reached for it but she pulled back.

"Sorry, but we've got to keep it wrapped up. It's safer that way."

Grayson let his hands fall. "Why?"

"It's a cursed object," Ms. Monroe said, pulling her glasses off her face and cleaning them with the bottom of her shirt. There was a smudge of dirt on the side of her nose. "A cursed object with one objective, to lure human sacrifices to The Crone Tree."

"Certainly looked that way from what I saw. The moment I looked at it, all I wanted to do was go to the tree," Abigail said. "But how could a book do that?"

Ms. Monroe pushed the glasses back up on her nose. "The printer, Bentley Yorkshire, believed that the demons might've tampered with his printing press as a joke. He recorded in his ledger that he found shards of strange tree bark in the press's gears and leftover sheets of paper that 'could absorb blood.'"

"I wonder how he discovered that trick," Dante said with a snort.

"Either way, the press made seven copies of that damned book before it was shut down. Most were gathered up and disposed of before they could get into human hands."

Grayson didn't miss the way she said human hands, as if that didn't include her.

Miriam lifted her hair off her neck, welcoming the breeze that rolled across the Heights. "Four copies have been found over the centuries—this one is the fifth. They were all disposed of properly, but there is a fear that the others might've made it out into the world."

"Maybe this is good news then," Dante said. "Maybe they're here in Castle Cove somewhere."

"I wish you'd been wearing the onyx I gave you." Ms. Monroe turned to Grayson. "Perhaps it would've protected you from the book's sway."

"No," Grayson piped up. He was beginning to feel better now that they were out of the woods and the book was away from him. "I was wearing it before we went into the forest. It didn't protect me from the stupid idea in the first place."

He thought of the night before, of the way he'd felt when he'd opened the book and began reading the story. Who knew a book could possess a person?

"I'm glad he didn't wear it," Naomi countered. "If he had, we would've never found you."

"You'd both be dead," Miriam agreed. She gave Grayson a disapproving look as if he was to blame.

"Thank you," he said, finding his manners at last. "Thank you for helping us."

They shrugged him off.

"What I want to know is why Hope is here. And by The Crone Tree of all places. There's no reason," Naomi said.

"Yes, it would help to know what she was after," Miriam said, her eyes looking across the road to the ocean beyond. "No doubt the trouble around town with the sirens and graveyard can be blamed on her."

"The Witching Blade," Abby said. She was looking at her arm, inspecting a scratch she'd received from a tree branch during their escape. "She said she wanted The Witching Blade."

The witches exchanged furtive glances, before Miriam fixed her with a hard gaze. "Are you sure?"

"Of course she's sure," Naomi said. "How would she even know that name unless she'd heard it?"

"This is bad," Ms. Monroe said. She squeezed the book tighter against her chest. "Really bad."

Miriam turned and considered the ocean for a long time. No one moved or spoke. Grayson wondered what that must be like, to have so much authority that people literally just stood around, waiting for you to give orders.

"We need to speak to Ethan," Miriam said finally.

"When?" Dante asked.

"Now." Miriam moved toward the cars. "Come on."

When Abby and Grayson hesitated, she jerked her head.

"You too," she said, throwing open her car door. "He might need to speak to you."

Reese

The trees broke open and the two-story Spanish villa sprang into view. The dirt road turned to beautiful paving stones that circled in front of the house. In the center of the roundabout was a fountain bubbling softly with turquoise water.

Liam parked his BMW in front of the cream-colored steps and Reese pulled up right behind him. They were out of their vehicles and on the steps a moment later. But they hesitated.

The front door to Ethan's house had a giant hole blasted out of it. It hung on its hinges.

"Hope had to make an entrance." Violet shrugged in her leather jacket. "Not surprising. Chaos demons like to blow shit up."

"Come on," Liam said. "We need to help him."

"Do we?" Violet said with arched eyebrows. "I thought Ethan was the baddest boy in town. And what are you going to do anyway, bloodsucker? Hope can incinerate you with a thought."

If Liam heard this taunt, he gave no sign. They followed him into the house as he led them through the labyrinth of lavish rooms straight to a study. In this room, the walls were replaced with floor-to-ceiling bookcases made of dark wood. Red fabric couches and highbacked chairs rounded out the decor.

Liam approached a fireplace with twin carved panthers of black stone flanking each side. He placed his hand on the right panther and the fireplace shifted. A passageway appeared behind the flames.

"It won't burn you," Liam whispered, presumably so Hope would not hear them. "Just step through."

Liam went first, followed by Violet. Reese trailed behind. The flames felt like a cool breeze on her skin as she passed through.

Ahead a spiral staircase appeared. They followed it down silently. Their feet slipped over the stone without making a sound. The air grew noticeably colder with each step. Reese was certain they'd gone underground.

When they reached the bottom of the stairs, she saw several things at once.

First, the walkway stretching before them led to a stone coffin. The lid of this coffin had been removed and thrown across the room. It lay broken in three large pieces against the far wall.

It had collided with some of the stone carvings lining the walls. The impact destroyed a section, revealing jagged rock beneath.

Ethan stood on the left side of the stone coffin. Hope stood on the right. Their gazes were locked on one another. Reese could feel the magic like electricity crackling in the air.

"Do not mind the mess, my friends," Ethan said calmly. But he didn't take his gaze off of the woman. "Hope is a mere chaos demon. She can hardly help herself."

"I'm so much more than that!" Hope's face contorted in a hideous snarl. "I'm *her* chevalier. Just as well as you! You have no more right to her than any of us!"

Hope jabbed her finger into the center of the coffin each time she said the word *her*.

"You have the Witching Blade and your blood. What do you mean to do now?" Ethan asked.

"It will work," Hope hissed. "It *will*."

"All that Ydril told you was untrue," Ethan said calmly. He placed one hand on the coffin's stone.

"He said the blade was in the ocean. That the sirens had it. But I figured out where it really was." Hope twisted the strange knife in her hand. It looked more like a stake than a blade to Reese.

"He deceived you," Ethan said. "So that you would give him the coin he sought. He can't go on hallowed ground. Did you know that?"

"Yeah, well, I didn't realize every piece of shit in this town was loyal to you." Her free hand gripped her edge of the coffin. "They won't be once they know what a coward you are."

"So how did you learn the blade was in the forest?" Ethan asked.

And with a sudden spark of clarity, Reese understood why he was asking. He wanted to know what mistake he'd made, and how his secret had been uncovered.

"It doesn't matter," Hope said. "*I'm* her chevalier. She *chose* me. You have no right to keep her."

"My queen does as she pleases," Ethan said calmly. "Six

months ago, Henry made the mistake of thinking he could also take her from this place."

Hope's lower lip began to tremble. "I've missed her. I want her back."

"This isn't the way."

But Hope had already pulled the long wooden blade above her head. Reese thought the demon meant to plunge it into the coffin, but no. She dragged the tip of the blade down her arm, splitting the skin. Blood welled up instantly, flowing over her flesh.

Hope extended her hand into the coffin.

For a moment there was only a dripping sound. *Tap, tap, tap.* Like a faucet leaking somewhere in this grand house.

Hope's pained expression gave over to pleasure. "See? You don't know her like you think you do. You think you know what she wants but—"

Hope's words were swallowed by a sudden intense scream. The volume of it echoed off the walls, colliding and overlapping with itself. Reese, Violet, and Liam all covered their ears.

Hope was yanked forward, her body slamming into the side of the stone coffin. Then the arm was wrenched entirely from her body and disappeared into the sarcophagus.

The chaos demon stumbled back, still wailing. She looked at her severed arm, now torn from her shoulder as if she couldn't believe it was gone. She opened and closed her mouth like a fish out of water.

Reese wasn't sure what she expected to crawl out of the coffin. Some creature worthy of a lifetime of nightmares.

But what she saw instead was a woman. A young woman, slowly rising. To Reese, she didn't look like the majestic living goddess Reese had always imagined Vendetta to be. Instead, she resembled like a child, no more than sixteen. Her eyes were large liquid pools of moonlight and her face cherubic. The hair flowing down her back, impossibly long, seemed to shine with a life of its own, as black as a moonless night.

Blood dribbled down her chin as she released her hold on the severed arm. It fell to the floor with a wet *splat*.

This was Vendetta. In the flesh. One moment she was standing in the coffin like a sleeping beauty just wakened. Then she was in front of Hope, wrenching the other woman into her embrace.

Vendetta tore open her throat with one ruthless bite.

"Please," Hope begged, tears streaming down her face. "Please, my queen. I only want to serve you. I only want—"

Vendetta tore her head off her shoulders the way one rips an annoying tag from the inside of a shirt. Pieces of the demon fell to the marble floor. Blood escaped the body in a red stream.

Go! A voice cried in Reese's mind. Violet startled beside her and Reese suspected she'd heard the same cry. Liam had already placed a hand on both of them, pushing them toward the stairs. *Go! Before she can—*

But Vendetta was in front of Reese. Her liquid brown eyes sparked with an internal fire. Not the hellfire Reese had come to know in the eyes of the demons around her.

Magic, she realized. *I'm seeing the golden burn of magic inside her. That's all she is in there...*

"Hello," Vendetta purred sweetly. She was almost a head shorter than Reese. She gazed lovingly up into Reese's eyes. "Did I make this one? She smells like mine."

"We are all yours," Ethan said. He was at her back now, one hand on her arm as if to pull her away. But he wasn't exerting any will over his queen.

"So beautiful," Vendetta said. She ran a blood-stained finger down Reese's cheek.

"Very beautiful. But look what you've done to your room, my lady. I will have to clean it up."

Vendetta turned and regarded the pool of blood and Hope's

destroyed body.

"I called her here. I called her like I called the other ones," she purred. Her words were in their minds, Reese realized. Her lips weren't moving at all. "More will come, Ethanu."

"I know," Ethan said. "You are very clever."

"I need more. I must be strong when she wakes up."

"Who, my treasure?" Ethan asked, mimicking her tone.

"Mother." A crystalline laugh like a bell echoed through the room. It was as if the idea delighted Vendetta to no end. "Were you afraid? You never liked Hope."

Vendetta slid her arms around Ethan's neck, slicking the collar with blood. It was a strangely sexual movement. It didn't match the child-like image in Reese's mind. "Do you think I will eat you next?"

"I'm not afraid." Ethan smiled sweetly. He wiped at her chin the way a father might for his daughter. "You may do what you want with me. My body and soul are yours."

"But I smell your fear. Why are you afraid, Ethanu?" She bent and smelled his chest. She moaned as if the smell was more than pleasant. "I am *so* hungry."

"I know," he said and put a hand on the back of her head. "You may feed on me, my queen, if you wish it."

Over her head, Ethan met our gazes. *Please,* his eyes begged. *Please get Liam out of here.*

Vendetta bent forward and sank her fangs into Ethan's neck.

"Come lie down," he said, gathering her up like one would a child. She didn't remove her fangs. "Rest now."

Violet shoved Liam up the staircase and pushed Reese up behind him. They fled as if their lives depended on it—and it was possible they did. No one spoke until they were in the pickup, rushing down the road at full speed.

"Christ," Liam sighed, removing his scarf the way one loosens a tie. "I thought we were dead. I thought she was going to drain every single one of us dry."

"You and me both, bloodsucker. Holy *shit* she's terrifying. More terrifying than I imagined."

She whooped and both Liam and Reese jumped.

"Take me to a bar," Violet demanded. "I need a fucking drink."

"Go to Setting Sun," Liam said. "Drinks on me."

"Is she going to drain him?" Reese asked. The world was beginning to solidify around her again. The blind panic seizing her left a cold chill in its wake.

"He's all right," Liam said. "But Hope is the second chevalier that Vendetta has killed."

"What the hell is a chevalier?" Reese asked, having heard that word twice tonight.

"Like her personal servants. Uh, minions maybe?" Liam tried.

"Like generals in hell," Violet said. "She created them to do her bidding. To protect and serve her."

"Why the hell would she kill her personal servants?" Reese asked.

"She's taking her power back," Liam said, darkly. His moody gaze regarded the ocean waves.

"Does this mean she'll kill Ethan too?"

"Someday," he said. "But he was her first chevalier. I have a feeling he'll also be the last one standing."

As the Castle Cove lights came back into view and a feeling of safety enveloped her once again, Reese relaxed.

"The goddess is waking up," Violet murmured from the backseat. "Any idea what that means?"

"No idea."

"What shall we do in the meantime?" Reese asked, slowing at the four-way stop outside Crossroads.

"Drink like it's the end of the world?" Liam offered.

Violet met her gaze in the rearview mirror, a wicked grin on her lips. "I can think of more than a few things to keep you busy."

Grayson

They departed Vendetta Heights with Grayson driving his car. Abby rode shotgun as they followed Miriam's Prius onto Canyon Road then Midnight Pass.

He thought they might make it all the way to the interstate when the Prius suddenly slowed and its blinker came on. It flashed, signaling a turn.

"There's nothing here," he said, incredulously.

"You can't see it?" Abby asked. She gave him a curious look. When he shook his head, she added. "There's a road there. On the left. It must be concealed with magic."

Again he was confronted with the idea that Abby was a witch. That Abby, unbeknownst to him, had crossed that line without his knowing.

Had they been heading for this shift even before the horrible night in the cove? Had it always been only a matter of time before they crossed the line between worlds?

Abby was fully on the other side of that line now. But where was he?

Maybe that's what his question about college—about what kind of life he saw his future self in—was really about. What kind of life did he want? Which world did he want to live in?

"What are you thinking about so hard?" Abby asked.

"Nothing," he said. He turned onto the dirt road.

The smell of salty ocean air filled the car.

The road was clogged with thick foliage from overgrown brush on both sides of the road. Grayson hissed as branches scraped at the sides of his car. He expected dips and ruts, but the road was smooth.

"He probably forces the branches back," Abby said.

"What do you mean?"

She makes a motion with her hands. "Like with his mind. Ethan is really powerful, probably the most powerful demon in town, from what I hear."

"We are driving to a demon's house?" he asked. He wasn't sure how he should feel about that.

"Honestly, no one can be sure of what he is. He walks in daylight, and demons can't do that." The trees broke open and a two-story Spanish villa sprang into view. The dirt road turned to beautiful paving stones that circled in front of the house. In the center of the roundabout was a fountain bubbling softly with turquoise water.

Miriam parked her car in front of the cream-colored steps. Grayson parked behind her and got out of the car. With his dirty clothes he felt wholly underdressed for a place like this. He was sure someone who'd just run more than half a marathon through the woods to save their lives didn't look or smell too great. But his self-consciousness was obliterated by the gorgeous ocean view. It sparkled like champagne in the late afternoon sun.

"Somethin' is wrong," Dante said behind him, breaking the spell.

"Yes, I see that," Miriam answered.

Grayson followed their gaze and found the front door to Ethan's house had a giant hole blasted out of it. It hung on its hinges.

"What in the world could do that?" Abby asked.

"Hope," said Naomi and Ms. Monroe at the same time.

"They should stay in the car," Miriam said and Grayson realized that she meant him and Abby.

"What if she finds 'im there and kills 'im?" Dante asked.

"I could stay with them," Ms. Monroe offered, a hand resting on top of her bristly orange hair. The hope was evident in her tone.

"No, Tabby, I want you to be my eyes." Miriam sighed. "We'd better stay together then."

Ms. Monroe visibly deflated as Miriam nodded toward the door. "You first."

"I was afraid you'd say that." Ms. Monroe sighed. "All right."

Then the woman who'd been Grayson's boss for the last two years did something he'd never expected. She transformed.

Into a cat.

The stark orange hair that always jutted uncontrollably from her head smoothed itself onto the sleek, lithe body of a house cat. And not just any cat. But the cat that he'd known as Pumpkin.

"She—" he began but could only point at the cat. "Shit."

Abby grinned. "You didn't know? At least I'm not the only one."

Ms. Monroe stepped out of her human clothes and trotted up the cream-colored steps into the house. The five of them—Miriam, Dante, Naomi, Abigail and himself—lingered on the steps, looking around at the approaching night darkening the distant horizon.

It was nearly fifteen minutes before Ms. Monroe returned. By then the cricket song had swollen to a full cacophony and the ocean waves had nearly lulled Grayson into a doze.

As soon as he realized Ms. Monroe was transforming back into her human form, Grayson turned around quickly. He didn't want to see the woman whose shelves he stocked, *naked*, even in twilight.

"Ethan asks that we come back later. Hope was here, she's been dealt with and he needs…to clean up."

Miriam nodded, conceding. "All right then. That's all for today. You're free to go."

They dispersed, returning to their cars. Before Grayson and Abigail climbed into his car, Miriam called out. "Abigail."

"Yes?" Abigail sounded nervous, even to Grayson.

"You did well today. Be proud of yourself."

Abigail beamed. "Thank you, Miriam."

They waved toward the departing coven and followed the car back to the road.

"Do you want me to take you straight home?" Grayson asked as Castle Cove's lights came into view. Night had arrived. The city was awake.

"No," she said. "I'm too wound up after everything. You would think I wouldn't be after the hike but—"

"I know what you mean," he said. "How about Sam's Soda and Shakes? We did cover like seventeen miles and a full-out monster battle—twice. I think that merits milkshakes."

It was a diner in Old Town a couple blocks from the First Night Theater. They specialized in burgers, fries and had an old-fashioned soda counter. After the long and physically exhausting day, Grayson thought he could eat three burgers alone.

Abigail smiled. "Sure. And then we'll live happily ever after."

Grayson couldn't keep the grin off his face.

"After we go to UCLA for four years," she said. "Of course."

"UCLA?" he stuttered.

"I was accepted. Or we could go to CCU if you want. I got in there, too. Oh, don't look so surprised. My grades are way better than yours." Abigail smiled and twined her fingers in his.

He wanted Abby, without a doubt. The events of the last few days had made her time with him seem incredibly precious. But he was still surprised that she wanted *him*.

"Are you sure you want to be with me?" he asked. "You can have anyone."

"But I deserve to have who I want, don't I?"

"Yes. But are you sure—?"

She didn't even let him finish. "Grayson. I've never been more sure of anything."

Get Your Free Story

Thank you so much for reading *Night Tide*. I hope you're enjoying your time in Castle Cove. If you'd like more, I have a free, exclusive Castle Cove story for you, featuring characters you've already met. It is not a pick-your-path story, but I think you'll enjoy this dark and delicious tale, nonetheless. Demons, vampires, and psychics, oh my.

You can only read this story by signing up for my newsletter. If you're interested, you can get your copy at ➜

www.korymshrum.com/castlecoveoffer

I will also send you free stories from the other series that I write. If you've signed up for my newsletter already, no need to sign up again. You should have already received this story from me. Check your email! Can't find it? ➜ Email me at kory@korymshrum.com and I'll take care of it.

As to the newsletter itself, I send out 2-3 a month and host a monthly giveaway exclusive to my subscribers. The prizes are usually signed books or other freebies that I think you'll enjoy. I also share information about my current projects, and personal anecdotes (like pictures of my dog).

If you want these free stories and access to the giveaways, you can sign up for the newsletter ➜

www.korymshrum.com/castlecoveoffer

If this is not your cup of tea (I love tea), you can follow me on Facebook or Bookbub in order to be notified of my new releases.

ACKNOWLEDGMENTS

Thank you first and foremost to the reader. Yes, you. You worked pretty hard this time around, didn't you? I hope it was a fun read for you—as that was certainly what I was aiming for.

As always thanks to my wife, Kim. She is my first reader and biggest cheerleader. Love you, Mimi.

Thank you to my pug Charley, who is the loveliest of writing companions and always remains dutifully by my side while I write. He makes the process so cozy—when he isn't trying to crawl *between* me and the laptop.

Thank you to my assistant extraordinaire, Alexandra Amor, who formatted the paperback, did some editing and offered countless hours of support, so that I can focus on doing what I do best: write.

Thank you to Silviya Yordanova for another perfectly creepy cover.

Thank you to my critique group The Four Horsemen of the Bookocalypse: Kathrine Pendleton, Angela Roquet, and Monica La Porta. They continue to wonderfully supportive women who I'm very grateful to have on hand for editing and writing support.

Thank you to my street team who are always eager to jump in line for ARCs. You guys are great at last minute suggestions and spreading the word about my new releases. And I'm so lucky to have your support.

I also relied on my lovely team of proofreaders to catch errors. There were hundreds of you, but shout out to Jo Lucas, Stan Hutchings, Valarie Moss, Chris Christoforou, Rosemary Kenny, G G, Maya Malone, T Mekko, Kristina Hawley, Alison Carminke, Dorkas Michaelis-Iske, and any others (who have sent in corrections after I made this acknowledgments page).

All remaining mistakes are my own.

ABOUT THE AUTHOR

Kory M. Shrum is author of the bestselling *Shadows in the Water* and *Dying for a Living* series, as well as several other novels. She has loved books and words all her life. She reads almost every genre you can think of, but when she writes, she writes science fiction, fantasy, and thrillers, or often something that's all of the above.

In 2020, she launched a true crime podcast "Who Killed My Mother?" sharing the true story of her mother's tragic death. You can listen for free on YouTube or your favorite podcast app.

When not writing or producing her show, she can usually be found under thick blankets with snacks. The kettle is almost always on. When she's not eating, reading, writing, or indulging in her true calling as a stay-at-home dog mom, she loves to plan her next adventure. (Travel.)

She lives in Michigan with her equally bookish wife, Kim, and their rescue pug, Charley.

She'd love to hear from you!
www.korymshrum.com

ALSO BY KORY M. SHRUM

Dying for a Living series

Dying for a Living

Dying by the Hour

Dying for Her: A Companion Novel

Dying Light

Worth Dying For

Dying Breath

Dying Day

Shadows in the Water: Lou Thorne Thrillers

Shadows in the Water

Under the Bones

Danse Macabre

Carnival

Devil's Luck

Design Your Destiny Castle Cove series

Welcome to Castle Cove

Night Tide

The City: the 2603 novels

The City Below

The City Within

Learn more about Kory's work at: www.korymshrum.com